THE
BLACK HOLE
PROJECT

by
C. Sandford Lowe
and
G. David Nordley

THE
BLACK HOLE
PROJECT

Brief Candle
Press

Publishing History: Analog Magazine Jul/Aug 2006-Sep 2007

First published in 2013 by Variations on a Theme

Cover design: Brief Candle Press

First Brief Candle Press edition published 2015
www.briefcandlepress.com

ISBN: 978-1-942319-10-8

ACKNOWLEDGEMENTS

Our special thanks go to the members of our writers group and our spouses, Gayle Wiesner and Ron Alford, who, over eight years, reviewed, commented, corrected, and advised us into getting this ready for publication. Thanks also go to Dr. Debra Fischer for advice on Epsilon Eridani; Dr. Geoff Landis, who suggested the original two stars be four, and many others whose web pages and papers helped us concoct an arguably physically plausible scenario. Any scientific exaggerations, mistakes, inventions, imagining, and oversights are, of course, the sole responsibility of the authors. Special thanks also to Stan Schmidt and Trevor Quachi for acquiring, preparing, and publishing the initial version of this novel as a series of novellas in *Analog Science Fiction & Fact*.

This work is dedicated to the late
Elizabeth Lowery
and
V. Gerald Nordley
who met only in their children's writing

THE BLACK HOLE PROJECT

PROLOGUE

About eight billion years ago, Shiva had been a Neptune-sized planet circling a newborn M3 star. But stars lie close at the time of their birth, and within a couple of million years, a neighbor star passed near the fledgling planetary system, perturbing it.

Nothing happened immediately, but as eccentricities waxed and waned in chaos, Shiva moved closer to another world until a hundred million years after their formation, they swung around each other in one final mad gravitational embrace and flew away from their former orbits.

One planet dropped in toward the star and the other fled outward with a few remaining moons to wander forever in the endless night.

In 2206, aboard the starship *Wilhelm Gliese* on a trip from UV Ceti to Ross 248, astronomer Chandra Rae found Shiva. Their trajectory passed near the center of an approximate tetrahedron of stars: Sol, Groombridge 34, Lacaille 9352, and Epsilon Eridani, and she knew a certain Dr. Zhau Tse Wen, a physicist who wished to use the energy of each of those stars to power a megalomaniacal experiment in physics. He was crazy, and in her opinion, grandiosity was only part of his craziness. But wonders were fashioned by crazy people.

She took some deep infrared images, analyzed the spectra, and judged that the lone planet's moon and ring system contained enough lithium, boron and hydrogen to supply the fusion reactors needed for a few decades worth of starship operations. She named the lone planet "Shiva" and the outer moon "Vertex," thinking Dr. Zhau and his staff would find it a suitable place for their very ambitious project.

They did, and sixty years later, Zhau headed a mammoth project to use streams of relativistic pellets from those four stars to push four billion-ton iron rods up to eighty-seven percent of light speed toward the most precise and energetic implosion ever arranged by human scientists. If all the calculations proved out, this would cram the mass of a small asteroid into the volume of an atomic nucleus.

Zhau Tse Wen was trying to make a black hole.

BOOK I
KREMER'S LIMIT

CHAPTER 1

Black Hole Project Headquarters
Santa Cruz Mountains
10 April 2257

"But what if you're wrong?" the reporter asked.

Hilda Kremer tried to compose herself. The Black Hole Project Auditorium became so silent that the gentle whoosh of maglev traffic on the grassway down the hill could be heard. Even the small gaggle of protesters outside the auditorium were quiet, leaving the air to the calls of birds about their business in the two-century-old redwoods that had grown up around the mountainside building. The four-story Mediterranean-style mansion had once served as a Buddhist retreat. The speaker's platform faced the rose window that once stood over the Buddhist altar, and Hilda often drew a sense of inner peace looking in that direction.

She needed it. They had spent twenty minutes explaining why making a black hole would not destroy the known universe, and here was yet another hostile question. A diabolically put question at that—a "what if" that assumed the very thing under question.

Dr. Zhau Tse Wen, who had the floor, turned to her. Did he want her to reply to the question? On one hand, his turning to her was a form of recognition; on the other, she didn't want to venture into the minefield of loaded questions. She shook her head. She made massive computer simulations; others made things happen. Desire was the enemy of equanimity and clear-headedness.

Tse Wen's mouth turned up just slightly at the corners. He winked and turned to the reporter who'd asked the question. "All of us depend on the forces between the electron shells of atoms to keep us from collapsing into a tiny ball of neutronium in the center of the Earth. What if we were wrong about that?"

A titter ran through the room. When Tse Wen smiled he reminded Hilda of a contented, if undernourished, Buddhist monk. He'd told her he had lost his hair before taking his initial telomerase treatments and preferred the look, as it simplified his life. His thinness was not from any asceticism; he simply forgot to eat for days on end. Not infrequently, Hilda and co-investigator Sarah Levine kidnapped him from his office and dragged him over to Sarah's room for a feast of chicken soup and bagel sandwiches filled with kosher sausage slices.

"We don't collapse..." the reporter started to say.

Tse Wen smiled and bowed slightly. "And neither has any naturally-formed black hole ever created a new universe on top of us. Please remember, we live here, too."

Tse Wen was a student of martial arts among many other things, but had the kind of mind that could apply those lessons to conflict with words and ideas. Here he had gotten the opponent going in one direction and effortlessly pulled him past his objective and onto the floor. But another reporter rose to take a shot.

"Dr. Zhau, is or is not the upcoming Ten-Ten experiment an attempt to create a black hole right in our own asteroid belt before final review of the project?"

"It is not. It is far too small, only ten milligrams, and its head-on geometry doesn't contain the mass. It can't create a black hole. Many years ago, it was thought that quantum black holes might form in such experiments, only to evaporate instantly. But according to the 2135 Wilson-Lu synthetic model of quantum gravity, the minimum area of an event horizon is approximately 1/720th that of a proton—far too big to be made with the amount of energy the Ten-Ten experiment provides.

"It should, however, help us calibrate the parameters of Kremer's Limit. I should let Dr. Kremer describe the need for calibration."

Tse Wen gave her a cautionary glance. 'Less technical,' she thought he meant. No escape this time. Hilda took a deep breath, stared up at great dark wooden beams, and imagined herself up there, calm and removed.

"Think of neutrons as tiny balloons filled with quarks; squeeze them and heat them enough, they dissolve into a 'quagma,' a kind of bubble of free quarks buzzing around like angry bees. Push more, and the quarks buzz around faster and push back. At a high enough pressure, there's a transition to an ultra-dense state of what we call 'strange matter' that is normally unstable but can exist under extreme pressure.

"Increase the pressure and we think one gets a condensed Planck-scale Lu superposition of all the original mass. I say 'think' because by this time a stellar mass is so dense it warps space-time around it to the point where light cannot escape, becoming the unobservable inside of a black hole. The central pressure of a quark star of 2.18 solar masses is enough to cause that collapse.

"To make a black hole without a stellar collapse, we need to force enough mass-energy into a small enough volume to exceed the critical pressure for long enough for the mass to implode within an event horizon. The Ten-Ten experiment shows us some of the process where we can see it. We need this information to design the final experiment."

Hilda touched the net for Sarah. *I'm getting into your territory now, and you* like *attention.* "Uh, Dr. Levine?"

Sarah beamed and brushed a wave of thick brunette hair aside. "When we try to make the black hole, we'll be using most of the interstellar propulsion power resources of four stars for several months to accelerate four iron rod impactors toward the collision vertex. To use more power would waste needed resources. Also, the resulting black hole would be heavier and harder to handle than needed. But if we use too little, we'd have to try again and decades of work would be lost. So we're going to calibrate the model first."

The reporter frowned and looked as if he were searching for a follow-up that would make news. Finally he just sighed, shook his head, and sat down. Hilda almost sympathized with him; the poor man had been looking for something sensational or at least controversial and what he'd ended up with was "... calibrate the model..." Granted, it sounded sexy when Sarah said it.

A tall, thin woman dressed all in black was next in queue; she rose and looked directly at Dr. Zhau.

"Silvia Opuerto, *O Investigador*. Why do this?"

Zhau was silent for a couple of seconds. Then he said, "Knowledge." After another moment of silence, he continued. "For almost two hundred years, physics has wandered the desert of testable speculations, a forest of competing models which cannot be downselected by any experiment we can perform. A mini black hole will change that.

"It should, once and for all, answer our remaining questions about event horizons and time travel.

"If certain models are confirmed, we may be able to use it to produce more black holes, and build gravity machines that would revolutionize interstellar communications.

"It may also tell us whether there are other universes with which we can communicate, and possibly even provide an escape from the extreme old age of our own universe. Philosophically, that would cause us to contemplate eternity and the meaning of our existence in ways not even indefinite biological life extension has forced."

Ms. Opuerto, still standing, "Eternity? Is there anything in our religions, in our philosophies, in our thousands of years of cultural traditions that will be safe against all this experimentation?"

Tse Wen smiled. "Of course. That which is not false has nothing to fear."

There were a few chuckles in the hall, and the questioner sat down. Hilda couldn't read the expression on her face very well, but perhaps it was a mixture of anger and sadness. Hilda found herself mulling over the question of whether any statement could be immune to testing.

"I think we should take one more question," Tse Wen said.

A well-groomed man stood up amongst the raised hands and stared almost accusingly at Hilda.

"Mr. Ried?"

"Yes, Torsten Ried from *Popular Issues*. Setting aside the uncertainties of the experiment and the possibility of wiping this universe out with a new big bang, have any of you considered what you might unleash if you succeed? Are the leaders of humanity ready for the kind of power having its own black hole would mean?"

Hilda sighed. *Popular Issues* was well known for its consolidationist-leaning reputation, and Ried was from the same family as Interplanetary Association Senator Lars Ried, a frequent project critic. But, despite his tie in to IPA politics, Torsten had legitimate press credentials and the last part of his question was fair—probably the fairest of the lot today, she thought. But it was the question of a man who thought mainly in terms of power over others. To move beyond that, she thought, humanity had to, well, move beyond that.

Dr. Zhau nodded to Bradford Adams. Brad was a gifted Australian engineer and practical problem solver. He'd thought and written more about what to do with a black hole, if they made one, than the rest of them.

"No problems, I think. Now we let people be people, so we still have gangs, power trips, and police actions here and there. But there has not been a war, or anything resembling one, among the advanced nations of the world, for almost two centuries. Our cybernetic tools for monitoring and preventing misuse of resources are increasingly effective.

"Anyway, the black hole will be created six light-years from any concentration of human population. No bloody politicians." The audience chuckled. Brad's normal standard English lapsed into Australian dialect, or 'strine' as he called it, when he got excited or wanted to sound folksy. "But now imagine these four ten-kilometer iron rods hurtling along at almost the speed of light, coming together in the most powerful explosive crunch human beings have ever made to make a brilliant speck of light, the size of an atomic nucleus, but with the weight of an asteroid. Everything will change. We may have relativistic starships the size of asteroids. Space-time itself may be bent to our will. It may even open portals to other universes.

"People *are* excited about this," Brad continued. "Even Bruce Macready, my old science history professor, wants in on it."

"The author of *Unification Quest*?" the reporter asked.

"Right you are. He's offered to leave Broadfield College on the Isle of Skye to go along on the Epsilon Eridani mission as an historian. That's probably the most challenging star in the project, technically, because it's so young..."

Dr. Zhau held up a hand. "I must thank you all for this fascinating discussion. So fascinating that, indeed, we have gone a bit overtime and our food is waiting. Please, everyone, join us for the reception in the atrium and perhaps these conversations can continue in a more relaxed setting."

He bowed and motioned for the team to rise, signaling the end of the press conference.

Hilda and Sarah were first on their feet and quickly off the podium and out the door at the rear of the stage to check on their handiwork. Sarah handed her jacket to a robot, revealing a dark low-cut strapless dress.

Hilda sighed. She hadn't considered looking any different at the reception than at the press conference, and her loose black tunic and pants, while simple and elegant, were about as unsexy as a nun's habit. Well, she thought, there was something to be said for truth in packaging. She touched the net to let Brad and Tse-Wen know they were ready.

The team lined up and the guests entered. After all the handshaking was done, knots of people formed. Sarah was surrounded by four major infonet editors, all male. Dr. Zhau had quietly slipped into a corner with the editors of *Scientific American* and *Nature* while Brad was sitting at a table in deep political discussions with some of the *Coriolis* media corps.

"Dr. Kremer?"

She turned. It was the reporter with the political point of view. She would have to watch what she said. Misquotes by a journalist with a political point of view could be a real problem. "Yes?"

"Torsten Ried. *Popular Issues.*"

"Oh, yes." They shook hands. Hilda forced a smile and focused in on him. He seemed normal enough, about 180 cm and trim. His slightly sun-bleached brown hair was short with a part on the left. He wore cologne, maybe a little too liberally for her taste.

"It's a nice spread," he said. "I detect a woman's touch in the programming."

She laughed. "Found us out, I'm afraid. Sarah Levine and I spent all afternoon yesterday on it."

"Dr. Levine, yes." Ried followed Hilda's eyes and did a double take.

"I'll need to talk to her, too, but she seems occupied just now." He turned back toward Hilda.

"Off the record, there's some real risk, isn't there?"

"Not in the Ten-Ten. The test is a little like this reception. The food was programmed down to the atom, but Sarah and I still had to slip in and taste it first."

He smiled disarmingly. "Is there any result that would cause you to give up the project?"

Hilda shook her head. "Black holes exist. The only question is how much trouble one needs to take to make one."

A deep resonant THUD broke the quiet. Almost at once, the floor lifted her up, then fell away from her. Antique glass exploded into the room from the high windows. Wine glasses toppled to the floor and food dishes followed. She wasn't conscious of falling; rather, the floor seemed to rise to strike her.

Smoke and dust filled the atrium instantly. People started to get up off the floor and head for the exits. Hilda sat where she was a moment, not realizing her mouth was open in shock until the dust began to tickle her throat. She tried to touch the net. *What happened?*

No answer. The building's communications systems must be down. She shivered—one got used to the near-instant wireless information access bioradio provided, and being cut off felt, momentarily, like suddenly being deaf, or in a lightless room.

"Dr. Kremer, are you okay?"

Hilda looked up at Ried's dust-covered face and clothes. "Ried? Yes, I'm okay. The local net's down."

He nodded and offered his hand, which she took and pulled herself up.

"Do you see Dr. Zhau or Dr. Levine?" She asked.

"He's okay—over by the buffet, I think. I'll see if I can find Dr. Levine."

Hilda found Brad and Dr. Zhau under the same table where she'd left them. Brad looked angry; Tse Wen looked calm but very, very serious. She felt another slight jolt then and some dust settled down on her. One look at the cracked wall towering over them and she slipped under the table between them.

"Aftershocks?" she asked.

"That was no bloody earthquake," Brad said. "I'd say it was a subterranean bomb and the cavity it created is collapsing. Hard to believe that level of animosity. Fortunately, it was matched by their level of incompetence; the damage seems pretty superficial."

Dr. Zhau shook his head. "We should not assume incompetence, but rather that it achieved exactly the physical result they wanted. Now, what purpose would that result serve? It would frighten people. It could also serve to make the political opposition seem more moderate by comparison."

Brad nodded. "A good cop, bad cop ploy. Just another argument for them—see, we still have these fanatics and therefore we shouldn't have black holes. Machiavellian, it is."

Hilda shuddered and looked up at the tabletop, then over at Tse Wen sitting cross-legged under it. She did a quick calculation and smiled. "Well, I think we should have black holes. If we had a 16-billion-ton black hole on top of this table, Tse Wen, you could levitate!"

Tse Wen smiled. "Truly an argument to silence the greatest critic."

Brad laughed and put an arm around her shoulder.

His body felt good next to hers, reminding her of the one night they'd spent together some twenty years earlier, when they'd gotten the go-ahead for the initial phase of the Black Hole Project. They'd been at a conference in Lillehammer, Norway, talked impactor design, and done simulations until the sun rose at nine the next morning. Then, when the maid knocked and they realized it was getting near checkout time, Brad had held her hands and suggested that, as they were going to have the name anyway, they may as well play the game.

It had made her happy to make him happy. But there'd somehow never been another such occasion with Brad. Now, feeling him next to her brought back that pleasant memory. She shut her eyes and tried to exist in the moment, banishing explosions from her mind.

When she opened her eyes, there was Ried, staring at her as if registering something that hadn't occurred to him before.

"I couldn't find Dr. Levine, but I think we're in the clear," he said. "The net's back up."

With a nonchalant smile she didn't feel at all, she extricated herself from Brad and from under the table. The two of them helped Dr. Zhau to his feet. Maintenance robots were already whirring around, picking up the debris.

She touched the net, comforted by its familiar presence. No one had been seriously hurt, the damage was superficial, and the building would be usable again tomorrow.

"Well, Mr. Ried," Dr. Zhau said while brushing the dust from his shirt and pants, "do you know anything about who might be behind this?"

Ried shut his eyes for a second. "Nothing yet."

"Really, mate?" Brad asked, his voice laced with irony.

"Look," Ried said. His face was hard. "My brother's politics are his business. We're just half-brothers anyway, and raised fifty years apart. I'm doing my best to be a reporter, that's all. But I think I can assure you that being connected with any kind of terrorism is the last thing he'd want politically."

Brad snorted. "Is that so? And why would anyone want to scare us?"

There was an embarrassed silence. Ried's brother was up for reelection, and if his coalition got a majority, he could be the new president of the Senate. Hilda shivered. Withdrawal of IPA support would kill the project. If the demographic analysis of consolidationist gains were right, humanity might be in for as profound an inward turn as that of China a millennium ago. She might get only one chance to make a black hole.

Ried looked rattled. "Look, the Public Safety Administration puts the explosion almost half a kilometer under the institute building—it's as if someone loaded a mining mole with a half-ton of chemical explosives. It was more likely intended to scare than injure."

Hilda reached for Brad's hand and gave a light squeeze. She'd never seen him so angry about something that didn't involve a steering magnet or a photon field lens.

Brad squeezed her hand back, shook his head, and offered a hand to Ried. "Sorry, mate... a bit shaken, it seems."

"Me too," Ried replied with a softer face and shook hands. "No offense taken."

Dr. Zhau smiled. "Well, Brad, Hilda, if things are back in harmony, perhaps we should check to see if our things are still on our shelves. The building is cleared for reentry, it seems."

Hilda shut her eyes. Not surprisingly, her office cam was still off line.

Then it hit. "Cleared for reentry?"

Dr. Zhau shrugged and smiled. "I thought there would be less chance of injury in a fairly mild shake if we took cover here. Everyone else was headed for the exits. Afterwards, we were not missed, except by you. It appears we were not as important as the events today might have led us to believe."

Sarah appeared. "Am I the only one here with the presence of mind to get out of the building?"

Brad started laughing uncontrollably. Soon they all joined in, and the tension drained away.

Ried put a hand on Hilda's shoulder. "They've ID'd the group responsible for this mess. Another small fringe group I've never heard of that wants recognition. Dr. Kremer, I'd be happy to help you put things back in order. Of course I might have a few more questions over dinner afterwards."

Hilda saw the reporter's face lighten up. It seemed an earnest offer. Brad gave her an 'it's okay' look.

"Okay, Ried," she said. "But only if you agree to call me Hilda. I've had about as much of 'Dr. Kremer' as I can take today."

"That," Brad added, "is another kind of Kremer's Limit."

Ried smiled and stuck out his hand towards Hilda. "Torsten, then."

Zhau Tse Wen gestured to the stairwell.

Hilda sighed. The elevators would be down for a few more hours.

••∞••

Dinner was at the Ridge House in North Boulder Creek. The meat was replicated, but the crepes and the soup were house made and the view sitting just above the pine tops was dramatic. As they ordered dessert from the tabletop display, the fog rolled in below like an alien flood.

Knowing Torsten would eventually break the quiet mood with questions, Hilda ventured one of her own first. "Tell me what it's like to be in a political family. I can't imagine the pressures it must place on everyone around your brother."

Torsten chuckled. "No, probably not. In my family, everything revolves around my brother's political career. He's the *vaterführer*. Anyone can do anything they want as long as it doesn't get in the way of his vision for the family."

"It sounds a little autocratic."

Torsten shrugged. "It takes a lot of effort to put someone in office. You need a support team, and what better team than a family? I'm kind of the black sheep because of my independence.

"Quite a sacrifice, I would think," Hilda said, feeling some sympathy. Her relationship with her own autocratic father had never been really smooth.

"Not for me. I always wanted to be a journalist. So I told them to leave me out of their political games. I just want to do my work the best way I know. Kate Avonford's daughter, aren't you, as well as Wotan Kremer's? You grew up in a famous family."

Hilda nodded. She knew about living with famous parents; her starship captain mother and planet-molding father couldn't live with each other and couldn't stay away from each other in a soap opera that had spread to every human habitation in known space.

"Left home at sixteen, when Mom left and Dad sent me back to Earth to go to school. I had other ideas; I wanted to come right back, so I asked the crew to let me stay awake on the voyage and I studied on my own. I pretty much grew up on that starship. I learned to pilot on the ship's runabout and learned zero g sports from the crew. The astrogator, Deb Fisher, got me started in celestial mechanics."

"Relationships?"

"Three women and a couple of very married men who weren't interested." She shrugged. "I wasn't that interested either and got a drug bug to keep me that way."

Torsten frowned deeply. "I don't like the idea of having some genetically engineered bacteria injected to make up for lack of self-control. I don't think that's the way we're intended to live."

"By whom?" Hilda asked. "Lots of astronauts do it—less personal conflict."

Torsten opened his mouth as if to argue, then closed it again. After a brief silence, he switched topics. "I see you don't have a school certificate or bachelor's degree."

"No, just the PhD. I passed all the tests for entrance to grad school by the time I arrived and went right into research. While I've gone to some lectures, I've never attended a regular class since leaving New Antarctica. So much for Dad sending me away to school!" She laughed. "At least your family's politics are external. You act like an objective journalist, but your questions seem, well, biased towards your brother's political bent."

"*Popular Issues* considers the consolidationist viewpoint a legitimate one. I try to ask the kind of questions my reading public would ask if they were here. Having a point of view doesn't make me unobjective or untruthful. Our readership has serious questions about what you folks are doing. My job is to address their concerns."

She nodded, trying to understand his point of view. "I suppose every new thing ever done has been terrifying to someone. Automobiles—people thought human beings wouldn't survive 50 kilometers an hour. Now we approach the speed of light. Some thought these genetically engineered radios we grow in our heads were going to turn us into computer-controlled zombies; now they're so natural to us, we forget about them. Change happens. We adjust."

"Look, Hilda," he said earnestly. "This Black Hole Project is terrifying to ordinary people who don't understand it. It's just way out of anyone's intuitive range. I don't know if I can really explain it, but at least help me understand it."

She made herself smile and replayed the press conference simulation on the tabletop display, pausing to add more explanation.

Finally he asked, "But a new universe is possible, isn't it? I mean, anything can come out of the quantum foam, can't it?"

"Look, according to statistical mechanics, every air molecule in this room might suddenly find itself on a trajectory toward the upper left corner of the room, leaving us in vacuum. Well, don't hold your breath."

Ried sighed. "Okay, I guess it's something I don't have to worry about right now. You don't mind if I use this interview on the net, do you?"

"Huh?"

"Watch the screen. I'll tap the restaurant's surveillance camera."

Hilda saw them from above, with the simulation running on their table screens, looking for all the world like some weird placemat art.

"But what about privacy?" she asked. "How can you do that?"

"I'm licensed media, remember; I have access. We can use security video because otherwise everyone would be running around with cameras making a nuisance of themselves."

"I didn't know." She mulled over his revelation.

"Most people don't. As for privacy, we have to ask before using it, or lose our license."

She smiled as she saw herself talk and gesture.

"No problem?" he asked.

Maybe it was the wine, but she looked all right to herself. "No problem." Hilda laughed. "But for the project information, Sarah's the key right now."

"Does she understand it as well as you do? How do you work as a team?"

Hilda thought about that one. "We all work well together; Dr. Zhau asks the right questions, Sarah generates all the possible answers, I winnow the answers down to those that make sense and can predict something. Brad figures out how to test the predictions. Then Dr. Zhau and I go over everything Brad does with anal-retentive thoroughness, and Sarah generates worst-case scenarios—she has the most imagination. Occasionally, I decide whether a worry is real or not."

"But if some new theoretical concern came up at the last minute, you'd be the one they'd turn to, wouldn't you?" Torsten pressed. "They'd be reluctant to go on without you."

Hilda laughed and waved a hand expansively, "Okay, I'll admit it. I'm probably essential." Four glasses of wine, she thought, was what it took to let her say something like that. "It's getting late."

Torsten nodded. "Yes. But I'd like to continue this someday."

The conversation had been pleasant and the offer sounded innocent enough. "Okay, when and where?"

"Well, maybe you'd like to get a taste of what's happening on the opposition side. I'm supposed to cover one of my quote brother's unquote speeches next week. Any chance you'd like to come hear it? Nobody needs to know who you are, of course. Then we can discuss it over dinner, on or off the record, as you like."

She did need to understand these people better. "Okay, it's a date."

They arrived at her car, the car door opened for her and she flowed languidly into it. Torsten grinned foolishly as he touched her shoulder, then let the door shut after her. She fell asleep against the seat as the car steered itself down the grassway and rocked gently as it caught the buried maglev track. Her last waking thoughts were she was going to feel a bit silly the next morning, assuming some idiot with a bomb didn't blow her up for real because if she was really as important as all that, maybe the opposition would... do... something.

CHAPTER 2

The hillside home of Rolf and Anna Messenger
Millbrae, California
12 April 2257

"Ever the day dreamer, eh?"

Torsten looked up from his chair on the deck, mildly irritated. He'd been working on the net—not daydreaming.

"Hi, Anna."

Anna Messenger, Cousin Rolf's wife and a distant Ried cousin herself, was Torsten's hostess when he was in the San Francisco Bay area. She was tall with straight auburn hair parted in the middle and casually dressed in a plain gray long shift. When she moved, it was pretty clear that was all she was wearing. Such casualness, he knew, was sheer art—as an actress, she had learned how to gain advantage with men, an advantage Torsten had long since conceded to her.

He waved a hand in the air. "On the net, studying Black Hole Project simulations."

"Full access? How did you get by the BHP blocks?"

"As far as I can tell, there are no blocks. No need. The explanatory text is in a foreign language—physics."

"Come on inside. The fog's rolling in and I'm chilly."

"I didn't get anywhere with Levine," Torsten said. "She's suspicious of me. But Kremer seemed less on guard. We may have the beginnings of a relationship, though. She's curious about us; she accepted an invitation to come to the forum next week. I need to sound like I've done some homework."

Anna shot a glance at him. "Kremer? The black hole science geek? A wonder she'd let you get close. Levine looked more amenable to drugs and seduction. Kremer doesn't look the type. You think she'll really come to the forum?"

Torsten shrugged. "She says she needs to understand why we're opposing the BHP."

Anna spat. "Now you're swallowing *her* BS. She more than anyone knows damn well they're rolling the dice with everyone's lives—and I mean everyone in creation—all for their own damn hubris. Torsten, politically, we need to get someone with inside credentials to say something embarrassing about the project. We don't have enough people scared yet. Did you get DNA samples?"

"We had dinner. I got her fork. What do you need that for?"

"Opposition research. The less you know about it the better. Anyway, Lars wants to see you about your reportage. He's downstairs."

"Here?"

Anna shrugged. "I didn't think that was a good idea either. He insisted on coming with me."

As they came down the stairs, Torsten saw Lars and Mono Tukapo, his bodyguard and political secretary. Lars was actually shorter than Torsten, but so toned and barrel-chested he looked bigger. His professionally styled hair was so neatly cropped he looked more artificial than a humanoid robot. He reeked of the presence and self-confidence of a successful politician, and had ever since Torsten had known him.

Torsten reached out a hand. "Hello, Lars. Something wrong with one of my stories?"

Lars flashed his best campaign commercial smile. "Hey, what kind of brother would I be if I didn't pester you once in a while? I'm worried that you might be doing the disinterested reporter bit a little too much, and thought we should have a chat. The polls being where they are, we could use a little more of a boost, and everyone knows *Popular Issues'* lean, anyway."

Anna chuckled and ordered some drinks.

Torsten shook his head. Only a tiny handful of physicists really challenged the physics, and they did so in a language he couldn't understand any better than Hilda's. "Lars, I've got a reputation to maintain. My stuff is much more effective if I appear objective—a point for their side for every two of ours."

A robot floated in with the drinks. Lars latched onto one and sipped it as he stared off into space. Anna played with her ice cubes. It was clearly up to Torsten to fill the silence.

"Maybe I could go to three points for our side for every one of theirs?"

Lars shook his head. "No, if anything, get the ratio more even. AIs look at ratios like that and report bias. No, the points for our side need to be more telling, the ones for the other side more trivial. Present the issue in our language instead of theirs. Weight it that way. The public's not concerned enough yet."

Torsten stifled a moment of irritation with Lars for telling him his own business—and worse, being right about it. He just nodded.

"Torsten, my committee is hearing rumors the BHP is carrying on some secret experiments, even more dangerous than the Ten-Ten. We're not ready to go public with that, so don't quote me."

"Funny thing," Anna said. "The same things have been going around my production set. The studio is owned by Wu-Davis Ltd.; one of their divisions is the prime contractor on the experiment instrumentation— the stuff that's supposed to take quarter-nanosecond pictures of the Ten-Ten experiment until it gets vaporized."

Torsten laughed. "I've looked, and there's nothing there. I couldn't..."

"Sounds like you have two independent sources, Torsten," Lars said.

Was Lars crazy? The sources were hardly independent. "You want me to go with that?"

Lars settled back against his chair and made himself comfortable. "Torsten, there's a time for objectivity, but this election is about pulling in all the resources of our family to help win. It's not about individual pride, status, and reputation. No, this is about our people and what we can give back to them, what we can give back to our world. This election is about much greater issues than making governmental policies and keeping the constituency happy. It could be about saving humanity itself. We need to sell people on the idea the public experiment is only the tip of the iceberg, that things are happening in the Black Hole Project that could destroy everyone if we don't expose this Ten-Ten experiment."

Torsten was silent for a while, contemplating his place in the family and the overall scheme of things. He had no choice. "Okay, you want a make-or-break issue to pull out of the hat just before the election? For that, timing is as important as content. You don't want to give them time to refute. Mark Twain said a lie can get halfway around the world before truth has even put its boots on. We have to time it so the boots come on *after* the election."

Anna smiled at Torsten as if to say, 'You're starting to enjoy this, aren't you?' Aloud she said, "Well, we're stuck five percent behind. We need to switch two percent to you and another two percent of the expansionist leaners to undecided. Simulations show a scandal on the Black Hole Project could do that, if it stinks enough."

Lars nodded. "Even the appearance of scandal, of stonewalling, or of something not entirely right could do it. Our side is the safe side."

Torsten sighed. "Okay. It's dueling experts and people-like-us can't decide. So, where there's smoke, there's fire. That will certainly bring in magazine hits; but..."

Lars cut him off with a wave of the hand. "This is the kind of gut-worry issue that binds voters together. Make them fear."

"As I said, it will be more effective closer to the election."

"Perhaps." Lars sighed. "We'll go with your judgment on that, for now. But make no mistake: this is a good cause to fight for. I believe in it. I'm told by some of the most brilliant scientists we have that existence itself is at stake here." Lars stopped for another dramatic pause.

He was convincing enough that Torsten wondered if he might be sincere.

Lars continued quietly, "This is big stuff. So big I'm pulling in the whole family on this one. I need you. Everything might depend on a few good breaks."

"I understand fully, Lars, and I'm on it. I just have to be a little subtle, or it could backfire before the election." He didn't add that it was certain to backfire sometime after the election; that was irrelevant. If Lars won, he'd be in power and he knew how to use it.

Anna touched him on the shoulder. "We may need to do something to this Kremer woman before she does something to us."

"Journalistically, of course," Lars added.

"Of course," Torsten answered. "But, if I'm going to gain Kremer's confidence, I can't irritate her too much now."

Lars raised an eyebrow, then nodded slowly.

••∞••

Torsten watched Kremer walk into the Mark Hopkins Hotel. Her costume was pedestrian, a black tunic and slacks—indistinguishable from what she'd been wearing at the news conference. A typical geek, he thought. She walked closer to the inner walls, looking up, and she wasn't the only one. The bomb at the institute had left its mark on everyone's thoughts—even at a Lars Ried rally. Anna's friends had meant to scare people about the BHP, but the immediate result was a kind of generalized fear that affected any potentially controversial gathering.

It was as if the bombers had let a genie out of the bottle, one that had supposedly been capped centuries ago. People were screaming for a review of antisurveillance laws and robotic restrictions. If Lars won, he'd probably get enough government policing power to prevent anyone from doing to him what his people had done to create the current mood. The irony of it made Torsten smile, however uncomfortably.

Kremer stopped and looked across the outer hallway through the transparent walls, a distinctive feature added in reconstruction after the 2221 quake. The view of San Francisco Bay was one of Torsten's favorite sights, too. The only visible security was signs at the entrances that said "by invitation only," but the party's AIs would discreetly check everyone entering with multispectral cameras and microwave scans from overhead. Plain-clothes operatives near the doors would be cued to offer gentle reminders to anyone who wandered in without reading the sign. Anna's work; she'd artfully arranged the appearance of openness and Kremer walked into the room unaware of the checks. Torsten went down to meet her.

She sat in the back of the room, running her hands through her short blond hair, clearly feeling uncomfortable. What would she know about Lars going in? He asked the net for a quick-look data scan to see what an outsider like Kremer might get. *Noted consolidationist within the Conservative Union Party —Geology degree—apolitical through grad school—gregarious—desire for order—politician since age of 42—drive for power came early—what did he want to be when he grew up? 'In charge,' quoted an undergraduate friend. Family home lies outside Leipzig...* Nothing particularly scary there. He went up to greet her.

"Hello, Torsten. I've been reading reviews of your brother's political life. Some aren't very flattering: 'unsophisticated,' 'a will to impose order,' and so on."

Torsten shrugged. "He's got a consolidationist constituency to play to. But beyond that, I think he's a pretty good leader."

"Is that your job, to balance the news?"

Torsten smiled and shook his head. For all her naïveté, this lady was quick—a lot quicker than he was, and he'd have to keep that in mind. He would have to work at his own pace and avoid getting into a contest of wits with her.

"I like to think I'm fair-minded about him. I don't know him as well as I should; he's more like a grandparent than a brother. Anyway, please keep in mind he's preaching to the choir here. His job is to pump these people up and motivate them to go out and work for the election."

Lars Ried strode into the room and waved to the crowd amid applause and cheers. Dressed in a high-fashion single-piece navy-blue suit in a loose-cut Scandinavian fashion over a powder-blue turtleneck set off by a red-jeweled medallion on a gold chain, he exuded urbane executive authority.

Political posters rose up as if on cue as he took the podium. Lars nodded in appreciation and finally held his hand up to quiet the room. "Tonight I would like to talk to you frankly about an issue that confronts each of us in this room and those I seek to represent. It is the undeniable and palpable suspicion, even fear, which divides the people of our Solar System today.

"Issues of pure scientific research that don't even have an economic value are dividing civilization.

"Too often, those of us who believe in letting humanity adjust to the changes technology has already made before embarking on new and questionable endeavors, may find ourselves caricatured and stereotyped as a danger to tolerance. Some have suggested the Conservative Union Party is motivated by political opportunism with the ultimate goal of denying freedom to researchers, many of whom are doing the enriching and rewarding work of consolidating, understanding, and applying the huge mass of data accumulated over the last two centuries.

"My friends, the Conservative Union seeks merely to point out the social and cultural implications of research can no longer be ignored. We say, let the people decide if they are ready for yet another new technology to complicate their lives. We say, let the people decide if they want to take the risk of playing around with the basic fabric of the universe when *there is no pressing need for it.*"

Kremer squirmed in her seat at the applause. Torsten patted her hand. Lars was in good form, Torsten thought, as the elder Ried's rhetoric flowed over its spellbound audience.

Kremer leaned over to Torsten and whispered. "I fear the beginnings of an inquisition."

Torsten settled his hand on hers. "Not an inquisition; a regaining of control. This isn't the Middle Ages. The AI infrastructure can't be the instrument of an inquisition and it will defend individuals who resist it. An inquisition is impossible. Lars just wants efforts refocused. Politics is perception, Hilda. Yours are different from most of these people's. Hear him out for me. Then we can talk, okay?"

Hilda rolled her eyes and returned her attention to the platform.

Lars Ried continued. "I come before this audience tonight with the explicit purpose of reconciliation with the scientific community.

"Let us bridge together the gap of misunderstanding. Let us help the scientific community understand humanity is in danger of losing itself and cannot afford the disruption the Black Hole Project might bring. Enough is enough."

"You call that reconciliation?" Kremer whispered to Torsten, who winked back at her.

"History has much to teach us about scientific research run amok," Lars continued.

"Friends, just as we have citizen oversight committees guiding our legislation, we need citizen oversight committees watching over scientific research projects. Even if they may be right, we have to hold back until at least a majority understands what they are doing! It's our necks on the line.

"My first priority if elected will be to put at least a temporary hold on any other experiments that may have societal implications, including, on the face of it, the Black Hole Project. My second priority will be to put in place a citizen watchdog committee to curtail aberrant research earlier. The expansionist coalition is on record opposing both initiatives. The choice of responsible people should be clear.

"Thank you for your support!"

The resulting ovation rang in Torsten's ears. Kremer sat shaking her head and looking distinctly unhappy.

"It's all about power, isn't it?" she said. "Who is the alpha male? Who gets to piss on who? Your brother reduces the work of the entire scientific community, never mind the Black Hole Project, to a political beauty contest, with him and his cohort as the judges."

He winced at this and the hostility it implied. "I'll ignore the moral issue for the moment, but at least consider it is simply impossible for a democratic politician to pander only to elitists and stay in office."

"Elitist? Look, I don't know the first thing about, say, hypnoactive kinetic art. Does that make the artists 'elitist'? It's just different areas of interest. Leave cobblers to their lasts."

Damn, she was bullheaded! "When the last is creation itself? I think not."

"But..." She seemed confused, and a bit angry. "You journalists can affect so many things yourselves. Are you really objective, or is that just a power trip, too? Excuse me a moment."

She whirled and walked off toward the toilets.

Torsten waited by the hotel foyer. He wondered once more if she was angry enough to duck out of their dinner date. But Kremer returned, noticeably more composed than when she left.

"I hope this doesn't mean we have to postpone dinner..." he began.

She shook her head and smiled fleetingly. "I'm fine."

They wandered downhill in silence and ended up, not so accidentally, at a small Thai restaurant Torsten knew. An elegant little hideaway on the third floor, it had leanings towards the exotic spices of

Pattaya—served, of course, by elegantly painted young men dressed in stunning silk dresses. He'd taken dates there before, often with good effect.

Kun Srichard, who knew the Ried men well, provided Torsten with a table in a quiet corner of the petite room with a secluded view of the ancient Golden Gate Bridge sinking into the fog, now rolling in from the ocean.

A message from Anna announced itself as they finished a dessert of candied rice and fruit. He touched the net for the playback.

Good news—they've got problems with the Ten-Ten experiment. Your sweetie doesn't know it yet, but she's going on a space voyage. And, so are we.

We? Space? he replied.

I'll tell you all about it when you get here.

His heart beat a little faster.

CHAPTER 3

Dr. Hilda Kremer's Office
BHP Headquarters
24 April 2257

Brad's image on Hilda's wall screen pointed to a section of the array imaged on the wall screen of his office. Hilda thought briefly of the nesting of images of ever-decreasing size and resolution collapsing to a precisely located point with no information content.

"If those radiation levels are isotropic," he said, "the experiment is putting out more energy in gamma radiation alone than we are putting in with kinetic energy." He turned to her. "I don't buy that, but I don't see how the results could be strongly directional. We've only collided milligrams; not nearly enough for any shielding effect."

Hilda shook her head, feeling frustrated; the results made no sense and screamed of bad data or bad instrumentation. But, she reminded herself, much great physics had come from results that were contrary to all expectations, at first. "Brad, even in these precursor collisions, we're into new territory—quagmas a million times denser than have ever been produced before. We ought to expect something new."

"I know," Brad said. "If we only didn't have the whole bloody world breathing down our necks expecting everything to be perfect and just like predicted or else. I look at the political sims and wonder if there will ever be another chance." He scratched his right temple.

"I know how you feel," Hilda said. "Bombs, grandstanding politicians, idiot journalists... I didn't think it would be such a fight." A pang of guilt joined her frustration. Dating Torsten Ried and getting a worm's-eye view of ultra-suspicious populism and its panderers had given Hilda lots of insight into the political problems they faced. In the last two weeks she'd seen political networking that put even academic kingdom-builders to shame. On her own part, she'd offered her services to the project's outreach group, talking to high schools, futurist groups, and even a convention for journalists.

Torsten, to his credit, had introduced her to several journalists who at least had an inkling of how the scientific community worked and encouraged her to reach out to them, while cautioning her not to voice too many technical words. But she hadn't touched her toroidal spin web transformations in two weeks, and she felt a growing void within her.

"It's a bloody law of nature; the bigger the advance, the more you have to fight for it," Brad said. "But we have to stay with it. You'll be able to concentrate a lot better when you get out to the test site, away from these distractions."

"Is that why Tse Wen is sending Sarah and me out?"

Brad shook his head in frustration. "I'm not sure what you two can do to the experiment on-site that you both can't do here. But it'll be a right place to think."

"Well, we're sure not getting anywhere here," Hilda said. "So maybe it will work. Maybe just seeing the stuff with our own eyes, touching the equipment with our own fingers..."

She recognized Tse Wen's wisdom in sending them to the experiment site. They needed focus, focus away from this political mess. But frustration crowded into her thoughts. She turned to her longtime friend. "Thirty years of work and things feel like they're coming completely unglued—bombs, Lars Ried's political pandering, crazy experiment results..." She sighed. "It's getting late. Talk to you later. I'm going to sleep." Hilda often stayed overnight and slept on a foldout cot. She pulled it vigorously from her closet.

Brad smiled. "Oh, she'll be right in the end, you'll see. G'night."

The screen went blank.

Chaos, I just hope I can sleep, she thought as she threw her clothes into the closet.

•●∞●•

Morning was bright in her window when she realized she hadn't thought about black holes, quantum gravity, or protesters for at least eight hours.

She took that thought back—she hadn't thought of it *consciously*. But from somewhere in her deep sleep at least three plausible explanations for what had happened had formed in her head. Smiling, she sat down at her terminal, grabbed her sketchpad, and started setting up the simulations.

Her stomach growled. She was, she noted, still stark naked and ravenously hungry. Time for a break. But plausibility started to change to possibility before her eyes, and she kept on. One of the possible explanations might mean the darker side of Lars Ried's political constituency may have penetrated into the project far deeper and with much more sophistication than any of them realized.

She sent a note to Tse Wen and grabbed her long shirt in case he called back.

He did.

"I was wondering if we might have lunch. There are things I'd like to talk to you about—in person."

"I am available," he said, with a smile.

•●∞●•

Tse Wen stroked the slight goatee he affected which, along with his baldhead and thinness, gave him the aura of an ageless oriental sage. He'd been about forty when the antiaging retrovirus was spread—it was all for effect, which he'd cheerfully admit if called on it.

"Now what is all this being mysterious about?" he asked.

Hilda's hamburger was too good to believe. Grill smoke leaking into the dining room of the cafe added to the taste of the food without being overly noticeable. She swallowed her last bite and had a sip of lemonade to clear her throat.

"I see three possibilities for what's happening at the experiment site. One, of course, is that it's new physics—perhaps a virtual quantum black hole did form and there was a kind of leak-through of energy from another universe, or another part of our universe."

Tse Wen nodded politely. He didn't think so either, she could tell, but completeness required mentioning the possibility.

"The second is that the anisotropy is caused by advanced wave Mota crystallization."

He frowned. "General relativity permits such a solution, but I think that is only because it is incomplete. Even at the Planck level, the causality implications are disturbing."

"Aren't they? I can't say there aren't any other possibilities for anisotropism, but that was the only one I could find that made even that much sense. Which brings me to my third idea." Her face sobered. "Maybe we aren't getting the real data."

Now Tse Wen really frowned. "The last thing a theorist should do is to claim that data is bad which does not fit previous theory."

Hilda nodded. "That's why I mentioned it last. But the falsification of data does fit within the existing theoretical structure, perhaps better and more simply than time travel or multidimensional teleportation."

Tse Wen shook his head, then grinned. "I would not put out press releases. But you have convinced me some caution is warranted. I shall have conversations. Do you still see the reporter, Torsten Ried?"

"Occasionally."

"Do you think that wise?"

Hilda ran a hand through her hair. "Torsten's a nice guy. Lovely smile, and he listens. I'm making progress; he's not certain the Black Hole Project is such an evil thing, he just doesn't know and he's got a lot of family pressure. And you know, I'm not sure Lars sees it as anything more than an issue that he can use. If it became a non-issue, or even worked for him in some way, I don't think he'd bother to oppose it. We just have to do a better job of educating people."

"Ah, very brilliant! After a few years of such an education program, the proportion of people who tunnel bombs under our building may decrease by a statistically significant amount!"

Hilda felt deflated. "I'm sorry."

"And I too, am sorry for using humor to disguise my frustration, which is as great as yours. I shall trust you and Sarah to deal with any possible physical causes of the anomaly, in the distraction-free field location. Brad will continue to supervise the work here. It will be left to me to talk to people to try to bring things back into harmony again. I think next year, *you* should chair the project."

Nobody had ever said or done anything to scare Hilda as much as that pronouncement. It left her open-mouthed and staring at Tse Wen in abject horror. She could not think of anything to say.

Tse Wen laughed and reached out to touch her. "No, no, I was only kidding."

Hilda began to giggle a bit in a reaction which soon dissolved into the kind of uncontrollable laughter that was for her but a micrometer from uncontrollable tears.

"You'll need to go soon," Tse Wen added. "You can work out the details of the investigation on the *Psi Naught* en route to the asteroid belt."

Hilda nodded. The institute's spacecraft had a fully equipped nanoscale fabrication facility.

••∞••

It took a week to clean up loose ends and get underway, but once the *Psi Naught* finished acceleration and settled into the routine of interplanetary travel, Hilda buried herself in simulations, changing parameters and discarding approximations in an effort to make theory fit the data. She came up only to eat and sleep. For her, this was what physics was all about—the driving compulsion to work through a compelling problem.

Three days after they departed, Sarah came to Hilda's cabin.

"Any luck with the theory?"

Hilda shook her head. "If those results are real, they don't fit theory. But the main data handling software seems very clean."

Sarah frowned "I think we can verify the anisotropy question by placing new Ragi probes away from the collision plane and firing another round of tests."

Hilda nodded. "That leaves bugs in the data stream itself." A century or two ago, spy services developed a very thin technology that could be inserted in an optical data bus. The bug could read data in the bus and then pass it on with or without modifications.

"It would have to be very sophisticated, possibly even a non-Asimovian AI," Sarah said.

The idea of an AI not limited by the laws of robotics disquieted Hilda. "Chaos, these people have blinders on if they'd do that!"

"You've seen them in action. Using an illegal AI would be exactly what consolidationists should be against. But power is what they're about, not principle."

Hilda shook her head. "They'd undercut themselves if it ever got out. Too big a risk, I think."

"So maybe they think that we wouldn't be looking for it," Sarah said. "Anyway, the Rieds aren't the whole story. The project is a big target. There are other more fanatic consolidationists and people who need to make their own mark on the cosmos. They could do anything."

"Our AIs should help us against that kind of threat."

Sarah shrugged. "They'd try to protect us, but remember that our opponents are people, too. Typically Asimovian AIs stay out of people conflicts until physical harm to someone becomes a real possibility, whatever their evaluation of the potential perpetrators."

"I'm not sure I'd want to change that," Hilda said after some thought.

"Me neither—which is why we have some work to do ourselves, and quietly." Sarah stood up. "I've got the equipment ready to go. Let's get it in place first thing before the opposition figures out that anything is happening, let alone what."

"Okay." Hilda nodded and smiled. "It's been a while since I did anything experimental. I may be all thumbs."

••∞••

Six weeks later, Hilda watched the fountain of glowing plasma behind the *Psi Naught* as it decelerated toward the main habitat for the Ten-Ten experiment personnel. Her weight fell as the spacecraft transferred its spin angular momentum to its exhaust.

From the ship's view port, Hilda watched long white tubes of the Ten-Ten experiment's pellet accelerators run off in either direction from the Macrocollider Experiment Station, fading to the thinness of spider silk but never quite vanishing, even ten thousand kilometers distant. The beauty of it never ceased to thrill her.

The project's cylindrical habitat and control center swung tethered to an asteroid about ten kilometers from the planned collision vertex. The complex seemed to grow as they got closer and she watched the cylinder of the habitat module swing around its asteroid anchor at once a minute like the second hand of a giant clock. A tiny elevator climbed inward from the habitat to meet them at the central rock.

The plasma fountain ceased as the *Psi Naught's* relative velocity decayed to a few meters per second, while Hilda and Sarah felt a momentary queasiness as they returned to zero gravity. Hilda took control of the docking for practice, goosing this thruster and that to bring them to the counter-rotating dock assembly at the north pole of the little asteroid. There were three other spacecraft present, including the InterplaNet News ship, *Gulliver*.

"I thought we were going to get away from that," Hilda said.

Sarah shrugged.

As she settled in among three other spacecraft, Hilda watched insect-like limbs deploy from a half dozen places around the *Psi Naught's* toroidal hull and grasp the open latticework of the docking platform. A flexible tube rose like a cobra from the platform and mated itself to the main door of the cabin. Sarah supervised the shutdown.

"Your helmet." Sarah handed Hilda her helmet with a slightly defiant look. The chances of her needing it were about as close to infinitesimal as any AI could calculate, but Sarah liked all her stones turned over.

Hilda laughed and took it. "I feel like I'm headed for another giant leap for womankind instead of a docking tube."

The entrance into the air-filled docking tube was as normal as ever, though, as was the trip down the elevator to the habitat cylinder. There was a surprise when they got there, however: Torsten Ried.

"Uh!" was all Hilda could manage.

"Mr. Ried," Sarah said, drawing out the "Ried."

"Torsten, we're going to be kind of busy," Hilda said apologetically.

He nodded, but looked at her more like a puppy than a predator. "Don't worry, the media room's on the *Gulliver*. We'll all be there, anchoring, when the thing actually happens. Besides, you don't have to work all the time, do you? Dinner's being served in the level six atrium now. That's where everyone is."

His questions over their last meetings had been getting less and less hostile, and their conversations had ranged over the known universe, from Hilda's memories of New Antarctica to the debate about the genetically unmodified New Reformationist colony at Proxima II. Hilda felt repelled at the loss of life and Torsten listened; he had been a good listener.

Hilda nodded. "Good. We'll be up after we get settled in. I didn't mean to be cold, Torsten. It was just, well, a surprise."

He laughed. "That was the general idea. May I offer you a tour?"

Sarah waved him off. "We spent a year out here helping set this place up."

"Oh. Well, okay, I'll see you ladies later."

The walk was a pleasant stretch. Hilda reviewed the layout on her net to locate their assigned quarters. The "Can," as they called the habitat, was about thirty meters in diameter with staterooms arranged in rings around the outside of each of the first nine levels. The center sections were given over to equipment, labs, and common functions. There were three elevators spaced equilaterally. The tenth level was a domed combination of park and vegetable garden, with a swimming pool that Hilda had been dreaming about since the *Psi Naught* shipped out. The corridors were lined with hydroponic flower boxes as well; a thornless yellow rose with just enough scent adorned either side of her room, Number 502. Sarah was in 503 next door, with petunias.

Later, they went through an uncomfortable dinner in which almost everyone was either a media jackal looking for meat, or a potential saboteur.

Hilda took Sarah's arm. "I'm not sure I can take another one of these."

"I know how you feel. Ready?"

"You mean, just go and do it? Now?"

Sarah grinned. "Now."

••◦◦••

They wandered out of the cafeteria separately, then checked out a shuttle, and arrived at the Macrocollider Experiment Station at 2300 universal. Formally, it was called the MES, informally, the "mess." The ten-meter-radius sphere of the MES was so covered with various protuberances, antennae, and boxes that it looked to Hilda as if someone had dipped a geckro covered volleyball into a bin of miscellaneous electronic parts. Their shuttle headed for a tubular protuberance that turned out to be an airlock. They docked.

Pressures equalized. The doors opened.

The spherical room was brightly lit. Narrow boxes, tubes, and lattice frames radiated from the very center of the complex like an outsized metallic forest growing from the tiniest asteroid imaginable—a one-meter-radius ball. It looked like random junk. But a second look showed Hilda that the long axes of most of the equipment lay in a circular plane centered on the vertex, as it should be to investigate a sheet of debris normal to the collision axis. Black patches of photovoltaic cells and infrared data bus windows glinted on most of the equipment.

Hilda examined one of several huge boxes around the outer wall of the sphere and found what she was looking for. "Sarah, neutrino detector. Neutrino radiation from the experiment *should* be approximately isotropic and proportional to the total energy. Let's see if this one is telling us the truth."

"Got it," Sarah said, and shoved herself over to the device.

Meanwhile, Hilda placed a number of simple, disk-shaped neutron detectors, each about two centimeters across and a couple of millimeters thick, at various places around the collision site.

"Good evening, ladies," a voice announced.

Hilda felt a chill down her back.

She turned and saw a large ruddy man wearing a BHP staff sweatshirt glide out from behind the central globe. He was calm, inexpressive, neither smiling nor frowning, but his eyes darted restlessly.

"Good evening," she said. "You are?"

"Dr. Vitaly Rossov, Dr. Kremer; I am new site engineer. Anything I can do to help?"

Sarah stopped her with a hand on her arm and smiled at Rossov. Hilda noted the front of Sarah's skintight pressure suit had opened almost down to her navel.

"Nothing we needed to bother you with, Dr. Rossov," Sarah said. "We're putting some equipment in place for tomorrow's test shots and adjusting camera fields. Trying to get a handle on the anomaly."

"I'll be about my calibrations then," he said. "We have a test shot at 0900 and everything should be ready. Not expecting visitors. Will be done in hour or so."

"We'll manage," Sarah said. "Thanks, Dr. Rossov."

Rossov nodded and floated back to where he'd come from.

Sarah made a hush gesture to Hilda, then pointed to the terminal end of the neutrino detector cable on the outer wall of the facility.

"Hold that," she whispered, positioning Hilda so her body hid the work site.

Sarah, Hilda decided, really didn't trust Rossov.

Silently, Hilda held the cable, floating so her body hid what they were doing while Sarah slipped the tiny, transparent disk over the optical cable end and reconnected. Then she followed Sarah to the airlock and the shuttle.

"Is Rossov a spy?" Hilda asked, in the privacy of the shuttle.

"Someone is," Sarah said. "He gives me the creeps, so that makes him a suspect. He's also in the right place. If Rossov were working for them, he'd know how to fake data. I'm going to set an agent watching with a radio link back to the Psi Naught. If there's any tampering, we should see it."

••∞••

Everyone gathered in the habitat auditorium to watch the data come in from the shot—staff, investigators, and press. Sarah wore a thin T-shirt and loose, clingy shorts—artlessly practical in the warm controlled temperature of the habitat, but Hilda thought it made her look like a teenage pinup instead of one of the top physicists in the Solar System.

Hilda wore a much more dignified plain black jumpsuit and had her vacuum tights underneath, in case they needed to go to the experiment site on short notice. What an odd couple we make, she thought. Hilda found a spot next to Sarah, then Torsten Ried planted himself next to them.

"Morning, Hilda! Hi, Sarah."

"Good morning, Torsten," they said, almost simultaneously, and with about the same weary inflection, then laughed.

He smiled. "Yes, uh, what are we going to find out new today?"

If we knew that, thought Hilda, we wouldn't be doing the experiment. But be nice, she told herself. "For one thing, we'll be able to put some limits on anisotropy and get a better idea of radiation losses."

"Anything that would detect the beginnings of a new universe?"

Some people, Hilda thought, had one-track minds. She shook her head.

"T minus three minutes and counting," the experiment control software reported.

Hilda scanned the situation display. A green color raced down the two beamline representations, indicating the accumulators for each set of coils along the line were fully charged, each coil ready to come on at the appropriate time to push the pellets ever faster.

The count reached ten. Torsten, she saw, looked confused. Too bad, she thought, I'm not going to launch into a lecture now.

"...three, two, one. Fire."

The green lights went off down the line at an accelerating rate until they were all off.

"Good shot," the controller reported.

I don't believe this, Sarah sent. *It's completely nominal. Hilda?*

Hilda was already comparing the readings from these instruments with those reported on the previous shots that had brought them out here. The anomaly had vanished entirely.

Nothing, she reported

"It looks completely nominal so far," Hilda said aloud.

"So far?" Torsten asked. "What does that mean? Why wasn't it like the first shot?"

Hilda stared at him, searching for words. She was not, she realized, ready to accuse nameless parties of falsifying the experimental results, even though that was what had clearly happened.

"Something in the instrumentation setup itself may have caused the first set of anomalous readings. That's the only thing that's changed."

"An observer effect? Like Schrödinger's cat—half dead and half alive until someone looks?"

Hilda groaned. "No, we physically moved the detectors. Besides, it's not 'half,' it's a superposition..."

"Excuse me, Mr. Ried," Sarah said. "Hilda and I need to have a chat. In private."

"You're in over your heads, then, aren't you?"

Sarah smiled. "Not exactly, Mr. Ried."

••∞••

Hilda followed Sarah, but instead of heading for their rooms, she headed for the airlock. Hilda smiled to herself—when Sarah said private, she meant private. Fifteen minutes later, they'd ascended the elevator, and set out gliding over the small asteroid's surface near in the two-year-long night of its south pole of rotation, with Sarah trailing an emergency survival pod along. Sarah said nothing for a while, but appeared to be looking for something. Finally she motioned for Hilda to follow her. Then, amazingly, Sarah seemed to vanish straight into the ground.

It was a cave entrance, Hilda discovered, as she got to where Sarah vanished. "Sarah?"

No response. The asteroid had a high nickel-iron content, though, and might be screening Sarah from her radio. There was no other cave entrance around, so Hilda gulped and pulled herself in afterward. It was pitch black.

"Sarah?"

An intermittent signal light started blinking on the display reflected in Hilda's helmet faceplate. As her eyes adapted to the dark, she began to detect a very dim glow and smiled. She activated her own suit lights so she could follow the passage, and in a minute was floating next to Sarah in a small, roughly spherical room.

Sarah put her helmet next to Hilda's.

"I think I know who," she said.

"Isn't this getting a bit melodramatic? I almost didn't follow you in here!"

Sarah laughed. "We might be bugged. The station net might be bugged. If your radio signal couldn't reach me in here, then the signal from any bug can't get out. Now, help me with the vacuum tent."

The two-person emergency tent was a tight fit, but they managed to wiggle inside and inflate it. As soon as the pressure was up, Sarah made a hush sign and started to take off everything, motioning for Hilda to do the same.

Their clothing might even be bugged, Hilda realized.

They pushed their clothes into a pallet, and sealed it. Donning the emergency gear, they deflated the tent and pushed the pallet out. Then they reinflated the tent.

"There's no reasonable theoretical explanation for this, is there?" Sarah asked.

Hilda thought hard, giving that question a lot more effort coming from Sarah than from Torsten. Maybe she owed him an apology. "The results are inconsistent and the second set are the right ones. It's Rossov."

Sarah nodded. "Besides, he may have intimate connections to the Ried family; he had an affair with one of the cousins, someone named Anna, years ago."

"Sarah, that's personal data. How did you... ?"

"Pillow talk."

"Sarah!"

She laughed again. "I got it from Irene Simmons; Rossov tends to brag after too many vodkas. Anyway, my cyberagent found Rossov was studying voice in Nürnberg then and appearing in low budget opera. This Anna was the only Ried of the right age in the area at the time. Rossov was not a very good singer, but a really clever set designer. Later he got a PhD in physics, but had problems with getting published and ended up in instrumentation. Professional jealousy and a sexual connection."

Hilda pondered this. "We can't let everyone know about the telltales."

Sarah nodded. "So we've got to play it like we don't know. With a couple more tests, we'll have enough information to argue convincingly the anomalous results aren't real. Or, we might catch him tampering again."

'What a tangled web we weave,' Hilda thought. But Sarah was right. "Okay. We can go ahead with the Ten-Ten without Rossov being aware that we're onto him, but we need him out of the picture before he can think of anything else to screw it up. Doesn't anyone have the authority to simply remove Rossov, without making explanations?"

"Tse Wen could, which I think he will, if we have data to convince the personnel review board," Sarah explained. "With Rossov out of the way, all we have to worry about is physics."

Hilda bit her lip. The election was less than a week away, and the Senate's control of the vast resources for the project was at stake. "What if Lars Ried becomes president?"

Sarah shook her head. "That's another worry. One more thing—we can't talk about this to anyone where they can plant micro bugs. Rossov is good at this kind of thing. The net here is his, so he can defeat that encryption, too. If we use another encryption, he'll think we're onto him. Nix on the net chat, too. Just in case. But we can bring dates here."

Hilda groaned. "Sarah, I just want to do physics."

Sarah grinned. "I'll take care of that. Let's get back."

On the surface, before entering the elevator, Hilda stopped and pointed up at the Great Square of Pegasus in the sky.

"Follow its eastern stars north, about one square's width. New Antarctica is up there somewhere."

"Homesick?" Sarah asked.

"Always, a little," Hilda replied. "Home" had been ripped away from her, first by her mother leaving, then by being sent to school on Earth. Something was missing, lost in time and distance, never to return.

"Lacaille 9352 is rising, down by Fomalhaut," Sarah said.

Like New Antarctica, it was too dim to see without optical aids, but she had one of the most brilliant stars in the sky to guide her to its neighborhood. To complete the picture, Hilda found Gamma Eridani southwest of Orion, and followed a short four-star trail to Epsilon Eridani. The asteroid's rotation had brought all three Black Hole Project stars above the horizon at once, briefly. She imagined four lines of fire, one from each star and one from the sun, meeting between them. The center of their huge triangle of stars. The vertex, about five point two light years away. Where it would all come together.

About there, she sent, *just above nu Ceti. We're going to make it happen, aren't we?* She asked.

Let's go find out, Sarah replied.

CHAPTER 4

BHP Solar System Experimental Station
3 June 2257

Hilda, in the holographic simulation room, found herself biting her nails for the first time since she was a teenager. The experiment itself was not the source of her nervousness. Three more runs at the milligram level showed no anomalies, and they got the go-ahead to do the Ten-Ten experiment—only two days before voting began in the senate election. The opposition was certain to do something, and there was no time to recover. She filed a final prediction run, leaned back to stretch, and saw Torsten Ried enter.

She fought irritation; there were no rules barring media from the work areas, but by a kind of implicit mutual consent, the physicists were allowed to work undisturbed in those areas. "We've got company."

Sarah sighed softly. "I noticed."

"Hilda, Sarah," Torsten said, "sorry for the intrusion, but we've got nineteen plus hours of virtual dead time to fill until you fire the Ten-Ten experiment, and I wondered if you'd help with a piece out at old Duluth Station—what things were like before the new facility—Captain Sally Duluth slept here and so on."

"Can we wiggle out of it?" Hilda asked Torsten. "There's still stuff to do."

"You're not completely ready?" Torsten suddenly seemed very serious.

Sarah shook her head. "We're more than ready enough, but we can always squeeze a little more out of the shot. Hilda, I have things in hand if you want to go."

Hilda nodded. Sarah was essential to their plans and having Torsten elsewhere would be a good thing.

"It won't be long," Torsten said. "I think we'll need three hours on site at the outside. We'll have her back here watching the MES eight hours before T = 0."

Hilda noted with a smile that, after a week out here, Torsten was calling the Macrocollider Experiment Station "the mess" and talking about "T = 0" like everyone else. "Tse Wen thinks it's a good idea to be as open with the media as we can and cooperate in every way possible. 'The silence of many hands not clapping is louder than the sound of few cheers,' he says."

Sarah sighed. "They won't applaud what they don't get. You've had practice with Torsten, of course."

Torsten smiled wryly and spread his hands as if to say that was simply the reality of his business.

Hilda shook her head. There were, she thought, people all alone in kuiperoid stations a thousand astronomical units from nowhere perfectly happy with research problems that could be done with one mind, a good cybersystem, and no interference. Why, she asked herself, had she chosen something so public? Or had it chosen her?

"Hilda?" Torsten asked and smiled. "You look frustrated."

"Just working things out." In spite of everything, the man still attracted her. A challenge? A response to the special attention he paid to her, even if it gave her a headache at times?

"Okay, I'll do it." She smiled at Torsten. "I'll meet you at the shuttle port in an hour."

●●∞●●

As they approached the Duluth Station airlock, Torsten said, "I hear your father's back on New Antarctica and wants you to go back to head up the project there."

Hilda looked at him quickly. "Word travels fast. That wasn't supposed to be announced until we finished up the Ten-Ten. I haven't really decided. There are still some issues between Wotan Kremer and me. That's off the record, though, please."

Torsten shrugged. "Don't worry. We'd just say you were weighing it."

Hilda nodded curtly. To give her mind something else to think about, she took manual control of their approach and swooped in on the shuttle's belly thrusters, pinning them to the floor with a gee and a half while the AI squawked helplessly. At the end of it, she kicked in the minus-x jets for a hard two seconds of eyeballs-out to leave them floating dead in space above the docking mechanism.

"Jesus!" Torsten exclaimed, looking green.

Hilda laughed. "I learned to drive on a starship's runabout, Torsten. It's what we do for recreation out here."

Once secured, they made their way to the lock. Hilda was almost into the tube, before turning back for her helmet. There was no net here, but it felt almost like Sarah was sending her a message. At the station entry lock they stowed their gear and headed for the old command center beneath the port area. Hilda floated over to a console and let microgravity bring her body into the footholds beside it.

She chuckled. "This is more advanced than it was in Duluth's day, but it seems primitive compared to what we use now."

Torsten looked at a bank of dead gray touch screens, wondering. "Can you explain what's changed in language people can understand?"

She felt irritated for only a moment. "I can try. This panel controlled a millimeter wave system; we could punch straight through an atmosphere with that, but the data rate was a millionth of the multiplexed x-ray frequencies we use now. Also, at the higher frequency, we can focus to a spot a million times smaller with the same size aperture at the same distance. That helps with the BHP's interstellar comm."

"That's done from here?"

"About fifty kilometers away."

"So right now, even though the project hasn't been approved yet, there are messages going out toward Groombridge 34, Epsilon Eridani, and, uh..." Torsten hesitated.

"... Lacaille 9352," Hilda filled in, "and Chandrasekhar Station at the BHP's vertex. The power systems being built there will be used for interstellar exploration, commerce, and settlements as well as for the Black Hole Project. This project requires a lot of lead time."

"You seem to have a great deal of confidence. Uh, zero gee is getting to me. Where's the..."

Hilda smiled. "Go out door three, then left."

Alone, she glanced around the room and remembered. Then she wondered what it would be like to remember it a million years from now, or a billion. Dr. Zhau often said the BHP was but part of the beginning of human history.

A dark spacesuited figure floated into the room and raised a spray can, which hissed. *Sarah...* There was no net in here. It got very dark as she fell slowly in the minuscule gravity.

••∞••

"Mr. Ried, Anna sent me," a low, slightly Russian-accented voice announced when Torsten emerged from the head into the passageway. It was Vitaly Rossov, the site engineer. He wondered what the man's relationship was to the family. He held out his hand.

"Why are you here?"

Rossov tossed him a duffel bag. "EVA kit. Put it on. I have something to show you. Channel 10."

Torsten complied and accessed Channel 10 in the suit's comm system. A star field filled his heads-up display. An arrow indicated one of the stars. A dim asteroid was moving toward it.

"Electing Lars is Plan A. This is Plan B. Arrow points to New Antarctica from Groombridge 34 antenna five years from now. Asteroid, we have just given a slight push, to cause an occultation."

Groombridge 34 dimmed and vanished for about thirty seconds as they watched. Then it blinked in again.

"How does this help anything?"

"When eclipse happens, we substitute our own message for a couple of milliseconds, in dead time before cut off. Then, fifteen years from now, the Groombridge 34 impactor has a new launch time. Wrong launch time. Clever, yes?"

Torsten nodded dumbly. Somehow it didn't seem fair. What possible good could it do Lars here in the Solar System? Well, he thought. Maybe it wouldn't work.

Rossov powered down the console to standby condition, then handed him a data stick.

"Codes. In case I am incapacitated, and the backup is not needed. It could give us away, so it shouldn't be used unless nothing else works. The AI inside knows what to do."

Torsten grimaced, wishing someone else had that mission.

Rossov put his helmet on and turned up the visor reflectivity. "You wait here."

"But Dr. Kremer..."

"She will join us shortly. You wait here."

••∞••

The first thing Hilda noticed as awareness slowly returned was that her head ached. She groaned and stretched. Then she remembered where she was—someone had done this to her. You should pretend you're still out until you get your bearings, she thought.

Too late. The figure with the spray can was in the room and headed for her. It had been six decades since she'd done any zero-g wrestling—but the fact that she'd done it at all might be an advantage. She took a deep breath, moved her legs against a nearby wall panel and with a quick movement, shoved off from the panel and lunged at him. He reached for her, but she caught his arm, pulled it by her, and wrapped herself over his back, starfish-like. The two tangled bodies cartwheeled toward the door while the spray can went flying across the room.

Hilda pulled on the release lock on his helmet and tried to twist it off.

"Who are you and what do you want? What did you do with Torsten?" she screamed.

The man grabbed the doorjamb to stop them, then tried to pull her arms away from his helmet.

With one foot planted, she stomped on the doorjamb, the sudden acceleration slamming his helmet into the doorjamb. He let go of her hands, then slammed his helmet back into her head, stunning her. Then he kicked himself free and went after the spray.

Hilda launched herself after him, but he remembered to avoid her starfish maneuver. They collided, grappled, and she went for his helmet. The clumsiness of his full vacuum gear and lack of purchase or leverage canceled any strength and size advantage he might have had, and the helmet began to turn. But he got his hands between them pushed her away and smashed a fist directly into her stomach.

She gasped and loosened her grip on his helmet and he kicked himself away. He reached the spray can before she could get to him again, and got her full in the face.

"Damn you!" she gasped, pushed him away and tried to jump for the door but lost consciousness before she got there.

••∞••

Torsten heard thuds, clangs, and what might have been a woman screaming. What the hell? He started to pull himself down the corridor back to the control room; but Rossov met him half way, going the other direction.

"Okay." Rossov said. "We go."

"But Dr. Kremer."

Rossov smiled. "She will not be around to interfere with our plans, now."

As the men left the old station's airlock for Hilda's shuttle, Rossov commanded the station into hibernation mode.

"Rossov, that's Hilda's air supply!"

Rossov snickered. "*Da.*"

Torsten grabbed Rossov's arm. Guilt feelings riddled him. "You only need her out of the way for a few hours."

Rossov pulled him aside. "We are going to alter the data to make the experiment look like failure. She could catch the phony data and blow whole thing. She probably cannot escape, but dead is safer."

Torsten reached out and touched Rossov. "I say no killing. It would ruin Lars if it got out."

"Calm down. Okay, I disable communications but leave life support system on." Rossov waved Torsten away.

Torsten pulled himself back through the connecting tube and into the runabout. Guilt picked at his mind. He wished an end to this nightmare.

But it came back with a vengeance.

"Going somewhere, Torsten?"

Torsten turned to see Hilda, smiling as if nothing had happened. His stomach knotted.

"J-just waiting for you."

She laughed. "I see I fooled you! I only need to fool a few others for a few hours."

"Anna!" Torsten could not believe her impersonation was so good.

"We're late, let's go," Anna said. "Vitaly will take the other spacecraft."

In Hilda's voice, she told the spacecraft to return. Torsten wondered, uncomfortably, what Lars really would have thought about this. How much had Anna taken on herself? Until now he'd never felt the psychological price of doing favors for his brother so heavily.

Anna seemed tense, too, but it might be more the anticipation of an actor ready to take the stage than worry about what might go wrong with her impersonation.

"Time to see if this works," she said. "Central Control, Central Control, this is Shuttle Two."

"Shuttle Two, Central. Dr. Kremer, has there been a problem? No one has been able to reach you. Dr. Levine is quite concerned. The experiment is on hold."

Torsten stifled a sigh of relief. Rossov must have added Anna's vocal database to Hilda's. The fact that Central Control's computer had accepted Anna as Hilda got them over the first big hurdle.

"Roger, Central," Anna replied. "I misjudged a zero gravity turn and hit my head pretty hard. I haven't been able to access the net; but they say a slight concussion can do that. I've taken some neurogen and it should clear in a few hours. It's a nuisance to be off-line, but I can make do with this." She touched the headset. "And aside from that, I seem to be fine. Tell Dr. Levine not to worry. I assume all the preparations are in order for the experiment? I haven't been able to reach Dr. Rossov."

"There are no problems with experiment preparations. Dr. Rossov is inbound to the MES. He is concentrating on some last-minute equipment items at the vertex and is not available for conversation now. Do you wish to speak with Dr. Levine?" Central continued.

"I'm sure Sarah's very busy, too," Anna answered. "Just tell her not to worry. I've been invited to do commentary on the media ship, so I'll be there if she needs me. Shuttle Two out."

Anna turned to Torsten. Flushed with the success of her impersonation, she grinned like a hungry tigress, floated over to him and ran a fingernail across his lower lip as she purred into his ear. "You don't seem to be in the spirit of things."

Torsten smiled apologetically. "Anna, I can't." He pulled her hand away from his face. "I'm worried about Kremer."

Anna laughed. "No worries there."

A chill went down Torsten's back. Had Rossov broken his promise?

"I'm not sure, Anna. This could all go wrong on us so fast."

She shrugged. "So it goes wrong? Even in the worst-case scenario, if I am discovered, I am on the press ship, vanish, and become Anna again. My skin now has both DNAs, and DNA is so reliable that nobody checks fingerprints anymore. You can deny knowing anything." She laughed. "If the Ten-Ten experiment is successful and the project is authorized anyway, we have a backup. If Lars loses, he can easily find his way back to the top again in twenty years or so. So whatever happens, we can still win. If you want power you have to take chances. Maybe you win, maybe not. But you never get anywhere by not trying. Immortality means never having to give up."

"But Dr. Kremer..."

Anna nibbled on his ear lobe, whispering, "You really don't want to know."

●●∞●●

Hilda awoke to a dry sensation in her throat. Then she felt a strong ache in her stomach and remembered the fight. Where was Torsten? She looked around. It was pitch black. Not a glimmer of light. She gingerly moved her arms and legs. Nothing broken. She pushed herself very gently up from the floor—all she had to orient herself was a thousandth of a gravity, and she didn't want to lose it. Where the hell was Torsten? What did they want with him?

Silence answered. Complete dead silence. That was wrong. Creepy.

"Override 10 A T 7." That was twenty-five years old, but why change it?

Still nothing. Whoever had shut this down had known what they were doing. Damn, she was a physicist, not a tech.

She felt herself gasp for a breath, and then another breath. Life support was down, and she'd probably used up all the oxygen in the immediate area. The silence—no fans, no circulation. Willing herself to be calm, she pushed herself away, down the hall, and was able to breathe more easily. 'You have to be like a shark,' she told herself, 'and keep moving to breathe.' But where? The airlock. She needed to find her helmet and an emergency suit. Back to the airlock. She felt her way along, blind, half-afraid to stumble across Torsten's body, but the floor was bare.

She reached the airlock, but couldn't find the emergency suit lock by feel.

How much time was left? She pressed the face of her wrist comp. Less than an hour, the numbers glowed at her. Glowed! She pressed the face again—her eyes were so well night adapted that she could see the wall clearly.

There! She pressed the emergency equipment panel, got the suit out, and released its tiny life support unit. Fortunately, the fittings were standard. Then she got her helmet from its niche, put it on, asked for max, breathed deeply, then turned it back to normal, as she felt fully recovered.

Now what? Her shuttle was gone, of course; a look through the airlock door window showed both that and the fact the outer airlock door had been left open. The bastards had been thorough. Maybe, with a clear head, she could get the station powered up again. There was a spare CPU...

Still suited up, she went back to the control center.

Working alone in a spacesuit, the CPU swap took an hour and a half. The new one knew nothing about any shutdown, so it quickly powered the system up. A comm light went on indicating the station's AI was standing by. "Computer, patch me through to operations."

"Visual and audio transmitting capability has been physically disabled. I can only receive visual and audio transmissions," the station's computer announced.

That had seemed too easy, and it was.

"What is the status of Ten-Ten?"

"The experiment has not been conducted, as indicated by the continued presence of the MES. I cannot query for data in a receive-only mode..."

"Computer, what is the status of the transmitter repair?"

"A full repair can be accomplished in two days."

"What's happening?"

"You are giving an interview to InterplaNet News," the AI told her.

"Me?"

CHAPTER 5

BHP Solar System Experimental Station
3 June 2257

The atmosphere on the press ship was tense, with all eyes glued to the data displays and the scene from BHP operations. The latter lacked the drama of bygone eras, Torsten thought. No consoles, no headsets, no big central display; the physicists just stood around in groups of two or three, occasionally saying something to each other. Rossov was back among them now, coolly going from one group to another and patting people on their backs as if he'd never been anywhere else. But the relaxed appearance was misleading; voice stress indicators were at 160% and nobody, but nobody was sitting down.

The south pole of BHP central faced the experiment and Dr. Sarah Levine was at a south-facing window, hands gripping the rail.

There were consoles aplenty in the nerve center of the media ship, a disk-shaped section of the spherical hull just below the observation dome. A half dozen had been bolted to the ceiling of the room, creating what was in effect another floor. They'd even, Torsten noted, tacked down a geckro walkway between the ceiling consoles and all but one of them had people hanging behind them. In zero gravity, as long as everyone watched their heads, that worked.

Torsten grabbed a towel someone had thoughtfully attached to the console and blotted up his sweat—it didn't run in zero gravity, just accumulated on his skin in great salty drops. Behind him was a chaotic mess of wires, conduits, and bodies careening this way and that; his editors would replace that with a giant version of the magazine logo. In the middle of all the chaos was a central desk, at which sat anchorman Ashira Nagato of InterplaNet News and Dr. Hilda Kremer—at least who they all thought was Dr. Hilda Kremer.

Torsten started his own voice-over. "This is Torsten Ried for *Popular Issues*. We are within minutes of the most breathtaking and potentially the most dangerous physics experiment ever initiated, the precursor of an even bigger experiment that will either, according to some, give humanity the power of gods or, if it goes wrong, destroy the entire universe. Let us leave that aside for the moment; this will be big enough. Not since the days of nuclear weapons has a man-made explosion so huge been attempted. Some think this threatens the very fabric of our existence, but the physicists have constantly assured us they know it will not. We shall have to hope they are right!"

With a glance of his eyes and a mental click, Torsten selected a view of the experiment vertex.

"This is where the collision will take place. The small structure you see will be totally vaporized in the explosion, but its instruments will send their important readings nanoseconds before they vanish. Physicists will use these readings to refine their model, the one that says there is no danger, and ask the IPA Senate for final approval to attempt to make a black hole.

"But what Senate? Whose viewpoint will this experiment support, the 'forward forever' liberals of President Owomba or the 'enough already' consolidationists led by Senator Lars Ried's Conservative Union Party? We should all know in about five minutes. In the meantime, we will join Mr. Ashira Nagato who is conducting the pool interview of Dr. Hilda Kremer, the chief theorist behind this gargantuan challenge to nature."

A nod to his AI took Torsten out of the flow. He sighed and turned his attention to his monitor. Anna looked very much like Hilda, but had a kind of snooty carriage that he'd never seen the real Hilda affect.

The audio fade-in caught her in mid-sentence. "...no problem whatsoever. It's really only a small nuclear explosion; bigger ones were conducted three centuries ago, right in Earth's atmosphere."

Nagato frowned. "Can you explain for new viewers, in words that we all can understand, what aspects of the standard model you hope to verify with this experiment?"

"Certainly. Our model predicts we can do the black hole experiment safely. It also predicts certain readings from this experiment. If they match, we maintain we can do the black hole experiment."

"But the black hole effort will be billions and billions of times bigger."

"You do what you can," Anna/Hilda said with a superior shrug.

Torsten found himself sweating. Anna/Hilda's answers had none of the depth that Hilda's would have had. By now Hilda would have explained what a "quagma" was and talked about compression constants and calibration. The general public might not have detected the difference, but someone like Dr. Levine certainly would. The whole house of cards was starting to fall apart in his mind.

"Mark one," someone said. "The accelerator coil field strengths are nominal."

I'm on, Torsten thought, suddenly too busy to worry about the deception.

"The biggest gun ever built by humankind is about ready to fire. Transient fields a billion times stronger than those that propel our starships will be applied in sequence to send its ten-gram bullets at ten times the speed of... I mean to a gamma of ten, that is to say to a speed so relativistic that they'll hit with ten times the mass they really have. I sincerely hope I am still here to report the results." Torsten took a deep breath. He was definitely rattled. What he had said was pure hype, but if there was even a chance in a billion that Hilda was wrong and the most vociferous of the critics right, they might have been his last words.

There was a momentary silence in the newsroom, as if the same thought had occurred to everyone else.

••∞••

A million nightmares raced through Hilda's mind. A recording? An experiment-induced time warp? A virtual doppelganger? "Let's see it."

She'd seen herself before, of course, recorded or through real-time monitors. But here she was, with Ashira Nagato no less, on InterplaNet News.

He asked, "We have reports about an abnormal amount of gamma rays on the preliminary tests. Can you confirm that?"

"Without using a lot of technical jargon," her double said, "the latest round of tests showed an unnatural, inexplicable amount of gamma rays escaping the collider collisions. Gamma rays are one of the most lethal forms of energy in the universe."

Hilda winced at how the double played up a danger that was nonexistent to anyone over a few hundred kilometers away from the experiment.

"Your calculations failed to predict this radiation?"

Hilda's image shrugged and gave a distracted look into the camera. "Yes, but it's not enough of a loss to keep us from making a black hole, so we don't consider it important."

"So we are going ahead with the final test anyway?"

"Of course," the double said with a voice that was dripping with contempt.

Hilda stared at the image, stunned and in shock. Not only the public image of the project, but her own reputation was being trashed by this impersonation. She smashed her fist into the palm of her open hand. Had Torsten been in on this sabotage all along? To set back everyone's work for at least a generation? To destroy the only life she'd known for the last thirty-five years? What kind of monster had she been playing with? How was she ever going to face Brad?

Academics and Earth were another life. Here she had to fight, to act, not react. But how?

If she could only get word to Sarah. Hilda thought furiously. She had a radio, in the suit. It was just a matter of gain. "What's the power of my suit radio transmitter?" she asked the AI.

"Three watts."

"Do you have a parabolic dish pointed at the station? How big?"

"I can point the north pole ten-meter radar dish at the station."

Hilda did the calculation herself—the suit antenna was essentially omnidirectional, so its three watts would be spread over... Maybe...

"Get the airlock ready. I'm going outside."

••○○••

It was hard to make good time over the dusty surface. If Hilda tried to stride or hop too hard, she would put herself on a trajectory taking many minutes to return to the surface. She found the best way was essentially to go hand over hand on the surface, pulling herself along from rock to rock as she emerged from the pitch-black shadow in her helmet light. But the surface of the asteroid's polar night was barely the temperature of liquid nitrogen and there was only so much the few nanometers of high-tech fabric of her gloves could do about that. Her fingers grew numb with cold. She flexed them furiously between grabs.

It took fifteen minutes to reach the dish. It was on a tower over a hundred meters tall with a despin platform on top of that. More hand-over-hand work. She looked down and shivered at the height despite the low gravity. She pulled herself over the rim of the dish, launched herself toward the feed horn at the focus of the dish, and grabbed hold.

"This is Hilda Kremer calling Dr. Sarah Levine. Emergency."

"Person calling on suit radio for Dr. Levine, your voice does not match Dr. Kremer's."

They'd hacked the database, Hilda realized. "Your database has been compromised. Get Dr. Levine. Tell her... tell her thanks for making me take my helmet with me..."

••○○••

Torsten stared at the time display; it didn't move. A hold, he guessed. The media deck was silent as if every comment that could be made had been. In the silence Torsten heard Anna/Hilda say, "I'm fine, Sarah, go ahead... let me check... no problem, that should be fine."

He could only hear this side of the headset conversation. Was Levine suspicious of something? Had Anna/Hilda allayed those suspicions?

"Resuming count at ten," someone called out.

Torsten stared at the image of the Ten-Ten's vertex, not trusting his voice.

"Five... four... three... two... one..."

"We have data!" someone shouted

"What the hell?"

"It's all neutral pions!"

"Look at the magnetic transient!"

The silence turned instantly into a babble.

Torsten stared at the facility.

It was still there. No ten-megaton nuclear explosion. But people all around him were yelling about data. Something was terribly, terribly wrong. Well, it was supposed to go wrong, to discredit the experiment. Maybe he had misunderstood how wrong. At any rate, he had better start talking.

"Something unexpected has happened," he intoned. "The experiment vertex is still intact, but instruments are reporting the results of a huge explosion, albeit not quite the kind of explosion expected. Perhaps time itself was affected; perhaps we aren't even in the same universe anymore!"

Steady, Ried, his producer said. *Keep your feet on the ground, you know.*

Torsten nodded and took a breath. "Or maybe there's some kind of massive instrumental problem." It occurred to him that Anna was prepared for this. "Let's see what Dr. Kremer has to say."

Anna/Hilda looked white-faced. The plan *was* for her to look confused and unconfident, but this looked too real. She talked, at any rate.

"The last round of tests showed an abnormal amount of gamma rays escaping the collider collisions. As I said, gammas are one of the most lethal forms of energy in the universe. They can also carry away the energy of collision before it has a chance to compress the matter enough. The fact that we have so many... uh... gammas..."

"Neutral pions," someone shouted, apparently trying to be helpful.

"They turn into gammas, right away," someone else said.

Anna/Hilda looked around. "Gamma, pions, we, uh, don't know what happened. Our models must be wrong. The energy could have gone into small black holes that consume ordinary matter, or produce something, uh, strange. I just hope this is contained."

Nagato jumped on that. "If the models are wrong, it would not be wise to go ahead with the Black Hole Project, would it?"

Anna/Hilda seemed to recover with that cue. "No, in all honesty, I think not."

He nodded. "The critics in the consolidationist alliance have a point then?"

"Yes, I'm afraid they do."

Anna/Hilda was now having trouble keeping a smile off her face; however unexpected this result was, it played right into their plan. It was time to get back into editorial mode. Torsten checked the setup and nodded to his AI to be ready to break in.

Nagato's frown was deep and angry. "I must then observe that these unexpected events harken back to the cautions the Conservative Union Party espouses. They say scientists do not really know what they are doing, and this is the apparent proof. We must now all consider our votes very carefully and take into consideration the power of these science experiments and their effect if left unchecked by proper oversight. Meanwhile, everyone here is still trying to figure out what happened."

Daring to hope, Torsten wondered how this was playing with the staff. He paged Rossov. No answer. He called up the monitor showing the scene in the station common area. There seemed to be none of the confusion and chaos there that was in the media center. Rossov was nowhere to be seen. Then he saw Dr. Sarah Levine's face. It was one great big grin.

She knew. They'd been set up. Oh, shit. *Anna, vanish. They're on to it.*

He looked back to the pressroom pool desk. Ashira Nagato seemed lost in concentration, listening to something. His mouth dropped open and his eyes got very big. Then his lips closed to a thin line of anger and he whirled around to the seat next to him. It was empty.

Torsten looked around; the room was a sea of floating bodies. Anna had somehow dropped her Hilda persona and vanished among them. He tried to imagine how—switch badges, let her hair out, wipe off some makeup? Anna Messenger would appear again. But there could be no such exit for him, he knew. He was hung out to dry.

Or was he? Was there any way he could backpedal himself out of this? And help Lars as well? Perhaps, he thought, perhaps. The knot grew in his stomach and he turned grimly to his pickup to try to talk his way out of it. He was good at that, he told himself—between Anna and his mother, he'd had to be.

"There have been some new developments," Torsten said. "Often, when nothing else can explain what has happened, the answer turns out to be some form of human manipulation, and that is apparently the case here. What we were told was to be the actual Ten-Ten experiment, was apparently not.

"Which leads to the question of where the data came from."

He sent a query toward Sarah Levine. *What happened?*

To his surprise, she answered. *As if you don't already know, Ried. Saboteurs apparently hoped to substitute false data for real data. We suspected that and did a precursor shot that triggered their mechanism, and revealed it. You can quote me. Levine out.*

He did quote her, and hoped he sounded innocent and confused. He certainly sounded rattled, no doubt about that. Text began scrolling on his monitor. Station security was looking for Rossov and the faux Hilda Kremer. Both were nowhere to be found.

"What this looks like now is an attempt to sabotage the experiment by very well-prepared opponents or, conceivably, if our imaginations run free, a staged sabotage attempt conducted by equally fanatic proponents seeking to embarrass consolidationist forces." He waved at all the media consoles, all occupied now with earnest people speaking rapidly. He could even smell, despite the best efforts of the *Gulliver's* environmental maintenance systems, the presence of too many excited bodies.

He looked back at the screen showing the common room to locate Sarah Levine. It didn't take long; she was facing a video pickup and seemed to be grinning right back at him.

You haven't seen anything yet, Ried, she sent.

Then she turned to her window as if to watch something.

What? In the middle of all this confusion? They couldn't... They wouldn't...

The countdown clock had started again, at T-60. The audacity of it took his breath. But what better time? He glanced at some of the other displays; he didn't understand the numbers, but they had all apparently recycled to pre-shot status. Rossov's false data had played itself out of the system and he would not have a chance to plant another set.

Or was he doing that now? If Rossov had slipped out on a small repair bot to the instrument module to cover his tracks or plant another set of spurious data, he'd be vaporized.

Torsten started to call security, to ask them to hold the experiment. Whatever Rossov was guilty of, for whatever reasons, he was still a human being, with a life to lead... Then Torsten stopped. If he called, he'd expose his own role in all this and involve Lars as well. Also, Rossov, if anyone, would know the real shot was in progress; if he was at the Ten-Ten's vertex, it was by his own choice. So be it.

Torsten realized that he, too, perhaps had a choice. At least for a while, he could be the professional he had always wanted to be, independent of his family, his own person. He was here, with an audience, with what could be the story of the dawn of a new era of history. It was not up to him to make the news. He had only to put everything else aside and report it.

"In the meantime," he began, "the research staff appear to be preparing to do the experiment for real. The data now show the beam lines are fully charged again. I am not getting a count but would guess that it will happen soon."

He had to fill, he realized; there were no more interviews to switch to. "The instrument module still floats suspended at the ends of the largest linear accelerator ever made. In a few moments, despite all the threats, sabotage efforts, and ethical concerns of opponents ranging from the fringe of political activism to sober physicists and interplanetary leaders, those accelerators may fire and lay the groundwork for a technological journey of Promethean significance that, like it or not, we all seem to be on."

He glanced at another monitor. "We have a count now—twenty seconds. The project staff members have crowded around their windows—windows, I should remind you, that are made of glass dense enough to stop ninety percent of cosmic radiation; you would not want to look at this with unprotected eyes... seven seconds... five... four..." He zoomed in on the vertex module. "...two... don't blink... one..." Suddenly, a brilliant white star sprang out of where the spherical instrument module had been. For the tiniest fraction of a second, he thought he saw a beautiful, iridescent hourglass shape expand from the vertex and rush at him, but it blew by almost instantly.

Did he feel a slight acceleration? Hilda had said there was not that much matter involved, even at its huge energies, compared to the mass of the station's asteroid.

"That was it! The instrument module has vanished—where the center of the Ten-Ten experiment was, where all the controversy, plans, and plots were focused, there is now nothing. There is nothing at all in that direction..." and he paused a moment as he realized the poetry of what he was about to say, and said it anyway, "... nothing between us and the distant stars."

"Mr. Ried?" It was a human voice, behind him. The idiot didn't realize he was interrupting a live feed. He held up a hand to indicate he was busy.

A hand touched his shoulder, lightly. "Mr. Ried."

What the hell? Well, it was a good place to break anyway. He faded his channel into the pool feed and turned angrily to confront his interrupter.

The young blond man behind him seemed suitably apologetic. "Please excuse me, Mr. Ried. I'm Simon Kalas, from BHP Central Security. Hilda Kremer, the real Hilda Kremer, said we should talk to you."

Torsten shut his eyes and took a deep breath. *Oh, shit.*

••∞••

A month later, when they landed back on Earth, it was Tse Wen and Brad's idea to quietly whisk Hilda and Sarah out to the Marin Headlands for a walk away from protesters and newsmongers who howled for news.

They walked up the dirt road towards a cliff overlooking the Golden Gate. With each step Hilda felt her muscles adjust to her Earth weight once more.

"Why such a windy place?" Sarah asked.

Brad deferred to Tse Wen, who was looking out over the cliff.

"The wind up here is strong because the topography has forced it up and given it a greater distance to cover. It is also hard on microphones and little things that fly. The wind has much to teach us about the source of strength, don't you think?"

It was coming from the East today, and was warm. Hilda touched Brad's arm.

He shrugged. "Like being in our faces. Hilda, your boyfriend's damage control efforts..."

Hilda winced. The history of her misjudgments with Torsten Ried now stood between them.

Brad shook his head. "Sorry Hilda. It's a bloody war of public opinion. Never mind truth."

"It's always been that way, Brad," Hilda said. She'd taken a vacation from physics on the voyage in from the asteroid belt, and had read a compilation of the correspondence between two American philosopher-Presidents, Adams and Jefferson, that Tse Wen had given her after the bomb attack. "Six hundred years ago Thomas Jefferson said that 'the inquisition of public opinion overwhelms in practice the freedoms assured by the laws in theory.'"

"Jefferson had it right," Brad said. "It's impossible to prove that anything is absolutely safe, and you'll never kill off all the wowsers. You just have t' out-argue and outlast 'em. Anyway, we've won, mates!"

"We have only won the right to keep trying," Sarah said. "Lars Ried keeps on stumping his platform and in a few years will be after the Presidency again and who knows how far they will try to reach." She looked up.

"You are worried about the other impactor launch sites," Tse Wen said. "We have people of unquestioned loyalty going out to take charge of those operations. Dr. G. P. Weaver, a former student of mine, is going to Epsilon Eridani. Hilda's sister, Elizabeth Avonford, will go to Lacaille 9352, and Hilda herself is going back to Groombridge 34. Beyond that, a wise combatant makes use of his opponents' energy."

Hilda smiled thoughtfully. "Thank you for teaching me that, Tse Wen."

"There is still no public word about the impostor and Rossov," Sarah commented.

The mention of Rossov saddened Hilda. There was no proof, of course, but everyone believed he'd been at the vertex when Sarah had triggered the real event. At least his death there would have been as nearly instantaneous as a death could be.

"Right," Brad added. "One or both of 'em are still out there. Hilda, did you know Rossov was sore at you about one of his papers not being accepted?"

"No, I didn't. All this for a paper?" She had reviewed thousands of papers over the years. She consulted her deep files through the net, "Oh!" A chill went down her.

"Hilda?" Sarah asked

"I trashed a paper. 'Quagma Energy Loss by Advanced Wave Emission,' submitted to Physika by V. I. Rossov, 2220. But that was over thirty years ago!"

Sarah laughed. "Advanced emission! Then he had a secondary agenda. He was still trying to get people to take his work seriously."

Tse Wen sighed. "When we made people immortal, we also made grudges immortal. Well, in the end, it would give me peace to think that Dr. Rossov may have killed his grudge the only way possible. I shall consider it a sufficient act of apology."

Hilda nodded in agreement. There was a justice to it after all, she thought, though she regretted the death greatly.

A warm gust of wind hit the group as they reached the apex of the hill. They turned their backs to it and looked out towards the Pacific Ocean and the Farallon Islands on the horizon.

"What do you think you'll miss the most about Earth?" Sarah asked as they got high enough to see most of San Francisco across the water.

"Besides us mates, o' course," Brad said, jokingly.

"Oh, I'll miss you all! Chaos help me, I will."

But instead of sadness, Hilda felt a rise of excitement. It was hard to contain. After all these years on Earth, she was finally going home to New Antarctica, to return to where she had been born, home to work with her father. Perhaps Kate Avonford's starship would stop there, too, some day. Too bad she would miss seeing her younger sister, Liz, who was shipping out to manage the impactor launch from Lacaille 9352.

Hilda picked up a sun-bleached Dungeness crab claw from the roadside where a seagull had dropped it. Playing with it absently, she looked first at Tse Wen, then at Brad. "And the wind," she said at last.

Sarah looked at her oddly. "The what?"

"I'll miss walking unprotected in the wind. New Antarctica is not misnamed. I'll miss this wonderful warm wind in my face."

••∞••

Torsten Ried glanced at the time display on his work screen. It was 1324, 7 August 2260. He wished he did not know what he knew would happen in three minutes. His stomach tightened.

Out in the asteroid belt, the inexorable laws of celestial mechanics would cause one small asteroid to come between the Black Hole Project's main x-ray communications laser and Groombridge 34. The occultation would only last a few minutes, and the AI had long ago predicted it; for those minutes, it would not transmit, lest its power slice a deep cut in the traversing asteroid's regolith and fog the entire area with droplets of frozen lava.

What the AI running the project's link to Groombridge 34 did not know, and what Torsten did know, was that there was another laser, hidden down on the occulting rock, that would transmit for about a millisecond on top of the main carrier between the last data and the interruption code. The AI that ran the bogus link knew all the right codes and modulations. It would also have a message, backed by terabytes of bogus experimental data and theoretical calculations, that would direct a delay in launching the Groombridge 34 impactor.

So Rossov's dark, ironic sense of humor would reach beyond his death. Did Hilda deserve this cruel revenge? Probably not, he thought, tightening his fingers into a grip.

It had taken all of his brother's influence to keep Torsten free after the Kremer kidnapping. If Torsten were to admit knowledge of the backup plan now, he would have to admit complicity in the kidnapping and he would betray his family in a way that they might correct very rapidly. He would also, once again, get involved in making news instead of reporting it. He thought of Hilda, Sarah, Lars, Anna and their Promethean agenda. Were they too big to stop?

To make the call or not? He opened his mouth to send a warning... then cleared his throat. Then he looked back at his time display and shook his head. Too late now.

BOOK II
THE SMALL POND

CHAPTER 1

In the Solar System's Kuiper Belt
9 May 2257

"Return? Return?! But we just got here! Nobody's even been down to the surface yet!"

The surface floated in the *Marsden's* observation window in front of her, forbidding, mysterious. And dark; three thousand times farther out than Earth, Sol itself was only a sixth as bright as a full moon. Still, she could see it floating dim and gray against a Milky Way brighter than it was. She put a hand on the view screen as if to touch the unknown planetoid below them. It drew Liz Avonford to it with a force far greater than its negligible gravity.

Salim shook his head firmly. "Orders from Dr. DeRoot. We have to go back."

She looked back at him intently, "But why?"

Salim shrugged his shoulders and opened his mouth to say something, but Liz held up her hand for him to stop.

"Nuts!" she said. "I'm going down for a couple of hours at least."

"I do not think that's a good idea. There will be hell to..."

Liz, halfway down the access tube toward the boat deck, didn't hear the rest. When she got to the red oval sliding door, she punched the button with far more force than needed to trigger the little mechanism.

"I am sorry, Dr. Avonford," Caroline, the *Marsden's* AI said. "But access has been denied."

"Salim!" Liz screamed, "Open the damn door!"

"Liz," Salim's voice came from the corridor speakers. "Rules are rules, orders are orders. We have to go back."

"We can go back. I just want to visit for a few minutes. Hell, they won't even know we got here for another two weeks."

"Seventeen days, eight hours," Caroline added, helpfully. "25 May 2257."

"They did the math," Salim said. "They didn't say so in so many words, but I think DeRoot would rather someone else be the first on the surface. This is the biggest thing that's been found in the Solar System in the last thirty years—it's 130 kilometers across! It's historically important. The institute would want to be involved in the landfall decision. We've got a big fish here, and we aren't supposed to be catching big fish. That's why DeRoot has us out here in nowhere."

"Nuts to the politics! I found it. I'm the commander here and I'm going to be the first one down."

Silence. But the door opened. What it came down to was that she was the expedition commander and the legal authority in place, unless Salim or someone relieved her. And not over this—no one had expressly ordered her not to make landfall.

Liz grabbed the doorjamb and projected herself across the boat deck to the nearest excursion vehicle. She checked herself smartly with a hand slap on the cockpit rim, pivoting her legs onto the seat. A quick visual showed the standard equipment was all present, including a helmet and coveralls in the wire mesh locker behind the pilot's station.

"Activate and close up," she told the module as she strapped herself in.

Two hours later, she was on the planetoid's surface, leaving the first human footprints on its regolith of coal-cosmic dust.

She crouched slowly to keep her feet on the ground, set an analyzer on the surface and waited for it to ingest some dirt and take isotope ratios.

"How old?" she queried.

The display inside her helmet projected 7.219 gigayears.

"Salim, if I believe this reading, this thing is older than the Solar System! Over seven billion years! It didn't come from here!"

Salim's groan echoed through her helmet, so loud it made her wince. She sighed. Bad enough to make an uncoordinated landfall on a big ice ball, but this was an uncoordinated landfall on a major discovery. She would go down in history instead of someone much more senior. She straightened her shoulders. That, she thought, was just tough.

••∞••

Two months later, Liz was back on Earth in Saint Petersburg, in Director Vitus DeRoot's office at the top of the very tall International Space Agency tower overlooking the Nevsky Prospekt that somehow still teemed with the cross roads of life from all over the world. DeRoot, director of the ISA Exploration division, was all the more terrifying because of the way his friendly, avuncular manner could mask his anger, she thought.

"Shall we go through the particulars?"

Liz willed her fisted hands to straighten and shook her head. She had a good idea of what would be on the list—every piece of negative information about her performance since she arrived in the Earth's Solar System.

He was going to do what he was going to do.

"The executive committee feels that we should take advantage of your family connections and the public attention your exploits have received in our education program."

Visions of intro classes and faculty teas rushed through her head. "With respect, Dr. DeRoot, I've not had any university experience. I did my degree on-ship, on the way in from 61 Cygni."

He smiled. "Not to worry. We can accommodate you in both respects. Ginny Lu has a long list of elementary schools over the entire planet that needs speakers. It would be a real treat for the children to meet someone who was born around another star, and is so famous. You'll be assigned to her. Anything else?"

"When does this all start? I have a milk run to the Black Hole Project in the asteroid belt."

DeRoot shrugged. "I wouldn't worry too much about the BHP; that's just too premature and grandiose—Director Zhau Tse Wen's political problems will shut them down before too long."

Liz felt a cold chill down her back. Was that what was behind this?

"Hilda Kremer, your sister, is on that project, is she not? I'm sorry." He frowned and looked down.

Liz bit her tongue.

"You colonials come back here with so much enthusiasm, but this is a very old Solar System and a very old planet with agendas that go way back." He shook his head. "One needs to tread carefully." He paused briefly. "Are we done?"

DeRoot had simply made a personnel move based on "needs within the institute." It had already been decided. What was done, was done.

She left DeRoot's office and went to her apartment on the thirty-second floor. There she opened a bottle of Mayagues Port, went out on her balcony, and looked out over the Ploshchad Ostrovskovo, awash in the late summer sun.

She thought about her mother, the near-legendary starship Captain Katherine Avonford, as she looked at the huge Russian monument to Catherine the Great. Its larger-than-life scale also reminded her of her planet-sculpting father, Wotan Kremer. She had vowed not be swallowed by her heritage but also, perversely, felt obliged to live up to it in some way, to be larger than life herself. She shuddered; time enough to get things back on track tomorrow. With that she set aside a couple of detox pills and proceeded to get smashed.

••∞••

The next morning, Liz went back to her small office in the exploration division. The door wouldn't open. She moaned, then wiped her hand and the handle to aid the ancient fingerprint recognition system's ability to recognize her.

It still wouldn't open.

A soft beep sounded that only the person standing in front of the door could hear. Liz touched the net for admin.

I am sorry, but you are not authorized entry to this office, came the reply.

Of course I am! Liz sent. *I'm Elizabeth Avonford and this is my office. For a while anyway...* Her stomach tightened as she realized what had happened. Chaos! It had only been ten lousy hours!

A young man, a tall blond, came down the hall toward her, followed by a cartload of boxes. As he reached her, he smiled winningly and stuck out his hand.

"David Levi." He pronounced it 'dah-FEED leh-VEE.' "A visitor already! As you see, I haven't moved in yet."

"It's my office," Liz said, knowing she was wrong.

Levi stared at her.

Liz sighed, deflated. "At least it was. I think my stuff is still in there."

"Oh, dear." Levi looked concerned. "Let's see."

He put this hand on the pad and the door opened. The office was bare.

"Damn!" Liz said. She'd only had it for three years, and most of that time she'd been in space. Still, there were memories—her first real job.

She looked at the wall where the pictures of her family had hung. The empty shelves that had held a few precious real books. Even her snow kitten doll was gone.

Levi looked mortified. "I'm sorry, I... They just assigned it."

Liz shook her head and wiped away a tear. "It's not your fault. I'm sure the service robots have stashed my things somewhere." She composed herself. "Well, what do you do?"

"Bio-nanotechnology. I got my doctorate at Jerusalem United thirty-five years ago and finally got a position." He stepped aside and the cart moved into the office with his things. "Only so much to do and a hundred and twenty-three billion people to do it."

Liz smiled and shuddered inwardly. She had a sudden insight into what resentment there might be towards her or any other colonials taking up positions.

"And, you are?" Levi asked.

Liz hesitated, then sighed. He'd find out soon enough. "Elizabeth Avonford."

His eyes went wide, "The person who just discovered the new planet three thousand AU's out? Captain Kate Avonford's daughter? And I'm taking your office? Geez, I'm sorry."

She smiled falsely. "Bureaucratic error. Uh, ten days before spring or after autumn equinox, the sun sets right behind the old fort. Enjoy it.

By the way, it's a kuiperoid or planetoid or whatever—not a planet." She turned and walked to the elevator.

As she entered her apartment, she realized she had to talk to someone. She touched the net for her older sister, Hilda.

The comm window blinked gray, then displayed the symbol of the Black Hole Project. The icon was a three-sided pyramid, nearly a perfect tetrahedron with a star at each corner. Two of the stars were yellow, two were red. A black dot in its middle was connected to the corners by four white lines. In half a century or so, four long, massive rods, each with a rest mass of about a hundred million tons, would be projected from each star, so fast they would weigh a thousand times their rest mass, to meet precisely in the center of that black dot, and, hopefully, form a mini black hole. Liz shivered when she thought about it—to think that her sister was in the middle of such a Promethean project. Her problems suddenly seemed very small. Compared to Hilda, even DeRoot was a microbe on Jupiter.

The site spoke to her: "You have reached the comm node of Brunhilda Kremer, PhD, and the Physics Section of the Black Hole Project. You may begin your message now."

Hilda, I just got my ass fired. She took a breath. *Help!*

A few minutes later, her sister was on her wall screen. Hilda had inherited from their father, Wotan, wide-set blue eyes and a long nose so much like her own that, in certain positions and lighting, it was almost like looking in a mirror. But Hilda's hair was an almost platinum gold, while her own locks were more reddish brown, attesting to Catherine Avonford's Celtic lineage. And Hilda had a strong chin. Liz often thought about having her own enhanced.

"Liz! Good morning. What's happened?"

Liz unloaded. "I don't know what to..."

She told Hilda everything, including DeRoot's personal affronts against the Project.

"Oh yes," Hilda said. "Dr. Vitus DeRoot... he's protecting his own job. If Lars Ried wins his bid for the Presidency of the IPA Senate, DeRoot wants to be seen as a supporter. By the way, Lars Ried's brother is a political hack writer."

Liz cocked her head, "Yes, but..."

"Your Dr. DeRoot was his fifteenth grade general science instructor at St. Louis Academy—Torsten mentioned Dr. DeRoot several times while I was trying to explain the project to him."

Liz' eye popped open. "Chaos! Out of 130-something billion people! The Rieds are trying to shut down your project so DeRoot has to put me in my place?"

Hilda apologetically shook her head. "Low odds, but yes, there's a connection. I haven't been much help in supporting their factoid about the BHP destroying the universe, so maybe it's another way of getting at me. I'm sorry. Is there any way I can..." she trailed off and looked thoughtful for a moment. "Look, Dr. Sarah Levine has changed her mind about going to Lacaille 9352 to work on the fabrication and the launch of its impactor for the BHP. You're an expert in space resources. Interested?"

Liz caught her breath in the thrill of the offer. Eleven light years away, at a start-up interstellar colony, she would likely have a major role. Then she hesitated. "Hilda, I don't work for people very well. I'm, well, kind of bullheaded."

Her older sister smiled knowingly, but instead replied, "You've led, let me see, about four expeditions since you got into Earth's Solar System, all successful, and the last one a spectacular success in everything, except, apparently the politics."

"Well, yes, but when I do an expedition, it's my show."

Hilda looked pointedly into the camera. "That's what I'm going to recommend."

Liz opened her mouth and couldn't close it. *In charge of the whole show? No boss, no politics? Eleven light years from Earth with nothing to do but make it happen?* She looked at her sister, excited, almost breathless. "You're kidding... You're not kidding. You think I'd have a shot?"

Hilda laughed. "That bullheadedness, along with your ability to improvise, is probably just what we need. There's a man out there named Gunheim, former PM of Queensland, given to grandiose schemes. He'll probably be in local politics out there, and if he starts interfering, it will take a strong will to stand up to him.

"We've got a planning meeting in a few minutes, so I've got to go. Should I ask Tse Wen?"

Liz caught her breath, then let it out slowly. She was all business now. Family business, in a way. Wotan had carefully nurtured his children, each of them, in daring to do big things in space. The responsibility would be huge; a monstrous projectile of precisely the right mass would have to leave Lacaille 9352 at just the right time and reach just the right velocity to meet the three other projectiles with nanosecond precision at the experiment vertex. A small pond, yes. But she would be the big fish in it. That excited her. And making the Black Hole Project happen would be an exquisite revenge on that arrogant, disingenuous bastard, Dr. DeRoot. But...

"Hilda, we haven't had a lot of time together. And this is the cradle of human civilization; I haven't seen a hundredth of it."

"I know. But I may be heading out, myself. Dad's headed back to New Antarctica; he and I have some issues to put behind us. The project needs a local lead; there are other political problems, though. Sis, we have all eternity ahead of us. Let's get together at New Antarctica when it's done. Maybe Mom will come."

Liz grinned. "Now *that* would be interesting. Okay, I'm in. If Tse Wen wants me, I'm ready."

She signed off and touched the net. *Any starships headed for Lacaille 9352 in the next year?*

One, the C.E. Singer, *Peter DeRoot commanding. Leaving Venus Equilateral in eight months.*

DeRoot? Any relation to the Director?

Brothers.

Probably irrelevant, Liz thought, but just bad luck if not. The *Singer* was her only choice. She stored the information and turned to her apartment window. Gold and pink clouds floated in the sky beyond the Ploshchad Ostrovskovo. She looked to the northwest, towards the lands of the Vikings and of Nansen and Amundsen. There was so much she hadn't taken time to see. Well, she told herself, as long as she avoided any fatal accidents, she would have the rest of eternity to do so.

CHAPTER 2

Between Sol and Lacaille 9352
23 September 2264 (Sidereal Reference)

In her third day after emerging from hibernation, Liz Avonford lay on a towel on the grass by a tiny pond under the warm artificial sun of the starship recreation dome, eyes closed. Linked to the computational power of the starship via bioradio and the local net, she was hard at work, simulating orbital motions in the Lacaille 9352 system.

At a time compression of 10,000, the planets of the system traced their orbits. Two small ones, Sunbeam and Canning, lay close in, surrounded by the orbits of a pair of larger worlds, Venus-like Carlisle and Mars-like Martin. Further out was a thin belt of asteroids, then a pair of gas giants, Munro and Spencer, that might have been twins to Uranus and Neptune. Beyond those rolled an icy plutonian world, Rayl, at the inner edge of a wide ring of kuiperoids.

A brilliant flash and afterglow in the inner system caught her eye. That must be it, she thought—the impact that would occur in the Lacaille 9352 system a decade from now. She replayed the last hours of the collision with real time speed and high magnification. The images coming through her bionet were so realistic they could not be distinguished from direct viewing and her subconscious quickly accepted the illusion of reality. A largish asteroid approached Martin, the Mars-sized world, slowly, gracefully taking a whole second to cover its own diameter to start with. But the asteroid sped up as it approached the planet until over the last two or so planet radii, it seemed to be sucked into the Mars-like body in a flash. Liz stared intently as a great enveloping black cloud boiled out of the wound and spread around the whirling planet. She zoomed in and replayed the simulation, slowing it down by a factor of sixty to real time.

She'd gotten out of hibernation six months before deceleration to hit the ground running, so to speak, and quickly became totally focused on her future environment. Next to sending the impactor for the Black Hole Project, the impending asteroid collision was the biggest thing happening in the Lacaille 9352 system. The simulation was based on data less than a year old in sidereal space—so it should still be fairly accurate, she thought. So far, her simulations showed the asteroid to have no effect on the power array they were building to propel the impactor up to speed.

The asteroid was nearly a tenth the radius of the target planet, and if the simulation was good enough, Liz thought, she would see the large rocky mass begin to break apart from tidal strain even before it struck. Sure enough, in the last minute it began to crack and elongate. Its forward edge flared in the upper atmosphere and contacted the surface in what was virtually a head-on impact about two seconds later. The energies involved were astronomical, but the scale was so huge it looked more like fluid drops merging than an explosion. The asteroid began to flatten itself against the planet as the back end caught up with its flattened front.

Shock waves began to spread, but were obscured by jets of matter in all forms that stabbed away from ground zero at impact velocity or higher and she had to turn her attention to lower, more penetrating frequencies. At first the ejecta fled perpendicular to the path of the vanishing asteroid in a terrible white flower, then the petals of this flower gradually rose from the surface looking for a moment like a medieval crown.

She checked the numbers; the impact area itself would be incredibly hot—perhaps as bright as the surface of a blue giant star. Except for the circular edge of the impact, that didn't happen immediately, however. The last of the asteroid vanished into a huge black circular hole. The whole process from first touch to vanishing took almost a minute. For a few seconds, there was nothing to see but the round dark hole and the jets of debris. Then the cavity began to glow with increasing ferocity. Pent-up thermal energy with nowhere else to go stripped the atoms of their electron shells. Although the computer rendered the plasma in a fluorescent violet, Liz knew that most of the radiation was in wavelengths too short for human eyes to see. She watched, fascinated, as a huge molten finger rose out of the hole and fell back. The minute-long movement seemed almost phallic and she had the briefest thought of impaling herself on it and being consumed from within in some kind of hideous flaming sacrificial ecstasy. She shivered at the feeling. *Where do such thoughts come from?* she wondered.

She replayed the simulation, watching from one radius out, ninety degrees west of the impact site. It took ten minutes to watch the shock wave spread around its victim. She shuddered. The work of eons undone in only ten minutes! The shock wave enveloped the planet, nearly blew away its atmosphere, and profoundly altered its surface, creating a vast tectonic jumble opposite the impact. The fire was now, the ice later.

Martin circled closer to Lacaille 9352 than Mercury did to Sol, but the red dwarf put out twenty times less energy; netting somewhat less than Mars' insolation. But unlike its distant cousin, Martin had a thick blanket of air. With a surface pressure of almost half an atmosphere, it had a much warmer surface than Mars, averaging about 10 kelvins below freezing—warm enough in spots for a few ice-covered lakes near the equator, but still very chilly. The impact would change that—for a while.

She sped up the simulation again, placing her virtual self ten planet radii overlooking the impact area. Lost in the moment, she watched billions of tons of rock melt and surge up in the center and in another crown-like ring, an Edgerton water droplet splash writ on a cosmic scale. The huge central peak subsided, then rebounded again, but much more slowly. Massive radiation to the sky robbed heat from the rock, making it more viscous. This was clearly visible through a plasma as tenuous as a good vacuum but so hot it had tremendous pressure. Eventually the oscillations and subsidences settled down as radiative cooling allowed the existence of solid rock again, leaving a huge multi-ring walled plane a thousand kilometers across, a somewhat larger version of Hellas on old Mars. The scraps of remaining atmosphere, incandescently hot from reentering debris and white with dust, finally rushed back in. It would block so much light the surface temperature would plummet below the freezing point of carbon dioxide.

So, not long after the impact, she thought, the atmosphere would be far more Mars-like, and Martin, on the verge of being habitable, would be branded with a new bull's eye and go into a near-permanent deep freeze. Liz sighed at the great stroke of cosmic luck that would let her be present at such an extraordinary cosmic catastrophe.

"Elizabeth Avonford?"

But the luck wasn't all good; it would happen just at the end of their BHP impactor's acceleration. Debris splashed from the collision could easily interfere with the vast solar arrays and beam drivers needed to send their impactor on its way. She asked the computer to light the array's position in vivid green, trailing and fading over several million virtual kilometers. The debris made a virtual cloud that spread from Martin inward and outward, and the edge of the cloud touched the ring of power stations that would power the Black Hole Project. Should they divert the asteroid for one revolution? Or change the time-mass-velocity profile to get the beam out before the impact?

"Elizabeth Avonford?"

The sound of her name penetrated. Dimly aware that it was the second time she'd been called, she groaned and opened her eyes, disoriented. Reality was calling her back from the virtual universe and it took a moment to adjust, like waking up from a dream.

Her eyes got into focus. The man who had spoken to her had a familiar accent, but she couldn't quite place him. "Yes?" she replied.

"David Levi."

She touched the ship's database and made the connection.

"Oh yes. You're the young man..."

"...from Israel, who took your office." He chuckled. "I quickly found out that was no place for anyone with an independent soul!"

They shared a rueful laugh.

"Your first time on a starship?" Liz asked.

David nodded. "I stayed awake; watched the Sun shrink to a point of light and redden. I didn't realize how red it was going to get. The safety lights in the observation bubble gave me the clue—when our gamma hit two, it seemed almost as red as they were."

At a gamma of two, the starship was moving at 86% of light speed—stretching the Sun's yellow light to red. "That's clever; I hadn't thought of doing that."

"We should get to see it again as we slow down approaching Campbell."

Liz's eyes widened. "Campbell?"

David smiled. "AKA Lacaille 9352."

"We?" Liz asked. She liked him instantly.

"Judi Lalande, Su Ahng-Lo, and the Captain—those of us who have been awake the whole trip. Lalande is an astrophysicist, she's doing research en route. I understudy Ahng-Lo with biosystems; I shall have my credential and experience by the time the voyage is over."

"Looking to ship out again, then?"

"I must see the universe and it is good to have as many qualifications as one can acquire. As soon as I solve the mystery of that kuiperoid you found."

Liz raised an eyebrow. "What mystery? Other than it's clearly something the Solar System picked up from somewhere else."

David grinned, delighted to pique the curiosity of a senior researcher.

Liz touched the net again; within the errors of measurement, the impacting planetoid was the same age as the rock she had discovered in the Solar System twenty years ago—7.392 billion years, plus about 3.6 million or minus 2.2 million.

"That could be a coincidence," she started.

David looked at her, a glint in his eye. "I think it is nearly a twin of the rock that is going to crash into Martin, maybe even the other half."

"The other half?"

"A rapidly rotating binary rock comes close to a giant planet, like Munro, and gets pulled apart. The slower half goes into a chaotic orbit around Campbell. The faster half gets ejected from the system entirely."

"This happened recently? Lacaille... er... Campbell... is moving very rapidly."

David nodded. "But in a halo orbit about the galactic center that turns out to be commensurable with that of Sol. They come close every 560 million years. Three times around for us, two for it."

"That's still an incredible coincidence."

He laughed. "Oh, I do not think it is so much. There are 500 billion plus stars or near stars floating around that big black hole in Sagittarius. What are the odds that none of them come close to Sol periodically?"

Liz chuckled. "Well, if you put it that way..."

He nodded and his eyes blazed. "Now I go a little off the path that is beaten. About 560 million years ago, life on Earth got a good, uh, kick in the trousers."

"The Cambrian explosion?" She began to roll her eyes. "That's way too much of a coincidence."

David shrugged. "That is why I tell no one my idea, officially, yet. But I think maybe I will find some biology around this red star we go to. And I wonder if it is biology we have already seen."

The importance of what he said sank into Liz. Archea native to Earth and the rest of the Solar System had closed loop DNA while some bacteria and the eukaryotes that made up multi-cell organisms and had loose string DNA terminated in telomeres—except for mitochondria. A debate had raged over two centuries about whether the eukaryotes were descended from archea and thus a radical evolutionary departure from the archea that made up, by mass, much of Earth life; or if eukaryotes were separately descended from eubacteria and archea had an earlier origin on Earth, or might even be an import from elsewhere. The tendency for bacteria to absorb each other and incorporate each other's genes made this difficult to discern from Earth life alone.

"Campbell *is* almost three billion years older than the Solar System..." Liz offered.

David's eyes glowed. "Ah, you understand!"

Liz thought about finding the kuiperoid, her chance meeting David at her old office, and now heading for Lacaille 9352 together plus sharing the same passion to do something significant. Perhaps there was something to fate.

"Are you busy for dinner?" she asked.

"What about lunch?" he countered, delighted by her attention. "It is almost lunch time now."

She laughed. He was as eager as she was. But she had an engagement. "The captain offered to show me his collection of ancient navigation equipment. He's going to establish a small museum at the Minot Space Colony around Campbell. I'll be in his quarters for lunch."

"Well, dinner, then?"

Liz allowed herself a slight smile. She had to be twice his age, even subtracting the years she'd spent in cold sleep. Was he looking forward to more than just dinner? The prospect was not entirely unpleasant.

"Okay," she smiled. "1900 in Sphere One."

Liz touched the net for a map. The *Singer's* habitable parts consisted of six spherical cabins spaced hexagonally around the tubular torus that carried the magnetic field generation lines and a passageway. The whole assembly spun about the torus axis for gravity, with the heavier lower half of the sphere rotating out and the airy park domes in. They were now in Sphere Three, with most of the other passengers. Sphere One, two spheres antispinward, was crew country.

"Captain's table, then?"

Liz nodded. Let him think he has competition.

••∞••

Liz looked forward to seeing the old hardware and was a little early to Captain DeRoot's quarters. On the way, she passed a woman who looked upset and gave Liz the strangest look imaginable, but said nothing and hurried down the access tube.

Judi Lalande, the AI identified.

Each sphere had four decks and a mess; the bottom contained a small swimming pool—actually a segment of the shielding water that surrounded each ball. The next deck up was given over to individual cabins. The third deck, comprising the central slice of the sphere, housed more cabins and a lounge area with readers, chairs, and mess facilities. Above that was an open dome covered with screens and floored with grass and shrubs.

By tradition, Room 131 on deck three of Sphere One was the captain's quarters in all ships of this design. In her voyage to Earth as a teenager, she'd never come close to Room 131; Captain Yuri Ivanov had been a serious, forbidding figure who smiled at girls maybe twice in a voyage. Remembering that sense of forbidden territory came back to her now. Liz had captained her own exploration craft in the Solar

System, but here in this moment on the *Singer*, she was an excited child again.

The captain's door slid silently open as she approached. He was at his desk, seated with his back to the door. Overhead was a set of shelves holding various pieces of metal equipment with dials, buttons, brass tubes, and lenses that all looked strange to her. The room itself was no bigger than her own.

"Come in, come in," he said, almost as if irritated. Then he turned and smiled. "Peter DeRoot, and you are the redoubtable Elizabeth Avonford?"

She nodded.

Instead of rising to shake her hand, he pulled a brass tube from his desk and offered it to her. "It's a telescope made four hundred years ago or so. A whaling ship captain out of Lisboa, Portugal, used it in the early eighteen hundreds. Go ahead, pull it out."

She grabbed the end of the tube and pulled; it slid easily out to a length of about half a meter. "That work?"

Captain DeRoot got up and motioned toward the side of his cabin. An ordinary-looking man, he wore his hair relatively long so it flopped over his forehead in a careless, boyish way. In contrast, his bearing and reserve spoke of self-confidence and authority.

A door opened revealing a room with a polished wood-grain table surrounded by plush chairs. She walked in and gazed around; the walls, except for one, were hung with real, framed pictures of sailing vessels and space ships. She smelled real wood.

The wall without pictures had a great box mounted on it with shiny brass fittings—hinges and a hook. The wood was varnished so deep and lustrous that it seemed still wet.

Captain DeRoot walked over to the box, lifted the hook, and swung its doors open, revealing a black shiny surface. "Lights," he said softly.

The lights went out and as her eyes adapted, Liz could see stars slowly spinning around, except for one bright one. A direct view window! She hadn't known there was one in any of the spherical hulls. But the hulls were double; the inner sphere rotated to accommodate whatever combination of thrust and spin the ship experienced while the outer hull stayed fixed. "How..."

"The inner and outer windows line up during the coast phase," Captain DeRoot said. "Go ahead, try the telescope."

She put the tube to her eye. After a slight adjustment of the length of the tube, she brought the golden point of light into focus. "Oh! A bright violet star," she said. "It seems impossibly small and intense. Is that Lacaille 9352?"

"That is its communications laser, blue shifted by our velocity. By the way, Roger Gunheim says Lacaille 9352 is called Campbell now, after an author who wrote a novel about using solar energy to power space flight about 300 years ago; the planets were named after characters in it."

She felt his hand find her waist in a gentle, if presumptuous, way. Her heart pounded. Was this really happening? She moved his hand away.

"I thought that wasn't official," she said, going back to the telescope.

"We're a long way from the Interplanetary Astronomical Union."

She felt his hand again.

Captain DeRoot laughed. "And, I am in charge here."

His hand moved up from her waist toward more intimate territory. It had been a very long time since a man had touched her that way and she felt both fear and excitement. But her mind told her this was too soon, way too soon. Liz pulled one hand free of the telescope and gently removed the captain's hand.

She felt momentarily rattled. He clearly meant it in a humorous manner, she tried to convince herself. But the captain's moves rang all sorts of alarm bells for her. Then she flashed back to the look on Judi's face. She pulled the telescope down and holding it in one hand, yanked the Captain's hand from her body. There was no resistance, but as she did so, his crotch bumped against her buttocks. He was, it seemed, ready for action. Again she was part repelled, part excited. She pulled her wits together and decided to give voice to what he'd done.

"We don't know each other," she tried.

"Well, that can be remedied," he said heartily and backed away from her. "Bring the lights up."

The ship's AI complied and when she could see again, Captain DeRoot was a couple of meters away from her.

"You're going to Campbell to take charge of the impactor project," DeRoot said, "to see that it gets made and flung toward the implosion site."

"Yes."

"There are people on site already with a lot more experience who are perfectly capable of doing that."

"Zhau Tse Wen sent me."

Captain DeRoot quietly chuckled. "At the risk of paraphrasing myself, we're a long way from Dr. Zhau. The man in charge at Campbell is Roger Gunheim. He's a nice enough man as long as you do what he says." DeRoot's smile was genuine, but his eyes were penetrating.

Liz carefully kept her voice level. "He's got a whole colony to worry about. I just have the BHP operation."

"Roger is a good friend of mine. We've made the Sol-Centauri voyage twice together, without hibernation. There is much time to think between the stars, about how things are... and how they should be. Now, I could put in a good word for you..."

Or not, she realized. Chaos! There it was, bald and simple. She could give the bastard what he wanted, or maybe risk everything she'd come for—everything she'd promised Hilda she'd do.

Liz went through her internal arguments pro and con. She craved power and she didn't want to risk losing it. She wanted to be in charge and wanted it in the worst way. It meant never getting kicked out of your own office at the drop of a hat, never being humiliated like that again. She could pay the price. She could take a shower afterward.

She let the captain lead her back into his room.

••∞••

The dinner table was almost full when she and Captain DeRoot arrived; she felt as if every eye were upon her. What did her face look like? Did they know? David seemed cheery and oblivious, but a dark knowingness in Judi's eyes screamed to Liz.

Liz sent her a message on the ship net. *It's not what you think. He wanted something from me. I wanted something from him. Nothing emotional. Besides, I've had worse.*

A nervous smile flickered across Judi's face.

"I got to see the brass telescope. We looked at Campbell and the comm laser."

What does he have on you?

What does he have on you? Liz countered.

Judi frowned. *My kid. A custody judgment. He could take the kid back to his father and leave me stranded.*

"Captain DeRoot has a really neat collection," Judi said aloud. "Did he show you his working reproduction of that ancient Greek computer? He made it himself." David, of course oblivious to the silent conversation, had replied to what she'd said aloud.

Liz touched the net for data on the device and recognized it; it had been on the top shelf in DeRoot's bedroom. She'd stared at it during his heaving climax.

"I saw it."

Come on, what's he got on you? Judi came back.

My job. She gave Judi the details.

"Uh, ladies, is something going on?" David asked.

It must have been transparent that they were exchanging net messages. Liz gave a quick glance toward Captain DeRoot, but he was explaining something to an entranced female passenger, one of the last to come out of hibernation.

Liz gently shook her head. Later. Aloud she bantered, "You wouldn't believe it. Well! Any luck with your panspermia studies?"

"Oh, sure. Did you know that there are at least forty stars that made visits to the solar neighborhood? Five of them came through at roughly the same time as Lacaille 9352."

••○○••

After dinner, David found himself walking back along the curve of the access tube with Elizabeth Avonford.

She seemed subdued and he tried to think of something to say to cheer her up, but when he opened his mouth he shut it again. What was one supposed to call her? Dr. Avonford, Elizabeth, or Liz. He deferred to his more normal upbringing and compromised on Avonford. Okay, maybe Elizabeth Avonford, he thought.

She looked increasingly upset, so he risked seeming foolish. "What's wrong?"

She stopped in the passageway and looked into his eyes, her face hard and weary. "I shouldn't say anything."

The passageway was covered with a tough aerogel that absorbed everything and weighed nothing. The space was utterly silent. Its curvature was such that here, halfway between spheres, neither end was visible; it felt utterly alone. David watched her sigh, knowing she needed to unload. He waited. Finally she began to talk.

"The captain has certain connections at Campbell. Those connections can help or hurt me. He also has certain... needs."

David risked touching her shoulder. "There was a threat implied?"

She nodded, holding back a quiet anger.

"I understand this well. It is not the act that bothers you so much, but the feeling that you have no choice in the act, am I right?"

She nodded.

Why, David wondered, should the artificial intelligence that really oversaw this starship permit such a transparent abuse of its human master's power? But he could answer his own question; ultimately people had insisted on a person being in control. And on a starship, there could only be one captain.

He spoke. "You have an interesting problem. For instance, if we were to present evidence to the second-in-command and demand that he take over, how would we know the second-in-command is not either complicit, or otherwise under the primary's control?"

Avonford shook her head. "We don't. What is the check on such people?"

"I think the threat of exposure would hold much weight with him," David told her. "He could find himself with nowhere in settled space to go. But, to fight this would not be without risk."

"If it was just me," she said, "I'd raise hell. But the whole human universe is counting on me to get this job done!"

This seemed a little much to David, who took a longer view of things, but her sincerity and enthusiasm were evident. He smiled and raised an eyebrow. "It is that important to study relativity? Why?"

"Look, if the Anderson, Lu, and Yoseph paper is right, we can use one asteroid-sized black hole to make more."

David shrugged. "And then what?"

Her eyes gleamed. "Look up Wheeler, Forward, Thornsen, and Zhau. With several black holes, we can make some of the gravitational machines the relativity theorists predicted. For instance, imagine a gravitational catapult that would send us up near the speed of light without our feeling any acceleration at all! Imagine..."

David held up a hand. He had his own doubts about what people might do with the fruits of the project. However, the Black Hole Project was a legitimate collective decision of the human race and he respected that. And anyway, it was obviously so important to Elizabeth that she was willing to be used for it. He was moved to concern.

"Look, we live forever these days. If there is a setback, it can be overcome in time. Besides, who knows where the captain's demands will stop? His behavior must be changed, or many more women will experience what you have. I think you must threaten to expose him. Then you will be in the driver's seat."

She raised her eyebrows, "It can't be just my word against his, and we can't count on the ship's AI."

David smiled. "I do biological nanotech. I have in my room all I need for bench level fabrication. What we need to do is record an hour or so of conversation with something too small and diffuse to be detected by all the usual precautions, which I'm sure that he will take. So I make a distributed network of nano cells. I could hide it under your skin, or in your hair."

Liz looked at him, worry in her face, but with anger and excitement, too. She nodded, not feeling powerless any longer.

He nodded back. "We shall go to my lab. The bug will run on your blood sugar and hemoglobin, just like your own cells."

He thought for a moment. "I shall put it just under your skin, where the room IR pickups can see it. I'll dump an encrypted file into the AI; it will not know what is in it and would thus not change it. And we would not be able to. So that would make convincing evidence, I think."

He looked at her expectantly. It was the moment of commitment.

"I'm invited for lunch again tomorrow. Can we have it done by then?"

"This is not a problem. The problem will be to get him to make his threat more explicit."

Elizabeth Avonford nodded. "I have all night to come up with something." Her lips curled into a faint smile. "Let's bug me!"

His nano bug, her lips, her commitment reeled in his head and excited him. Liz was, apparently, one who could drink deeply from the cup of experience. He had thoughts of moths drawn to flames, but was she the moth? Or the flame?

••∞••

David met Liz again the following evening. They listened to the recording of Avonford's noon encounter. DeRoot had walked right into it.

"What would Gunheim do for me if I did this?" Avonford had asked in a totally playful and innocent voice.

"Let you run your project, most likely," DeRoot had said.

"And if not?" she'd asked, laughingly, but David noticed a hint of strain.

"Well, the converse, I would suppose. Will you take off your clothes, now?"

"Enough," David said. He had what he needed. She could have walked out right then, he told himself, and if she had not... Well, he didn't want to know.

••∞••

All locked in, Liz told herself. They had the voice file, and the evidence was already on its way to both Earth and Campbell, encrypted, but in a way that would be released if the AIs involved did not get positive instructions from her to not release it. David had been very clever to come up with that insurance policy.

In the last 24 hours, she and David had developed a closeness she'd never felt before. No man had gone to bat for her like this and she allowed the pure warm feeling to wash through her for a moment.

Still, she felt nervous as hell. David might not have anticipated everything. Judi had declined to be a part of it. She still had too much at stake. DeRoot could get back at her without anyone being the wiser, she'd said. David had reluctantly agreed. Besides, they had enough without her, hopefully.

They walked into the Sphere One Commons. DeRoot, waiting for her, frowned a bit. Not expecting David, Liz thought.

The captain recovered quickly. "Ms. Avonford, good to see you. Mr. Levi?"

"Captain," David said, "I suggest that we sit down. We must discuss something with you. I suggest you tell the AI to not record what we have to say. I think you understand what this is about."

DeRoot frowned and tightened his lips, then he looked at her. The threat was silent, understood.

She looked back, just as cold, just as firm of lip. She hoped her refusal to back off was every bit as clear.

At length, DeRoot nodded.

Without any further word, David produced a comm card and played back the segment with the incriminating language. "We have taken the necessary and obvious precautions, and have supporting evidence of other kinds concerning other events, not involving anyone on this ship," he said afterward.

The last was a complete lie, Liz knew, but one that might give Judi some protection.

"You will understand the implications for both you and Mr. Gunheim," David said.

DeRoot stared coldly at her, ignoring David. "You goddamn whore." His voice rumbled in anger.

Liz stared, unable to help the start of a tear, but willing herself not to give an inch in this contest of wills.

No one spoke. Each looked at the other. DeRoot's face tinged pink. David watched in amazement. Liz valiantly worked on a poker face, wondering if this was the first time the captain's persona and behavior had been questioned to such a degree. He was a smart man; surely he would take this no further. Liz watched quietly. Only when she thought the steam had gone out of DeRoot did she glance at David.

"It's your show, now," the younger man said.

She nodded. "Captain DeRoot, I want your assurance, and Mr. Gunheim's, that there will be no interference with my work in the Lacaille 9352 system in support of the Black Hole Project."

He snorted. "That's beyond my power."

"You had best hope not," Liz countered.

"It may be in the best interest of the ship to have you two hibernate for the remainder of the journey."

He might, Liz realized, be able to order the ship's AI to do just that. Then, while they were totally out of touch, any sort of revenge might be orchestrated.

"Then," David said calmly, "we would be unable to keep the encrypted data from being released where we have sent it."

The captain shut his eyes again. Then he nodded. "You're a competent goddamn blackmailing whore."

Liz allowed the slightest hint of a smile to touch her lips.

The captain had challenged the very core of her raison d'être, her greater reason for being, her very soul. If it had not been for the threat to the project, the threat of her part, even her control... She decided not to go there.

"A moment." DeRoot turned away from them and stared at a wall screen that showed stars gliding by with the ship's rotation. They waited.

Then he turned back and smiled. "Very well. I apologize. I'll speak to Roger and the project deputy, Cyan Mutori; I'm sure there will be no problem." He sighed. "Eternity is a long time, and if our paths cross again, perhaps I won't make such a mess of it."

"For the rest of this trip, don't even think about it," she replied coldly.

DeRoot rolled his eyes up and nodded. "Well, enjoy the rest of the trip, Ms. Avonford, Mr. Levi. If you need anything from your Captain, don't hesitate to ask."

They were back on record, Liz surmised. She nodded and led David away.

As soon as they were halfway around the tube and out of sight and sound of anything, she jumped him, wrapping her legs around him, squeezing with all her not inconsiderable strength.

"Eliz..." he choked out.

She released her grip and reached for his tunic collar, already shamelessly out of control and reveling in it. It was a victory, a complete victory and she intended to celebrate. "You're my goddamn hero, David."

CHAPTER 3

Minot
Lacaille 9352 (Campbell) System
5 October 2272

David couldn't help but gasp as their shuttle exited the access tunnel into Minot, the main Campbell system residential habitat. He, Liz, and Judi had flown in from the south pole, where the landing docks were, into what looked like a huge Chinese lantern, its insides filled with fields, forests, and streams. Beside them was a snow-covered alpine terrain in the shadow of a huge dark disk that floated ahead of them.

"That's the back end of the secondary reflector," their guide shouted over the hum of the shuttle's fans.

David nodded and smiled; they'd retracted the shuttle canopy and were sitting in the crisp open air, feeling and smelling very much like a bright, late winter day in St. Petersburg. The scale still overwhelmed him.

Liz Avonford grinned at him as the crisp breeze of their flight streamed her hair behind her. His heart beat faster, anticipating. She had long since succeeded in convincing him that she wasn't just being grateful for helping her, but was deeply into the erotic arts. She initiated everything—instructed, taught, and occasionally used him to achieve her own erotic nirvana. He worried a bit about being so totally dominated, about just being along for the ride. But what a ride!

They nosed down and began scudding over the sculpted, snow-covered crags of polar Minot.

"Ten minutes to Lenore," their guide announced.

They crossed the sun line. Rock and gravel gave way to terraces of meadow and soon the first trees shot by beneath them. The vastness of the habitat spread out around him and he thought about Moses on the mountain viewing the Promised Land. That reminded him of the New Israel space colony, orbiting Proxima, and Ben Shalom, the messianic anti-Moses who had led so many of the orthodox to the stars. The debates about that had filled the coffee houses of Ashqelon in David's childhood. It had been the first of what were now over a thousand exclusive ethnic or religious settlements among the nearby stars, and not everyone was happy about it. Children raised in such places faced the same kinds of survival challenges as youngsters in cults on Earth.

Liz touched him and pointed.

He looked in that direction and saw a small rustic cabin by a stream between waterfalls; the first sign of human habitation he'd seen. He knew that this habitat had an equatorial radius of only ten kilometers, about half the size and a quarter the area of New Israel. Of course, then, the interior area of New Israel was actually larger than what was left of old Israel on Earth. Above a certain scale, David thought, the eye and the mind give up. Something is simply big.

"Getting warmer," Liz shouted; their weight was increasing as they moved further and further from Minot's rotational axis and the shuttle's fans had gotten louder as they revved up to carry the load.

He looked up at the reflected image of the star. The illusion was perfect; the mirror itself could not be seen in the glare and it seemed as if the star itself were suspended above them. Though he knew it was much cooler than the Sun, there was nothing to compare it with and it was so bright it saturated his color vision; it looked white. David touched the local net. 19 Celsius outside now, at latitude of 45 degrees. It would get up to 24-25 along the equatorial sea coast. The smell of pine forest yielded to the more complex orders of deciduous trees.

Liz smiled and pointed to her head.

David opened his address.

Only about five thousand people so far, Liz sent. *L-5 Grissom has fifty-seven million, and its area is a little smaller.*

The land lay mostly flat below them now, a calico patchwork of forests and fields, some tended by cultivating robots.

A herd of kangaroos! Liz noted.

Roger Gunheim is Australian, David sent. *There's a town coming up. A broad, winding river circled the inside of the habitat at its widest part.* A large clearing with wide, low, modernistic architecture lay ahead of them on a thumb of land.

That's Lenore, Judi sent. *Named for Lenore LeBois. She was the first system exec and she died mysteriously. I guess you have to die to get something named for you.*

Judi, what do you think happened? Liz asked.

Gunheim had his way with her all the way out. They'd just finished the colony when his buddy, DeRoot, arrived with another thousand passengers. That was forty years ago. The two of them got a council formed which made Gunheim the executive. Lenore objected and she was found dead in the river near the town, not three weeks after it started flowing.

Suicide? David asked.

Ruled an accident. But her personnel files disappeared.

This isn't all on the net.

That's right, Judi said. Then she leaned forward in her seat so he could hear her voice over the buzz of the shuttle's fans. "DeRoot told me. Trying to scare me, I think. It worked."

David shivered.

The shuttle passed over a town that would not have appeared out of place in Australia four centuries ago, and settled onto a well-manicured grass field. A group of horseback riders came out to meet them, with spare mounts. DeRoot, who'd come in earlier, and Gunheim were among them along with a Eurasian woman.

"G'day and welcome to Lenore," Gunheim shouted, all ebullience and smiles. "Mount up! It's Suits-off Day; 39 years since we moved in here. There's roo on the barbie for you."

••∞••

The smell of roast meat, well-seasoned and basted, wafted in a gentle breeze from the barbecue pits along the river. Liz looked around at the 40th celebration of Suits-off Day. What a difference a year made! She knew most of the people; everyone connected with something outside Minot itself along with their friends and relatives, maybe a couple of hundred people altogether. Suits-off Day marked the auspicious moment that Minot had been declared habitable and the first colonists had left the crowded confines of their starship to occupy the great spherical shell. Liz sat at a wooden table with her deputy, Cyan Mutori, David, Judi Lalande and her son Oscar. The last looked incredibly primitive as he chewed on an emu rib.

Roger Gunheim strode up a small hill near the tables in full outback regalia—safari shirt, walking shorts and a wide-brim hat with one brim buttoned to its crown. He lifted a ridiculously large mug of local brew with a Bavarian-style conical metal cap and shouted, "To the success of all our projects!" Then he flipped the cap back and chugged.

Liz laughed, lifted her much smaller glass of Lenore stout, and took a sip. The reflection of Campbell, as much a heat lamp as a light, warmed her skin.

As BHP director, her project for the last twelve months had been to supervise some twenty people scattered around various asteroids to make key architecture decisions for their busy but not-all-that-creative robot laborers. The fabrication of the impactor was ahead of schedule, and the combined power/beam modules were on a schedule that had at least some margin. They'd become like a family—all dedicated to accomplishing the greatest human project since terraforming Mars.

With one exception.

"Gotta lid on Terry Peal?" Judi asked.

Liz laughed. That particular exception was more interested in setting robot armies one against the other than in mining. He'd also been spouting anti-project propaganda to anyone who'd listen. "He's been eased aside, and others have taken up the slack. We're on schedule."

Here comes da boss, Judi warned.

"G'day, mind if I join you?"

Liz looked up at Gunheim.

"You shot this?"

"With a crossbow. A fair shot and it was near the end of its natural life span," Gunheim told her.

Oscar, Judi's son, looked confused and moved closer to his mother.

David leaned towards him. "When deer become old and feeble, they hurt a lot. That is where hunters come in and end suffering. It is either hunters or wolves, I think."

"Oh," Oscar said, with a furtive glance at Gunheim.

"You have wolves here?" Liz asked.

Judi looked at Liz. *With Gunheim's kind around, you don't need wolves.*

Liz frowned. As far as she could see, Gunheim was all glad-handing and bluster; a little shallow, but harmless. But that was likely an act.

"Dingoes, it would be. But we haven't introduced large predators yet, mate, and may not for a while. The grass contains a weak contraceptive, so the herds grow more slowly," Gunheim said. "Well, I didn't come over to talk about hunting. Liz, we're a kind of family around here."

"Great to be part of it," Liz said, feeling all warm and relaxed with the stout. A splash from the shore caught her attention; shorts and halters littered the riverbank beach and shouts of laughter and splashes beckoned her. She'd worn a red towel kilt and matching halter and was beginning to feel overdressed.

Gunheim nodded and beamed, but his eyes were sharp. "Well, in families one shares, and, well, the council and I think it's time to share a little of your workload, let some others get some more of the action."

Liz couldn't believe what she'd just heard. The warm fuzzy feeling evaporated almost instantly, replaced with a cold knot in her stomach. She smiled weakly and tried to hide her feelings. "I'm not exactly overworked."

Gunheim shrugged. "Well, maybe it's just that some other very capable people have been underworked. At any rate, there's been some friction, and whenever anything like that happens, those of us who are in charge have to make some response, tweak the organization, do something of that nature, just to let people know we're on the job."

Liz suddenly felt naked, and cold.

The table fell silent, everyone looking at Gunheim.

"Now don't take this too personally. I don't think anyone can really fault you for not doing something about Terry Peal and his bloody robot wars, but you're pretty young yet and sometimes it takes a little more subtlety to keep everyone happy."

"Chaos, how subtle did I have to be! I just let Ivan Marenkov take over the stuff Peal wasn't doing anyway."

Gunheim shook his head. "And you left him off the production achievement list."

"But he wasn't producing."

"You could have lowered the threshold instead of bloody humiliating him." Gunheim's last few words had a bit of snap in them. "But then," he went back to his avuncular style, "these are things some experience brings. You're doing fair on the impactor fabrication now so we thought we might let you concentrate on that and let Mutori take over the people management chores."

"You don't understand, Mr. Gunheim," Liz said, trying to keep a mixture of anger and fear out of her voice. "My sister, Dr. Zhau Tse Wen, and the whole project expect me to see the efforts in this system are completed on schedule. When you come down to it, the BHP is why this colony exists at all. I can't just walk away from that."

"And you aren't. The decision has been taken out of your hands, so you aren't breaking any promises. No worries. And really, it's better for the project if some more experienced managers help out."

Liz shot a look at Cyan Mutori, who smiled sympathetically, but said nothing. Judi left the table with her son so quietly that Liz didn't realize she was gone. David sat open-mouthed. He was running the biosurvey on the asteroid that would soon impact Martin and was, she knew, very vulnerable to what had just occurred to her.

Payback time, Judi sent. *He just needed an excuse.*

••∞••

A wave of rain clouds spiraling down from the south pole darkened the sky over Liz's dome, transparent when not in use as a display screen. Under it was her one-room office, kitchen, bedroom, and entertainment center; a small high-tech outhouse hid behind some shrubbery. In actuality, the shrubbery formed the walls of her abode; in the warm tropical climate of the low latitudes of Minot, an occasional splash of warm rain was an easily acceptable trade for the feeling of openness and freedom this style of living gave her.

But not today. Today, she wanted a cave. Noon and still in bed, Liz lay under the sheets, head in the pillow, reliving every moment of her life from when she decided to go down to that rogue kuiperoid in the Solar System, to losing her office, to staring at DeRoot's ancient Greek computer while he used her body. At least that had been partly voluntary; a choice, a trade. This time she had been truly raped without a stitch of clothing touched—utterly humiliated in front of her friends in a format so public and genteel that she couldn't even have thought of screaming.

Well, she could scream now! Out in the woods over a kilometer from the nearest other home she spun in her bed, flung her arms out and screamed a nameless, primal scream until her throat hurt.

"Liz?"

She caught her breath and screamed again, cutting herself off when it sunk into her that someone had called her name.

"Liz, are you okay?"

It was David. Chaos, she was no mood to be social. No, maybe she was—but not the normal thing, no, something dark, onerous, and degrading.

"Are you okay?"

"Does it sound like it?" she snapped and regretted it. Suddenly, she didn't want to be alone. "Oh, come on in."

He came through the short entrance maze and walked under the dome rim just as large gray raindrops began to splash all over it, drumming in a way that made it sound like more of a storm than it was. She got up to meet him and collapsed on him, sobbing.

He held her until she collected herself.

Finally, when her face had dried and she'd started thinking again, he disengaged slightly and put a hand on her chin. "Liz, it has been three days. Have you eaten anything?"

Three days? She could still taste the emu in her mouth.

"We are all concerned," David said, "but we are being very circumspect. Mutori wants you to know she had no idea this would happen. Judi is terrified."

"I haven't had a message from her since..."

David nodded. "We think Gunheim is reading these messages. One wrong move and Oscar is in cold sleep on the next starship to his father.

Look, I'm uncomfortable." He waved his hands around him, and smiled wryly. "What do you do about bugs in here?"

"All the insects here are genetically engineered to avoid human pheromones so I don't need..." Liz thought about the other kind of bugs, then shrugged her shoulders. "Oh. You want to take a walk in the rain?"

David smiled and nodded.

A bird chirped. The smell of wet vegetation perfumed with flowers flowed into Liz's dome on a gentle breeze. The rain lessened to a warm mist and overhead the reflected disk of Campbell seemed to coast through the thinning clouds. Liz's blue funk had dissipated as well; just getting out of her dome and talking with David had gotten her mind engaged. She was, she realized, ready to move forward. Ready to gather information. It was the first step in starting to work the problem.

"Okay," she said, to herself as much as to David. "What are my options?"

"Your options? For what?"

"To get back in charge of the project. To put Gunheim in his place. To get my life back."

"Brainstorm?"

"Yeah. Let's have some ideas. Everything on the table. I could kill the bastard. Don't look at me that way; we'll deselect later. Maybe we could just kidnap him, put him on ice until after the impactor flies."

David shrugged but didn't look very encouraging.

"Okay. Am I good in bed? Good enough so that someone as experienced as Gunheim would do stuff for me?"

"Liz, you are not serious..."

"It's on the table."

"I am not experienced enough to know. You are only my third lover and it is hard for me to tell."

"Well, it's on the table, anyway."

"As a last measure, I hope."

Liz laughed. "If that. Now, could I invoke authority?"

"Earth is a long way away."

"But life is a lot longer these days. Twenty-five years, back and forth, can go just like that. Does he really want to have the most powerful people in the Galaxy pissed off at him forever?"

David shook his head. "If he were rational, I would think not. Okay, on the table." He grinned at her.

"That's the spirit." How was it that she was now cheering him up?

"We could try blackmail again. It worked once."

They looked at each other.

"For a while," they said almost simultaneously and laughed.

"Back to the authority option," David said. "Gunheim is not an absolute authority here. He must answer to a council."

Liz shook her head. "Which has been very compliant, it seems."

"We could at least argue the case. Show his relationship to DeRoot and their history. We put all the facts before them. They are people."

"They are Gunheim's people."

David shrugged. "That does not mean that their brains have ceased to work. Anyway, they are the ultimate authority here."

Liz shook her head. They were not the ultimate authority. "David, they are elected. He doesn't have to control ten people, he has to control ten thousand! If I can get an election called, the AI will recognize the electorate as the ultimate human authority. He won't be able to fix it."

David frowned. "Perhaps. But are you suggesting a frontal, public assault? That burns any hope of making any of the other options work. It would be a gamble."

"But a clean, open gamble. We can expose him and DeRoot."

"Liz, he is a good politician. Somehow, I think, you will end up looking like a dirty whore. And many people who agree with you will not be able to say so publicly. Judi and myself for instance."

"You won't back me?"

"I can't. I would lose my project. I am taking great risks even talking to you about it."

"But you are talking."

He nodded. "There are people here he can't threaten so easily, and people who remember Lenore."

That was true, she knew. She couldn't blame David; if the positions were reversed, she would do the same. She sighed, then mischievously led him back to her dome and pushed him down on her bed. "Suppose there was a bug in that tree, right there, with a camera." She pointed over the end of her bed to the forest beyond her dome.

"It is possible."

Mischievously, she reached between his legs. "Ever done it with someone watching?"

"No." He shivered, but did not remove her hand. "The dome, Liz. Opaque..."

She stared into his eyes, unblinking, and gave him her most predatory grin. "Nuts." All the emotion of the last three days seemed to roll through her then, driving her to seek one immediate, cathartic release. Her body, she realized, was incredibly ready. She pushed his shoulders to the sheets, straddled him with her bum toward the imagined bug in the trees, and ferociously pushed against him.

Then he started to push back, almost angrily. To her surprise, she wanted that. She wanted it very much.

Release took her almost by surprise, and was still throbbing through her when his came so that they fed on each other, back and forth until they were totally, totally exhausted. She rolled off him and, still breathing heavily, spread-eagled herself on the sheets to try to cool down in the warm, moist, flower-scented air. David's fingers still touched hers. Above, between her and the distant, mist-covered landscape of the opposite hemisphere, someone glided by on gossamer wings not that far over her dome. She held up an age-old finger curse. *I hope you have a good view.* On that thought, she fell asleep.

••∞••

Three weeks later, in Liz's now-certified bug-free home environment, David glanced at the latest projections, displayed in various graphs on her dome. The good news was that in plastering the truth about DeRoot and Gunheim's escapades all over the colony, Liz had gotten two council members to support her and enough signatures on an election petition to start a campaign. Out of a hundred and fifty supporters she found enough candidates for a reform slate that, if elected, would control the Campbell system governing council. That had gotten the AI to override DeRoot on monitoring political activity. The bad news was that Liz had, at best, maybe twenty percent support. Forty-six percent of the electorate either thought she was a troublemaker or didn't believe the charges at all and thirty-four percent didn't know what to think, or weren't saying.

"Liz?" Cyan Mutori's voice rang out from outside the hedge. That she was using voice instead of net was interesting, David mused.

Liz nodded to him. He got up and slipped quietly into the nearby woods. Cyan Mutori was probably the last person who should know he was actively helping Liz in her campaign. Gunheim had made it very clear to him that while he recognized, with a wink, David's personal relationship to Liz, any public attacks from David would, in Gunheim's words, "be a mite disruptive to your research program, mate."

"Hello, Cyan. Come on in," Liz said, when he was safely out of sight. Her voice carried clearly in the still evening. "How's the project going?"

David felt for Liz. Gunheim's next move, of course, had been to remove Liz from her remaining role as impactor fabrication specialist. She'd been reduced to following things on the public net and getting reports from friends.

"I would like David to hear what I have to say," Cyan said. "I understand the precautions you take. I am not offended."

David was startled. Had she seen him? Or did she just reason he would be here? There was much more to Cyan Mutori than one realized.

"Come on back, David," Liz said.

He reappeared from the woods.

Cyan nodded to him, with no hint of a smile or a frown. She wore a green sarong with white flowers and a white orchid in her long, jet black hair—South Pacific, squared. She'd even browned her skin somehow; lamps, probably, David thought. Campbell didn't put out enough ultraviolet light to make a tan.

"Physically, the project is a little behind schedule, but okay," Cyan began.

"Behind?" he asked.

"Deliberate delays, I think. If I counter them completely, I fear I may be removed because these delays represent the will of someone powerful." Cyan shut her eyes for a moment, then opened them. "If I let them become too great, the project will be in jeopardy and I will be the scapegoat. It is a very delicate situation."

David shook his head. "You are risking a lot. Look, as I understand it, the worst thing that can happen is that, if we don't launch, the other impactors get diverted and, thirty years later, we all try again. It's not worth a whole lot of suffering. Pun not intended."

Liz shook her head. "David, I don't know that there will be another chance. Human politics. It takes so much discipline and it's so visible. Every one of the launch sites has to be able to push the project through at the same time, without any more coordination than a twenty-two-year round trip communications delay... We have to do it here if we possibly can."

"Liz, you're fixated," David countered.

Cyan shook her head. "Liz, David. Gunheim is not trying to stop the project. It is, I think, a worse problem, and that is why I am here."

Liz turned to her and stared. "What could be worse?"

"He came to me yesterday with a question. 'Now,' he asks, 'if one impactor hits a little less hard than the other three impactors, there would be a little momentum bias in the final product, wouldn't there be?'" Mutori shook her head. "He does not understand several things."

Liz said nothing, but stared at Mutori, shock all over her face.

"What?" David said, uncertainly. "He has done simulations, of course."

Liz looked at him, white-faced. "You can't just 'do' simulations. You have to know when approximations are good enough and when you need another couple of days of number crunching. And," she paused, "there is still too much we don't know about how matter behaves at such energies and densities. It's hard enough to do a symmetrical zero-biased simulation. Chaos only can tell what would happen if something was even as much as a nanosecond off."

Mutori shook her head. "He is talking momentum, Liz. Hitting at the right time, but with just a little less momentum. A slight amount of momentum bias would send the hole back this way, where he could gain control over it. It may be possible to use one small black hole to make others—Kaufmann's modified Kerr-Newman solution with an omega sub-Lambda field. He would then have, I think, very great power."

David gave her a blank look, consulted the net, frowned grimly and said, "Oh."

"Power, literally and figuratively," Liz said. "David, this isn't just about me and my job anymore. The reason Hilda sent me out here was because I'd be absolutely loyal to her and ensure that everything be done exactly right. I don't mean to insult you, Cyan. You're a good person. But the project needed that certainty. Humanity needed that certainty."

Cyan looked down. "I took entirely too local a view of things. I compromised. I am sorry."

David tried to digest what he heard. "Gunheim. In charge of a black hole!"

Liz snorted. "That's hardly the worst case of what could happen. One other thing that might happen is hole is too small to last long, and comes jetting this way. It would be unstoppable and ready to explode in a final burst of Hawking radiation, converting millions of tons of mass into hard radiation in a fraction of a second. Perhaps right in our faces."

"It sounds like a good argument for not trying this at all. What if someone else has the same idea? Maybe we *should* shut it down."

"David!" Liz sounded horrified.

He gave her a lopsided grin. "Just thinking out loud. Okay, I'll give up my project and support your reform slate publicly. Do we have any more options?"

"Black hole formation is not all that Gunheim does not understand. I think he thinks I will want to share his power with him—that I will be his compliant partner in exploiting the black hole and... in other ways."

David looked at her expressionless face. Why am I surprised, he thought.

"I came to make an apology," Cyan said. "I shall make my apology in this way. I am local, a first colonist. Some think that by watching much, and saying little, I have leadership qualities. So, like David, I will sacrifice my position and I shall run for the council on your reform slate as its leader. That may change the political dynamics in some small way. If I am so lucky as to be chosen by our people and the council as System Executive, I shall give the project back to you, Liz. Will you accept such an offering?"

"Cyan!"

Cyan raised her head, smiled, and opened her arms to Liz. The two women embraced so shamelessly that David thought he should turn around. Except that his eyes were riveted to the beauty of it. It was only much later that David realized what he'd been witness to. That demure, self-effacing, shy speech by the achingly beautiful, vulnerable Cyan Mutori might prove to be one of the most devastatingly effective power grabs in the history of any democracy.

CHAPTER 4

At Minot
15 March 2274

David looked at each of the three hundred eighty-two tension-filled faces in the LeBois Amphitheater waiting for the debate to begin. Nervous whispers filled the air. Vid pickups shot the scene to an excited ninety-seven hundred other colonists unable to physically attend. Never had a local election debate caused so much stir.

The whispers hushed as Gunheim and Cyan Mutori walked onto the stage that was decorated by "Campbell" flags. Designed by Gunheim's council for the debate, the flags sported a traditional Campbell clan tartan with a red circle in the center. A row of them lined the back of the stage, flying in a light breeze ordered up from the colony weather masters just for the occasion.

Gunheim shook Cyan Mutori's hand with a politically confident smile. Cyan reciprocated. They turned and walked to opposite sides of the stage as a band of faithful followers for Gunheim clapped and cheered their candidate on.

The debate had been Gunheim's idea and he'd gone after it with all the small town boosterism and enthusiasm he could muster. The incumbent, apparently, had no doubt that his charismatic, glad-handing personality would overwhelm the small, quiet, and far more reserved woman.

David looked at Liz and Judi, who were talking to some of their supporters, a small group in what seemed a very large crowd. He touched his campaign button, a simple blue background with three white block letters arranged in a triangle. The letters, C. M. R., stood for Cyan Mutori, Reform. There were not many of them among this crowd. But, in small consolation, there were not many of the others, either.

Young Su-Li, Captain of the just-arrived starship *Poul Anderson*, had been dragooned to play moderator. Standing at a mid-stage lectern, he let the gavel fall. Then he banged it again to silence the remaining voices.

Here we go, David sent to Liz. *Scared?*

Nervous. I won't underestimate Cyan, but our main issues are too outrageous to believe and impossible to prove, Liz answered.

Well, yes, but I think word of mouth has gotten around, David sent. *I don't think anyone really doubts the harassment stuff. Whether it's really that important, we can't tell. But no, she can't bring it up directly. People would react against that kind of gutter politics. What Cyan has to do, mainly, is to convince people that she's a viable alternative.*

Cyan won the coin flip but elected to go second, David mused.

Gunheim rattled off the colony's accomplishments and even played a bit to his rakish reputation. "It is wonderful to have a contested election, of course, and we've had a great deal of fun with it. But there is a serious side to this as well, mates. We have here," he ended, "an election the main issue of which is, in the great tradition of colonies spun off from mother civilizations, whether we decide who calls the shots or continue to accept whoever Earth sends us from eleven-and-a-half light years away.

"The Black Hole Project is not at stake; we shall bloody well do our share and do it proudly. Make no mistake about that. But we need to let history know that it's our project too, to be done in our way by our people. This is a new civilization here and with your vote, this will be our independence day!"

David started to clap out of polite habit, then stopped himself. The applause was loud enough, he thought, with lots of cheers and tartan waving. When it died down, the starship captain motioned for Cyan to begin.

"We do agree about one thing. This is about who is selected to be in charge of things..." Cyan turned toward her opponent and smiled, "...and why."

The laughter began in the front where they could see Cyan's expression clearly, and it rolled toward the back until everyone, even Gunheim's supporters, was chuckling.

Effective, David sent.

Not to be underestimated, Liz replied.

She did it! Judi Lalande sent. *She got the bastard's behavior on the front burner without going in the gutter!*

Lots of debate to go, David reminded them.

Cyan followed up her opening with a positive approach, detailing in simple declarative sentences how she would handle management and personnel issues, emphasizing metrics and fairness. Her manner was controlled and careful, but the clarity and substance of her words seemed to hold people's attention; she was, after all, talking about their opportunities.

She moved beyond management technicalities in the summation of her opening remarks. "The great challenge before us is coping with time. As individual minds, we now expect to last indefinitely. We are too new to this and still think of years as a great gulf. But the eleven-and-a-half light years between us and Sol are really as nothing. Who are we? We are human beings. We came here, specifically, to be part of what, by most measures, is the greatest collective human project in history. It may lead to an increase in our knowledge and a resulting increase in our capabilities even transcending that of agriculture, navigation, nuclear physics, and robotics. The spotlight of history indeed shines on us here and now; and it is a history which will be in your own memories as long as they last. We have choices to make in this election that will be remembered forever. Let us make them with great vision and great wisdom."

Complete silence followed this. Then Judi Lalande started clapping. David's trance broke and he started clapping too. He nudged Liz into action. Others began clapping as well until the crowd reaction seemed to match that following Gunheim's speech, but without the cheering. Good, a thoughtful crowd, David considered.

The rest of the debate followed that pattern. The candidates elaborated on their positions in response to questions. Gunheim had more one-liners, but Cyan's answers struck deeper and were more notable by contrast to her normally serious demeanor. The contrast in personalities could not have been clearer, but in the end, there was little difference in goals or substance. It was anyone's guess who had "won."

David squeezed Liz's hand on the walk back to her house. "She certainly held her own, I thought. And I think we had a lead going in."

Liz didn't say anything, but held his hand more tightly.

••∞••

Liz stared at the numbers floating in the air. Cyan's slate was still marginally ahead, but...

"The undecided have the real lead," David remarked.

"People don't want to contribute to a bandwagon effect, whoever they support," Judi said, while throwing a Frisbee to her son, Oscar.

"A bandwagon would be fine with me," Liz said.

Liz, this is Cyan.

Liz pointed to her head, letting the others know she was getting a transmission. *Go ahead.*

We have a problem out on Canning. Terry Peal went off the deep end.

Liz registered the name with a start. *The robot wars guy? What's he done?*

He kidnapped a dozen people in a construction shack. He has decided the Black Hole Project is a bad idea and should be shut down. There may be some political pressure to do that if people's lives are at risk.

Crap, Liz replied. *Are the people really in danger?*

Our psychometric filter has Peal at 8 out of 10 on the Kaczynski-McVeigh scale. He could think those who do not agree with him, or simply work on the project, are morally complicit, or can be sacrificed. My friend, we must do something immediately. Unfortunately, I think I will need to stay here because of the politics. Would it be possible for you to go to Canning and deal with this as my emissary?

Liz touched the net quickly—the KM scale had been around since the 21st century and measured a propensity for rationalized violence. Peal sounded like a problem that needed fixing, but...

Cyan, I'm not, officially, part of the mining operation anymore.

You are now. This is an emergency. You know Peal.

Gunheim will unappoint me fast, and maybe you, too!

I do not think he would do anything so arbitrary during the campaign. He would, however, make me pay for it if I am not successful. You are the most logical choice because you have the greatest commitment. Also, having you involved may make Roger angry, and angry men sometimes act unwisely, to the profit of their opponents.

Persuasive arguments, Liz thought. *I'm on my way. Liz out.*

"What was that?" David asked.

Liz pursed her lips. How much should she say now? "Terry Peal again. David, have you ever heard of a couple of psychiatrists named Kaczynski and McVeigh? There's a scale relating to antisocial conflict..."

David's eyes went wide. "Liz, Kaczynski and McVeigh were not psychiatrists."

Liz felt another chill.

"20th century American political killers," Judi said. "Liz, what gives?"

She told them. "David, can you arrange a shuttle berth to Canning for me?"

He nodded. "What do you have in mind?"

"Making a hero out of myself."

"How?"

"Don't know yet, but I'll have to do it there. I'll need to get on my way before Gunheim figures it out."

"It might be better if I came with you."

She gave him a brief embrace and whispered in his hear, "Cyan needs you, here." She turned and ran for the Lenore Landing Field.

It took her forty precious minutes to get a fan car, then another twenty for it to glide its way to the North Pole port facility. When her fan car arrived at the port facility, the human attendant was grinning ear to ear.

Her heart jumped. The man worked for Gunheim. Was she already too late?

"I get a nice break today, it seems. You've got the last shuttle."

"Really," Liz said, wondering how close they'd come to disaster.

"Dr. Lalande's people just reserved all the others for various astronomical missions. Something about getting a wide baseline for a predicted supernova in a Fornax dwarf galaxy."

All right, Judi! Liz quickly wiped off her smile, nodded smartly and climbed into the spacecraft.

••∞••

She was worried she might be stopped until the count reached zero and three gravities of launch acceleration pressed her into her seat. That fell to a single gravity as the nuclear rockets took over. In a few minutes, she was weightless and heading for her destination on a fifty-kilometer per second trajectory that made only a slight allowance for orbital mechanics.

She catnapped, then watched the Canning news feed on her 30-hour journey.

Gunheim's handpicked team was at least 12 hours behind her—Cyan had managed to hold things back for almost two hours, and it had taken another 9 hours to get an interplanetary shuttle.

Liz followed the news for a while. The politics had gone as predicted with Gunheim criticizing Liz for earlier mismanagement and Cyan patiently explaining how things had developed—making sure the media 'uncovered' how Peal had used his friends' influence to amass a lot of robotic parts. Gunheim had started talking about the destiny of mankind and how everything had to be on the table as long as people's lives were at stake. Cyan had quietly asked just how much people were willing to be governed by fear. Liz nodded off.

When she woke, the brilliant crescent of Canning, rugged with impact craters and massive shield volcanoes, filled the forward view screen, with Campbell beside it. From this close orbit, the star appeared almost twice the Sun's area and about as bright, visually despite having most of its radiant energy at invisible infrared wavelengths. It poured onto the planet and the co-orbiting array almost two and a half times more energy per square meter than the Sun gave Earth. Even if she succeeded in stopping Peal, she realized, they would need every joule of it. She strapped in for deceleration.

••∞••

It was late at local night when the Canning Base spaceport passenger-access-tube snaked its way to Liz's shuttle. The only one to meet her at the inner door was Todd "Mac" MacGregor, a nervous, sandy-haired young medic whose wife was one of the hostages.

"Why," he asked choking down his emotion, "is this impactor schedule so damn important?"

Liz bit her lip and answered carefully. "The impactor your people are making," Liz explained, "has to match perfectly the other impactors in density and dimension as well as velocity to produce the necessary symmetry at the impact point. It's slow work, even for robots, and once our margin is used up, no way to make up the time. Peal's cut off the flow of iron to its assemblers, so we've already lost most of the margin. Further delay could ruin the efforts of thousands of people over the last four decades."

"But, my wife..."

Liz shook her head and put a hand on his shoulder. "If he gets away with this, it will just be something else next time. We have to deal with it now. I think I can do it."

The young man looked at her quizzically. "How? Peal's a master of technology."

Her mind suddenly clicked. "Mac..."

"What?"

"He's looking for a technological assault. Not a physical one. I could go personally and offer to exchange myself for as many hostages as he's willing to let go. Once I'm in... he's soft, maybe thirty kilos overweight. I train to one gee. Maybe I can take him out with my bare hands."

The young medic looked aghast. "And maybe you'll get yourself killed! He has robots, and the ability to get around the laws of robotics."

Liz nodded, almost surprised at herself. "He's got the project by its throat and I promised I'd get it done. It's worth taking the chance." Liz stared at him a moment and made a decision. "Mac, can you give me an edge?" There was a drug, she knew, that would give a person what used to be called hysterical strength, to lift beams of people crushed in a structure collapse, or a table to plug a blowout, or to pull open the last door to safety.

"A gamma stimulant? They're illegal..."

"They're for emergencies, Mac, and your wife's life *is* at stake."

He tightened his lips, then said, "Okay, it's worth a try. You getting killed wouldn't put my wife in any more danger, and might get her out right away." He paused and nodded, apparently making up his mind. "Wait a moment. I need to get the drug myself instead of ordering it the usual way. Peal has probably compromised the system and we don't want to make him suspicious."

The moment turned into several minutes—precious minutes in which either Peal or Gunheim might do something to make what she planned impossible. Finally, Mac returned. He held out a small blue capsule to her and she took it in her hand. It stuck to her.

"Geckro surface. You can hide it in your mouth and it will stay put. Bite it hard just before you need it. You'd better get going."

Liz nodded in acknowledgment. "Don't tell Cyan until I'm in." She turned and headed for the Canning base airlock.

••∞••

Three hours later, Liz came through an airlock and faced Peal. She'd gotten three others freed in exchange for herself—not as many as she'd hoped—before she went in. The five left were in the back of the lounge module Peal had occupied, normally a place for crews to take a break from vacuum work. It was essentially a spacecraft with everything but a propulsion system. The chunky beady-eyed man stared back at her, his mouth set, looking like a rebellious teenager. A dull-finished utilitarian humanoid robot, anatomically correct in one important feature, stood quietly beside him. Peal's sick sense of humor, she thought. The hostages were in plain view sitting on a couch and chairs in the room behind him. They weren't bound, but Peal had erected a transparent barrier between their part of the lounge and his. Handcuffs lay on the table in front of them.

A hummingbird-sized robot hovered about her on nearly silent fans, undoubtedly probing for anything technological down to the size limit of autonomous robotics. Steady, girl, Liz told herself as she let herself be inspected.

"Okay, you pass," Peal finally said. "So here we have one of these would-be gods that want to play with universes! Do you feel godlike now?"

He wanted to humiliate her! Maybe she could play that angle. "Let these people go, please. Then I'll do whatever you want."

Peal laughed. "Really? Wu and Markovitch, get your suits on and get out of here. Simmons Kefli, and MacGregor, you stay for now."

Mac's wife was a petite brunette, her face a mask of determined calm.

"Everyone, Peal. Please."

"No. I may want some more fun later. Are you going to keep your bargain?"

Liz bit her lip. She didn't want anyone else around but, she told herself, the gain was worth the risk. "Okay. What do you want?"

He leered at her. "Take your shipsuit off. Put a set of handcuffs on and come in here."

Liz complied. The handcuffs clicked ever so softly as she shut them around her wrists. The material felt like basalt fiber composite— standard 3D lithography material. It was strong enough, but brittle, she thought.

When she got the cuffs on, a section of the barrier slid aside.

"Come in," Peal said with a grin. As she reached the opening in the barrier, the humanoid robot began to move toward her. "A modification of the virtual reality glove. What it feels, I feel. Now turn around. Do you know what 'black hole' means in Russian?"

Now or never, Liz thought. She bit down on the capsule as she complied with Peal's order, moving back against the barrier as she did so. She shivered to elevate her heart rate and hyperventilated. Strength flowed into her. Steady, she told herself, thirty seconds for maximum effect. She felt her muscles quiver in preparation.

"So, you think you're going to play with the universe, do you?"

This wasn't going to be easy. Okay, she thought. She'd never get to Peal before the robot got to her, take the robot first. She allowed it to close the distance. Four meters... three. Now! With a scream, she snapped her wrists apart then forward as hard as she could, and fell back against the barrier. The handcuffs cracked open and the line holding them together pulled out of the right one. Pain stabbed up her arm like a hot knife. She ignored it. The robot snapped toward her almost faster than could be seen, but her right leg was already up to meet it. Her heel hit right in its mechanical pelvis hard. Something snapped in her leg. More searing pain. Damn, Hilda, I tried. I really tried, she thought.

But in a second she realized she wasn't done yet. The robot had rebounded from the collision and was sailing across the room in the low gravity. Before it could bounce and get back, she launched herself at the startled Peal, ignoring the pain in her leg.

No time for fancy stuff. Her balled fist caught him squarely in the jaw, going through it as if it were balsa. Her momentum crashed them both into the mini galley at the end of the room, a coffee pot bouncing away spewing hot liquid all over. The impact knocked the breath out of her. Already she was beginning to feel lightheaded and tired; but the robot would be back for her. She whirled Peal's limp body around to put him between her and the robot.

The machine crashed into them and bounced away, inanimate.

Dead man switch? A look at what was left of Peal's head told the story. There was gray matter on her fist. She shook it off automatically, revulsed.

Boost and adrenaline spent, the pain from a broken leg and broken wrist hit her hard. She felt nauseated, and fainted. The last thing she remembered was the smell of spilled coffee.

••∞••

When Liz regained consciousness a week later, her wounds were healed, she was a hero, and Cyan Mutori was the new chief executive of the Campbell system. Roger Gunheim had left the Campbell system with DeRoot and some of their cronies, bound for the BHP vertex to see the implosion, and then on to a new colony at Stein 2051, 25 light years distant.

CHAPTER 5

In Space, at the Impactor Launch Site
26 October 2275

The impactor looked like a long thin filament that seemed to run out to infinity. At high magnification, Liz and David could see a slight texture to it; individually controlled superconducting solenoid rings were placed every few meters to stretch the wire taut to just the right tension, giving it some rigidity for maneuvers and providing a fine control on its density. Somewhere, out toward the end of the rod, was the main magnetic reflector. Any time now, David thought.

Cyan's term as chief executive had begun well. The impactor launch was back on schedule, albeit with the smallest of windows. No more delays could be tolerated, but so far, so good. He, Judi, Cyan, and Liz took a shuttle out to the launch site, a point high over the asteroid belt where the impactor coasted, waiting for the main beam. While far from the revelry, they had all wanted to, well, be there.

They waited in blackness, their eyes adapted to the star spangled night. Some constellations he could recognize despite the distortions of distance: the hook of Scorpius, belted Orion, and the mane and haunches of Leo. He smiled. From here, Leo had acquired a knee; Rigel

Kentaurus, Alpha Centauri's other name, was now Rigel Leonis! And between the lion and a barely recognizable big dipper was the Sun. *If I forget thee, oh Jerusalem,* he thought.

Liz announced, "About now."

He looked south to the impactor, below the lion and its new knee. At its far distant end a tiny blue star appeared and gradually grew to an iridescent flower, brighter and brighter with its far edges fading into a deep violet.

In the close-up optics, the impactor began to move across the field of view. Faster and faster it went. The view zoomed back.

It was bright enough now that David risked a look at Campbell and the ring of beam projectors around it. Only a few of them were active at this early stage, he knew, but already the power was a million times that used to launch a starship. And it would grow by many orders of magnitude over the next nine months. By that time, he would be deeply into analyzing the results of the planetoid's impending impact on Martin.

He felt Liz's arms around him and smiled. Time enough for work later. Her face was glowing—he kissed her. Cyan Mutori glanced at them and looked away.

They watched for an hour or so, until the violet flower had faded into the interstellar depths. Then their shuttle turned back for Minot.

Once home David put his full energies into his own projects. To the victors went the spoils, David thought. His work, which he'd worried about losing altogether, was now getting high priority; such was his reward for backing the winners.

An urgent message awaited him—results from his Prospector Probes deep in the icy mantle of Martin. They'd struck water. No question about it; 11.36 kilometers under the ice surface was a huge lake, filling the bed of an ancient caldera. No, he thought, not all that ancient. Martin must not be completely stone cold. There was some tidal stress from its eccentric orbit, and its radioactive ores still put out a fair amount of heat. It had to get out somewhere, and the readings pointed to several vents across the bottom of the lake. There could be life down there, he thought.

The thought hit him in the gut. Oh, God! If Martin had water and heat, then... his imagination ran wild.

Far from being the agent of a temporary rebirth of this planet, the impending collision might mean the destruction of one of the six independently evolved biologies known.

●●∞●●

Liz stared up at the sky in her dome with restless anticipation. She touched the net to check the countdown... 1205013 seconds... about two standard weeks... the particle projectors would finish their job—and hers. Then what?

A beep on her comm sounded. A message from David in his new lab in Lenore.

"Liz, come over, please. I need your help!"

She found him staring at a micrograph of a rock sample brought up from a deep borehole on the planetoid falling toward Martin. He hadn't noticed her coming in, but instead continued to stare at the dark rock. She found herself staring at it, too.

Liz saw a number of what looked like tiny microbes, squirming around. "From the planetoid?" she asked.

"Liz." They kissed cheek to cheek, not on the mouth, Liz noted. He was all business.

"The center of the planetoid is now above the melting point of water. It would be boiling in a near vacuum; but here and there, the vapor can't get out fast enough and the pressure rises to the point where liquid water exists. They thaw out once every hundred and eighty-three thousand years, and they're thriving, for the last time."

"In the wild anyway. What are they?" she asked.

"Archea. Almost eighty percent identical to those in the Solar System and thirteen other star systems. Their DNA forms loops instead of the strings capped with telomeres that we use. They're rugged; that's why so many of them are extremophiles."

Liz looked at him quizzically.

"Their DNA doesn't wear out."

"Wow! Neat." She knew the whole astrobiology team was in a race to study every facet of the colliding worlds before the collision destroyed the incoming planetoid and utterly transformed Martin as well.

"Expected. We find them on Martin too, and on that planetoid you found back in the Solar System. But there is something else in some of the volcanically-warmed lakes on Martin: multicellular archea with knobby-loop DNA. See?"

Liz couldn't tell if the stringy stuff she was looking at were loops or not, but they appeared to have knots in them.

"God knows how long these little critters have survived protected by that layer of ice, Liz. We'll probably never know their earliest beginnings. What could they have shown us?"

Liz squeezed his hand. "I think they've shown us that life is everywhere."

He squeezed her hand back. "I need your help badly, Liz."

"How?"

"I know I was against changing the trajectory of the incoming asteroid originally. But I did not know about the knobby DNA then. We have to stop the collision."

"What? David? How? The BHP impactor needs the entire array output for the next ten days. And look at the simulations. Even if we were to turn the array on the planetoid now, without time for any preparation there's no guarantee it would accomplish anything."

"There must be a way! That is your field. Give us a chance to study Martin biology in situ!"

Liz shook her head. "I'm truly sorry, David."

He looked at her, anguish written all over his face. "That is all I get? 'I'm sorry?'"

Liz felt torn. "David, my job is to make sure the impactor gets exactly what it needs. There are three other impactors headed for the experiment site. If any one of them is off, a half-century of work goes down the drain. I can't think of anything we can do at this point that wouldn't jeopardize that. But I'll ask the staff. Anyway, the geometry is wrong; the planetoid's trajectory is in the local ecliptic plane, so half the array is blocked by the other half. The gap is on the one side, and Martin blocks the other side. We won't be able to get a significant push on the planetoid for another three days in any event. Maybe you'll have enough samples by then."

He abruptly got up. "I need a break."

She took his hand and held it tightly.

"Make it enough time, Liz, please," he said. "I am going out to the remote lab to do what I can."

••∞••

Three weeks later, David greeted Liz at his remote lab deep inside the only natural satellite of Martin, and gave her a quick tour. The moon was a captured nickel-iron asteroid about seventy kilometers by fifty by thirty. Robots had hollowed out a 500-meter spherical cavity deep beneath the surface. They also built a rotating drum that was 200 meters in radius to provide enough gravity to keep the researchers' bones solid and to settle the various fluids of life in and outside the isolation lab. Construction was still going on, and people were working out of cubicles. Plantings and roofs would come later, he explained.

She looked grim and troubled, he thought—and steeled himself for bad news. He showed her a seat in a bare cubicle he used as a staff conference room. Cyan Mutori was on screen, seated with a couple of council members and three or four people he thought might be project engineers. Cyan looked as poised as ever, with no hint as to the position she might take. He took a deep breath.

Cyan started. "David, for those of us who are not exobiologists, perhaps you could start this conversation with a little background."

"Thank you, Cyan. We have found multicellular life on Martin. Worms, actually, primitive, but with a pass-through tube for a gut and the beginnings of a primitive nervous system. We suspect there are more complicated life forms."

The light speed delay between the lab and Minot was almost a minute. It seemed more like an hour. Finally, the people on his screen reacted with a murmur, but it was not as loud as he'd hoped for.

He tried again. "You must understand the importance of this. We have found the first multi-celled life form that humanity has ever found off-Earth."

Another minute, more murmur.

Cyan beamed at him. "David, this is great news, and your team is to be congratulated for all their hard work. Wouldn't everyone agree?"

Louder murmuring and congratulations poured toward him. "Could we have some additional perspective of your discovery?"

Gehenna. What else could he tell them? He spread his arms. "Look, it's a given that all the life we know spawned from single cells. That's the beginning. What we have here are multi-celled organisms. So the problem to investigate is: Where did they evolve? Near the thermal vents at the bottom of the lakes on Martin, or somewhere else? And if so, why were they able to survive on this particular planet?"

Liz leaned forward. "These life forms may have come from someplace else?"

He had expected his good news would set everyone's enthusiasm on fire. Instead he was getting polite questions.

"They have loop DNA like extremophiles but we aren't sure whether they are descended from archea. That means we have another, entirely different architecture of life floating around the galaxy. But the gene trace diagrams indicate a recent origin, pointing toward a development unique to Martin. I'm betting that life for these worms started right on this planet."

Another wait, then someone else asked, "Have you looked into the geologic history of this planet enough to be able to substantiate this thesis?"

He shook his head. "We do not have data enough to decide one way or the other. We need more bore holes, more lakes, and more samples. We need an intact planet on which to do this."

"But we don't have the time," Liz said simply.

He shot her a look, then looked back to Mutori. "That's where you all come in. We have to divert the incoming planetoid. It would be nice if this could be done without affecting the Black Hole Project, but this has to take priority.

"Look, I've studied the project plans and there is some margin built in. The impactors lock into beacons as they approach the impact point and start exchanging vectors. They can all decelerate a little to recover synchronicity if one is a little off. We can make up the total momentum after diverting the planetoid and let the impactor control system get things back in sync again. But even if that doesn't work, would it really matter if it takes another century to make a black hole? This is something that may never come our way again."

Liz shook her head. "I can't endorse that approach. What if we aren't the only ones with some kind of problem? Yes, there is some margin, but not enough to cover things if all four impactors make changes as big as we are contemplating here. We can't just grab all the margin of error for ourselves. We have to put that impactor on exactly the prescribed profile if we humanly can."

After the light speed delay, a project engineer shook his head. "It would be better to destroy the impactor and start over again than to be slightly off. A great many things could happen with an asymmetric impact, some of them very dangerous indeed, and to people other than ourselves."

Cyan Mutori nodded gravely.

David's heart sank. They just couldn't see how important it was! Of course not, he thought. They were mostly physical scientists and engineers. They had different values. Against all logic, he searched Cyan's face for a hopeful sign, but her face, of course, gave nothing away.

There were more questions and answers, but in reality everyone was well-informed. This was not a question of facts, but one of value and perspective. His, he realized, was not theirs.

One of the council members made a motion to adjourn without acting on the diversion proposal. They voted silently.

Finally, Cyan looked at him. "The consensus of the Council is to continue with the original mission plan. We'll put all available resources into getting as large a physical sample of pre-collision Martin as we can, right up to the last minute. I am sorry, David, but it is the best we can do for you. I know human team members will want to stay until the last minute, so we need to be fairly firm about getting them off. Please inform everyone that all human team members should plan to be off of Martin within 24 hours of impact, for safety."

David nodded dumbly and sighed. "I understand. Thank you for considering this. Since there is so little time, I should get back to work."

••∞••

Liz went jogging. The track circled the small habitat—if you ran spinward you were heavier. She ran spinward—punishing her body helped with the frustration. They had enough power to divert the planetoid now, but no way to couple that power efficiently to the planetoid. It would require engineering a new reflector to couple the beam's momentum to the planetoid. But if they waited until they could get one installed, it would take so much power the project would be compromised. The dilemma seemed to have no solution.

David, of course, would never understand that. Liz continued going in circles, mentally and physically. Finally exhausted, she stopped at the locker room, showered, dressed, and headed back to David's quarters.

David wasn't there.

••∞••

David stowed his Martin suit and a big duffel bag behind a bulkhead then geckroed his feet by the airlock as the last shuttle from Martin's surface docked. His course was settled, but he wanted to make sure no one else would be harmed. He waved to them as they came out of the access tube and pulled themselves down the corridor, accompanied by robots pulling bags of samples and gear. They all smelled of dust from the surface.

"Is everyone off the planet now?" David asked the last one off, a stocky man named Ned Oh.

He nodded. "Everyone's here and accounted for."

"Very good. I will try to get back before departure for Minot, but if not, go ahead without me; I may be some time, and can take this shuttle back."

Ned looked at David oddly, then smiled. "You? Late?"

David forced a smile. "The collision apparently will *not* be late, and there is still much to do."

Ned patted him on the shoulder; the lack of an effort to divert the planetoid had been a disappointment for all of them. They shook hands and Ned followed his group down the corridor.

David boarded the shuttle and stowed his gear. Settling in at the controls, he contacted the busy port manager. "I need to make a fast trip down to the surface. There is a last minute discovery at a new ice lake."

The man, tall and light-haired with a bushy mustache and an easygoing manner, squinted and smiled. "Well now, someone might think you just wanted to be the last one off the planet."

David smiled back nervously and didn't say anything. Let him believe what he wanted.

The man shrugged. "Okay, it's fueled and ready. No other traffic, so you're cleared."

The trip down to the planet took four hours. The ice lake actually existed; he landed on its shore. If nothing else, he would find out one or two more things about this world. He pulled one of two boxes out of the duffel bag and replaced it with a survival tent and a couple days' worth of rations. He carried the box down the ladder and set it down outside the shuttle's airlock. Then he went back up, opened the panel to the ship's main processor, and disconnected it. That should set some alarms going, he thought.

On his way out he touched the box and hesitated, going over everything again. No, he had to do it this way. There could be only one way to get him off the planet alive, and that would be to divert the planetoid. He took a breath, threw the switch on the timer, climbed down the ladder, picked up his gear, and headed for the lakeshore.

Ten minutes later, the blast severed his only way off the planet.

They had not really listened before; perhaps they would listen now.

Later, on a small rise, he looked out over the lake. At early evening by local time, the scenery here, in one of the few places on Martin's surface not covered with ice, was breathtaking. The steep sides of the caldera were a study in deep red and black, with glints here and there of volcanic glass. The ground was cracked and brittle—he would have to watch his step; getting himself killed too soon would defeat the whole purpose of this mad exercise.

Would Liz or Mutori pull out the stops and divert the planetoid? Or, would they let him be blown to smithereens along with the planet? He looked at the still lake, reflecting the glowing crags of the caldera's rim. Was it really still, he thought, or was it, too, teaming with life, every bit as deserving of saving as the damned, all too important, Black Hole Project?

••∞••

Liz was deep in concentration on an idea that just might work. Array construction robots in orbit about Canning were hurriedly fabricating a huge net, a thousand kilometers in radius. A large magsail, meant for a starship, would be attached to the net; along with several million tons of ballast, weighted around the rim of the net. If everything went right, the whole assembly could be pushed with planetary transport beams to intercept the planetoid about a hundred planetary radii from collision with enough momentum to cause it to graze Martin's atmosphere instead of colliding directly. But it would be very, very close.

Something was trying to get her attention. Amongst the numbers and trajectories, a signal light was flashing.

"Yes?"

"It's Ned. I'm at the door. I thought I should deliver this news in person."

That didn't sound good. "Come in."

One look at his face confirmed that he was the bearer of bad news.

"Liz, have you heard about David?"

She shook her head.

"He's gone to the surface of Martin, making a human shield out of himself."

"Oh... crap! I'm sorry, I should have seen this coming. He's never... he..."

"I didn't see it coming either."

"I'll need to talk to Cyan."

Ned nodded. "Let me know if there's anything I can do."

As he left, Liz touched the net. *Cyan, emergency, Cyan, we have a problem,* she sent. The light speed delay was maddening.

What, Liz? What is the matter?

David has gone human shield on us.

Wait.

Human shield?

He's gone down to Martin in hopes we'll divert the beam projector to save his life.

Wait.

You know him better than any of us, Liz. Can you talk him out of it?

I'll do what I can. I'll get absolutely nowhere talking on the radio. I'll have to do this in person.

Wait.

The momentum exchange mesh—the big net—is almost ready, Cyan said. *Hopefully we can spread the push over the entire area and hold the major pieces together. If we use BHP projectors, we can load less ballast and launch it now, then give it a major push.*

No! Keep the projectors on the impactor. We can't risk screwing with that. I'll go down to Martin myself and try to bring David back.

Wait.

Liz, do you think that is wise? Much could go wrong.

Liz remembered how David had helped her stand up to DeRoot, how he'd been at her side when things had seemed darkest, and all the wonderful, sweet moments of lovemaking they'd shared.

Cyan, I owe him too much. I have to try. I'd never forgive myself if I didn't.

Wait.

I understand. You will take several robots, of course, armed with tranquilizer darts; I will authorize the exception to the Asimovian rules. I know you will try to get his voluntary cooperation first, but time is short. And Liz we've been over David's recent communications. Voice stress analysis, word patterns, and other things. He doesn't seem to be well.

Chaos! What?

People still occasionally got brain tumors, Liz knew. They were quickly cured when detected, but they had to be detected first. Then there was the stuff he was working with; the quarantine was very good, and the human immune system should be totally lethal to anything that hadn't evolved ways to counter it. But there was still a chance. Deep in thought, Liz barely noticed the light speed delay.

We don't know without doing a scan and taking samples—it could be strictly psychological, stress-induced. But I think it's important to know if he's been affected by anything in the environment, because a layer of that environment will be plastered all over this planetary system in a few years as a result of impact debris. At any rate, he's presenting the beginning stages of classic paranoid schizophrenia, progressing rapidly. Also, whatever he does, you should not blame him, or yourself. I know this is hard when it happens to someone you love, but tragedies happen. If the worst happens, remember him as he was. Finally, and I am very sorry to say this, but he may strike out irrationally. Remember that if he does, it's not him. But still, be very careful. And remember that it is not always possible to fix everything. If it gets too late, come back.

I will, Cyan. Thank you.

Could she hunt down David as if he were a zoo animal out of his cage? Could she leave him to die? Did she have any choice?

••○○••

David found that he was off the net. The relays may have been removed or someone may have thought that denying him access would give them an advantage. That meant they were going to try to resolve this by force instead of negotiation. His heart sank; that would cost several hours. No, he thought, they might work the problem in parallel; even now some way to divert the planetoid might be in the works, something that could be turned on or off at the last moment.

Night fell. The planetoid was less than a day away, near the ecliptic plane, coming posigrade. He looked to the west and found it easily—it had a huge coma of gas, like a comet. The nucleus was already a small disk. It would stay there, fixed among the stars. That was how one could tell if something was going to hit you—the angles stay the same.

Very well. If they were going to try to force him off, they would come with robots, sensors—the whole nine yards. They would succeed, unless he could somehow anticipate them and strike first. He had dealt with terrorists back in the Israeli defense force; he was on the other side now, but he knew the territory. Maybe they would not anticipate that.

To get a surprise, he would have to make them think he was here but actually be there. He took a reflective blanket and some line, then climbed up a small lava dome until he could see the landing site. He built a couple of small towers with flat volcanic rocks and anchored the top of the reflective blanket to them. Then he anchored the bottom of it at about forty-five degrees so it formed a kind of lean-to. He went back down and moved his campsite until he could see the distorted reflection of the still-glowing wreck of his shuttle in this jerrybuilt mirror. The radio in the emergency stores had both infrared and radio frequency bands, as did the suit. He set it up in sight of the mirror. If this worked, he'd be able to speak on infrared from his suit, the infrared would reflect off the mirror to the emergency comm pack, and his voice would come out on the radio from the campsite.

He took a second box from the duffel bag and headed for the landing site.

Halfway there he keyed the infrared channel in his helmet. "Hello everyone. Liz, Cyan. You know I am very sorry to cause you so much trouble. You must also know that this is more important than your inconvenience, or even my life, if it comes to that. You must do what you can to prevent the impact. I must do everything I can to make you do that. I have no choice in this. I hope you understand this. I am sorry."

He heard his little speech on the radio as he said it; a distracting echo, but it proved his system worked. Unless they had managed to deploy a very sophisticated surveillance system on very short notice, they should think he was at the campsite on the shore of the lake; he'd left a heater on there, and the radio would be coming from there.

"David, this is Liz. I'm coming to get you. We've figured out a way to divert the planetoid; a huge mesh net is on its way from Canning. It will probably work, but if the planetoid breaks up in the net, some of it may get through. It's too dangerous to stay on the surface of Martin."

David's heart beat rapidly. There was hope. Then he thought again. What proof did he have that anything was actually being done? They'd cut him off from the net. She could be lying. Why not? She would do anything to save her damn project.

"Liz," he said. "That sounds very hopeful. Thank you for making the effort, if it is true. But I must take the risk that it is not true, or I give up all my leverage. Please go back and get me after the impact is diverted."

"David, you might be dead!"

"I know this. I have thought this through very carefully. It is my choice."

"David, I am coming to get you. That is my choice."

He could think of nothing to say to that. He quickly covered the distance to the landing site and hid himself in a broken lava tube near the wrecked shuttle. None too soon; just as he settled in, he heard the sonic boom of the approaching shuttle, and soon the glow of its engines lit up the landscape. He watched the bullet-shaped vehicle's landing gear extend as it set smoothly down, the hatch side turned mostly toward him.

David agonized. But he would have to do what he had to do; he had come too far to waver now. If Liz were lying to him, she had sealed her own fate as well.

As soon as the shuttle landed and Liz had popped the hatch, he opened his comm line. "Liz, my camp is on the shore of the lake, about ten minutes walk from here, uh, I mean from where your shuttle is coming down."

"I see it, David. Please come meet me at the landing site. We're doing everything we can."

He shook his head automatically, even though she couldn't see him. "I cannot take that chance. I am sorry. If you want to talk, come to the camp. We still have several hours."

Liz didn't answer him. The hatch swung open and she descended, followed by three black circular robots hovering on their fans. He could barely see them, but this close he could hear them.

She strode off toward the camp, her path lit by a helmet light. The robots, presumably invisible now, followed. He patted a device in his pocket; he had an answer for those, but now was not the time to reveal it.

David judged the distance to the shuttle. He didn't dare use the infrared to talk now; Liz would pick that up in her helmet and immediately know what he was doing. Would she suspect? Had she left a guard? The best strategy would be to approach the shuttle in an unthreatening way. His box with the bomb was a standard sample box, and should be recognized as such.

He waited until she was halfway to the camp, then got up and walked as calmly as he could to the shuttle. He opened the standard infrared channel for robotic interface and positioned his body so the beam would not carry to Liz or his own radio relay setup, he hoped.

"Hello. I'm David Levi. I have some samples to go to the lab."

"Mr. Levi. Please do not enter the shuttle; you are not authorized. I have notified Captain Avonford of your presence."

"David!" Liz screamed. "I thought you were at the camp. What are you doing at the shuttle?"

"I changed my mind," he said, using the radio channel from his suit. He took two more steps closer to the shuttle, reaching the right landing gear. "I really wanted to see you again, Liz." He turned away from the shuttle, triggered the switch, and set the sample case down as carefully as he could. He started running toward Liz, not daring to look back. Five... four... three... two... one...

The blast wave almost knocked him over. Now he looked back and watched the shuttle topple to the ground. Back to square one, he thought. He turned back toward Liz and stood motionless, trying to figure out what to say. She would probably be upset.

A sudden sting in his arm told him just how upset.

••∞••

Liz had skimmed along the regolith toward David, wanting to believe him, wanting to get him and get out of here. But she'd been deceived. Should have had the robots tranquilize him earlier, she thought. But she'd held back. Maybe there was an explanation that made sense. Once he was in her arms again, surely he would listen to reason. He had run toward her; she could see the light on his helmet bob up and down with each long stride. Surely they could still sort things out.

The blast took her totally by surprise and she watched in horror as the shuttle toppled to the ground. There was no second explosion and its navigation lights stayed on. The port light created a pool of red on the lava and showed the crumpled side of the vehicle in high relief.

Liz brought herself to a halt. *Take him down,* she sent to the hovering robots. Talk about closing the barn door after the horse escaped.

Liz, Ned. Are you okay?

I'm fine. He got the shuttle before I got him. Can you get another one down here?

We'll have to try, won't we? The port manager and I've got it in works, but it looks like an hour to fuel and check out and four hours—make that four point three—down to the surface where you are. That's collision time, I'm afraid.

Her heart skipped a beat and a knot suddenly tightened in her gut. *Chaos, try to shave ten minutes off that somewhere, will you?*

I'll try my best. Do you want me to tell Cyan?

So it's down to this, Liz thought. What would Cyan Mutori do? A word from her now, and the full power of the beam could be thrown against the planetoid, possibly breaking it up, possibly pushing it away. But that diversion would also throw the impactor off profile, perhaps irretrievably so. Damn Peal! There was no margin, none.

Not just yet. See where you get on the spare shuttle.

Are you sure, Liz?

It could mean the difference between probably living and probably dying, for both her and David. But it could also be the difference between carrying out her mission with certainty, and leaving humanity's greatest project to chance. She'd wanted to be the big fish in the small pond, to have the big decisions. Well, this was one that would echo through the rest of history.

Yes, I'm sure. Ned, if it doesn't work out... It's not your fault. But get that damn shuttle here!

It's been on its way since you asked. Everything optimized for minimum time. Good luck. Ned out.

Liz looked up at the oncoming planetoid and its halo of gas, rising high over the eastern horizon. It would not, if she remembered the simulations correctly, quite reach the zenith from her location. In the last minutes, it would begin plunging back down to the horizon. Then a hypersonic detonation wave would jet out above her and the blast wave would roll over the horizon at the local speed of sound, some twenty minutes later.

Human beings had voluntarily gone to their deaths before, for a big enough cause. She had not ever quite thought of herself that way. All told, she would rather not. But one of the things that human beings were about was will. We were out here because of will, she thought.

Liz, Cyan. What's going on down there?

Liz sighed. It hadn't taken her long to find out.

A small delay. He's tranked now. I'm going after him.

Wait.

You are stranded!

Maybe. Cyan, am I still in charge? Is it my call? You know what is at stake. This situation is my responsibility, and I have chosen to keep the Project on profile. On our friendship, please honor that choice.

Wait—much longer, this time, than required for just the light speed delay.

I understand what is at stake. If it were my responsibility, I would, I hope, have the courage to choose as you have. But we will do everything we can short of affecting the project to get you out of there. The net has been launched; it should arrive three hours before impact. The planetoid will still be half as far away as the moon is from Earth. If everything holds, it should get enough delta-v to just graze Martin's atmosphere. Roche forces will pull the planetoid apart, but the net may hold it together for a while. We can't tell whether it will be captured or not—too many uncertainties.

You're giving me some hope, anyway. Between that and the relief shuttle, I'm going to assume I'll make it, Liz answered.

Liz had kept walking as she talked. David's helmet light glowed softly, nearer and nearer.

When she got there, that was all there was—the helmet light.

Where's David? she asked the robots.

The one designated "Alpha" answered. *We have a command authority conflict.*

"Chaos!" Liz struggled to regain her temper.

Cyan, could you reset the command authority override on my robots? David has pulled another fast one on me.

Wait, agonizingly long.

Done. Use the prefix "Sunbeam" if you have any more problems.

Thanks.

To the robots: *Sunbeam. Where's David?*

Mr. Levi is proceeding on foot to the lake. He apparently has a trank antidote.

No kidding! Keep him in sight. I'm following.

Liz, Cyan. We can still boost the net a little more.

Chaos, Liz thought. Why couldn't they just let the decision stand?

No, Cyan. Thank you, but no. The whole thing's chancy and the last thing I'd want is to screw up the Project and get killed.

Wait.

Liz! Judi Lalande broke the quiet. *In one hour, we can no longer accelerate the net. Martin's moon is getting in the way.*

Yes, Judi, Liz here. I understand. I may end up seeing this explosion first hand. You know what? I'm not scared. It's like letting go. Liberating in a way. What will happen will happen. I accept that.

Silence. It gave her a momentary chill. Would they respect her wishes? She tried to contemplate her humiliation if they did not and the Project got screwed up. Much better to die a martyr. She smiled to herself. Risky behavior was nothing new to her, and here it was, the ultimate. Triumph or die. No. Triumph and die. Glory.

As if floating on air, Liz started running towards David. There was still time to grab him and at least get away from Martin, she thought. But if not, glory.

She stopped bouncing and opened a radio channel to David.

"David. What's going to happen is going to happen. There's nothing more that anyone can physically do. The net is on its way; we should be able to see the intercept. It may work. Meanwhile there's a crewless shuttle on its way to take us off. It may get here in time even if the net doesn't work. There's no point in running from me anymore."

"I can't believe you."

Liz looked up into the sky and asked for a reticular circle where the net was. It floated in front of her eyes at infinity, a faint red circle. There, in its center, was a tiny spider web. "David, believe your own eyes then. Look up. In Ursa Major, a little left of Mizar and Alcor, there's a faint, tiny web."

It grew even as she watched. Liz touched the net. Forty minutes until impact. Even without additional boost from the Project projectors, the device was traveling at a hundred and thirty kilometers a second.

Maybe too fast, she realized. She looked at the projections; ninety percent of the net cords were predicted to fail on impact. Would the remaining ten percent be enough? Things would stretch, of course.

David materialized from the dark into the glow of her helmet light. "You planned it this way, didn't you! You all did."

Liz didn't bother to answer that. He was here; that was all that counted. "Let's get to the shuttle rendezvous."

David caught up to her and they both turned towards the dark sky standing side by side. "When?"

"Thirty minutes for the net impact, about three hours for the main event and the shuttle landing."

Wordlessly, they returned to the landing field.

The net zoomed by overhead, moving at the apparent rate of a high-altitude aircraft or a satellite; but it was much farther away and moving much faster. As it approached the planetoid, its angular rate grew less and less; a trick of perspective, Liz realized. The net now moved almost directly away from them. It would have been better, she thought, if it could have hit the planetoid from the side, but this would be almost as good. It only had to slow it a little, just enough for Martin to move a little further from under it.

The net vanished, invisible against the glowing gas surrounding the planetoid.

It happened slowly. The planetoid slowly split into two, then three, then five pieces. Some of them seemed to be drifting off to the right, others not at all.

Liz, Cyan...

I saw, Cyan. It looks like part of it is still going to hit.

Wait.

Yes. There was a small delay on the shuttle trajectory to let the net go by. It will be very close. Be ready to run for it. In the meantime, perhaps you would wish to settle whatever you need to settle. I've opened the net back up to David.

She didn't think they would make it. *Thank you, very much, Cyan, for everything. Thank you.*

Two hours, forty minutes. A message to Mom, of course. *To Captain Katherine Avonford on whatever starship she may be flying to wherever. Mom. You've probably heard what happened off the media. By the time you read this, I will have become so much interstellar gas flowing out of the Lacaille 9352 system. Perhaps we will run into each other. I'll say something general about how I feel about this—it's not really bad at all. I've let go. I'm accepting it, at peace with it, even in a strange way, looking forward to the experience. I always wanted to be important, to make a mark, to be remembered. But I'd rather have stayed around for the party. I forgot how so many of history's legends bought fame with their lives. Martyrdom isn't worth it. Tell everyone that. Martyrdom isn't worth it.*

And to Hilda. *I made a mess of it, Sis, but I got it done. Enjoy the physics.*

And to so many others.

She looked at David, silent, concentrating on his own good-byes.

Five minutes. Death hurtled towards them. It was huge now, a constellation of comets with a single coma falling toward the horizon, visibly moving, passing what brightest stars still shone through its vapors. One by one, they slipped below the horizon.

Time to impact?

The first contact has occurred.

A sudden glow lit the horizon. Then a ghostly curtain began to spread from some point below it, like an aurora, but a thousand times brighter. Jets of debris and gasses tangent to the globe of Martin at the impact point moved at tens of kilometers per second.

Heart in her throat, she sent a last message to Cyan. *I guess this is it. Thanks for trying.*

Wait.

Hang in there, Liz. The shuttle's almost down and it will take several minutes for the blast wave to reach you. But be ready for five gees flat on your back in the airlock.

Shuttle on approach, be prepared to board.

She looked up and the deep blue of its jets lanced down from the sky. She reached over and grabbed David.

"Time to go."

"Go yourself. It's hopeless."

"Come on, we've got to try."

While David lingered in awe of its horrible beauty, Liz grabbed his arm and gave it a tug.

"Come on! Run for the shuttle!" It settled down fifty meters from them, its hot exhaust flapping their Martin suits.

She felt David pull her hand loose. "Go," he told her. You can't save this place, you can't save me." And he pushed her towards the shuttle. "Just go!"

It was futile, they both knew it. Regardless, Liz focused. She could not give up completely. How close could she come to getting away?

Prepare for immediate lift off as soon as I get in the hatch, she told the shuttle. Without David's weight, she reached the shuttle as the debris curtain spread overhead. The trick would be to get between that and the blast wave.

The ladder hung out of the hatch. David got up, at last, and tried to run toward her.

"Hurry!" she screamed.

He tripped over a small rock and fell. He picked himself up. A second lost. "I'm going to be the martyr here, Liz. Get lost!"

A strange orange light flooded the horizon. She turned. Ah, yes. This was it. She sent what she saw streaming into the net. Roiling clouds zoomed toward the zenith as if in a time-lapse video of normal weather. It glowed. Everything glowed. She felt like she was in an oven.

Air slammed into her and sent her skyward, the shuttle and David tumbling nearby. She felt surreal.

Hot—very, very hot. Her visor melted, bowed in, a blowtorch played on her face. Everything went dark. She took a last breath, a breath of pure fire. She willed herself to take it deep, so as not to prolong the pain. *So I pass into legend.*

BOOK III

IMPERFECT GODS

CHAPTER 1

Spaceport, Planet New Antarctica
Erebus (Groombridge 34A) Star System
12 April 2272

She's on that ship, Naomi Abila thought as she watched the incoming interplanetary shuttle rise slowly in the far north like a supernova kicked loose from the firmament, a brilliant point of light that got higher and brighter every second. As it grew brighter and nearer, it began a majestic sweep eastward and inscribed a thin, glowing trace across Canis Major and then Orion. Gently, its path curved back until it was again headed directly for their base on New Antarctica.

Naomi smiled at her son, Sasha. She worried that he might resent having another person becoming, effectively, lead on New Antarctica's part of the Black Hole Project to create a mini black hole. That had been pretty much hers up to now. On the other hand, he idolized Dr. Brunhilda Kremer, all the more since the story had arrived of how she helped derail an attempt to sabotage the project back in Sol's System. And, of course, in a time where age difference no longer mattered, Dr. Kremer was single.

The glow faded from blue-white to dull red to nothing. Flood beams stabbed up past the tiny yellow disk of their local giant planet, Amundsen, into the Milky Way and found their target, a tiny ball so reflective it might have been made of liquid mercury. Rapidly it descended toward them. At first it seemed like a small chromium moon, then, as it dropped lower, Naomi's perspective changed and she saw the light scatter off a teardrop hull that seemed as big as a hill and shiny as a mirror.

A beam of brilliant green-glowing plasma lanced up from the landing area and blossomed into a violet flower just beneath the broad part of the hull where its force spent itself against a silent expanse. Distant ice fields around their "dry island" city glowed in response.

The spacecraft slowed and followed the beam down toward the landing zone with the ponderous stateliness of objects of its scale. A hundred meters up, the plasma flickered out and the two-hundred-meter-long teardrop settled down through wind-whipped snow as if held by some giant hand. The sight of a thousand tons of mass effortlessly floating on magnetic fields never failed to inspire awe in Naomi. At times like this her mind went back to ancient legends; we are heirs of Prometheus, she thought.

The port dome flowed up and around the ship as it slipped down into the colony docks.

Naomi turned to Sasha. "Let's go meet the new boss."

"Us?"

Naomi laughed. "Your Uncle Ted is out at the site and Wotan Kremer's tied up in a meeting about ice sheet slippage."

"Dr. Kremer is his daughter, isn't she? Hard to imagine Grandpa Abila staying away if it were you."

Indeed it would. Dad was always there to greet her, even when coming back from a few weeks at the construction site. But Wotan Kremer was notorious for not letting personal matters interfere with business. "Yes, but melting planets has to be done just right. He'll probably see her tomorrow."

"I wonder what they'll call New Antarctica when they're done melting the ice."

Naomi sparkled. "Come on. You'll want to make a good impression."

He chuckled and followed her into the elevator.

She'd reserved a table on the upper level where they could watch the disembarkation. She liked to watch the new arrivals and imagine who they might be and what their personalities would be like. Sasha shared that general interest, but today was a little more special.

They arrived in the great cylindrical cavern just as massive sections of the shuttle's hull swung aside, exposing its innards to the business of unloading. The hull was covered with frost and there was a sharp nippy smell to air just mixed with the icy nitrogen above. They could even see their breath. Sasha tried blowing a ring of mist.

They walked to their table, a semicircle that curved away from the low, transparent guard wall. Four pod chairs rimmed the table and they took the middle two. She settled into the infrared warmth of the chair and savored the sensation of breathing crisp air. They ordered coffee and watched four ramps slide out from the sides of the cylinder into the ship. A host of robot unloaders rolled down three of them to get to the cargo. Above them was a large sign, "Welcome to New Antarctica, Erebus (Groombridge 34A) Star System." The name they'd given the star was that new.

A dozen folks emerged on the fourth ramp, hooded against the chill of the still-warming air."Do you know which one she is?" Sasha asked. When she didn't answer he slung his arm on her shoulder. "Mom?"

"Huh? Oh, sorry. I was just checking with the site on how the impactor fabrication is doing. *Icestar* is reporting a concern about defect frequency."

"Mom, those pop media gadflies would make a scandal out of someone's hangnail."

His mother kept listening to the net intently.

When Sasha cocked his head at her, she chuckled. "It's not really important; we'd like the impactor to be a single crystal, but that's not a requirement. An impactor traveling that close to light speed, its mechanical properties are almost irrelevant."

Sasha shook his head. "Whatever." Then he looked back at the disembarking passengers.

A hood fell back from a passenger revealing a tall blond with wide-set eyes and a long nose. She didn't seem to mind the chill, and she was grinning from ear to ear. She glanced around and Sasha's eyes met hers momentarily.

"Mom?"

"Dr. Kremer's the tall one." Naomi waved. The woman waved back and headed for the elevator.

"Not bad," Sasha said. "She'll melt someone's icecap."

Naomi smiled. At twenty, her son was somewhat of a man-child, brilliant enough in his architectural studies but never quite connecting socially. She worried that she was too close to him, that she hadn't quite lived up to her weaning responsibilities.

Dr. Kremer reappeared on the terrace and headed for their table. She'd shed the hooded cape on the elevator, to reveal a trim figure in a standard gray unisuit. She carried herself with a grace that spoke of diligent exercise.

"Mom, is she an athlete?" Sasha asked. "Thirteen years on a starship and she looks like she could run a marathon!"

Naomi laughed. "About seven years ship time—remember your physics—and people have a lot of time for exercise on interstellar voyages. Sasha, don't jump into the personal stuff right away, okay?"

Kremer held out a hand as she reached the table. "Naomi Abila! How good to see you in person. And, this must be Sasha!"

"Welcome to New Antarctica," Sasha said, holding out his hand.

Kremer shook it, smiling broadly, then added, "I just heard everyone voted to change the star name to Erebus when I came out of deep sleep. I love the change—I think."

Naomi patted her on the arm. "You'll get used to it!"

They sat and ordered more coffee, which a robot vendor brought in short order.

"It's good to be home," Kremer said to Sasha. "You've just graduated, haven't you? Architecture?"

Sasha nodded. "First year in grad school now, macroarchitecture."

"He wants to design space colonies," Naomi added.

Kremer smiled warmly at her friend's son. "I'm sure he will. What do you think of the Black Hole Project, Sasha?"

"The BHP's just mind boggling, Dr. Kremer," Sasha said, "trying to get such a precise collision with four billion-ton impactors six light years away."

She laughed easily. "You can call me Hilda. And that's about all there's left to do in physics—mind boggling things. All the easy stuff was done before we were born. But this shouldn't be too hard on our end. All we have to do is to get the impactor up to speed and going in the right direction. Vertex Station, where the impact point will be, provides the vernier beams and guidance points for the final approach. Then, on December 23, 2284, all four impactors meet the target as planned, and boom! We get a mini black hole."

Sasha shuddered. "Or, boom! The universe blows up!"

Naomi grimaced and tried to think of something diplomatic to say as Kremer's jaw dropped.

"Just kidding," Sasha said quickly. "But we've got some ice-heads here, too, who think it's possible."

"Well!" Kremer shook her head. "I didn't think I'd escape them entirely."

"Anyway, we've got an extra six months," Sasha said.

Naomi stared at him in shock. "What do you mean by that?" No one had mentioned a delay to her. She looked at Hilda, who shook her head.

"Ginny Wu at *Icestar* says a message came in delaying the impact time by six months. Says they're reviewing the calculations and that Wotan asked them to hold it until he gets a chance to talk to you, Dr. Kremer."

Naomi watched Kremer's face go ashen for a brief moment. "Ginny Wu is Sasha's best friend's cousin," Naomi quickly bridged. "It's still a small town here."

Kremer smiled at Naomi's effort to smooth things over. "You should have seen it when I was here. Morris Wu—he started *Icestar*—and I went to school together half a century ago. A delay doesn't sound right, though; I should have gotten word directly. Let me double check... nothing."

Naomi shook her head. "Dr. Kremer, uh, Hilda, it could be a rumor or a complete invention on someone's part. Ginny can get a little in front of things at times."

Sasha laughed. "Like when she said the Maluks were New Reformationists and they were just Baptists!"

"Well, I hope that's all there is to it," Hilda said. "You'll let me know before doing anything about it?"

Naomi grinned. "Absolutely! When are you going to meet your father?"

Hilda shook her head. "He's still in a meeting about tidal waves and ice sheet collapse. Said he'd be here tomorrow. Naomi, I haven't heard anything about a delay, which is surpassingly strange. It's a major change. Brad Adams and Sarah Levine back at Sol's BHP would have sent messages to me. All the traffic I've gotten is completely normal."

"Including the impact date?" Naomi asked.

"That was set seventeen years ago," Hilda said. "The impactor state vector targets are cast in concrete; they're the fixed star about which everything else in the project revolves. The only reason to send a new one would be some major change."

Naomi shivered. "Hilda, we do have some Consolidationists here, including three of the ten planetary Councilors. Hans Bluth, the security minister, is one of them. Wotan figured that was a good place for a conservative."

Hilda shook her head. "Some of those people think they're so right anything they do is justified."

Sasha's head was turning between them like a spectator watching a tennis match. "What happens if we launch late?" he asked.

Naomi looked at Hilda and both women shook their heads.

"Complete disaster," Hilda said finally, "of varying flavors depending on how late and what is done about it, but as far as the project is concerned, complete disaster."

CHAPTER 2

New Antarctica
12 April 2772

Hilda found quarters in the Hadley Hotel, overlooking the large lake in the center of Dome II, east of the spaceport. The hotel was a re-creation of the hotel in Hobart where Amundsen had stayed after his return from the South Pole. It was staffed by pleasant android robots with cockney accents. After brunch with Naomi and Sasha, she'd spent the day getting her things in storage and connecting with Shira Hassan, an old schoolgirl friend and BHP team member who promised to call on her.

"I'll be the one in the head scarf and long dress," Shira laughed.

"You always had the most beautiful long silk scarves." Hilda remembered them fondly.

Storage chores done, she took a break and walked around the lakeshore where she and Mom had played.

Still there was the fountain where Mom had told her of her decision to head the first expedition to Ross 128...

••∞••

"I have to do this, Hildy. Kyle Perot got himself killed in a skiing accident and they need another starship captain. It will be the first-ever discovery voyage not mounted from the Solar System; and after sixteen years on my butt, it's an opportunity I can't pass up. You can come too, if you want."

"Will Dad come?" she'd asked.

Mom had been silent for a while. "Your father and I... well, sometimes two strong people need to get away from each other for a while."

"Mom," she had said, "I love Dad. All my friends are here. School— I'm playing clarinet in the band. Song-Do Chun wants me to go to the Waltz Festival with him."

"I understand, dear," she'd said with a smile. "'Feathered and flown with projects of your own.'"

"Huh?"

"Look up Millay. Don't worry, dear, we'll have more time together some day."

"When are you going?"

"Tomorrow," Kate Avonford had said. "Tomorrow."

••∞••

Hilda felt the moment as clearly as if it had been yesterday. Her face felt warm in the cold air. Even so, she threw her arms around herself as she did that day. It had been the end of her childhood. She finished the walk with moist eyes and headed up to her room, to bury herself in the details of expanding the solar power and beam projector array that would push Erebus' impactor to its rendezvous some six years hence. She worked through dinner but made it down to the Lakeside Grill for supper with Sasha. The starship had been on New Antarctica's 38-hour, four-meal day since deceleration, but she still felt a bit of a disconnect after all the years on Earth.

She watched a show until the wee hours, and fell asleep easily enough.

A crash of cutlery woke her the next morning. Her room overlooked a large courtyard full of diners busy with their breakfasts; someone must have knocked over a cup. She opened her eyes and decided it was well past time to get up. Dad would be coming by at noon.

The knock on the door came at 19.6 hours, precisely. Heart in her throat, she opened it.

"Dad!"

Wotan Kremer had not changed physically since Hilda had last seen him, but he gave the appearance of a somewhat more youthful person than she'd remembered. His shoulders were more square, his posture better, his face more ruddy and self-assured.

Of course, the man who had sent her away to Earth at the age of sixteen had been a very sad person trying to put a failed marriage behind him. That had been six decades ago, with a reunion, two more children, and another split. Those who are larger than life live by their own rules, Hilda thought. One looks up in wonder and tries to stay out from under their feet.

"Hildy!" He opened his arms and Hilda rushed into them. Sixty years of heartache were suddenly set aside and she was ten years old again, back in the time of birthdays, Christmas trees, and trips out to see the stars. Her eyes filled with tears as she laid her head on his broad shoulders. At length they parted. She rubbed her eyes. Should she mention Mom? What wounds would that open in both of them? Yet to say nothing was like trying to ignore an elephant in the room.

"Katherine sends her greetings from Luyten something or other, wherever she is now, Hildy. She's very proud of what you've accomplished, as I am."

"I'm... I'm glad you're speaking to each other."

"Hmph. Well there are times when I think one year between messages is about right. But, *ja*, we communicate. I should have been more realistic; the only way one can keep a butterfly forever is to put a pin through it."

They had *Mittagessen* of vegetable cake and salad, then talked into the afternoon about family, about Liz going to Lacaille 9352 to manage the final effort there and Konrad, the brother she'd never met, leading a colony at Ross 128. They wended their way back to Hilda's room. Finally it was time to talk about the business at hand.

"Dad, there's a rumor that Earth's directed a delay."

Wotan nodded gravely. "We received it five days ago. I wanted to talk to you about it before I released it."

"I'm glad you did," Hilda said. "Things don't seem right—I would have gotten a message, too. From Zhau Tse Wen, from Brad, or from Sarah—from all of them."

Wotan shrugged. "Our people had some reservations as well. But the orders came right from the BHP transmitter location—our interferometers pinned it down to within a couple of kilometers in the Sol system. The multichannel signal was continuous, with all the right synchronization codes. There are occasional dropouts, but that happens going through an asteroid belt. I've released it to your access. Go ahead and take a look."

She touched the local net and scanned the numbers. It was basically their standard state vector update, of which there had been several early on but none in the last ten years. Standard except the launch epoch was almost six earth months later. The comments field said the change was due to a recalculation of the ten sigma coupling to the probability field for fluctuation inflation.

Hilda's stomach suddenly knotted up. "Dad, there's no such thing as 'coupling to the probability field for fluctuation inflation,' and the BHP certainly hasn't done any tests to look for anything like that."

"Hmm. Well, that's not really my area, but I understand that many physicists think the big bang couldn't have happened by itself, that something external, some first cause, had to trigger the initial period of inflation."

Hilda was about to say she'd never heard of such nonsense when she remembered she had, and where. "Dad, there was a Dr. Hiram Kokos working with the consolidationists... I think he was making those kinds of noises. He's a planetary astronomer, not a theoretical physicist, and no real physicist takes his stuff seriously. Ask your local physics community."

Wotan shook his head. "Hildy, that would be Brian Lobov, who runs the physics department at our university, and maybe a couple of others who make it a hobby. He's pretty good; I rely on him." He smiled and shrugged. "But there is just not much of a physics community on New Antarctica, even now. We only have about half a million people in the whole system! Why do you think I sent you to Earth?"

Hilda's eye's opened wide.

"Mom left. I thought I was, well, in the way. A reminder."

"Oh, no, Hildy, never that! It was for your physics—you didn't want to do anything else, no boys, no dances, just your equations and your experiments. Hildy, do you remember the argument you had with Alex Leparc about relativity? I thought you two would come to blows! You were, what, eight years old?"

Hilda winced. She *had* dated a couple of times; he hadn't noticed. Alex and she *had* come to blows, later, and nobody had ever heard about it because young men don't like losing fights with girls.

"For physics, Hildy, you had to go to Earth. All these years, you never said..."

He was completely right, she realized. She could never have done what she did at New Antarctica. But she had not felt that way at the time. Emotions held back for years raced through her. She didn't know what to say.

As if he'd forgotten how old she was, Wotan sat next to her and put his arm around her. Then he seemed to remember she was no longer a little girl, and straightened up, awkwardly removing his arm and straightening out his shirt.

"I'm sorry, Dad. I just..." She took a deep breath to bridge back into the present. "Perhaps I should order some drinks?"

Wotan sighed and smiled. "Dry sherry. Our vines have done well."

She placed the order on her bionet. Wotan segued in to his work.

"Have you noticed the glaciers are starting to retreat? Air pressure went over 0.6 bars a couple of months ago, and our mean surface temperature is up to 254, and up to 274 within fifteen degrees of the equator. Things should proceed quite rapidly now."

Hilda's mind shifted gears. "274? Above freezing? Open water? Do you have open water?" New Antarctica had started with a surface temperature of 233 K at the equator with spots below 173 K at the poles.

Wotan laughed—the deep-throated, powerful, thunderous laugh she remembered from the good times of her childhood. "Not yet, but they've created a betting pool. The bets will peak for a time a few months from now. People keep asking me; I tell them I'm not saying because I don't want to bias the pool. Can you imagine that? It is far too complicated to predict precisely, but they think I know and am not saying!"

Hilda shook her head.

"This is the most Earth-like planet humanity has ever found! Mass, gravity, tectonics, everything. All we had to do was give it a little push, *ja!*"

Their drinks arrived. Wotan swished the dark fluid around his mouth, then abruptly swallowed.

"You must come on an air trip with me and I will show you this world I am building for you."

"For me?"

"Of course for you, if you want it. Why do parents do anything?"

Hilda laughed. No person could own a planet, but as a first generation founder's daughter, and having made a small mark in human history, she would occupy a unique position here for as long as she wanted. "Okay, but it will have to be tomorrow; I'll be leaving for the site the next day."

Wotan drained what remained of his sherry.

"Done. We'll leave about eight, from West Dome Airport."

After Wotan left, Hilda remembered that they'd left the conversation about the delay unfinished. She touched the net to find Dr. Brian Lobov.

Somewhere, the fates were having fun with her. Dr. Lobov had been a student of none other than Hiram Kokos. Whoever had sent that message had sent it to fertile ground.

The next day, they left early and flew over the ice pack and emerging islands of New Antarctica's Great Equatorial Sea. Their aircraft was a high-wing delta design with a mostly transparent fuselage. Wotan flew with manual controls. He was born before genetically engineered bioradio and had an irritable distaste for prostheses. As long as Hilda could remember, he preferred to do things with his hands.

Wotan pointed out to her where the first open-air settlements would be. "It's a volcanic island chain, with the hot spot migrating southeast, somewhat like the Hawaiian Islands, but a bit larger. You see, the big caldera, Novetna, is now free of ice!"

At his touch the aircraft banked left over the gigantic sharp-edged depression on the top of the mountain. They were cruising at fifteen kilometers above sea level, but the mountain was almost twelve kilometers, and a red-orange glow from a spot in the huge caldera was easily visible.

"It has a lava lake!" Hilda exclaimed.

"*Ja*, more than one. We will not build too permanently near that one! The next island west is not so active. The government and the university, they will go there. I call it Avonford Island, after your mother."

"You miss her sometimes?"

"I miss the good times. But, Hildy, you must remember she and I are two stubborn people who found we could not make always the compromises two people must make to live together. We both had to be in charge, and that was impossible. Impossible. The fights, those I do not miss."

Together, they watched the ice fields flow by below in silence. Hilda brought up the subject again.

"Dad, the university..."

"There will be a place for you there, Hildy, if you want it. Dr. Lobov will be glad to have you; he has many new ideas he would like to discuss with you."

"Uh, Dad. I've looked at a couple of his papers. You don't have much in the way of peer review out here, and..."

Wotan held up a hand, with a laugh. "Hildy, I cannot get into any physics discussions—not my area—but I am sure that is something you physicists will work out! Perhaps the experiments done with this black hole we are making will clarify things, no?"

Hilda nodded, with the unspoken reservation that some people find it very hard to give up cherished ideas, even with contrary data staring them in the face.

"Dad, I'm convinced there's something wrong with the delay message. The physics justifying it is wrong, but it's wrong in such a way that may not be clear to Dr. Lobov."

"He is a good man, Hildy. You are suggesting that someone has deliberately sent a false message, to sabotage the project?"

"I think so. There's been no subsequent confirmation."

"Hmmm. Hildy, would there be?"

"It's such a major change, I'm sure I would have gotten a personal message from Tse Wen, Sarah, or Brad. The physics is such a departure from the standard model, that it would be the most important thing happening in physics. But we have no news."

Wotan was silent for a while, then said, "If we send our impactor at the wrong time, it would be bad."

"Very bad."

"I am looking forward to using mini black holes to make a new kind of world, like a ring world, but one that can use the energy conversion properties of a black hole to provide light and propel itself among the stars, or maybe even to another galaxy."

"Dad, that would take millions of years."

Wotan laughed. "When I was growing up, people got old and died in a few decades; everyone was in a hurry. 'We aren't getting any younger, are we?' they would say about delays. Now we say 'we aren't getting any older, are we?' There is time enough." He reached out and touched her hand. "Hildy, people look up to me here. I have to be responsible and responsive."

He chuckled as if he did not take it very seriously, but Hilda saw the steel in his eyes and thought otherwise.

"I do very much want the black hole to be created," Wotan continued, "and it is a unique honor to be Chairman of the Erebus System Commonwealth Council when it is happening. But that means I am not free to do exactly as I please, even where you are concerned, my Hildy."

"Dad, if our impactor is late, and the other impactors aren't diverted, they will make a beam of relativistic matter and radiation that could squirt out our way, spraying over this planetary system. Everyone will have to take shelter. Some of the larger pieces of debris could hit like nuclear warheads. It would be moving so fast the first of it would arrive only hours after the flash of the explosion. Very little warning would be possible."

Wotan thought for a while. "There is time," he said finally. "The Impactor does not launch for eighteen months yet, even on the old schedule. So no changes need to be made now. We will discuss and evaluate this. Meanwhile, I have something to show you. Ahead, we approach the shadow line."

Their aircraft had overrun morning, racing into night. As the sky darkened, Hilda saw the Vasili range rise before them, painted blood red by the rising star behind them.

"Oh!"

"*Ja*, but wait a moment now as we go over."

Darkness fell and Hilda sought out the Sun. She knew the routine from childhood; find the Milky Way, then to the right of Eta Carina, the

Southern Cross. Its long axis pointed toward the bright pair of Alpha and Gamma Centauri, in the Centaur's hump. Above and right of that extended line she found a second magnitude yellow white star, bright in its isolation. Sol. She felt a brief tug of homesickness, for the many years she'd lived among its planets. But this was her home, wasn't it?"

"Wilkes is rising," Wotan said, "over those peaks."

"Yes," Hilda murmured. Almost as bright as Venus from Earth, the frozen world was easy to spot low in the crystal clear sky.

"That one is near opposition. A pretty sight. But now look down."

She did, and the ice below glowed red as far as she could see, as if lit from beneath. A network of brilliant yellow lines could be seen here and there.

"You have heard of the Deccan Traps of India?" Wotan asked.

"The huge lava field?"

He nodded. "Something like that is happening here, beneath the ice. We have removed an immense weight from the local geology. New Antarctica is smaller, denser, and younger than Earth and the demons of its core are less tame." He chuckled at the metaphor. "We have loosed their chains, and this ice is now melting from both below and above. It will be gone here in a few weeks, I think."

"And with it the clear skies," Hilda remarked.

"*Ja*, for a while, cloudy it will be."

A meteor streaked through the dark sky, and then another. Soon the sky was full of them.

"More nitrogen," Wotan said, "that was once ammonia ice in the Krietzerbelt."

The planet was transforming before her eyes. How many years would she live, Hilda thought, how many star systems might she see, before she saw the likes of this again!

••∞••

Hilda caught her breath as she approached the nearly completed impactor with staff members Phil Stavros, Shira Hassan, Naomi Abila, and her brother Ted Abila. From ten kilometers out, it looked like an incredibly long, thin beam of light with a spiderweb at one end.

"How did it go with your dad?" Naomi asked Hilda as they approached its dull gray cylindrical surface.

"I was awed by the progress he's made," she answered softly, thinking about progress in all its various guises.

"What about the project schedule?" Phil Stavros asked, swiveling his seat around. He was nominally their pilot, but he handled everything through AIs and the net. A youngster of 40, he'd mastered the ability to carry on a verbal conversation while interfacing visually with the net.

"We can keep going for now, but he's not convinced the message is phony. The physics rationale is apparently credible to Dr. Lobov, whom he trusts."

"But Lobov doesn't have..." Naomi paused and started again. "He's a nice avuncular showman and students love him, but I know physics better than he does!"

"I know, Naomi. But Lobov has a PhD from Earth. That makes him a god as far as Dad is concerned."

Ted shook his head. "A rather imperfect god, if you ask me. I have an idea."

"Yes?"

"We can add another deflector ring to the design. It will let us push fifty percent harder and give the control system fifty percent more drag to use when it reaches the vertex. We may need some added flexibility—in case there are schedule problems."

Hilda thought long and hard. There was only one thing more important than not getting into a contest of wills with her father, and that was the BHP itself. She closed her eyes. If Wotan were held responsible for the failure of the BHP, his reputation would be ruined forever. Humanity had not yet gotten used to the implications of that word "forever." The ancient words came to her mind: *Cattle die, kinsmen die, a man himself must likewise die, but one thing lasts forever, the doom on each man's life.* Nowadays, one could not even count on death for escape from one's critics. It would be up to her to keep her father from becoming the laughingstock and fool of history.

But even in fighting for his own doom, Wotan Kremer could be a formidable opponent. And he was the law, here. Hilda touched Naomi's hand. "We need more of a contingency, and one that is less obviously a challenge to his authority."

"What did you have in mind?"

Hilda shook her head. She tried to remember what she could about leadership. An American general, Patton, had once said something like,

Don't tell people how to do something, tell them what you want done and they will surprise you with their ingenuity. That seemed to fit the circumstance.

"It's probably best that I don't know," Hilda went on. "Dad can be very clever, and I don't think I could lie if he asked me a direct question. Meanwhile, Ted, I need a favor. You're more attuned to AIs and what they can and can't be made to do."

He nodded, looking at her with dark shiny eyes from beneath a mop of short wavy black hair. He was, she thought, very handsome.

"What do you want me to do?" he asked.

"I've sent you a link to the postponement message. I'd like you to analyze it front and back. See if you can find anything suspicious at all that might indicate a fake—besides the content, of course."

"You mean like using a different version of the spread-spectrum encoding protocol?"

"The what?" Hilda touched the net and was greeted by a two-line definition, half the words of which she didn't know, and a menu of menus the titles of which would require a trip to a dictionary. She shivered. Just as soon as you think you're hell on wheels in this universe, something comes along to humble you.

"Uh, a spread spectrum protocol is something that determines which bits go where on which frequency," Ted said. "Different protocols work better than others depending on what part of the Solar System the beam is going through and what the solar activity is—separate AIs might differ on what protocol to use, so an abrupt change in protocol could indicate a different choice, or just a change in conditions. But it could be an indicator of a different source."

"Yeah, that kind of thing," Hilda said. "Indicators. Lots of good, solid indicators."

A slight tug on their seat harnesses told them the runabout had reached the end of the impactor. The lines holding the superconducting loops that would pull the impactor up to a gamma of ten looked exceedingly thin, but up close, Hilda could see they were more complex.

"The stays are like lace tubes."

"Yup," said Ted, "almost two meters across. The lacy pattern is due to cross-connections—you could cut any of these stays in a thousand different places, and still tow the impactor. The carbon nanotubes that bear the weight are even thinner. Most of what you see is matrix and shielding. The Groombridge 34 system is fairly young still, 2.734 gigayears by the last measurements, and there's a fair amount of debris around. So we have to design for more contingencies. By the way, have you looked at Bee?"

"Bee?"

"Our other red dwarf. Out that way." Ted waved toward the rear of the impactor.

Hilda followed the motion of his arm and soon spotted a very brilliant orangish star.

"Pull up a visual from astroview and zoom in," he told her.

Hilda did so.

"It's only about a tenth the brightness of A," Ted said. "Not much more than a brown dwarf, and the biggest thing in its planetary system is a micro-giant with a Mars-sized core, about three Earth masses of ice on top of that and two Earth masses of hydrogen, etcetera, on top of that. But it's got a huge asteroid belt—almost a ring system, really— about two tenths of an AU out."

Hilda noticed a dark curved line across the southern hemisphere. "It seems to have a ring."

"Yup. The first planet out is a bit off the equatorial plane—probably an escaped moon, an interloper. Anyway, it makes the ring thicker than it would be otherwise."

"Anyone out there now?"

"Less than a hundred researchers and the usual infrastructure," Naomi said. "The main habitat is a toroid—only three hundred meters across." She grinned. "It contains the smallest population of an inhabited star system that we know of. My other brother's out there and says they're lost in it. It's a good place for independent minds that want to get away from it all."

Hilda thought about the opportunity such seclusion would give her. Time to think. Time to wrestle with the universe without having to worry about projects, schedules, and politics.

"You look wistful," Ted said, laughing. "Are we already such a pain?"

She shook her head. "No, no. It's just that, well, not everyone is made for what they have to do in life." She sighed.

Their craft rounded the impactor in silence.

"I may have to oppose Dad to make the project happen," Hilda finally said. "I'll need your support and it won't be without risk. Tolerating disobedience isn't one of Dad's virtues; he can be gentle, but only when his control isn't threatened."

"Wotan's our elected leader," Naomi said. "You can't just say no, Hilda. You have to think about the rest of the colony and your responsibility to them!"

"Oh God, Naomi! I've thought of nothing else. But that's the point, isn't it? That message is bogus. If we follow it, we'll have had a role in sabotaging the most important project humanity has ever attempted. It passes all the authentication tests; but Tse Wen and all would never send out something like that without a viable explanation."

"I can't remember any group, never mind an individual, openly defying the Council President before," Ted said in a hushed voice.

Shira Hassan spoke up. "We made him give in on allowing traditional clothing."

Hilda nodded. If it had been up to Wotan, there would probably have been a dress code. As it was, the colony colorfully reflected the varied national origins of its people. Her father was stubborn and autocratic, but not impossible when others were clearly in the right.

"He may not feel free to do what he suspects should be done," Hilda said. "You would be saving his name and his reputation as well, though don't expect to be thanked for it."

"Well," Ted said, "it hasn't come to all that yet, and we'll proceed as if this delay order is going to go away. I've got a feast programmed back at the construction shack. Strap in!"

Hilda laughed and had barely gotten her belt around herself when the runabout leapt forward at what must have been a full gee. The construction shack, a golden ring spinning on top of what looked like a beehive of robots, grew before them. Now that she thought about it, she was hungry.

Most of the crew were there to meet her, and over coffee after lunch, Hilda laid it out.

A younger woman laughed nervously. "We're just going to buy some time, right, Dr. Kremer? Until something from project HQ clears this up. That's not defiance, I mean we wouldn't really be doing anything irreversible. It's not any worse than, say, pretending you're out of touch when someone rings you. Once it gets cleared up, we say, 'Oh, sorry, there must have been some miscommunication,' and because shutting down would have been a disaster, they wouldn't look any deeper than that."

Hilda shook her head. "That impactor has to be on its proper vector come whatever, or the project may be dead for a long, long time. The consolidationists are within a razor's edge of a majority back in the Solar System. We may never get another chance."

One of the older researchers raised a hand. Hilda nodded.

"Jake Jabowsky, Dr. Kremer. What if we're all wrong? What if we send our impactor into that asteroid against legitimate orders? What then? Our collective butts will all be persona non grata here from now to kingdom come!"

"Cool it, Jabowsky," Phil Stavros said. "That would be nothing compared to what would happen if we're not wrong and *don't* send an impactor!"

Hilda shook her head. "We're not wrong, and I'll be available here for the next ten days to walk anyone interested through the physics. But that's a good point about the consequences. I know we all believe in this project. We wouldn't be here if we didn't believe in it. But those of you who don't think you can survive the consequences should leave now before you are further involved. I hope I can trust you enough to not talk about our intent prematurely." Hilda looked at each her team members in turn. And then she looked at them again. "Who's with me?"

Jake grabbed his jacket and headed for the exit. He might be a useful witness when this is all over, she thought ruefully. No one else left.

Ted raised his coffee cup. "To launching on time, come honor or chaos."

"To launch!" a dozen voices cried, and they all clinked their coffee cups together.

"Looks like we're in with you, Hilda," Ted declared.

Hilda allowed a few nanoseconds for relief to drain tension from her shoulders. Then she smiled at her team. "Let's get back to work then, and be thinking about how we do this."

••∞••

Weeks full of quiet tension became months of quiet tension. Impactor launch preparations were coming to a head, but Hilda still had nothing other than physics and faith in her colleagues that they would prove the message was, indeed, fake. The camaraderie she enjoyed with her father had become strained; there was a new elephant in the room, but if either of them mentioned it, they argued.

Finally, just to ease the stress, she agreed to go swimming with Sasha in the dome's center lake where she had swum as a child. Too late, she realized that swimsuits were forty years out of style here, and looked studiously straight ahead as she walked naked into the icy water and quickly submerged her body up to her neck. *It couldn't have been this cold when I was a kid,* she thought, between ragged gasps. Finally, she got used to the temperature and began to relax.

"Something's bothering you," Sasha said, swimming over next to Hilda. "Something more than cradle robbing, I hope?"

His young impetuousness made her laugh. It was much needed. "Cradle robbing? If you were sixty-five and I were twenty, would that be cradle robbing?"

"I guess so. It's okay as long as it's fun, I think. I mean, we'll live forever and if I were a million and eighteen and you were a million and sixty-five it wouldn't make much difference."

Hilda laughed. "It's hard to imagine what we'll think when we're a million years old."

"I really don't care if you're old enough to be my grandmother. I'm a dirty old man trapped in the body of a grad student."

Sasha had a cute mouth, Hilda mused. You had to give him that. She wondered what the conservative journalist, Torsten Ried, back on Earth, would think of her cavorting naked with this young Hercules. Cultures differed, and as she looked around the lake, she noted another couple or two, freely and shamelessly expressing affection—or lust—for each other. Nobody seemed to mind. "And thanks to genetic engineering, I'm a septuagenarian old maid trapped in the body of a nymphet," she replied. "I should dye my hair gray." She rubbed her shoulders for a bit of warmth.

"Are you cold? Do you want to warm up on the sand?" Sasha asked. He began to lead the way towards the shore.

She shook her head and glided back away from the shore. Sasha joined her. He took one of her hands and rubbed it as if warming it. The floor of the lake had fallen away and they were treading water.

He turned his body and brushed himself against her. "I can warm you up a bit more. Doing it with people watching slides easy, here." He took her other hand and rubbed it. "Uh, you don't mind do you?" he asked.

She didn't mind it, she realized, any more than she needed it. Her mind was far elsewhere, fragmented in time and space. She was in her room, three-quarters of a century ago, simulating Solar Systems while other kids went swimming. She was watching the data come in from the black hole they were making, a dozen years from now. She was skimming over endless fields of solar arrays last week, drinking in the power to make it. She was listening, then and now, to her father telling her to pay attention to other people's ideas and not act as if she knew everything. She was with Brad in Lillehammer, a long time ago, taking one drink from his cup, but somehow never again. Her whole life was of one cloth, including the urgent young man beside her whose attentions she did not, in some existential sense, object; they just were.

His hand caressed her cool skin and she didn't mind.

But she had better pretend she *did* mind, or things could slide down the slippery slope of major embarrassment. She pushed him back and laughed. "Give me another year or two to get used to the idea. Meanwhile, the impactor launch will be excitement enough."

Sasha's eyes went wide. "The old man give the okay?"

Hilda shook her head. "I'm going to talk to Lobov and see if I can convince him to help us persuade Dad."

"Terri's in Lobov's class—thinks his ice is clear."

"Which means?" The metaphor didn't ring a bell with Hilda, as familiar as the colony on New Antarctica was, it was different, too. Her mother had never been topless in public, that she knew of, let alone totally naked. But there was not one swimsuit in sight. She'd been away.

"He can see all the way to the bottom of things—real deep."

"And Terri is?" Always check the quality of the data...

"One of Jennreh Poi's cocks," Sasha said, as if that explained something.

"Students?" Hilda asked.

"Huh? Oh sure. Terri's a grinder. He's talking about going back to Earth to study under Dr. Kokos. The First Causes guy."

Despite the warm male body next to her, Hilda shivered. "Sasha, I don't think it's a good idea to mix religion and physics, but it's even worse to mix them and not be honest about what you are doing. This Jennreh... is she a lover of yours?"

"No such luck. She's an artist, Kama Sutra and all."

Hilda looked at him. "I didn't really mean to pry. Everything is so much more open than before. It's just not a big part of my life."

"Sex?" He looked incredulous.

"That. Not a big part of my life."

Hilda felt his hand leave her skin. 'Damn, why had she said that' was written all over his face. "Look," she said, "Jennreh and Terri, do they talk about Lobov? What he says in class?"

Sasha pulled back to the moment. "Some. Uh, they are into something they call 'intuitional science.'"

Hilda looked at him with a raised eyebrow.

"It's the idea that the broad sweep of things must first make sense at some higher intuitive level so that if you're really in tune you can just, uh, *understand* the fundamentals of what's going on and the details, equations, and math aren't really as important. Dr. Lobov kind of smiles at that and makes them work quantitative problems anyway. But Terri says Dr. Lobov has a lot of questions about the assumptions behind things, like he's not sure the standard model is right."

"Anything about the BHP?"

"Terri said Lobov said the BHP isn't necessary for science unless it shows the theory is wrong. But if it can show the theory was wrong, it shouldn't be done because it would be unsafe. Uh, that's kind of complex." Sasha sighed and frowned. "If you want to talk to Terri, I guess I could set that up. But watch out for his come-on."

Hilda looked into Sasha's brown, pleading puppy eyes and placed a quick kiss on his cheek. She sighed. "There's not much time, so I'm going to have to go with what I've got. Thanks for giving me an idea of, uh, how clear Lobov's ice is."

Sasha smiled. "That's okay." He hesitated, but only for a moment. "Uh, do you want me? Even a little bit? Or am I acting like a complete idiot?"

Hilda laughed. "What would your mother think?"

Sasha rolled his eyes. "I think she'd be relieved. She keeps trying to fix me up and it keeps not working."

"Oh? Why is that?" Hilda instantly berated herself for teasing. She needed Naomi's good will and her guess was the mother doted on the son.

"I guess I don't have the timing right. Like with you now. Or like when a girl wants to do stuff, maybe, and I keep talking. That kind of stuff."

Hilda put an arm around him and kissed him again on the cheek. *Why not,* she thought. *It would be an act of grace.* She smiled to herself and reached her fingers out as if to touch Sasha one more time. She stopped herself and let the water cool her down. *First things first,* she told herself.

"Can you meet me tonight? After my meeting with Lobov?"

"You... Really?"

"Really! In my room in the Hadley Hotel. About 3130?"

"Yeah. Sure. I mean if you really..."

Hilda put a finger on his lips, then, with as much dignity as she could muster, stood up, and walked to her towel on the beach.

••∞••

Dr. Lobov gushed disarmingly, friendly and ebullient as he ushered Hilda into his simply furnished open office area overlooking Dome 4's central park area.

"Well, well, well! At last, a colleague from Earth! Ever since your father told me you were coming... Well, suffice it to say we're all thrilled and I'm sure you'll find our research at this University every bit as robust as at your college—Stanford, wasn't it?" He laughed at his joke, eyes twinkling.

Academic humor. Still alive and well even in the far reaches.

As Lobov pulled up a pod chair for her, Hilda noted his long torso, wide shoulders, and deep blue eyes. He wore an immaculate jet-black jumpsuit, unrelieved except for a polished silver cross within a circle decorating his belt buckle. She wondered if it might be an Earth symbol, a Christian symbol, or just a design.

"Wotan tells me you might consider joining our faculty!"

Hilda smiled. Young people moved in and out of the area freely, except for a serious young man with a dark goatee beard sitting in a lounge chair in a corner staring off into space. Having been there, Hilda knew he was likely working his virtual rear end off in some simulation that only he could see.

"I haven't taught in years, but as long as I'm here..." She shrugged.

"We'll have thirty-two incoming major students next year. We really should have two introductory sessions. You know how we do it here?"

Hilda shook her head.

"The whole class meets once a week and just talks about concepts and ideas." Lobov waived an arm in the air. "The programs take the students through at their own pace, and alert us if someone is having trouble. Then we have appointments to help them through."

Hilda nodded. "I did my undergraduate work on a starship that way. The captain helped me at first, but I'm afraid I got ahead of him a bit. I took my degree exam after deceleration, did my senior orals, and graduated the first week I was on the Farm."

"The Farm?"

"Stanford," she paused ever so briefly, "University."

He winked at her. "Good one!

"Ah, yes! Your educational path albeit unorthodox certainly seems to work okay. But here, we mentor."

"I'm sure it helps, and I do look forward to talking with students again. I haven't had any experience with undergraduates, though..."

"You'll love it! Fresh minds ready to be shown the way!"

Hilda laughed, then brought up what she came for. "Dr. Lobov, I need your help. Are you aware of the political problems the Black Hole Project has had on Earth?"

Lobov frowned immediately and nodded gravely. "Not everyone here feels we are ready for it, either."

She gave him a wry smile. "I'm very sure the delay message was a covert product of the opposition and does not reflect the views of the leadership of the BHP, nor the position of the government. I need to convince Father of that. I know you think highly of Dr. Kokos, and the reason given for the delay seems to follow from his work."

He nodded. "Yes, so it seems. But I think there is a but to this, no?" He flashed a quick smile.

Hilda sighed. "If we look at Kokos' paper with Sun and Kreshkov in 2102, the threshold they calculate for what they call a "seeded inflationary fluctuation" is three orders of magnitude higher than what the BHP can generate. So this isn't really consistent with Kokos, either. I've put the work up under my name and Kokos'. I'd like you to take a look at it."

He frowned more deeply and waved at his wall screen, which promptly displayed the equations. He studied them, nodding, then shook his head. "When we are so close to the cutting edge of what we know, maybe three orders of magnitude is not so much." He rubbed his chin slowly. "I will have to look at this more carefully. It has, you will appreciate, been some time..."

She deftly disguised her shock with a smile. Any undergraduate at Stanford, Hilda thought, would have had no trouble with what she had given him at all. Trouble was, she needed this man's help.

"Of course, Dr. Lobov."

He nodded. "There may be something to it, but what your people back in the Solar System..." he raised a hand... "Peace. I acknowledge that you think the change did not come from your people. But the argument itself *is* in the scope of the broad, intuitional thrust of Kokos' work, the modeling details..."

Hilda could contain herself no longer. "Dr. Lobov, that's a fourth power in the denominator! To reduce the triggering threshold by three orders of magnitude, the Johanssen quintessence multiplier field would have to be *twelve* orders of magnitude higher!" Not that there was any evidence for any such "quintessence multiplier field" in the first place; she bit her tongue on that because it was one of Dr. Kokos' pet hypotheses. One did not win a physicist's support by attacking the pet hypotheses of his mentor.

"Do we know that it is not?"

"But I think we do. A QMF that high would produce billions of little universes at every gamma ray burst! That clearly doesn't happen!"

Lobov shook his head. "I'm not sure... I... I'm just not sure." He smiled weakly. "Perhaps, you... we... are missing something obvious. QMF seeding is such an elegant, clear solution to the first cause problem that it *feels* right."

"But I'm not asking you to give up QMF, just to recognize that, quantitatively, it can't apply to the BHP."

Lobov sighed. "I'll have to study it more. You do raise some interesting points."

"Will you say that much to Father?"

He shrugged and grinned. "That would not be so much backtracking for me. I have never claimed certainty about the universe-seeding concern, only that it was defensible in light of the first cause principles—qualitatively, of course. Well, now!" He brightened as if a storm cloud had passed. "Can I at least talk you into a seminar series next year? On the famous Kremer's Limit?"

By that time, she realized, the impactor would be launched and the last pusher pellets en route to it. Suddenly, she appreciated that her role in the Black Hole Project would be over. She would be just one of many investigators at the end of a fire hose of data—most of which would be of more interest to engineers and relativicists than someone whose specialty was ultradense matter.

She was home. She had a new life ahead of her. It was time to start thinking of that.

"Of course. Let's talk about schedule after you've got your new class settled in."

Lobov laughed. "Speaking of which, the day has moved on a bit, hasn't it?"

Hilda smiled and nodded as she rose. It was approaching 3000. The student with the beard was still sitting in the chair as she left. As she turned to wave from the door, her eye happened to fall on an old-fashioned 2D image hanging in a frame on Lobov's wall. She turned quickly and walked away so Lobov would not see the shock on her face. It had to be fifty years old at least. Lobov had been on New Antarctica for some thirty-eight years. A lot of time for things to change by some standards, less by others.

The picture was of Lobov with two men and a woman in a residence, probably on Earth—Earth, because the other men in the picture were Torsten Ried and his older brother Lars, leader of the anti-BHP Consolidationist Alliance.

••∞••

Hilda wasted no time leaving the building. Once outside, she called Wotan, then rushed toward his place in Dome Three. Short, dim-red lights illuminated the darkened evening pathways. Brilliant stars of the Southern Cross and Eta Carina overhead provided enough light to make out the various features of the landscape. Someone briefly opened a door across the lake from her and the brilliance of that little bit of artificial light hurt her eyes. She blinked hard and saw the reflection of Scorpius on the still lake, remembering that, as a child, she had imagined it a sea monster about to emerge and devour her. The air was crisp; New Antarcticans had always enjoyed a vigorous diurnal temperature change. Alas, this was no time for her to tarry, with two appointments yet for the long local evening.

As she neared the passageway connecting Dome Two with Dome Three, she heard footsteps behind her and turned. A dark, unrecognizable shadow was right behind her.

"Dr. Kremer," the person said. It was a man, by his voice—a cold, flat, unwavering voice.

"Yes? Who are you?"

"I am a warning. The impactor launch will be delayed. The message will be obeyed."

Suddenly, the night seemed chillier.

"The message is a fraud," she said. Quickly she touched the net and asked it to record what she heard and saw.

"We are not concerned with who the message comes from, only that it is obeyed and that you do nothing to subvert your father's direction that it be obeyed."

"He hasn't given that direction."

The figure began walking away. It was real enough. She could hear the crunch of sand under his feet. No, that could be faked, if needed. Should she chase it? Run in the other direction? Or keep her composure as if nothing had happened? She decided on the last, and began walking briskly to Wotan's home. On the way, she queried the net and found the voice was untraceable. What was she dealing with?

••∞••

Wotan had a glass of wine waiting for her and was not in the mood to talk about the BHP. Rather, he talked about the growing colony and how, in a few decades, people would walk around on New Antarctica in shirtsleeves and the only ice would be near the poles or on the tops of mountains.

"Then," he mused, "maybe I will move to Bee and start all over again. I will have to build a whole planet there, do you know? It will not be a big one—maybe the size of Luna. If they let me, that is."

"But you're..."

"I'm not in charge there. It is a separate star, no? There are only a few people living there, but they decide their own things. Maybe they will surprise me! They are building their own starport—did you know?"

Hilda shook her head.

Wotan laughed. "It will be a long time before a starship stops there that does not come here first, but it is a symbol for them. Everyone gets to dream, no?"

"Father, we need to talk about the Black Hole Project schedule."

Wotan frowned.

"If we do not launch our impactor on schedule..."

"I am all for launching the impactor on schedule. The question is whose schedule? Yours, or the one the project sent you?"

"They didn't send that."

"Hildy, who else would have?"

"The consolidationists. Lars Ried and his crew. Lobov knows them— he has a picture of the Ried brothers hanging up in his office."

Wotan shook his head again. "Now we have conspiracy theories!"

"Backed by the fact the message cites physics that are wrong."

Wotan kept shaking his head. "I have only your opinion for that, against that of every other physicist in the system."

She couldn't believe what she was hearing. "Have you polled them? How many have you talked to?"

Wotan's face clouded as if he were going to yell at her the way he had when she'd been late for family outings or forgotten her housekeeping chores. Surprisingly, he said nothing, and his features softened.

"I forget sometimes that you are not who you were, Hildy. You have been around the block some and have a right to your thoughts. Please remember, however, I have been around much more than you, and I must make the decision. Absent any proof other than what only physicists can quarrel about, I have to take the message as valid. If I were to do otherwise..." He shook his head. "There are people here who think I have been leader too long. What I do must be understandable, or I lose the support."

Hilda saw her dream begin to crumble before her eyes. This stubborn old man who could not see, who would not think.

No, that wasn't fair. She was the only one who knew, the only one in the whole damn planetary system who *knew*. For everyone else, it was politics, dueling experts, and belief. Very well, what political argument could she make?

"Father, you know that verse from the Havalmal? *Cattle die, kinsmen die, so must oneself must likewise die...*"

"*...but what dies not is what is said, the doom that lies on each man's head,*" Wotan finished.

"If you are the cause of the BHP failing, what will history have to say about you, down through eternity?"

"Not good, I grant, if you continue to oppose me, Hildy. If we are both wrong together, then neither of us will hurt too badly. If we both insist on being right in opposite ways, then only one of us will be right and the other will suffer greatly."

"There is time yet."

"*Ja*, there is time. Do you know there is enough open water now that plankton may survive? Maybe next month we will seed the equatorial sea!"

So, Hilda thought, wryly. When it gets uncomfortable, Wotan changes the subject. They still had not had a good talk about her mother.

••∞••

Hilda reached the door of her room feeling drained, betrayed, hopeless, and on the verge of tears. As the 19th century style door swung open, she saw Sasha was waiting for her in a T-shirt and running shorts. "Sasha! How..."

"It's a small town, Dr. uh, Hilda. The desk clerk is Holly Wu's aunt. She let me in. Uh, if this is a bad time..."

They had a date. A million years ago, she'd made a date with him for 3130 and it was almost 3200.

"Looks like you had a bad meeting," Sasha said, worry written on his face.

Hilda smiled wryly. "It did not go well, but we're still alive for the time being. Why? Do I look like I just got out of a three gee simulator?"

"You're kind of drooping a bit. Could you use a hug?"

He stepped forward and opened his arms. Without really thinking, she did the same and met him halfway.

The door swung shut behind her on its own—only the appearances of the Hadley Hotel were early 20th century.

She let him stroke her back and laid her head on his shoulder, more in exhaustion than anything else.

But gradually, the tension left her, and she let herself melt into him, pressing her breasts into his strong young chest, and feeling his thigh firm between her legs. After the tense, cold, confrontation she'd just had, it felt surpassingly good. Somewhat to her surprise, she did feel, if not in the mood for sex, at least having no need to resist. Let it happen. Why not?

She lifted her head up, and his lips sought hers. Out of nowhere, passion emerged. She thrust her tongue into his mouth and moved her lips around as her hand moved down to his buttocks. She pushed him closer and felt his hardness against her thigh. A fleeting rapidly dissolving part of her consciousness wondered what was happening to her. All of a sudden she wanted him. Urgently, desperately, she began taking their clothes off.

CHAPTER 3

New Antarctica
23 October 2273

Over the following year, a few brave pioneers had moved to the equatorial islands as spectacular icebergs fell into the newly open seas of New Antarctica. Hardy plankton had begun to grow there and Wotan was predicting fish within a decade.

Meanwhile, impactor launch preparations were coming to a head, but Hilda still had nothing other than physics and faith in her colleagues that they would prove the delay message was, indeed, fake.

And Sasha continued to ask Hilda for dates. Her status as Wotan Kremer's daughter and Chief BHP scientist in residence allowed barriers to be erected to most such distractions, but since Sasha was Naomi's son, he had access. And Hilda gave in, more often than not.

Thus, when Woton asked to see her on a serious matter, she thought it was Sasha, and not the project schedule, he wished to lecture on. But no.

"It is time to make a decision, Hildy. In my position, I cannot, absolutely cannot, go against the direction from Earth and the guidance of the best scientific advice available."

"Father, *I am* the best scientific advice available."

Wotan shook his head. "No, Hildy, you are my headstrong little girl, too stubborn, too committed, too involved. I know you." He tried to smile kindly. "Even if maybe you are right, why are you so impatient? The project will be tried again, in fifty years, in five hundred. What does it matter, now that we live so long? I am sorry, dear, but your efforts to get people to try to make me change my mind have not had much effect. I am saying no."

How did he know? Not that she'd made any great secret of her visit to Lobov, or the University chancellor or the local news outlet people; but she hadn't done that publicly and AIs weren't supposed to spy on personal communications. Then she thought about the quiet student in Lobov's office and the mysterious warning she'd gotten on the way. The conclusion that led to chilled her.

"Father, are you having me followed?"

He smiled. "The security service, such as it is, has someone keep an eye on you, yes. It is precautionary only, for your own protection. This they do for me, and the other council members and their families too, so it is nothing to be worried about."

Oh chaos, security was in the hands of a consolidationist! Hilda couldn't find words. Everything fit together now in the wrong way. She gritted her teeth. Tse Wen, Brad, and Sarah were counting on her to make this impactor launch happen. A knot grew in her stomach. Come on girl, she told herself, you're supposed to be a genius. There has to be a way out. Oh, where was the way out of this? She thought about timelines, construction rates, terminal guidance, ways to cheat, crazy stuff that she didn't have time to analyze. Time. Then it hit her.

"Father. Look, we can have it both ways. I can have a second impactor built and we can launch the first one at the old time and the second one at the new time, and divert or hold the second one when confirmation of the original schedule comes in."

He shook his head. "Which it will not. Then we'll have this whole conversation over again!"

"I can live with that." But could she? It cut through her like a knife.

Wotan laughed. "You are like the condemned prisoner who put off his execution by promising to teach the king's horse to talk. I will not die. You will not die. And I doubt very much this horse will learn to talk." He scrunched his face in thought. "This idea of yours will give you, what, 23 days? No, I think that would be too late. We will make that 20 days—before we step up to peak power. You have 20 days to prove beyond any doubt that the day after tomorrow is the correct impactor launch date, or you will shut down the impactor propulsion."

"But the other impactors..."

"Brunhilda Beatrice Kremer, I am enough of an engineer to know that in the very unlikely event you are right, they will have made provision to divert the other impactors as soon as they see ours isn't there. 20 days. This is what we plan, this is what we will do."

"New Antarctica days," Hilda said. That would make it just over a terrestrial month. She smiled inwardly at her small victory. Sarah had sent personal messages all along, and her last message had arrived in the final stages of impactor launch preparation. The next one should arrive just before the final power ramp-up.

Wotan shook his head with a laugh. "*Ja*, New Antarctica days."

••∞••

Hilda found Sasha waiting for her with drinks when she returned to the Hadley. She suspected that, over months, he'd even started to anticipate her moods. That usually pleased her, but tonight she felt drained, betrayed, hopeless and yes, even a bit desperate.

He handed her a glass of dark red liquid with a twinkle in his eye. "They just started distributing this new vintage from our grape vines. I got us a bottle!"

"Thanks," she said. "Sasha, I..."

His lips covered hers, stopping her from saying she wasn't in the mood. With a sigh, she kissed him back perfunctorily. Then she drained her glass.

He filled it again. "Something wrong? Want to talk?"

She took another drink and shook her head. "Later." The stress seemed to become a little less unbearable. Sasha's young hands were all over her, she noted almost abstractly. The initial buzz of the wine was warming her, and she made no effort to dissuade him.

The petting felt good, maybe just what she needed. Getting in the mood, she pulled on his waistband and guided him to her bed. But, as their clothes found their way to the floor, she glanced at the camera pickups in the room and tensed up. Of course, the system had eyes everywhere. There were very good, unbreachable safeguards built into the artificial intelligences that ran the system and normally, nobody thought of them. But her father, she knew all too well, often considered himself above the limits imposed on ordinary people. She imagined the safeguards breached and Dad, his agents, and all their friends watching.

"Hilda?" Sasha asked. "What's wrong?"

She looked at him. Still maybe three or four years from full maturity, he was beautiful as well as handsome. Maybe because of the wine, or pheromones, or just reaching some limit on how much she was willing to fear, she felt her attitude change. To hell with them. She gave into desire.

"Ouch!"

"Oh, sorry!" Hilda pulled her fingernails out of Sasha's skin, stroked him soothingly—she hoped—and laid her head on his shoulder. "Too much happening today; I'm somewhat mixed up inside."

"Well, I'm not."

She laughed and went along for the ride.

Afterward, she let her head relax into the softness of his neck. Sanity faded back in and with it all the worries, all the things that had to be done. How much could she ask of Sasha?

"I'm using you," she said, staring him in the eye. "And I know that's what I'm doing."

Sasha grinned, his wide glistening eyes boring into hers, and he squeezed her hands. "If this is being used, use me! Whenever you want me, Hilda. Go ahead. It's okay."

"I hope you don't hold it against me later."

He shook his head and chuckled softly. "Actually I was hoping someday we could share space or something. Maybe a trial contract? Maybe..."

She put a finger on his lips and shook her head. "Maybe, some day, when I'm not three times your age and you know a little better who you are."

He sighed and looked pleadingly at her. "Whenever you want me. Whenever."

She bit her lip. There was using and then there was really using. But she was in a bind.

"Do you like Bach?" She reached over the bed for her bag and pulled out a music wand.

"Oh. Classical music?"

She nodded and a fugue filled the room. Then she nuzzled her head into the pillow beneath his. They'd have to have sensors in the pillow, or on their faces, to pick up what she'd say now. Not impossible, but maybe more of a departure from civility than her father was capable of. The codes of Earth and the charter of New Antarctica forbade unwarranted government bugging of people and their rooms.

"Can I really trust you?" she whispered in his ear. "Completely?"

"Sure," he said. "What is it?"

"Do you believe me when I say the impactor has to be launched on time, that the delay message was bogus, and the entire project depends on that impactor getting pushed to the impact point at the right time with the right velocity vector?"

"Uh, sure, Dr. Kremer."

She laughed softly. So in his mind, the Dr. Kremer that ran the BHP was not the same woman as the naked woman beside him. Like an ancient Greek goddess, her various aspects must be given separate names.

"We may have to defy local authority to do it. There will probably be consequences."

"For you, anything!"

"You know how pushing the impactor works—by shooting a torrent of tiny pellets at the reflector fields? Like pushing a paper cup with a water hose?"

"Yeah, that's pretty basic."

"Right. Well, the launch time and velocities of the pellets are arranged so that they arrive in a steady beam to provide constant thrust. The last pellets to arrive at the impactor have the longest distance to go, and they need a head start. Power requirements almost triple at that point. Anyway, Wotan is giving me until then to find evidence the delay message is wrong."

"That's... uh, only 20 days from now!"

"Yes. The problem is that the only jury Dad will believe is loaded against me: Dr. Lobov and his students. I'm reduced to hoping for some message from Sol to come in that explicitly mentions the schedule, which no message is likely to do because the schedule has been fixed for years! I need you to help me keep it going anyway."

"Let me get this straight. When..."

"Quietly. I want you to help me do that."

"I could end up frozen," he whispered.

She hugged his body closer to hers. "They wouldn't execute you..."

Sasha laughed. "No, no, that's 'ennay' talk for being put on ice—uh, they take you off the net and confine you to quarters. That's the worst, unless, of course, you want to be terminated. That's only been done once—a girl had a baby by someone that dumped her, so she dumped the baby. Outside. When her ice got clear, she didn't want to live with that memory. So instead of being frozen, she asked to be allowed to die. She took some pills. Anyway, getting frozen is still pretty bad." He looked her directly. "But I haven't said anything. What is it you'd want me to do?"

Hilda kissed him softly and whispered, "Ask your mother if she can find a way to prevent the AI controlling the beam driver arrays from following Wotan's orders for a couple of days."

"Sure, but why me?"

Hilda put a finger to his lips. "I have a feeling everything I say to your mother is very closely monitored." She told him about the incident on the way to her conference with Wotan. "So this may be my last chance to communicate honestly, and I'm taking a chance on that. You need to tell her that everything I say to her from now on, I will say with the expectation that our consolidationist friends, Wotan's security people, or both, are listening in."

All languidness had fled. Sasha was wide-eyed. He looked around the room, as if searching for bugs. "Do you think that they, ah, are watching us?" he whispered.

Hilda laughed. "I don't know." To the room, she said, "Are you?" and watched Sasha's expression. "Just kidding," she added, wishing she meant it.

Sasha kissed her cheek. "What do you think Mom can do?" he whispered.

Hilda thought hard. On one hand, the less Sasha knew, the less trouble he would be in. On the other, it was likely her last best chance to communicate freely to Naomi. "Okay. An AI is supposed to obey authority as long as it doesn't get anyone hurt. When authorities conflict, it obeys the higher one. I'd argue that since the BHP is a project of all humanity, and I am its representative, I outrank Wotan as far as the BHP is concerned. That's the case she needs to make. I've already filed all my physics objections."

"Aren't the AIs smart enough to choose because of that?"

"Not where human orders are concerned. What I'm counting on is that first, the fact that I'm right means people might be harmed if it doesn't go as planned. That appeals to the first law of AI ethics. Second, I have a case to be in charge, and that should work for the second law."

"Sounds like a lock to me."

Hilda shook her head. "If I can think of it, Father will think of it and so will other people who will come up with a way to counter it. Your mom or your Uncle Ted might come up with something better. Sasha, I'm a physicist. I want to see if all the little strings sing the way we tell them to. This cloak and dagger stuff leaves me with a pain in my gut. I wish Sarah were here."

"Sarah?"

"Dr. Sarah Levine. She's a lot more, well, enthusiastic than I am. She'd be having fun with this." And, Sasha, too. Hilda thought. Oh, would Sarah have fun with this young man.

Said young man put his lips on hers. She melted into him, then found herself sobbing uncontrollably. In a few days, he would leave for the launch. Then she would be really alone.

CHAPTER 4

Hadley's Hotel
New Antarctica
14 November 2273

Hilda watched the impactor launch from the Hadley, alone. It was less dramatic than the launch of a starship. The program brought up the pellet wind slowly, to avoid exciting any vibrational modes in the long thin structure. It took an hour for the violet reflection plume to grow bright enough for the cameras to see.

Okay, we're off, Hilda sent to the operations crew at the control center. It was all deliberately low key, given Wotan's reluctance and possible political problems for anyone associated with the project.

Naomi sent back a feed full of cheers, totally innocent. Except that Sasha gave Hilda a big wink. Hilda smiled, poured herself a brandy, and went to sleep.

●●∞●●

A month later, Ted Abila looked at the highly magnified and enhanced view of the departing impactor relayed from a big interferometer telescope in the orbit of the giant planet Amundsen. The pellet streams of a hundred thousand plus beam projectors converged in a very narrow, ghostly cone on the head of the impactor, visible only by the red lights strung out along its length. At the tip of the cone an intense glowing ring sparkled with the detonations of millions of particles each second and gave rise to a diaphanous rose of varicolored light, an ever-shifting aurora of recombining ions that trailed back along the length of the impactor. Delicate as it looked, the ethereal flower represented a wind of billions of Newtons pushing on the immaterial magnetic sails of their baby. The long iron rod had absorbed an unbelievable amount of energy from the solar arrays circling Erebus, almost as much energy by now as its entire rest mass. Possibly all for naught.

The beauty of it made Ted sigh. Already two light days distant, its velocity was up to eight-tenths of light speed with three days to go. There still had been no confirmation of the launch dates, new or old, however, and Wotan was still adamant about turning the beam drivers off, as Hilda was about keeping them on. He knew that she was right; the delay message cited fringe physics that very few who knew anything took seriously. He had hoped he wouldn't be forced to act on his knowledge.

The time had come, however, to choose between his career, his position here at New Antarctica, the trust of its leadership and the completion of what was the most ambitious project begun by humanity since the terraforming of Venus started. He had made that choice and would honor it.

He touched the net for the AI controlling the beam array. *Thorin, confirm shutdown cancellation authority.*

Shutdown cancellation may be ordered by the designated representative of the Erebus Council chairman, currently Wotan Kremer. It may also be ordered by this AI if needed to save human life. Finally, Dr. Hilda Kremer, as representative of the Human Commonwealth for the Black Hole Project, may cancel shutdown if needed for the continuity of the project, if physically present at the control center and not under duress.

Thank you, Ted answered.

Ted stared at the beam reflection aurora for another minute, then sent a prearranged message to Sasha. They had debated whether Hilda should have come and camped out at the project control center, but had decided against that as being too risky. It might signal their intent to defy authority. The cover story—that she was coming out to tell the staff about the shutdown in person—should be plausible enough.

But Ted had thought long and hard about the words "should" and "plausible enough." He had decided he was not going to risk everything without a fallback position. So he also sent a message to his brother at Bee, innocuous enough, but containing the word 'disestablishment.'

The next four days, he thought wryly, would be very interesting.

●●∞●●

Two days later, by simple chance, Hilda happened to be looking down from her balcony into the courtyard of the Hadley when Sasha, just back from the operations center, walked through on his way to the elevator. The staff was replacing the breakfast tables with casual rounds, creating somewhat of an obstacle for him to weave his way through.

They rarely met casually anymore—not a falling-out but simply reflecting mutually incompatible schedules and the fact that Sasha had other more appropriate "projects of his own." Nonetheless Hilda felt a kind of parental—or sisterly—fondness, and she was very happy to see him. Her eyes followed him across the courtyard.

She suspected why he had come; the truce between her and Wotan was over and the war she did not want was about to begin. The look on his face told it all. He was miserable about something.

One of the staff turned to speak to Sasha. The face looked familiar. In a moment she had it. He was the lean, goateed "student" in the corner of Dr. Lobov's office when she had first come. As Sasha left the courtyard, the man waited a bit, then left his table. With an almost military bearing, he followed Sasha—as did two other workers. Hilda stepped back from the balcony, her mind awhirl piecing it together.

Security. Minders. They could be there only for one purpose—to keep her from going off planet. It meant they knew about the plan.

She smiled to herself. They didn't know she knew they knew, at least not for a couple more minutes. She looked down; there was another balcony below her. Almost without thinking, she snatched a sheet from the bed, tied it on her rail, and was over and on the way down as the room announced Sasha's presence at the door.

The lady in the room below had the double doors. She looked up from a puzzle with wide-eyed shock as Hilda plopped down on her balcony.

"Dr. Kremer! Is there something wrong?"

"Yes, but I can't take time to explain. I need to use your room portal to get out!" Hilda said as she brushed by.

"Of course, but..."

Hilda was out the door and didn't hear the rest as she fled to the right. Security would be watching the outside, she imagined. So if she simply ran out of the building, it would likely be into the arms of her father's security forces.

"Sorry!"

Lost in thought, she'd bumped a group of Moslem women headed into the women's room. Hilda looked at the long dresses and beautiful headscarves and wished she had time to ask about Shira.

"My fault. Not paying attention to where I was going... Shira?"

"Hilda! I hoped you might be here. My mother and aunt wanted to..."

The two friends looked at each other.

Shira pulled Hilda close to her ear. "What's wrong?"

Hilda squeezed her arm. "It's too complicated to explain, but I have to get out of the building quickly, without someone seeing me."

Hilda stared into her old friend's dark eyes, silently pleading. Shira would be risking a lot to help her.

Shira didn't hesitate. "You could wear my scarf and coat, then leave with our group."

Hilda was dumbfounded, but there was no time to argue. She nodded. "That might work."

"Come!" Shira urged.

The little tone in Hilda's head signaled an urgent message. It was from Sasha.

Hilda, are you home? It's urgent!

He must know about the people following him. They had gotten to him, of course. There's no way a twenty-year-old could resist that kind of pressure from authority.

I'm with a friend, Sasha. Is everything okay?

I'd better talk to you in person. Can't explain.

It's going to have to wait a couple of hours. Make yourself at home. I'll be back about 1900.

Then she exercised her option to drop off the net.

Five minutes later, covered from head to toe and in the middle of a group of similarly costumed women, Hilda walked out of the lobby. Ten minutes later, with only the scarf, she was on the tube headed for the spaceport.

The *Fram* was in dock under the mammoth dome, due out in three hours, but getting on it would be a problem. If she tried to sign on the normal way, security would have her in a moment. Touching the net would immediately reveal her location, as would using any comm station. She made do with keeping her head down to avoid public safety cameras—those generally looked down from elevated positions.

Finally, she spotted a tall man in a uniform with a *Fram* crew patch on the margin of the landing field watching some robots maneuver a large piece of equipment onto a dolly. Hilda removed her scarf altogether. She decided to take the chance and walked up to him.

"Hello. I need your help."

"Huh? You are?" He brushed a shock of sandy hair from his forehead and scratched his head. He had a thick moustache that wiggled a bit when he spoke.

"Dr. Hilda Kremer. I have to get out to the project control center. Hans Bluth is trying to stop me, so the less I have to tell you about it, the less you'll be involved."

"Security! What makes you think I won't call them right now?"

"I've gotten lucky twice today. Once more is all I need."

He laughed and offered his hand. "Vanya Karinoff. Are you sure you want to do this?"

Hilda nodded.

Karinoff sighed. "Well, I'm about done here and I think this is something I should bump up to the Captain. Of course, he's on the ship." He gestured to the huge dark egg standing to the side of the field.

Hilda smiled. "Let's go."

They had to walk almost a hundred meters across the cold polished rock, utterly alone in the crisp still air. This would never work, Hilda thought. She felt totally exposed. They would be watching for her. At any moment she expected a squad of security officers to surround her.

It was the longest hundred meters she'd ever walked in her life. She watched her breath condense into a thin fog. Through it, hundreds of people wandered, ate, talked in the upper galleries around the landing field, eating. Most watching her casually, some not so casually.

Then, finally, they reached the ramp, climbed it, and were in the ship.

"This way." Her escort led her down the toroidal corridor that circled the base of the ship.

Hilda breathed a sigh of relief as they moved out of view of the entrance. With a great deal of good fortune, she would be in orbit by the time Sasha and his security escort ran out of patience.

"Outboard #10," Karinoff said. "Captain Martee's in and will see you. I've got to run."

He tipped his cap.

"Take care, and thank you, thank you!" Hilda gushed.

He gave her a quizzical smile and a brief wave as he disappeared quickly around the bend.

Was there a warning in that smile? Hilda knew nothing at all about Captain Martee. She briefly considered fleeing around the bend the other way and ducking into a closet or something to stow away. Probably wouldn't work, she decided. There'd be cameras and other sensors in every place big enough for a person. Instead, she focused her mind on the task at hand. She had one more person to sell on the merits of her cause. She touched the entrance pad of the door, and it hissed upwards.

What she saw hit her like a brick in the stomach. The room was nicely appointed, with pictures of historical spacecraft on its curved walls and comfortable-looking aerogel furniture with shiny metal tables and a desk placed throne-like in its center. There, behind what was presumably Captain Martee's desk, sat her father, Wotan Kremer. He was not smiling.

"You are going to answer some questions, Brunhilda," he said.

Focus vanished, she felt a renewed chill in her veins. Time momentarily stopped. Then a light jet of odorless gas caught her in the face.

••∞••

Four days later, Hilda and Naomi were brought to the council chamber by security escorts. Wotan was there, with Naomi's father Akaabe, Dr. Lobov, Security Minister Hans Bluth and several council members. The wall at the end of the chamber displayed an image of the still-accelerating impactor. The place smelled of a fresh cleaning.

That smell reminded her of the hospital room where she had spent three of the last four days—in a drug-induced stupor. Presumably, she had told them everything she knew, but she couldn't remember anything more than soft lights, quiet voices, and the clean, antiseptic smell of the place.

Yesterday, she'd woken in her bed to find her hotel room turned into a prison cell. The doors would not open and she had no net access. The last time Wotan had done that to her, she'd been eight years old. He was all smiles now. The beam projectors had been shut off four days ago, the off pulse arrived at the distant object two days ago, and the view of what happened would reach New Antarctica in a few minutes. He wanted to rub it in, she suspected.

A very determined self-destruction, Hilda thought. Her father's reputation would never recover from this—he would pay for his role in sabotaging the project through as much of eternity as he cared to live. So let him have his fun now. She walked stiffly to a seat and glared at him, wondering if he would see any of the pity in her anger.

"We are a community of laws and of authority deriving from the collective," Wotan declared after everyone had been seated. "Five of us have tried to put themselves above those laws…"

Naomi's father jumped in before Wotan could say anything else. "Wotan, your daughter represented the collective of humanity. One can make the case that it is you who have defied *it*."

Wotan sighed. "Akaabe, I have the floor. Does disrespect run through your entire family? Wait your turn."

Wotan straightened his back and looked at the people assembled. "If legitimate authority is not heeded, we have chaos. Is there some small chance the message directing us to delay the impactor launch was not genuine? Perhaps. But the decision concerning what to do about it lies with the collective and not with individuals.

"We are here today to show that legitimate authority succeeds because it represents the will of many, and many have cooperated to uphold it. Colonel Maluk." Wotan gestured to a man that Hilda recognized as the bearded "student" in Lobov's office, who now wore some kind of gray jumpsuit uniform with discrete pips on its shoulders along with the New Antarctica patch below his right shoulder.

"Thank you, Mr. President. Formally, this is a disciplinary hearing to state charges and recommendations concerning the behavior of Brunhilda Kremer and Naomi Abila in willfully disobeying lawful directives of the representative of the council. A jury of peers will be assembled to judge the gravity of the offense, the prospects of a repeat, and the appropriate action, unless the respondents waive that procedure in favor of a determination by the Council President. Which, I might add, would save a great deal of trouble in an open and shut case. The three who have fled in exile to Bee have, for all intents and purposes, chosen their own fate."

Hilda barely heard a word, the voice itself taking all of her attention. It was that of the dark stranger who had accosted her on the way to visit her father after the conversation with Dr. Lobov. Colonel Maluk, of course, was a consolidationist and probably had been promoted as such by Hans Bluth.

Wotan nodded. "Thank you, Colonel. We will hear from the respondents and representatives in a moment. Now is the time to see the futility of their efforts. In precisely ten seconds, the beam will cease to push the impactor."

All eyes went to the screen. At the appointed second, the glowing ring at the head of the impactor vanished and a wave of darkness shot backward, extinguishing the aurora of its progress.

"Thy will be done," intoned Hans Bluth.

Wotan frowned at him. "We have a secular proceeding here. And it was our collective will."

The security minister smiled. "As you will have it, Mr. President."

"Damn!" Colonel Maluk shouted and pointed at the wall, his face turning red. "That isn't funny. Give us the real feed again."

Hilda turned to the wall screen again and gasped. The reflection aurora was back again, somewhat wider, she noted, and the cone looked like it was coming in at an angle to the impactor, as if from a different direction.

Wotan closed his eyes momentarily, then said in low, measured tones. "It is not, apparently, a jest. The beam that has resumed pushing the impactor is coming from Bee."

He glared down from the council table, first at Naomi, then at Hilda, looking like a cornered animal prepared to deal death to its tormenter at the first opportunity.

"Ted did it!" Naomi squealed. "He's got Bee to keep pushing the impactor."

Wotan brought his ceremonial gavel down on the desk so hard that it broke, but nobody so much as tittered in the silence that followed.

"We are still in session here," he said, "the stakes of which have been raised considerably by this *unforeseen* treachery." He turned to Maluk.

"The respondents didn't know about this," growled the Colonel. "Our methods are reliable."

"Wotan," Hans Bluth said, "this is what *you* get for being so sanguine about those elitists setting up their own government."

"And what would you have done," Wotan snapped back. "Organized some kind of an expedition against them? Start interstellar warfare?" He turned to Hilda. "Brunhilda, I don't care if you didn't know about this... this scheme. You are responsible for it. I hold you completely responsible."

Then he sighed and shook his head. "For chaos' sake, what can we do now? Allow me for a moment the fantasy of thinking I have been correct in this and assume that we have sent an impactor six months ahead of schedule. What are our options?"

Hilda spoke as evenly as she could. "We send word ahead. Our transmissions will arrive months before the impactor. The impactor wouldn't receive terminal guidance anyway and would miss the impact site by several astronomical units. Then we send another impactor on the revised schedule. This is what we should have planned to do anyway; the effort to not send the impactor on the original schedule was never anything more than a consolidationist plot to sabotage the project!"

"The remorsefulness of the respondents is noted," the security minister intoned, getting nervous chuckles throughout the room for his irony.

"Enough, Hans," Wotan said. "Brunhilda, I suppose you would maintain that it isn't necessary, but would you humor me and send word forward as to what has happened?"

"I'll need to have my net access back."

"Wotan..." the Colonel growled.

"Peace, Maluk," the security minister said. "She's done all the harm she can. Your access is restored, Dr. Kremer."

It was like having her sight restored. Hilda quickly had the incoming backlog sorted for messages from the Solar System; there were a dozen text messages and a video of a celebration at the BHP institute. Tse Wen, Sarah, and Brad were there. Hilda checked the time date and smiled inwardly.

"This needs to go on screen, everyone," Hilda announced seriously.

Wotan shrugged and nodded.

The party scene lit up the room in contrast to the previous spacescape. Dr. Sarah Levine, in a painted-on black thing with an impossibly plunging neckline, came to the fore.

"Hi, Hilda, and everyone, from 11.63 years ago. We've timed this party scene to arrive as you celebrate the completion of your impactor launch..."

There was an audible gasp from Wotan and several others. Dr. Lobov got up and made his way out of the room.

"...when ours will be on its way too," Sarah's image concluded.

The screen went dark. "You've made your point, Brunhilda," Wotan said.

"Can we go now?" Hilda asked.

"This is still a disciplinary hearing," Colonel Maluk said. "The merits of the issue are beside the point. I will remind you that a number of people here and in the Solar System do not regard a success of the BHP as a good thing. At any rate, you broke our laws."

Wotan nodded. "You are out of order, Colonel Maluk, but correct."

"Dad!" Hilda shouted. "We've saved your reputation. We saved you from the consequences of the biggest..."

"Quiet!" Wotan shouted. Then he added, more gently, "Some things, however true, are better left unsaid. I appear to be acquiring some hard-earned wisdom in that respect. Unlawfulness is still intolerable, whatever the result. Will you accept my judgment? And will you, Naomi? Or do we have to go to trial?"

Such a trial would savage her father, Hilda realized. He would lose his council presidency. Someone else would preside over the completion of the terraforming project. She couldn't do that to him or to those who supported her. Wotan's blood was still strong in her, after all.

"Mr. President," she said formally, "Naomi and the others followed my direction. I had both project and local authority under you. What was done was my responsibility. Leave them alone and I will submit without trial."

Wotan looked at his ministers who, under the circumstances, appeared to want a trial no more than he did. At any rate, Hilda saw all the heads nod. Colonel Maluk sat, impassive, lips tight.

They were, Hilda knew, rapidly exchanging views over the net of what should be done with her. She had a pretty good idea of what the decision would be as well. It seemed the only one possible. All her dreams of coming home again, of reconciliation, of seeing New Antarctica bloom, were likely gone.

Finally, Wotan tapped the gavel head on the desk, waited for quiet, and said one word, hard and cold. "Exile." He looked to his right and left. No one objected. Then he got up and left.

Hans Bluth reached over and took the remains of the gavel. "I, I will entertain a motion to adjourn."

One of the other members mumbled something.

"Hearing no objection, these proceedings are adjourned." He shrugged and set, rather than pounded, the amputated gavel head down. Everyone started talking as the Councilors unceremoniously filed out of the room.

As the chamber emptied, Naomi and her father came up to Hilda, who still had her security escort. The guard backed away a few feet to give her space.

Naomi hugged her. "This will blow over. He'll get over it."

Hilda shook her head as tears ran down her face. "I'll go to the Vertex, I think. Try to make myself useful there. Maybe I can come back some day."

"I'll miss you. We'll all be thinking of you twelve years from now, you can count on that."

Twelve years, Hilda thought bitterly. Twelve years was the time it would take the impactor to get to Vertex plus the time the news of what happened would take to get back. One fifth of her lifetime so far.

She smiled inwardly at that thought and tried to imagine how she would view the passage of twelve years when she was a million years old, or a billion. Then she thought of some unfinished business with someone for whom a dozen years was still half a lifetime. The sentence

C. Sanford Lowe ∞ G. David Nordley

would take effect quickly, she realized, and she might not get another chance.

"Sasha?"

He came over to her, looking miserable. "I'm sorry. They ordered me to cooperate, Dr. Kremer, and..."

Hilda placed her finger on his lips, then wrapped her arms around him and gave him a long, sensual, unabashed hug. "No hard feelings," she said. "Take care of yourself. Have fun. We'll see each other again, some day. Okay?"

He smiled. There were the beginnings of tears in his eyes.

She brushed her lips against his briefly, then wordlessly turned and left the room. Naomi walked back to the Hadley with Hilda, past the school, the lake, and the other places of their childhood. She had been home such a short time.

She was off planet again by 3400 that day.

●●∞●●

From her room a week later Naomi pulled up a view from the Amundsen astrogation facility. Under moderate magnification and viewed from almost directly behind, the back-splash of a departing starship looked like a ring of fire, or rather a circular aurora, with the ship itself a particularly brilliant spark in its middle. Hilda is there, she thought, probably cold-sleeping through the high acceleration departure. At four gravities, she would be near enough to Vertex to see the impact within hours of the event.

It was, she noted with some irony, Father's Day on the New Antarctica calendar, and she reminded herself to send a message... no, she would walk over. It had been at least a week. He would lecture her about getting involved in politics and then smile because he was secretly proud that his daughter had done something wonderful. They would share a hug that was all the more precious for the cold edge in Wotan Kremer's voice when he had sent *his* daughter away again. Naomi asked whatever gods there might be that a tiny bright new star lay at the end of Hilda's journey—that Wotan had not sent her from one broken dream to another.

BOOK IV
LOKI'S REALM

CHAPTER 1

Broadford
Isle of Skye, Scotland
2260

I suppose it's more interesting when, in the words of Robert Burns, "the best laid schemes o' mice an' men gang aft agley" than otherwise. I'll have no quarrel with that, though I do have to say that had everything gone according to plan, it still would have been quite an adventure. What we learn from this effort is that while the universe still has a lot of surprises to throw at us, we'll match that from time to time with the surprises we throw at ourselves. But that would be getting a wee bit ahead of myself.

I'm Bruce Macready, historian of the Epsilon Eridani mission to build and launch one of the four impactors intended to produce a miniature black hole. Though smaller than an atomic nucleus, it would mass billions of tons—enough to stay around long enough for the physicists to play with it and someday, perhaps, use its progeny to construct vast Faustian machines that will manipulate the very fabric of space itself to humanity's purposes.

Aye, that was the hope.

How, you might ask, did a Scottish professor, who had not left the Isle of Skye more than a half dozen times in his 147 years—let alone go into *space*—become involved in this? Well, I had taught the history of science and technology at Broadford College for over half *its* existence, and held every position including chancellor at one time or another. I thought the human race was in a flat place of late, not making history like it had done before. Earth was pacified. Mars was only just terraformed and already a hotbed of cultish agrarian politics. It would be centuries yet before Venus offered a similar opportunity. I sensed that, short of the possibility of alien contact, the making of a black hole would be the signal event in even my extended lifetime.

Year after year, Tsiolkovsky thundered down the ages to my students—in my voice—saying that one could not live in a cradle forever. The original words had only to do with the planet Earth, long since transcended. However, in a broader sense, the idea of a cradle is relative; it is wherever you start from.

It had taken me the better part of a century, but now, I realized, Tsiolkovsky was speaking to me. My journeys until then had all been virtual and vicarious. Always the observer, never the participant. What might I make of myself out there? It was time.

I found that among the BHP principle investigators was one Bradford Adams, an Australian physicist who had attended Broadford for a year on exchange and taken one of my classes.

I took it on myself to contact Brad and offer my services as an historian on the 50-year expedition to Epsilon Eridani—a star about a third of the Sun's luminosity, which, due to its extreme youth, was not suitable for a colony and thus had no indigenous historians.

To my great surprise, the project leader, Dr. Zhau Tse Wen, showed up at Broadford to interview me. We hit it off well, and over a glass of 14-year Talisker, my proposal was accepted. So, with a little more fuss than I need to relate here, I made my good-byes to my elder brother at Macready Manor, to Broadford College, and to my past life.

I sent a few personal things ahead and began this journey of some thirteen light years on foot, hiking the ten kilometers to Kyle of Lochalsh with all the clothes I would need for a couple of days on my back. One travels light among the stars, and I wanted to savor what little time I had left on Skye. It was October, clear, bright, and nippy and the view of Skye from the height of the bridge almost made me turn in my tracks and head back.

But, no, I have an inertia in me that is legendary and my path I'd chosen. I sighed and marched down the mainland side of the span and on to the transit station. There, I caught a fan bus to Glasgow and took an orbital shuttle—much faster than the freight elevator—to Sheffield Spaceport, 400 kilometers up, where the *Admiral Byrd* was then keeping station.

As I left the shuttle, a smiling attendant met me. "Dr. Macready? You're wanted on the starship."

I was surprised; the *Admiral Byrd* wasn't due out for two more days, and I'd anticipated some time to explore Sheffield Spaceport.

The attendant handed me a pair of old-fashioned-looking spectacles. Smart glasses, I realized. They'd been around for a couple centuries, but I'd never had need of them at Broadford, an old-fashioned wrist comp having met all my needs. I frowned.

"Your orientation," he said. "They're for those who haven't had bioradios installed."

Of course. I'd been born a wee bit early to have the genetic modification that allows people nowadays to send and receive radio waves and talk directly to computers. The spectacles were a prosthesis for those of us so handicapped. I put them on with a frown. Nothing appeared.

"Speak the name of what you want to know as quietly as you like, or stare at something for more than a second, down the hall, for instance."

I looked at the attendant. The glasses identified him as "Lane Woo, flight attendant. Cislunar Transportation Service."

"Thank you, Mr. Woo. This will take some getting used to."

He nodded with a smile and went about his business leaving me to bumble about mine, feeling as out of place as a penguin at Miami Beach. I'll concede the gadget may avoid many an awkward social occasion, but the art of a pleasant introduction must suffer greatly. Why are we in such a hurry now that we all live forever?

The glasses led me to an elevator down, or out, rather, to the 0.1 gee level and through a long park-like transit lounge to the shuttle gate. In a few minutes, a crewless runabout whisked me off to the starship.

Up close, the *Admiral Byrd* was impressively weird. Through its transparent hull, I saw a hundred-meter-wide crown of six half-kilometer-long icicles that were evenly spaced. At the wide end of each icicle was a ten-meter-radius sphere, which housed the habitable parts of the starship. This entire arrangement rotated majestically. From my point of view, the icicles occasionally eclipsed each other, separated, and eclipsed each other again, making me think of the blades on wool shears.

As I got closer, I could see the band of the crown that joined them all was thick enough for people to pass through. Closer still, and I saw the forward ring sitting about a quarter of the way between the main ring and the tips of the icicle. Thin "legs" slanted in and forward to attach this smaller ring to the rest of the ship.

The forward ring was a magnetic choke that would increase the ship's ability to reflect the ions that would push it along—this magnetic mirror design actually dated back to the 20th century, though not realized until the 22nd. The second ring's magnetic field also helped deflect any debris in front of the ship.

It is one thing to study the history of such things, or see them on some video display, and entirely a different thing to see them with one's own eyes. I was awestruck. This was a real starship and I was going to ride on it.

The runabout set down on the inside of the small ring in a complicated maneuver which its AI handled flawlessly, leaving me with about a tenth of a gee of spin gravity. I wondered if such a maneuver could even be attempted manually.

Dock and seal were quickly announced, and my smart glasses guided me down a long sloping corridor that ran inside one of the choke-ring supports to the passageway in the main ring and something approaching lunar gravity. From there they conducted me into the middle of Sphere One, a living-room-like common area surrounded by doors to private quarters and a fireman's pole in the center leading to decks above and below. I had barely begun to wonder which door was mine when one to my left opened unbidden. An AI somewhere was responsible, of course.

To be truthful, I was beginning to feel uneasy. Were there any people on this starship? Not wishing to appear unsophisticated, I resisted the temptation to call out "Hello, is anyone home?"

The cabin was tiny; a two-meter-long fold-down bunk took up the entire outboard side. A well-disguised lavatory fit snugly to the right of the door at the foot of the bed and a small desk and chair pod was to the left of the door.

I checked to see if my personal stores had been stowed, and they had—as part of the shield mass. Included was a precious case of my native island whisky, Talisker. I licked my lips but set aside my thirst for the nonce.

"Hello, Dr. Macready. Rumor is I'm in charge of this zoo."

I turned. Outside my door was our expedition commander, G. P. Weaver, a tall man with close-cropped steel-gray hair. By his biography, he was a horseman, a Texan, with PhDs in animal husbandry and systems management. He still had vestiges of a Texas accent, but this was well-smoothed to the aerospace standard of English that had evolved to sound not too unlike the Canadian of the Toronto region. He offered me the calloused hand of a sincere physical hobbyist, with a correspondingly firm grip.

"Glad to meet you, sir," I replied, wondering what he'd think of my rather unsmoothed Scots accent, "and there'll be no need for the "doctor" so far from the classroom. It's Bruce."

He gave me a long look as if judging whether he was ready to be on a first name basis.

"Right, Macready... uh, Bruce. Brad Adams arranged for you to have this stateroom."

"Aye."

"Did you intend to ride out the acceleration?"

It was clear that he didn't think it was a good idea. Neither, it happened, did I. I shook my head. "I dinna think so. Others have reported on the joys of living at three gravities for three months far better than I might, and dealt even more convincingly with the boredom of the long coast through the great black." I smiled at him and waved a hand to indicate it was no matter. "So I've chosen to experience the journey in cold sleep."

"Good call. We'll be doing five gees, not three."

"Is there some urgency, then?"

"No. Some worries. Let's just say that in the current climate, we're leaving as little to chance as necessary."

"Aye." There'd been the bombing and the attempt to sabotage the Ten-Ten experiment. As an unknown, and an outsider, I was probably not above suspicion myself. "No question about me as long as I'm on ice, is it?"

He pursed his lips, but didn't say anything.

"Very well, but there's an agreement with the project management that I be thawed out should anything of significance happen. They provided me a stateroom in that eventuality."

Weaver raised an eyebrow. "Project management will soon be a long, long way away. We have ninety-six scientists with us who want to study the Epsilon Eridani system in detail. They're in cold storage and will stay there until we're ready for them."

"Aye," I replied, matching his seriousness. "I hope my arrangement meets with your approval, then."

His face remained impassive.

"Ah, once I've sorted myself, I hope to ask Dr. Davra about the finer points of what the robotic minions at Epsilon Eridani can do on their own and what might require our direction." Davra, a comely lass, was the chief roboticist.

He looked at me a bit, then nodded as if making a judgment. "I see you've homed in on the central issue already. The short answer is, their programming *can't* anticipate everything. That's why Doc Zhau sent us."

Dr. Zhau and Weaver had a history that went back several decades, and when Zhau had wanted someone he could completely rely on to ensure the Epsilon Eridani impactor went on time, he'd picked Weaver as he'd told me over a whisky at our interview.

"I'm afraid Davra's on ice already, as is everyone else."

"I've been wondering if she had a last name. I didn't see one on the crew list."

"Nope. She claims she doesn't need one. It's not the name she was born with, of course."

When I raised my eyebrow, he laughed.

"Some Hindu thing. You'll understand when you meet her and everyone else after deceleration—maybe three weeks, subjective time."

"We're leaving so soon?"

"You're the last one on board. Captain Lee says we can move up a slot if we leave now—saves us three months. We catch an interplanetary pusher beam tomorrow morning and coast out to somewhere between Earth and Mars' orbit where we'll pick up the interstellar boost."

"No one said anything! I might have made you late!"

Weaver laughed coldly. "Not hardly."

"So if I'm late, yer gone?" The most momentous decision in my life might have been brushed off without so much as an afterthought! I imagined the looks of pity I'd have endured, slinking back to Broadford like that.

"Consider it a test. We weren't at all sure you belong here. Anyway, you weren't late. No hurry on the cold sleep; but if you have any goodbye calls to make, do it now before the light speed lag gets too big. I'd go up and use the park. Great view to describe if you can't think of anything else to say. Just ask the *Admiral* if you need anything."

"He's always listening? Like Big Brother?"

"Not really. It's for security and safety. The audio pickups are bright enough to identify a request and connect if required. Also, the *Admiral* doesn't share without permission. You'll get used to it. Anyway, you won't be overheard; the *Admiral* will fix you up with an implant."

"No thank you, sir. I've resisted having a radio grown in my head for over a century and I'm not about to relent now."

"I said implant. A subcutaneous chip with a network of electrodes. It's no more intrusive than a wrist comp. We won't touch your genome, and besides, it's a safety item; we can't have people incommunicado on a starship. This is nonnegotiable, Macready. The runabout's still on the ring. Your call."

"But..." It was suddenly very clear to me I was no longer in academia. The principle of the thing grated on me, especially having it pulled on me now. But it was probably not the only of my many foibles and eccentricities that I would have to leave behind. "...never ye mind. I'm staying."

He nodded. "I'll give you some time for your calls now." With that he turned and left.

That, I felt, had not been a good start. This man would be the ultimate human authority for the next four waking years of my life. Och, I thought, if the whole mission went like this, I would have very little to write about. Perhaps Barton would come to my rescue; if his Bruce could make something of watching a spider build a web, so could I. Things could not be like this the whole time. This was most likely just a bit of hazing.

Given our precipitous departure, I did have some calls to make, and thought to make a point of taking Weaver's advice, in case he was watching. So I took the center pole upward and emerged into a dome-like room under the top of the sphere with some plantings and a small pool. The dome ceiling was tiled with display screens and generally gave the illusion of being out in space itself. I lay down on the grass and watched the Earth rise and set over me as I asked the *Admiral Byrd* to place my calls and began a round of uncomfortable conversations with people I'd had breakfast with only hours ago.

My twelve-year-old great-great niece Alice wanted to know where I'd put a book she'd wanted to read. No, I hadn't taken it with me. Try the spare room bookshelf.

My brother-in-law, Ian, had a couple of last minute things concerning my power of attorney. I was not abandoning my share of the estate—I would be gone for only half a century or so—but I had to allow for all contingencies. Our lives diverged now, and we had to get on with it.

Maggie, bless her, asked if I'd liked the breakfast. It was so delicious I could still taste it.

It was the evening of what had started as my last day on Earth as I said my final goodbyes and reflected on just what I'd done. This morning, I had rolled out of my old oak frame bed, just as I'd done for a hundred years or more and had my eggs and bangers no differently than almost half a million times before. I could even still feel a bit of sausage in my teeth.

Done, I lay on the grass, looked at the stars, and rubbed a little moisture from my eyes.

••∞••

Cold sleep is a very civilized process. You simply take a pill and fall asleep in your stateroom. Someone or something comes along in the middle of the night, gives you a shot you never feel and carts you away to your cold sleep unit—a CSU as they call it—an uncomfortably sarcophagal-looking thing that you never see, if all goes well. On arrival, the process would be reversed. I'd wake up in the local in-processing facility—a hotel-like place—on the space colony the robots were building for us around Epsilon Eridani.

So, before turning in, I poked around the ship a bit; if things went according to plan this would likely be the last I'd see of it. It was like rattling around in some strange, lifeless museum.

Curiosity satisfied, I went back to my stateroom and showered in an ingenious pull-down tube. Then I followed the instructions to put on my shipsuit—kind of a smart fabric second skin that would actually hold you together against the vacuum, should some emergency arise. Finally, I lay down to wait for sleep. My last thought was that I'd have spent less than a waking hour in the tiny room.

CHAPTER 2

Aboard the *Admiral Byrd*
between stars
22 June 2266 (Sidereal reference)

The first clue I had that things had indeed gone "agley" was when I woke up. Sounds penetrated my awareness, mainly a barely perceptible low thrum not unlike that of the *Admiral Byrd's* air circulation system. I opened my eyes; the light level was quite low, but enough for me to see that, indeed, I was still in my stateroom aboard the *Admiral Byrd*. I noticed a slight metallic taste in my mouth, presumably a legacy of a cold sleep experience. Otherwise, I might have been woken up from an afternoon nap.

Spin gravity was still about lunar level; my earth-trained arm shot up as I cast the sheet aside and took care not to bump my head while sitting up. I kept hearing a tone, but couldn't see where it was coming from. Then I remembered—I could talk to the ship!

"*Admiral*, what's that bloody noise?"

The noise stopped instantly. *That is the attention tone from the communications implant installed while you were in cold sleep. Do you hear me satisfactorily?*

I nodded. But it wasn't coming from my ears. Ah, the implant. "Aye," I answered.

In a few days, you'll be able to communicate subvocally. But for now, continue to talk to me aloud; this will let your chip learn your nerve impulse patterns. You have an urgent message from G. P. Weaver.

I blinked hard, shook my head, stretched to wake myself. "Okay, please play it."

"The latest data from the Epsilon Eridani system indicates problems. Come to the project staff meeting to discuss the situation. The *Admiral* will give you the details."

Weaver, apparently, was honoring the conditions of my presence on the expedition. This, I told myself, was a good thing, though having my sleep disturbed didn't make it feel that way.

"What's up, *Admiral*?" I queried.

A very violent and entirely unpredicted collision in the Epsilon Eridani system has increased the amount of meteoric debris in the system by two orders of magnitude, an order of magnitude more than the array-building system has been designed to withstand.

"Indeed! I'll be right along."

I wondered how the artificial intelligences that were building the array would cope with this. What plans should we make? Was the project itself in jeopardy? I got myself up to speed as much as I could. Then it was time to go to the Sphere Three park.

Getting there was no problem; the hollow main ring led through the center of each sphere. A woman by the name of Jill Davenport, head of biology, soon followed me on the pole and assured me this was the way.

As I came up into the dome I was greeted by a shapely lass of dusky complexion wearing a glossy purple shipsuit that looked like it had been painted on her body. It had a white shoulder-to-hip slash; broken where it was, the suit was open nearly down to her navel. With the iron discipline of a century of interaction with female college students, I kept my eyes on her head. I recognized her from my study of the crew.

"Dr. Davra, I presume?" I said, somewhat stuffily.

"Hello, Dr. Macready." She smiled at me curiously and motioned to a spot on the grass. "We're about ready to start."

I nodded, sat down on the grass like everyone else, and looked up at displays of comets and collisions spread all over the dome display.

"Damn, Emma." Weaver said at length, "How'd this happen?"

Dr. Lewis, our astrophysicist, stood up so she could see everyone. She reminded me of my kindergarten teacher so many years ago, save for a London accent. She was dressed, much as I was, in plain walking shorts and a loose pullover tunic that gave little hint of any figure.

"Essentially bad luck. I think the recent increase in activity of Epsilon Eridani—it's up almost an order of magnitude from the baseline—has modified the orbits of several comets and perhaps larger bodies. The big collision followed a bolometric luminosity spike of almost twelve percent—a huge flare by solar standards—that occurred the year we left. This likely increased cometary activity of all sorts, leading to random non-gravitational accelerations, lots of orbit crossings, a significant increase in collision rate and debris. It's a feedback process—exponential as long as a reservoir of material exists. Epsilon Eridani's planet, Loki, now has an eccentric orbit that continually stirs things up. A collision that big might not have happened for tens of thousands of years. Instead, it happened now."

"So, what do you think we should do about it?" Davra asked pointedly.

Lewis took a breath. She seemed a bit intimidated by Davra, but determined nevertheless.

"Study it for now. Something is going on we don't quite understand. We'll come up with a better solution if we do."

"Meanwhile, we're losing ground," Davra complained. "Simulations show the response of the AI systems will be to divert power array production to beam drivers, up to the point where that's all that's being made. Without replacement array panels and any new arrays, we'll be losing ground. We'll have to come up with some creative solutions."

She was answered by a tall, angular, man with a shock of boyish hair. After a moment's cobweb cleaning in the cold-sleep-dusty cells of my memory, I recognized Dr. Daggert Dickson, an engineer and expert in propulsion systems.

"The AIs won't? I thought these systems were fairly creative," he said.

"We cut back on their creativity," Davra responded. "We didn't want them thinking up new purposes in a thirty-year management control loop."

"Definitely not," Dickson agreed. "If we don't watch out they might invent sex..."

"Hmph." Weaver interjected. "Well, our starship isn't under any such constraints... on creativity that is. *Admiral*, do you have any ideas?"

"About sex and the array construction systems?"

Dickson and Davra laughed, Weaver coughed, and Dr. Lewis groaned.

The *Admiral* continued as if unaware that anything humorous had occurred. It was, of course, by no means unaware, but had merely evolved a deadpan strategy for dealing with Dickson's version of humor.

"The current system is already at an optimum production-reproduction balance. It would lose ground under any change in allocation of manufacturing effort. Therefore, to complete the project, with the planned performance margins, the current system will need to be changed.

"There are three things being produced; factories, array panels, and beam drivers. One change would be to add something else to the system. The effect of that additional thing would need to be to attenuate the debris flux. One could build spacecraft to find and divert collision fragments before they come into range of the impact protection systems of the arrays. This would enable the array system to grow again, but not as fast. However, you asked for ideas, not solutions."

Dickson chuckled. "Thanks, *Admiral*." He turned to Emma and frowned. "Look, the composition of the debris appears to be mainly S and C type asteroidal material right?"

"Carbonaceous chondrites. True."

"Okay. They're rocks, like the raw material we're using for manufacturing. *Admiral*, what if we collect that, instead of going after more asteroids? That takes more propulsion, but we'd be able to put less effort into mining and get kind of a two-fer."

"I show sufficient growth. That was a good idea, Dr. Dickson," the ship said.

I frowned. AIs are programmed to praise humans because it makes them seem more human themselves. However, in practice, I've always found the effect a bit cloying.

Davra sighed. "Of course it was, *Admiral*. And so was yours. I liked that."

"Why don't you ask him what he's doing tonight?" Dickson quipped.

Everyone laughed except Emma, who simply tightened her lips and waited for it to stop.

Weaver held up a hand. "Okay, Davra and Dickson, can you get together and polish this off? Give us a look tomorrow morning?"

Emma looked like she wanted to say something, but held off when Weaver looked at her.

"And now," Weaver said, "For those who haven't met him yet, I'd like to introduce our captive historian, Dr. Bruce Macready, late of Broadford College, Isle of Skye, in Scotland."

Davra sat up and looked right at me and smiled so come-hither she might have been a sophomore female student in danger of flunking a course she needed very, very badly. She had done nothing to hold the front of her suit in place and the outward fold in her shipsuit showed just about all of her left breast. I'm not sure what my facial response looked like to her, but, so help me, she giggled. I took it to be a friendly giggle.

Emma looked my way, expressionless except for a slightly raised eyebrow.

Dickson shrugged and said, "Hi, Bruce."

"Uh, hello everyone."

And that was that. We all stood up and chatted with each other for a while. Whether by chance, natural reticence, or intent Dr. Lewis was the last to greet me.

"Bruce, is it? Please call me Emma."

She gave me a warm smile and by the time we'd exchanged pleasantries, the others had left.

I suddenly realized I was ravenously hungry. "Cold sleep, apparently, gives one an appetite. I thought I'd head to the cantina. Would you like to join me? You could explain again to me just what's happening in the Epsilon Eridani system."

She looked at me as if I'd said something exceedingly strange, but then said. "I don't know that I'll be able to take you much beyond the background material you've already studied, but..." She shrugged and gave me a slight smile. "I'm hungry too."

Once our canteen sandwiches were devoured, I asked what had been bothering me.

"A great amount of planning has gone into this. So much so that for there to be a problem of this magnitude seems inconceivable."

Emma nodded, very seriously. "The system has been studied, modeled, and monitored for over two hundred years with increasing accuracy. What happened was unprecedented. I suppose we have to remind ourselves that two hundred years is a near infinitesimal part of the life of a star. But that doesn't make me feel much better."

"Oh, it would appear to be a serious matter, but I dinna think it one for which you should bear any particular blame just for being an astrophysicist."

She shook her head. "You don't understand. I led the modeling team. It was my call, my assurances..."

Och! So it did weigh heavy on her. I am not sure how to explain what I did next, other than that Davra's display had put me in the mood. Davra, herself, seemed clearly untouchable to me. Those subtle things that sort us males from alpha to zed had made clear to me from my wee years that women like Davra belong only to the alpha sort. To assume she was other than untouchable would only invite heartache. But Emma was more like another professor, of similar disposition to my own, I thought. And she was clearly unspoken for and in need of some tenderness. So I had motive and opportunity. And, alas, I had also the means.

"In that case, bonnie lass, you'll be needing a wee bit of fortification. Now, have you ever tasted the whisky of my native isle? It is called Talisker and I have brought a supply with me."

"Whisky? I'll have a bit of wine now and then, but..."

"It is only technically whisky. Really one consumes it as a liquor, or a cordial. There's a touch of sherry to it, some say, and a thickness and a sweetness that will put you in mind of no whisky you have ever tasted before. You really must try some."

She gave me a wan smile. "Dr. Macready..."

"Bruce."

"Bruce. I'm 123 years old. Been around the block, haven't I?"

The way she said it, I didn't believe a word of it. "Then come along, lass, will you?"

She laughed a bit. "Oh, why not?"

She followed me out of the canteen. "How did you happen to come on this expedition?"

I laughed. "I knew someone on the project and I asked. To my surprise, I seemed to have been the only one to have this idea." We'd reached my stateroom and its door glided open at my approach. I gestured for her to precede me and continued. "In short, they said yes."

I put a scene of Loch Ness on the far wall, a sunny day in late October full of autumn color.

Emma sighed. "So whatever errors I make, whatever consequences my mistakes have, you'll be there to write all about it for all eternity to read."

They dinna send idiots out to the stars. "Now, lass, I'm a fair man, and there'll be no need to dwell on things of little matter. Besides, for such inquisitions there would always be the official logs. My job, as an historian, is to make what all happens comprehensible to the general reader. I'll not be passing negative judgments on people just because they're people."

She simply looked at my view of Loch Ness. "You mentioned some local libation?"

I smiled, glad for the change of subject. "I did indeed. Talisker, a single malt Scots whisky..." I explained about aging, sherry cask wood, local grains, and all as I poured us a finger each.

So there I was, not a week out of the manor by my subjective time, with a woman in my room yet. Macready, I told myself, you are indeed a long way from Skye. The staterooms are compact as you might imagine, and the bed doubles as a couch when one isn't sleeping. So we sat on that.

"Dr. Macready, I can detect very faint echoes of some of the qualities you mentioned, but my overwhelming impression is more of... of some kind of mouthwash. And my mouth burns." She rolled her eyes up, then gave me a kind of wry little smile. "But it does make me warm."

I put my hand on hers and sighed.

She made no move to remove it, but simply shook her head. "I'm not sure what's gone wrong. Epsilon Eridani is a very young star system, and it's suffered some recent pathology. The planetary orbits haven't settled down. It's still very hard to tell what happened or when. A passing star or rogue planet may have disturbed the system. Or the system may be disrupting itself chaotically."

"Disrupting itself?"

She shrugged. "Orbits evolve. Planets perturb each other. Eccentricities vary in cycles. A system may clank along alone like that for millions or even billions of years, then someday all the cycles match up the wrong way and two planets come too close to each other and..." she spread her arms as if to encompass some unimaginable disaster.

I took another sip of the Talisker and looked into her eyes, sympathetically.

This, I realized, was probably a time to do something. But the last thing I wanted to do was to offend her, or scare her off, by being too forward.

"Uh, what happens then."

She sighed. "There is a brief gravitational embrace, they whirl around each other, and one or the other planet gets thrown into an orbit that leads into the cold dark or maybe into the central star. The other, in this case Epsilon Eridani's big giant planet, Loki, is left swinging wildly in and out. "

"So Loki might ha'e a wee affair and t'other planet's no more there." I hadn't actually meant to do a rhyme, it just rolled on out that way, as Talisker is wont to inspire.

Emma raised her eyebrow, smiled briefly, but carried on. "Most likely in the cold night. If the other planet fell into Epsilon Eridani, the metallicity would likely be higher. Stuff falling into a larger star tends to stay near the surface." She leaned forward as if formulating an explanation. "It's an evolving planetary system. If we increase the speed of building the array, we should be able to stay ahead of this mess, but..." She drained her glass. "This stuff does grow on you."

I poured another round. "But what?"

"Oh, nothing." She raised an eyebrow at me. "Must remember I'm on the record..." Somehow she had moved near me, her arm lightly touching mine.

It burned where we touched in a way I remembered from close dancing in the days of my youth. I mulled over whether she might welcome an invitation to become more intimate, or whether that would be too forward for now.

She turned to me. "You're a professor of history?"

I brought up on the wall pictures of Skye, Broadford, Portree, and the family.

It was then that the terrible reality of what I'd done hit home. "It's just been a couple of days to me, but they've not seen or heard a thing from me for, what, a dozen years now. Like that star system you describe, all of a sudden things come together then, boom, I'm off into the cold dark. History can be like that, do you know? The lives of those who have done things of note oft' get a bit messy in the process. But I left no other complications behind, if ye ken."

"Me neither. If you think about it, that's probably true of most of us on this mission."

"Davra?" I asked.

Emma rolled her eyes. "I'd guess life is *very* simple and uncomplicated for people like her, and Dagger. No need for anything deep or long term. No need to waste time."

"Dagger?"

"Dr. Dickson's nickname. Well earned, I might add," she said with a smug smile.

"Och! Ye ken Davra might ha'e, uh, Dagger, 'round her little finger?"

"And Weaver. Any man. And any robot, too. She knows just how to pull what she wants out of the *Admiral*, too." Emma sipped. "So we off and do something when we don't really know what we're dealing with."

"Maybe you should have a talk with G. P., privately."

Emma looked into the bottom of her cup then gave me one of those subtle but suave know-it-all looks the English are so good at. "It's too late, Bruce. Davra's already convinced Dagger to go for her robotic solution and G. P. has no strong view himself. It's a majority."

"Weaver's a widower," I said, changing the subject.

Emma nodded and took another sip. "Yes. That was awful. His wife was thrown from one of his horses twenty years ago. I imagine he blames himself."

I shrugged. "I dinna know. Hmm... twenty years."

"It makes you wonder. The star we're going to will likely stay much as it is for twenty billion years. We don't die of natural causes any more. So he may well be blaming himself twenty billion years from now."

"Aye, he might. If he dinna fall off a horse himself." I smiled

Emma laughed slightly and moved away from me. I missed her touch, but at the same time felt relieved. "The universe, I think, needs some stable people in it. Those that don't fall off horses."

"Aye."

"I enjoyed this, Dr. Macready... Bruce. We should talk again some time." She stood up.

"It's been a good conversation, yes." I stood up. There was no walking her to the portal as it was only a meter or so from us. So she simply walked out. The portal closed behind her, and I sat back on my couch. Two minutes ago a real woman had been sitting next to me ready for anything as far as I could tell and I had not as much as put my arm around her. Sadly, such was typical of my history to that time, if the truth be known.

I finished my drink and noted that we'd done in a quarter of a liter. With several years to go, I'd need to be a bit more parsimonious from here on.

••∞••

The next day, with a few technical modifications, Dagger and Davra's plan was adopted and the *Admiral* sent it to the system. It would be a minimum of several, well, exactly 3.2184 years, ship time, before confirmation of its implementation could reach us, and we'd be but a wee bit under half a light year out from Epsilon Eridani, and into deceleration by then.

Naught more to do, but we were to remain up and about long enough for our bodies to repair whatever minor damage had occurred during our last round of cold sleep. I had several more conversations with Emma, all in public places. I felt awkward and the contacts grew less and less. Meanwhile, I learned how to "touch the net," to ask for information and send messages to people. It was not telepathy—no group mind or anything like that; it was much more like using a wrist comp without having to raise your arm to look at it or speak to it.

The morning before we were to return to our long sleep, I ran into Weaver at the canteen. I'd come to like him. He had the air of the American cowboy with his no-nonsense attitude and could set you right at ease without losing his dignity of command.

"Morning, Macready. This your work area?" He said that with a grin on his face the likes of which put you in mind of a brilliant morning sun chasing the mists away from the bay at Portree, that or twenty year Talisker.

"Och, I'm here a lot. But, in a way, as an historian I ken that it is *my* work area."

I did not add that sitting alone in my stateroom reminded me too much of how I'd flubbed my opportunity with Emma.

"You look like you had a descent sleep last night, Weaver." I could not call him G. P. as long as he kept calling me "Macready."

Weaver hunkered over the coffee thermos thoughtfully then poured a cup of coffee. He straightened and raised up a seat next to mine. "I don't usually talk about my private life much, professor, especially to someone with that recorder-like brain you got in your noggin."

"I dinna mean to pry. Just you seemed happily contented. She's a bonny lass. Jill, is it?"

He shook his head and smiled. "It's been a long time, Macready. Felt real good."

Back in my stateroom, I poured myself a finger of Talisker. Then I edited and filed my writings, taking me well into the evening—best do it now before cold sleep messed with me.

Done, I poured one more shot and secured the bottle with some other things I'd rather pack myself than leave to our robotic minions. I used that shot to wash down the pill that insured that I would not wake prematurely. Homesick already, I pulled up a view of the wood near Broadford, pulled the sheet up over my shoulders and waited for my eyelids to drop. Everything, no doubt, will soon have sorted itself and be back on track, so this interlude could easily prove the most interesting piece of the whole history and I counted myself fortunate to have lived it. The next time I opened my eyes, I thought, I'd be in my quarters in the habitat being built in orbit around Epsilon Eridani, reporting on the private and professional lives of the researchers as the robots finished their business of making and launching the impactor.

It did not exactly happen that way.

CHAPTER 3

Aboard the *Admiral Byrd*
Epsilon Eridani system
20 November, 2272

Consciousness dawned and I started to think about where I was.

Our trip to Epsilon Eridani would be over and I should be in some kind of house or apartment in the great rugby-ball-shaped habitat the robots had been building for us, along with a hundred other freshly thawed people.

Sounds penetrated my awareness, mainly a barely perceptible low thrum not unlike that of the *Admiral Byrd*. Every second or so, I heard a distant, hollow thump—a construction device of some sort, I thought. I was not entirely motionless but the accelerations were slight. Had I not been on a mattress, I doubt I'd have felt anything.

I opened my eyes; the light level was quite low, but enough for me to see that I was still in my stateroom aboard the *Admiral Byrd*. My first thought was that something more had gone wrong.

"*Admiral?* Why am I not in the habitat? Haven't we made it to Epsilon Eridani?"

"Dr. Macready, we are indeed in the Epsilon Eridani system. Unfortunately, the habitat is not ready yet. Priority needed to be given to array construction and the drivers needed to decelerate this starship."

"Are we under way? I feel a very slight jostling."

"Plasma clouds from debris are being vaporized by our lasers. These still retain their momentum the deceleration shock of which is absorbed by our magnetic fields and their current loops, which pass it onto the general structure as a significantly broadened and attenuated shock wave, sensible nevertheless."

"You mean to say we're being hit by something big enough to move the whole ship every second?"

"Essentially. Anything that hits us will move us a slight amount. Your threshold for sensing acceleration appears to be about 3 microgravities."

"There's a fair amount of debris then?"

"Much more than anticipated. Work on the habitat had to be suspended."

"I'd like to have been awake and informed earlier."

"Captain Lee decided to not waken anyone. Dr. Weaver made an exception for you due to your arrangement with the project management. That is why you've been wakened now. We have just taken up station behind the unfinished habitat and the project staff will be meeting for lunch in the Sphere Two drawing room in an hour. You are invited."

"Well, I accept the invitation! Meanwhile let's see what's out there. Let's see this unfinished habitat."

The *Admiral* put its image on my wall screen.

I saw a glowing Medusa—a black disk surrounded by curling wavy streams of light. It took me a few seconds to register what I saw with what I knew.

"We're in the shadow of this habitat?"

"Yes. The outward end of the shell has been covered; that is the black disk; I can amplify it if you like but it is smooth and featureless at this magnification."

"Never mind. All those streams..."

"Comets. There are about 973 of them in your field of view."

"They're all heading right into the star?"

"That is mostly perspective," the *Admiral* answered. "Only 311 have perihelia within the photosphere. All but 15 of those are actually ammonia saturated slag balls from our mining operations."

The *Admiral's* comments notwithstanding, I was in awe of this picture, of all this cosmic debris falling toward the star, and feeling not a little uneasy.

●●∞●●

I headed to Sphere Two a little early hoping to speak to Weaver first; to thank him for waking me, but also to diplomatically express my concern for being so late about it. I announced myself to Weaver's portal and it slid open. The stateroom was one of the backups for the captain's quarters and large for a ship—a suite, actually, with a separate bedroom and a small living room. The walls held scenes of plains and horses from the American West, but there was hardly any other decoration. He was rarely there, so why bother to decorate, I surmised.

Then I spotted a pot of purple and white flowers on a shelf with a grow light overhead.

Weaver strode in from the bedroom, shook my hand, and waved at the flowers offhandedly.

"Never seen flowers in an expedition commander's quarters before?"

"Aye," I smiled at him. "But that's more from not being in an expedition commander's quarters before as from not seeing flowers in one. From Davra, is it?"

It was Weaver's turn to smile. "Jill Davenport brought it in; calls it a 'lady's slipper.' Damn plants have been living in her botany lab ever since we left Earth—she's determined we remember where we come from." He shook his head. "Meeting's in fifteen minutes. What'cha got?"

"I've been, well, a wee bit out of the loop so I wanted to go over the master plan before we go in. Now, I've scanned Davra's notes on the system feedback loops and I wanted to fit it into the big picture from your perspective."

Weaver waved me to seat and ordered coffee from his replicator. He turned back at me. "Coffee?"

"Tea. Earl Grey with a bit of cream and sugar, if it wouldn't be a bother. I prefer to lighten with cream as it doesn't dilute the tea as much."

I liked Weaver's no-nonsense stance; another old American west trait. He might affect some rustic crudeness, but he could cut to the chase faster than Broadford's chancellor did, which was saying something, indeed.

He related that, as our rate of construction had gone up, so had the rate of solar storms and impacts, leaving what should have been a marginal gain as yet a net loss.

"We're about three months behind where we should be, even with the habitat construction delayed. I reckon it's manageable, but it's worrisome." He had the face of one who didn't need such worries.

"The research crew stays frozen then?" I asked.

"Until that habitat is ready, we've got nowhere to bunk 'em."

"Is there nobody in there with expertise that we might use, say, in a brainstorming session?"

Weaver looked me in the eye. "I've got what I think are the best experts on this already. The group is about the right size—I don't want too many cooks. And I definitely don't want any more politics. I also, Dr. Macready, do not want there to be anything to *encourage* the politics I've already got. Savvy?"

That last may have been an attempt at French, but no matter, I could read the context. "I think I've been very careful not to take sides, G. P."

He pursed his lips and nodded. "Time," he said.

We went into the meeting, which went much like the first. About midway through, Davra pointed out that the collector array didn't really have to be in the plane of the ecliptic where most of the junk was.

Emma countered that non-ecliptic orbits would be perturbed into uselessness.

"Wait a minute," Dagger said. "Just how long would it take to perturb them into uselessness? Say, if we went to fifteen degrees, or, well, whatever the optimum is."

Emma blushed and held up a hand to consult her celestial mechanics simulators.

"If we put the node about 135 degrees from the impact center, we'll get a couple of millennia of line of sight at..."

"Sounds good enough for me." Dagger said. "Unless you're planning on hanging around..."

We all kind of laughed. The *Admiral* figured a new array orbital inclination for minimum impact flux. We'd start loading the new orbit immediately, and move existing arrays gradually, using their beam drivers as reaction engines with dumb pellets made of slag as reaction mass.

••∞••

About a week after the meeting, Weaver took me aside.

"We have a break in the solar weather coming up and Dagger's going to take a look-see at the habitat tomorrow, hoping to get some ideas to speed up construction. You up for the trip?"

All my life, I had been oriented toward processing information, not going out and doing things. I'd not a thought about going off the ship, but the idea did arouse a bit of curiosity in me, and would probably intrigue my readers.

"Huh? I dinna see why not."

Weaver nodded with a smile. "You two might find a thing or two to chat about on the way."

The thing or two being Davra and Emma, I surmised. My last couple of 'dates' with Emma had gone much like the first; however, as neither of us were in the habit of disclosing our private lives, the others had assumed things were a bit more exciting than they in fact were.

"We might at that," I answered with a shrug.

Weaver grinned and clapped me on the back. "Let's mosey."

••∞••

When not underway, the *Admiral Byrd* extends a tube with multiple docking collars toward its spin center from the upper torus. I met Dagger at the lift leading up through one of the upper torus support spars.

"So, Bruce, Emma treating you all right?" He looked at me as if testing to see my reaction.

I was duly taken aback. "Well, she's a wonderful person and I've indeed learned a lot from her. As a matter of fact, she thought we might watch a big slagheap from the prograde feed path hit Epsilon Eridani today. She thinks the carbon might make a temporary dim patch."

"Like a star spot? The only star spots I know of come from huge magnetic fields, so I don't..." Dagger held up a hand; the lift had arrived. We got on it and announced our destination.

Dagger turned to me again. "Now, Bruce, you gotta keep in mind that this is a relationship with a woman, and there are some things that, well, naturally go along with that. Can't run away from that. Body won't let you."

"Aye... Well, mine has never been all that needy, if ye ken. Anyway, I'll admit to be hoping for a wee bit more experience in that area now that every female I see isn't out of bounds for one reason or another."

Dagger slapped his leg and guffawed out loud. "We're here. Let's check this bugger out and I'll tell you all about it."

I found that a bit rude at the time, but he was an American, after all.

The runabouts were stored in the long hollow cones and were winched up to the center and attached themselves to the docking port. A runabout is, essentially, a rectangle of equipment with a clear half cylinder with rounded ends stuck over one side. To me, it looked like half a transparent sausage lying on a small version of Clarke's rectangular monoliths.

A person came in through a lock in the bottom center of the rectangular part and entered the transparent half-sausage. There were ten pairs of seats in this cabin with an aisle down the middle. The ends were quarter-sphere domes. We floated in through the lock and used hand holds to propel ourselves to the front where we strapped ourselves in. Despite complete automation, Dagger looked over the boards very carefully.

"Okay, let's go," he said at length. The runabout detached itself, rotated and jetted out toward the habitat with the slightest of acceleration.

Satisfied with our progress, he fixed his eyes on mine with a big grin on his face. "So really, you doing okay with Emma?"

I shivered at his crudeness but resolved to not play the tyro. "Aye and then not aye. She's a wonderful person, but matches my reserve all too well, if ye ken."

To my surprise, he nodded quietly and sat for a moment thinking. At last he looked at me, dead in the eye again, and said, "So you both wait 'till hell freezes over before either of you makes a first move. I kinda figured something like that. So throw a line in another pond."

I could not bring myself to answer and left the moment to silence.

As the runabout approached the mammoth incomplete habitat, I felt like a fledgling leaving the nest for its first trial flight. Yes, I'd ridden in the runabout out to the starship from the station—it seemed like a million years ago now, and that had been exciting enough. But that was really a glorified taxi ride. Now here I was in an alien star system with but a handful of other people heading out to look at the results of a problem for which no one had the measure. My heart beat faster.

"Bruce?"

"Uh... Wee bit new to this is all. Ye were saying."

"Just if it's not gonna work, it's not gonna work. Hedge your bets. Spend time with someone else."

Dagger was persistent. I had to give him that.

"Och! That would seem disloyal at this point."

"Women, they understand that kind of thing. Sometimes I think that's about all they do understand. Look at this mess we're in. Emma did the astronomy and Davra did the robotics."

"I'll not be traveling that road with ye, Dagger," I said, shocked. "There were many, many other eyes on those plans and most of them men, I'd think."

"But not since we started having problems. Things haven't gotten better, they've gotten worse. I don't think either of them have the big picture. They try to deal with it by intuition, and whatever it is, it's outside their intuition's box."

"Aye, there may something to that. Not that anyone else seems to know either, mind you. I thought of suggesting to our chief that he might be getting a wee bit more help on this, and he nearly bit my bloody head off, so to speak."

"Probably because I suggested the same thing. G. P. is a bit touchy when it comes to critiquing his leadership."

A huge comet tail came into view just before we came around the edge of the habitat. I couldn't see the coma—indeed, it may have already hit the star. A pebble splashing in the sea, I thought, contemplating the relative nature of violence in the Universe.

We came around the edge of the habitat. A slice of Epsilon Eridani came into view. In a blink, stars and comets vanished as my eyes adapted. Our future home was not solid, but the composite sheathing—basalt fiber in a polymer hydrocarbon matrix—had given way to the unfinished latticework of aluminum beams. Our shuttle glided around this smooth outside shell and finally gave us a clear shot of the inside.

"Take us across the diameter, for a first look," Dagger told the runabout. "Then we'll fly back along the surface that's been built so far. Align our roll axis to the habitat-sun line."

The runabout performed the last of these maneuvers first, then canceled what remained of our sunward velocity, leaving us nose first to see a "full" habitat. A topography of sorts had begun to emerge. You could tell where a large lake was going to be. I could see the sculpting of the far end—what would become tree and grass covered highlands sloping down to the higher gravity lowlands of its equator.

"Tell me, Bruce, did you bring one of those kilts with you?"

"No, but it would be easy enough to replicate; there are many patterns on file. Getting a bit warm?" The star on one side and the reflection from several square kilometers of unfinished habitat on the other were warming the insides of our transparent bubble rather rapidly.

"Yes, a little. The fans will kick on in a bit. About the kilts, I've always been meaning to ask a Scot..."

I laughed. "In my case, generally a well-used pair of walking shorts, as I'm not so fond of embarrassing accidents."

Dagger laughed. "Well, you could make an exception for Davra."

Now *that* was the nature of the man.

I coughed politely. "I'd need to know her a wee bit better."

"She hasn't made a move on you yet?" Dagger seemed astounded

"No. I'm not very tall, my voice is a bit high, and I tend to lecture, so it's no surprise."

"Hmm. She has a purpose in life and she knows what it is."

"She's an excellent roboticist."

Dagger shrugged. "That too."

"Emma seems more my type."

Dagger laughed. "Coward! Emma makes love like she writes a scientific paper. Everything precise and in its place and a soft little squeal if she gets something out of it. I asked her once what would happen if she let go. She said, and I think she meant it, that she *was* letting go."

"You've been intimate with Emma? I dinna..."

As it so often happens, when you discuss someone, they pop up. The ship's attention tone sounded again and there she was on the console screen. She could not have heard our discussion, I had to remind myself, but my guilt must have been written all over my face!

"You look as if you've swallowed a canary, Bruce."

"Good day, Emma," I said.

Dagger waved at the video pickup.

"The habitat looks an awesome sight from where you are," Emma said. "Pity we haven't finished the other half."

When finished, the habitat would be the same shape as the Campbell space colony but a tenth the radius and a hundredth the living area. Still, it would provide a decent living space once the rest of the passengers were defrosted. While our crew's work would be done in a few years, the people who'd come to study the star system might remain here for decades, perhaps permanently. The full kilometer from the center to the empty half-finished bed of the equatorial pond was a very impressive sight.

"Golf," Dagger said. "I'm looking forward to making some wings to scope out a golf course. Maybe have the robots make me a little split-level on a riverbank. You should see the slobber marks all over the canopy. Getting hard to see," Dagger told her.

"You'll find serviettes in the mess module. Now, there's a major new magnetic disturbance rotating into view on Epsilon Eridani's equator. No clue as to where it came from, but it's going to move the particle stream from the last major flare in our direction, with the particle flux hitting in about two hours. It might be more than the runabout can handle, so Captain Lee wants you both back at the ship before then."

"Uh, right." Dagger said. "Tell her we both plan to be back aboard and in our beds by then. Unless, of course she prefers it some other way…"

"Message received, Emma," I said. "Thank you."

"Cheerio."

"Let's hang out here a while," Dagger said. "I want to pick out a place for my little mansion."

"Deceleration in three seconds," the AI responded. "Two, one…"

A soft '*thonk*' and a lean to the side announced the maneuver.

"We'll pass somewhat to the side of the geometric center of the habitat," Dagger said. "The concave inside of this half-finished egg focuses heat and light there."

As I sat composing descriptions to go with the video files, I was conscious of the noise of the runabout's air circulation fans. The habitat reminded me of a cleaned-out eggshell in an eggcup, almost that white, with the ragged latticework of the equator serving as the rough edge of such a shell. "Impressive bunch of real estate," Dagger said.

"Aye, that it is, Dagger, that it is. What?" A sudden *'snap'* got my attention.

With no more warning than that, miniature lightning bolts began to jump from place to place across the control panel, between seat frames, and even off my fingers toward anything remotely conducting.

"What the hell?" Dagger said.

"Emma?" I called.

No sound.

Dagger gave me a quick look that said trouble. "Shuttle, what's our status?"

The AI said nothing. I looked over at the instrumentation console. It was as dark and bleak as a November morning fog on Skye.

"I think we're looking at a real power loss here," Dagger said in measured, professional tones that did nothing to disguise the tension in his voice.

"Ouch!"

I felt a surge up my spine. Electricity or fear, I knew not.

Gradually, the fireworks subsided to be replaced by dead silence.

"Have we been hit?" I asked

Dagger shook his head. "Didn't feel anything like that."

"They'll miss us, right?"

I could see Dagger's face reflected off the canopy. He was scanning the boards, looking for anything.

"Yeah, they should. If they're okay themselves. Looks like a complete electrical failure here."

"What does that give us?" I asked quietly.

"Well," Dagger scratched his head. "The good news is we're alive with enough breathable cabin oxygen for 30 minutes or so. The bad news is, we can't hang here. Notice it getting hotter? Reflection from the habitat and Epsilon Eridani, I'd say. Getting insolation from both sides."

Our shuttle had begun to tumble. "Can we get away?"

"Maybe. Let's get our emergency suits on. They've got a cooling system that's body-heat driven, a marvel of fluidics."

I found the cabinet—marked Emergency in big red letters—pulled the panel away and grabbed the suits. "Helmets?" I asked.

"Not yet, but let's keep them handy. Gotta move this thing somehow."

"Fluidics...Dagger, if I remember properly, there are valves..."

"Yeah, of course." Dagger dove for a panel in the floor. "Can you get the universal wrench from the tool kit?"

I found it and gave it to him. He squeezed himself under the floor. In a few minutes, punctuated by groans and expletives, he bellowed, "Hold on to something!"

I grabbed a seat. "Holding."

There was a kind of boom and we jerked up. I almost fell.

"I think I've found the plus-Z peroxide feed. Now, what you'll need to do is look straight up and tell me when the edge of the habitat is overhead."

"What part?" I asked.

"Any part!" he yelled back.

"Aye, I hear you." I looked up. It seemed to take forever but eventually our slow rotation precessed to the point where the unfinished edge of the habitat was overhead.

"I've got an edge overhead now," I said.

"Hang on."

I did so, and this time there was a sustained push for maybe two seconds.

"What's happening?" he asked.

It was hard to tell how much movement we got from it by eye; but I did notice something. "We're spinning faster and it's getting a bit cooler," I said. "I'd say we're off dead center, so to speak."

Dagger groaned.

"Well, I dinna think it was that bad."

"No, damn it, not you. I've lost the wrench."

"Och! Well, at least we are moving. They'll come get us for sure."

"I'm not so sure. The flare..."

"You think the flare did this?"

"Maybe... lots of magnetic fields and stuff. How close are we to the habitat wall?"

We had moved noticeably. It was very hard to judge by eye, but it seemed as though we were twice as close to the side toward which we were moving as the other side. "Maybe 700 meters and closing," I responded.

Dagger emerged from the hole in the floor. "Can't find it. How are we doing?"

"Maybe 600 meters, now. Done in a about a minute," I said. "About a hundred meters a minute. We should be there in about six minutes."

Dagger and I watched the habitat get closer, and drift slightly off to the right, "I don't think we're going to hit it, Doc."

"Well, a bit of good news!"

"That's not good news. Without power, this runabout is a death trap. If someone doesn't rescue us, we've gotta get some mass between us and that particle storm before it gets here." He pointed at the habitat. "That mass."

Epsilon Eridani rotated into view. It was covered with ominous spots. The runabout air was beginning to smell sweaty and stale—the canopy was large, but would contain only so much oxygen. I thought about all the years I'd spent at Broadford and the inexplicable humor of a cosmos that might end me so far from the Isle of Skye.

"How are we bloody going to get there?"

Dagger looked at me like a man possessed. "We'll have to jump for it. Grab your helmet."

It looked a bit chancy, but it was clearly the only choice, and one that was fast approaching. We got our helmets on and began to check each other, as the manual called for.

"Bet this is as fast as you've ever had to do this," Dagger said as I inspected the neck seal behind his head."

"Easily, but that would be unfair."

"How so?"

"Well, laddie, this would have to be the fastest time for reason of it being the only time."

Dagger sounded for a moment like he was choking, so much so that my eyes went to his air hoses with concern.

"Doc, there's no orange showing on the seal, is there?"

"None at all. I did read the manual."

"That's a good thing... a good thing. Well, Doc, do you happen to remember where the manual canopy bleed is?"

I thought for a moment, calling forth a fuzzy image of the schematics in my mind; but I could not see it so clearly. My memory of text has always been far superior to my memory of images.

"Sorry, I cannot. Why don't we just go out the lock?"

"It needs power, Bruce."

"Oh." Of course it did. "Uh, how *are* we going to get out?"

"There's a canopy door for use inside the habitat. It opens in, so we've gotta let the air out first; otherwise we'll never be able to pull it open against the pressure."

"Oh."

Our rotation brought us around to a close up view of the edge of the habitat.

"Geez we're almost there." Dagger flipped upside down and started working on the base of one of the runabout's chairs."

"Dagger..." I had no idea of what he was doing, and we had to get out of here in a couple of minutes or be fried by the particle storm. Some anxiety must have slipped into my voice.

"Stifle it, Bruce and grab this chair so it doesn't float away."

Having no idea what he intended, I did so. Then, the chair came free and he flipped back feet-to-the-floor."

"Now hold onto me. Use my backpack harness."

I grabbed it with one hand and a still-attached chair with the other.

Dagger grabbed the backrest of the chair with both hands. With a mighty heave, he swung its titanium legs into the canopy. There was a satisfying crack. He did this again and a small crater appeared in the transparent cover. Two more swings and there was a slight pop and a noise like a balloon deflating. Necessity is indeed the mother of invention.

We were almost even with the girders of the habitat.

"Come on, give me a hand with the door." Dagger said, his voice noticeably fainter.

We both pulled the hatch in as hard as we could. Finally it moved. Air rushed past me from the shuttle. We pulled harder and it swung open. The remaining air blew out with a ghastly whoosh as I hung on for dear life. It was then I saw we were no longer racing past the habitat, but just drifting by.

Our emergency suits had kits with dispensers of what looked like brilliant orange cloth measuring tape. Dagger pulled a tape from his suit and attached it to mine.

"If one of us catches on, we both do. Get ready."

Our rotation brought the habitat's bare frame in front of the hatch.

Dagger pointed to a girder. He mouthed, "Jump!" Then he pushed me out the door and I glided to the girder. Dagger jumped a bit later, before the tether between us went taut.

Terrified, all I could do was reach out and hope to find a grab-hold. It took forever—we were further away and the structure was bigger than it had first seemed. I closed in on a girder, finally saw a crosspiece come within reach, and grabbed. My feet swung to the frame. I gasped with relief, then looked back.

Dagger floated toward me, arms stretched out waiting for a girder, but none came within reach. Then the tether pulled taut and he swung onto my girder, feet first, like he'd been born to it.

Dagger tethered us both to the girder, then he pointed at our runabout tumbling away into space. The escaping air and our jumps had propelled it away from the habitat at right angles to its original motion, that is, slanting away off to our right. There, save for some very good luck, went I! We allowed ourselves a minute to catch a breath.

Dagger touched his helmet to mine. "Radios don't work. Life support's on fluidic backup, so take it easy—it's just a steady cycle. Won't respond to greater demand. First time EVA?"

"Aye."

"Well, best that it's us rather than the girls. Kinda hard to imagine Emma coping with that, isn't it?"

"Oh I dinna know, Dagger. Wreck the boat and get themselves stranded on a bunch of bare girders waiting to be fried by a particle storm? Och, that I suppose they might have done."

Dagger guffawed so hard his helmet came away from mine, and I was treated to what looked a silent movie of a man in convulsions. Finally he calmed down and looked around.

I did as well. Our only immediate protection was the junction of two girders—maybe a square meter of shadow space. The silence was deafening, and through the silence came a feeling, a fast beating of my heart. It pounded. At least I'm alive, I thought.

But for how long? We'd had two hours until the particle storm was due to hit, but no telling how much of that was gone with the cron on my wrist inside the suit, and the suit's electronics out.

We were probably going to die anyway, I realized. I was going to miss out on half of the biggest adventure of my life. And then where would I be? The chronicle would never be finished. It was the one thing I'd wanted—a book of my own about something really important. With a bit of time to think, I'd quickly gone from relief, to profound regret.

Dagger touched helmets again.

"Gotta get in the shadow... should be able to see the starship... only a couple of kilometers."

"How?"

"Leapfrog. I'll skim on ahead and out on the tether. You stop me and I should swing down to the surface. I'll tie down there, then you release and jump out. The line will swing you back in an arc and you'll land ahead of me—be sure to land feet first. Then you tie down and I'll do the same thing."

"Aye, I understand. Any idea of the time?"

"Thirty minutes to the particle storm arrival, maybe. Didn't think to take my cron off before I put the gloves on. Well, I'm off. I'll pull on the line a couple of times when I'm ready for you."

I watched carefully as he jumped over the unfinished habitat latticework toward the portion that was solid and might provide more protection. After some time, the line went taut and he swung down to the surface.

Then the line jerked twice. My turn. I found I could grab an edge of the beam with each hand and assume a kind of squatting position. Then I just let go and stood up; that got me going as fast as I wanted. The tether pulled taut in a second or two and I swung forward over Dagger and down toward the habitat. With some doing, I was able to get my feet "under" me again.

As I descended, I realized I would miss anything solid and "land" in a gap between the beams. Judging the matter as best as I could, I pulled on the tether tape to bring me down a little closer to Dagger, where there was a solid girder. I missed with my feet, but was able to grab it with my hand as it went by. Whew!

I tied down, pulled the line twice. Dagger made his jump, with much the same results as the first, except that he vanished near the end of his swing—we'd reached the shadow of the habitat.

I took another jump, swung down, and went blind as I entered the shadow before my eyes had adapted. I bounced in the dark and I floated out, helpless. Then Dagger reeled me in.

We touched helmets. "Gotta absorb the impact with your legs. Shit, pull the protective covers off the geckro patches on your boots!" Dagger said, showing me the gray circles on the bottom of his space boots. Normally the geckro patches—areas of artificial nanofibers that cling to things in space like the microscopic hairs on gecko feet—are protected by special plastic covers so the boots don't stick to everything.

"Och. I dinna think of it." I quickly reached down and pulled them off. Memory is a tricky thing. There's a fine difference between knowing something, and thinking of it under pressure in unusual circumstances.

"Yeah. We're on the completed part of the habitat shell, now. There should be a line of handholds every ten meters," Dagger said. "Latitude and longitude—it's a standard safety feature on the outsides of these things."

Latitude and longitude, I realized, referred to the habitat's outer surface. The "north pole" would be the completed end of the half-egg shape, with longitude lines running from it, and latitude lines at right angles to those. I looked around but was unable to spot anything.

"Bloody hard to spot. They should have lights."

"They do," Dagger said. "But there's no power yet. Where the devil..." Dagger started. "Bruce, move your foot."

I did so, and there, right under it, was a hand-sized depression with a small bar running across its diameter.

Using the handholds as tether attach points, we were able to continue our journey. Soon, we saw the starship rise over our tiny horizon. As the rising was due to *our* motion and not its, this event was not that much of a comfort.

"I'm exhausted," Dagger said. "Need to rest."

"Right." When exercising, the CO_2 built up faster than our self-powered life back-up support systems could handle.

After a couple of minutes, Dagger said, "Look, I got an idea. We take a mylar blanket from the emergency kit, jump out into the sunlight, and use the shiny side to reflect a bright spot down on the habitat. The *Admiral* should see it moving around and tell someone."

"If it's still functioning." I was in a gloomy mood. "And if the someone doing the reflecting doesn't get fried when the particle storm gets here."

"Hell, Bruce. Sometimes you gotta take a chance. Think of it like a date. You make a move, and maybe you get slapped and maybe you get laid. But you sure as hell don't get laid if you don't make a move, do you?"

"Can ye lay off the sex jokes and put your full mind on the problem at hand?" I said in momentary irritation. Also, he was hitting a little too close to where I lived.

I pulled my helmet away before he replied, fumbled the kit open, pulled out the blanket and flattened it. I could see stars in the reflection of the shiny side. I touched helmets again.

"It should work. Maybe if we both jump, put our boots together and stretch it between us?"

"Yeah. Let's do it."

We tethered ourselves to a handhold and gave it a try. It seemed to go well enough; we didn't feel like we got fried and a bright spot of light danced around on the shadow side of the habitat. Then we pulled ourselves back down to wait.

I touched helmets. "I'm sorry, Dagger, but my sense of humor must be suffering from a wee lack of oxygen."

"You're sorry? Who am I kidding! Can't help it, though. It's how I get rid of tension. Sometime you've gotta either laugh or cry."

"Aye, or commune a bit with the bottle," I allowed.

"That too. Or sex. Sex works. Let's face it, there's nothing like sex after a hard day at the office."

"How would I know?" I asked.

"I thought you and Emma..."

"Och, it's never *got* to that stage."

The way we had to keep our helmets together to talk kept me from seeing his face, but I could imagine his shock at this revelation of mine.

"Let me see if I understand. It's never got that far with Emma, or not ever?"

"Alas, not ever. I'd be quite willing under the proper circumstances, I assure you."

"In a century and a half?" he asked, wonder in his voice.

"It's just that every woman I met was a student or a married professor or a colleague with whom I would not want to embarrass myself, or too dull to interest me, or... och, I don't know. Look, Emma may need a little more effort than I'm ready for. Anyway, there is no hurry, these days."

"She's a bit of a cold fish at times—just needs some leadership. But Davra now. She takes charge, more than even I can handle sometimes. Of course, maybe that's her real purpose."

I winced at his rough assessment. "Aye, with the robots and AIs taking care of themselves, she wouldn't really have that much else to do."

"You should give her a try."

I winced again, this time for Davra. "Och, I'd not be her type, I assure you—sophisticated things beyond my imaginings." I could adore her from afar, I realized, but the thought of actually having to contend with her experience might be an exercise in humiliation.

"I have some video files," Dagger offered. "Training material. I dated this girl once who starred in..."

"I'll pass, thank you. Look at these stars, now. I've never quite seen a sky like this." My eyes had fully adapted to the dark, and the Milky Way was right across my field of view, but much brighter, I thought, than I'd ever seen on Earth. It was repeatedly crossed by comet tails every bit as bright as it was. Some were long and thin, some double, some fans of gold light.

"Do you see Scorpius and Antares? Low, toward the hull?" Dagger asked.

It was difficult as there were too many bright stars to easily see the asterism, but I finally located it. "Aye. But there seem to be more bright stars in Libra."

"Yeah. One of them is Alpha Centauri, the yellow-white one. Nothing much brighter around it. Now look north of that, over east of Arcturus. See a pair of yellow stars."

I looked north and found brilliant orange Arcturus, though it's ice-cream-cone-shaped asterism seemed to be a bit scrunched. A spread hand's width to its left were a pair of golden stars, maybe three or four degrees apart. "Aye..."

"The upper right one is Sol."

Somewhere, orbiting that tiny speck of light was a far tinier speck called Earth, and on that a yet far tinier speck called Skye. The suit was keeping me comfortable, but I shivered anyway.

"We're a long, long way from home," I said after a bit, unable to come up with anything more profound. "What do we e'en think we're doing out here? It's humbling."

"Yeah, you're right. Even wall screens don't do it justice. Not enough field of view. God, look at all the comets. And all the space junk; half the stars in the sky look like they're moving, like we're near some kind of airport. Speaking of which, LAX is a great place..."

I shuddered and broke contact. Those weren't airplanes moving at a few hundred meters per second; each slowly moving point of light was the size of a mountain or larger and moving hundreds of times as fast. We were waiting for a radiation storm to hit us in a sky full of would-be dinosaur killers and Dagger wanted to talk about sex. I shook my head. It was probably the most bizarre moment of my life.

One of the stars seemed to be getting bigger, or brighter. I bumped Dagger's elbow and pointed at it. We touched helmets again.

"I see. It's not moving. Just getting closer," he said.

"That means it's going to hit us, doesn't it?"

"Yeah. It's coming right for us."

We watched as it got brighter and brighter, closer and closer.

"Too bad about the habitat. Too bad about everything," Dagger whispered.

"We could jump."

He grunted. "No. Get flat as you can and hang on. Half the chance of shrapnel."

I grabbed a handhold and watched in silence as the oncoming object suddenly vanished into the shadow of the habitat. My eyes adjusted and I thought I could make out its black shadow against a comet's tail. Is this how it would end? I thought bitterly. Would our hopes be dashed by a futile spot in the sky?

Then brilliant light suddenly exploded around us. I braced for the shock.

Dagger's helmet bumped mine. "Hang on, Doc, it's a searchlight!"

"They've come for us then?" My eyes adjusted and I could see the dark shape of the space vehicle with Davra's face lit by light from the controls. She was so beautiful. In that moment, life seemed wonderful and Davra particularly so.

Positioning jets spit from the side of the little craft as it slowed, swung around, and gently drifted down to us.

Dagger bumped my helmet, laughing with relief. "Let's go. Our limo has arrived!"

We stood up just as the airlock in the bottom of the little runabout opened up. Emma, bless her, motioned us to jump in and we did. Never had a wee bit of ship's noise sounded so good.

Topside, we pulled our helmets off. Emma's face could have been the model for the Mona Lisa. She motioned us toward the seats.

"You have the most beautiful face I've seen in the last three hours!" Dagger said, grabbing her for a big kiss. "I can't believe we're alive!"

"Emma, Davra, what the bloody hell happened?" I asked.

Davra turned around and shook her head. "We got a major electromagnetic pulse from the flare—collapsing filaments—and the half-finished habitat acted like a parabolic mirror. Every wavelength over a centimeter came right back at you, several million times stronger."

"We weren't in the exact center!"

"But neither was the pulse from the center of Epsilon Eridani's disk! Probably ten thousand kilometers above the left limb. We'll go over it all later, but first we've got to hurry back to the ship before the particle radiation storm hits."

"Buckle up," Davra said. "*Admiral*, get us out of here!"

I grabbed seat arm and pulled myself in just in time. The shuttle reacted as if an unseen hand had grabbed us and thrown us at the starship. The *Admiral* began to grow larger ahead of us.

"Uh, Davra, Emma, thanks," I shouted over the jet roar.

Davra turned and gave me a smile that would take the mist off a moor, but there was a bit of cat-that-caught the canary to it. "Sure, Bruce. A piece of cake! You guys gave us a bit of excitement out there!"

"The particle flux has arrived and is increasing," the *Admiral* told us. "Ten millisieverts a second now, with lethal levels predicted in approximately seven minutes."

"Is this all the faster she can go?" Dagger muttered. "Where's a fast woman when I need one?"

No one laughed or said anything. We kept looking at our wrist comps as the *Admiral* grew from a toy to a full-sized spaceship.

A hundred millisieverts a second. Somewhere I remembered that, even with our genetic mods for radiation tolerance, a prompt dose of 50 sieverts was fatal. I could take about a minute of this. But the ship filled the sky. About 600 meters from the ship's center, the *Admiral* announced, "Down to two millisieverts a second."

"Home free, pretty much." Davra said. "We're within the ship's magnetic field. But it would be better to get down to the spheres where we're behind some water."

The runabout glided neatly onto the docking attachment with a satisfying clank. Air whooshed into the airlock.

We were greeted by G. P. Weaver and a very tall, oriental woman with dramatically long hair, wearing a simple black jumpsuit. Her face seemed familiar, but that my European-trained eyes couldn't place her for certain.

"Welcome back, folks." Weaver said.

His voice sounded very good.

The woman asked how we were, seemed satisfied, then told us very gently we would not get many second chances out here. She looked at Weaver the way a disapproving parent would look at a child, shook her head and left. I'd thought she was the ship's physician until I'd gotten a clear look at the name tape on her jump suit. Despite nearly a decade of being no further from her than the length of a football field, that was the first time and only time I met Captain Lee Hyun Sil face to face.

"Let's get downstairs," Weaver said. "And check with the *Admiral*; you'll be on a med program."

Tension drained from me as we entered the Sphere Three park area. I turned to Emma. "You saw our light spot, then?"

She looked at Davra. They giggled.

"We had a better homing beacon," Emma said. "uh, 'cold fish,' I recall."

"'...wouldn't really have that much else to do...'" Davra added.

"'...just needs some leadership?'" Emma raised an eyebrow.

"'...likely into sophisticated things?'" Davra stuck out her tongue at me and wiggled it.

"Your suit receivers were blown," she added, "but the microphone preamps worked just fine."

••∞••

Meeting in the Sphere Three park the next day, we put the banter all behind us.

"We aren't achieving exponential growth," Weaver said. "Between an increasing impact rate and particle storm damage, we're barely achieving any growth at all."

Emma sighed. "Star weather, like all weather, is chaotic. In all likelihood, our best strategy may be simply to slog on and wait for it to get better."

Dagger shook his head. "And when will that be? The impactor should start on its way in less than two years and we'll need to have the array up to full power within a month of that."

Davra, for once entirely serious, nodded. "We try to optimize for one set of conditions, and the conditions change, with no rhyme or reason to it."

I laughed bitterly. "Aye, it's as if the whole system has consciously turned against us. More spots, flare damage up, cometary activity up, collisions of all sorts up. It's like trying to build in a sandstorm." That sounded a wee more spooky than I meant it to be, but it was all too easy from where I stood to see the opponent as conscious.

Weaver's face looked grim. "We've got to come up with something, folks. I'm counting on you—along with people on three other planets, not to mention the impact station."

I looked at him. This was leadership, aye. But where were the ideas going to come from? Everyone sat there silent.

Well, this was not so different from uncounted faculty meetings. I could at least get a ball rolling. "I'm no technical genius, but if you don't mind some input from an historian, there's an old engineering problem-solving technique called brainstorming. You sit around and throw out ideas, no matter how crazy. No criticism, just throw out ideas. One suggests another and things get a bit crazy and you record all of it. Then you display what you got, and you note the problems and maybe solutions to the problems. Those that have no solutions, you winnow out."

Silence. Och but this was very elementary stuff. I looked at Weaver— stared, really

"I reckon that sounds like a way to start," he said at last. "Let's try it."

"But everything reasonable has already been proposed, hasn't it?" Emma said, throwing up her hands.

I nodded agreement. "Aye, and if so, it's time we start looking at the unreasonable things, no? I'll start out. We seem to be fighting a hostile intelligence. Maybe we can communicate with it?"

Emma groaned.

Dagger laughed. "Can't critique yet, if I got the gist of the rules. Okay. Maybe Davra here is in cahoots with all the anti-black hole project people back on Earth and is secretly sabotaging the robots. We can her and then it gets better. We're going round robin on this? You're next, Davra."

She clenched her hands together in front of her and stared down, then took a deep breath. "We don't need the power right now. Maybe we can store everything in one protected place, then unfold it when we really need it. G. P.?"

Weaver seemed surprised at the notion that he would participate in the brainstorming session, but he smiled. "Haven't had to saddle that stallion for a while. Well, now. If we think there may be an optimum strategy outside our search area... something extreme... Maybe we don't make any more arrays at all, just grow array makers exponentially. Less area to worry about. Then we turn 'em loose all at once." He smiled again and shrugged his shoulders. "Emma?"

She gave a short laugh. "It's an engineering problem, really. I don't recall reading of any similar situations."

Everyone looked at her.

"Oh, very well. Impact damage goes as the square of velocity. So we could start over further out where the relative velocities are lower and the particle cloud is less dense. We'd use thin film reflectors to concentrate light and make up for the loss of insolation."

We went round and round in this way for an hour. I had trouble visualizing the problem, so I asked the *Admiral* for a view of the Epsilon Eridani system and the cloud of debris.

The *Admiral* portrayed the system on the dome ceiling.

"It's not a sphere, is it now? It looks more like a fat donut," I noted.

Emma sighed. "The donut is the debris cloud. Imagine a thin flat disk with Epsilon Eridani in the center, slicing through the donut the way one would slice a bagel. The disk is some 4 billion kilometers across, but only 40 million or so kilometers thick; that's because of the planet Loki's gravity. All the major planets are found in this disk. The asteroids, comets, and other debris form a torus—the donut-shaped cloud you see—around this disk. It gets less and less dense the further one gets from the disk."

"Pity we can't orbit the arrays over the poles." I said.

Emma groaned. "Basic astrodynamics. Sorry, Bruce. Critiquing, aren't I. But the project plan is for an equatorial ring, and even in a polar orbit, the arrays still must pass through the debris torus, and then there will be precession..."

"Okay, okay," Dagger said. "But they only have to pass through the debris cloud twice an orbit, right? Most of the time the array is out in the clear. That's better than being in the mess all the time, isn't it?"

We all looked at him.

"*Admiral?*" Weaver said with renewed interest.

"The problem is one of rates. Lowering the exposure lowers the rates, giving the robots a chance to catch up. We should be back into exponential growth in a few weeks. As far as visibility toward the impact station, we can tilt the array ring up to 37 degrees inclination and still give the beam drivers a clear shot at the impactor."

Everyone leaned forward as they threw out their ideas. Good, I thought, as the ideas flew across the grassy floor of the dome.

"Don't we want to critique the rest of the ideas?" Emma said. "If it's a good process, the process should be served."

I thought about enduring a critique of my hostile intelligence idea. "'Tis not always necessary, if ye hit on something that looks good right away," I offered.

Davra grinned at me. She'd caught the excitement of a potential solution. I winked back, happy to be noticed by her and relieved the team seemed be reinvigorated and pulling together.

Emma didn't react; she had that faraway look of one communing with the computer over her neural net. "Very well. In these conditions, we should need at least 28.75 degrees inclination to cut the impact rate down enough for exponential growth. The reaction mass needed to push the array elements into the new orbit would be about as much as the mass of the array itself."

"Yeah, well I've got an idea about that," Dagger said. "We can have array elements north and south of the orbital plane push on each other by tossing mass back and forth with rotating tethers. It's like a couple of sailboats with fans, each blowing the same wind back and forth at each other."

Emma frowned. "But half of the array segments would go into an orbit tilted one way and the other half would go in an orbit tilted in the opposite direction."

"So?" Dagger replied. "All we care about is that the orbits are out of the debris most of the time."

"Hmm," Weaver said. "This begins to sound like it might work. *Admiral?*"

The group dynamic was still working, I thought, but with some unvoiced concern. Weaver looked relieved. I was partly worried, and partly impressed, by how hands-off he was. There were lots of smiles and nods, but very little involvement in the discussion or even managing the discussion. There are techniques for leading problem solving efforts, but he seemed to rely mainly on his personality and aura of command. Would that take him far enough? I wondered.

"Dr. Dickson's idea would significantly reduce the time to achieve exponential array growth."

"Davra?" Weaver nodded her way.

"Coaxial electromagnetic launchers would make more sense than tethers," Davra said. "Simpler."

Dagger laughed. "Only if you're fixated on things going in and out..."

"I fail to get your point," Emma said. "What does that... Oh, my!"

Davra gave her a lopsided ironical grin. "I don't think anyone's been getting Dagger's point lately."

Groans all around signified the end of the meeting. But they were groans with smiles.

••∞••

Two months passed. Schemes may unfold in one's mind in an instant, and be communicated in a few minutes. But when such schemes involve the rearrangement of the heavens, some time is required.

At my bidding the *Admiral* obligingly drew a picture of the Epsilon Eridani debris disk on my neural net page. The power ring was now at an angle to the disk of almost thirty degrees, so that most of the time the power stations would be well above or below the thickest parts of the cloud.

As its inclination increased, our robot hordes could spend more of their time making more array elements, beam projectors, and more robots instead of fending off debris impacts. By the by, we got ahead of the game enough to allocate some resources to finishing the habitat.

About two hundred fifty days after our arrival in the system, the habitat shell was finally completed and we all piled into a runabout to watch the flipover and spinup. It lay before us like a huge silver egg, with one long end toward the star. Brilliant violet plumes erupted around the shell's shadow line—fusion rocket exhaust. The rockets began the spinup with their initial thrust vectors just enough canted that the shell slowly swung up as the applied forces and moments of inertia performed their complex, carefully calculated dance. After three hours of ponderous, majestic twisting, the fusion flames vanished and the habitat was left with its long axis at right angles to its orbital plane and spinning fast enough to provide one-third of an Earth gravity. We were all suitably impressed.

Over the next few days, a thin film mirror, angled to reflect sunlight down into the habitat, was erected over its north pole on a "despin platform" that rotated in the opposite sense of the habitat, to keep it pointed at the star and to provide a landing place for the various runabouts and shuttles. Magnetic fields sprang up to protect the area from particle storms, and robots busied themselves in finishing the habitat's interior.

CHAPTER 4

Asgard
Epsilon Eridani System
25 March 2274

Finally, near the first anniversary of our arrival, Weaver gave the welcome command to defrost the rest of the crew and move everyone to the newly completed habitat. I moved my things into my new quarters, a cottage on a tributary to the equatorial lake surrounded by saplings.

But grass still grows more quickly than trees, and Dagger soon had a place for his second-favorite recreational activity—the game of golf. The course was laid out in a great circle a couple of kilometers north of the central river so that one almost always struck the ball in the direction of the habitat's rotation; this brought a drive down about as quickly as it would have come down on Earth, despite the lower centrifugal gravity of the habitat. Dagger was a fanatic, and I soon found that, embarrassing as it was for a Scot, I could not play at his level.

The habitat needed a name. In line with the Norse mythology theme of the rest of the system, it became Asgard. Trees, aided by modified genes and soil additives, grew rapidly. So did the culture, for which we had plenty of time. That culture, as one might suspect, had much in common with that of remote outposts throughout the history of exploration. Our small cohort was no exception. Since the habitat was up and running, our original group had blended into the general populace. While I still took careful note of what was going on, a certain routine had set in.

I'd taken up my previous profession, and begun a class on the history and philosophy of astronautics. In my spare time, I took on the formidable task of replenishing my dwindling supply of Talisker with a replicated variety. The replicant wouldn't be the real thing, but nary another soul would know the difference, and even I might not know after the third glass. I had just finished giving the *Admiral* a fairly decent recipe when Emma called.

On screen.

There was a rather un-Emma-like twinkle in the astrophysicist's eye. "We're having a little reunion of the early birds at Dagger's place tomorrow, for old times' sake. Can you come?"

"Aye, it would be good to see everyone. I have a few papers to grade, but should be done by then if I get to it."

"1000 hours, tomorrow. You'll not mention this to Dagger now?"

"You mean a surprise party?"

"Indeed. Cheers!"

If Dagger reacted true to form, I thought, it could be fun. Dagger enjoyed pulling practical jokes, so getting one back on him would be quite the ticket.

"We'll meet where his path turns off the West River."

"Aye, see you then."

●●∞●●

Dagger's cottage of cast stone looked something like one might find in the middle of his native Maine. It even had a replicated stone wall along the front of the house with wild roses lovingly tended by microbots. We were kept outside for a couple of minutes—long enough to wonder who else might be there.

The front door, a large piece of solid replicated wood, opened and Dagger, looking half-asleep, looked out at us. I saw that his right arm was covered with what appeared to be a hard white wrap.

"Surprise!" we all shouted.

He suddenly awoke, shook his head and blinked his eyes.

"That'll teach me to run simulations past midnight. Well, come on in!"

We filed in and took seats around Dagger's grand stone fireplace, complete with simulated fire. It was cool enough in here that the warmth was welcome. We ordered drinks and his domestic robot brought them.

Dagger thrust the appliance on his arm toward me. "Will you look at this, Bruce!" Dagger's face was a mixture of mock disbelief and outrage. I went to bed in perfect health and woke up with this! You're an historian of technology. Do you know what this is?"

I dutifully looked the appliance over. "It's a 'cast.' I saw one in a medical museum once. They were made to immobilize the arm to allow it to heal from a break. But nowadays, of course, we'd simply have a robosurgeon glue the bones back together. But I gained my comm implant in a similar way, so I'm sure there must be some other medical explanation. Jill?"

The biologist shrugged, but the twinkle in her eye told me she was in on it.

"Oh come on," Dagger implored. "Something's up, someone knows!"

"Ladies," Emma said, "I think we're being asked for a diagnosis."

"Better tell our Don Juan what this appliance is for," Jill said, "or he's likely to go crazy."

Davra grinned. "*Admiral?*"

"It had come to my attention that Dagger's hand was in danger of repetition stress syndrome caused from his efforts to modify his golf swing to compensate for Coriolis force."

We could hold our laughter no more. Seeing which way this was going, I touched the net to ask the *Admiral* to send us some of my replicated Talisker.

Dagger looked at us with disgust. "So that's it now. I'm warning you, I'll be getting even."

"Dagger dear," Davra cooed, "you could just let it ride and call it even."

"Oh no. Letting things ride, that's not me. The chase is on."

I looked at him in apprehension, then he broke out in a laugh. "Just kidding. Maybe. I think she wants you next, Bruce. If I were you, I'd look out."

The whisky arrived. "I'll be trying a bit of bribery instead," I said. "Shall we toast to the balancing of the books?" The robotic servant produced glasses of the amber liquid, and I passed them out.

Weaver arrived as I did so. He seemed unhappy, but not, perhaps, about our escapade.

"Sorry I'm late, folks. What's this about retribution?"

We told him and he shook his head. "Folks, this is a 50-year mission." Then he raised his glass of whisky and joined the party.

••∞••

Within our diverse community of scientists and engineers, there was a great sharing of cultural conditions. About six months after Dagger got his cast, I let him, Emma and Davra talk me into a rendition or two of the bagpipes. I remembered that Emma had not done badly on the lute herself the previous month, while wearing an Elizabethan dress, even.

I had invited the gang over for libations, but my real purpose was to fill in some details on our debris problem. They were having fun sidetracking me, of course.

"So, having done my duty," Emma continued, "why don't you consider upholding your end of the British Isles. Do you play the bagpipes?"

I smiled. If you would know the truth, I am a wee bit more of science historian than Scots culture historian, but I had played the pipes a time or two and could do serviceable renditions of "Highland Laddie" and "Scotland the Brave" along with a few lesser known tunes requiring a more cultivated ear. "Some," I replied.

"And you could come up with suitable national dress?" Dagger wanted to know. "You'd look nice in a dress."

I gave him a withering look. So, I thought, if I was going to do the bagpipes, I'd have to come up with a kilt. "I dinna bring one with me, but with the help of the replicator, I should be able to manage that as well. And, it is not a dress!"

"Okay, okay," Davra said. "Pipes and kilt at 1900 Thursday?"

"It shall be done." I was eager to get back to my job as an historian. "How are things going?" I asked her.

"Our doubling period is down to about 45 days, and pretty much holding there. The more robots we make, the higher the debris flux gets." She looked at Emma. "Tell him about your sims."

Emma shrugged her shoulders. "My simulations show the system had been moving toward resonance before the latest increase in magnetic activity. Things were settling into rings, Lagrange points and so on. But the increase in flare activity, starting about six years ago, caused a lot of out-gassing and non-gravitational accelerations."

"Heat up an asteroid with a lot of ice in it, and it turns into a steam rocket," Davra commented.

"Thank you, I've read my Whipple," I told her with a smile. "I ken what non-gravitational accelerations are about."

She raised an eyebrow.

"They move into different orbits and run into things," Dagger added.

Emma nodded. "The debris population goes up by orders of magnitude. A lot of the stuff further out gets perturbed into Loki's sphere of influence, and not a small amount of that stuff has been flung into the inner system in retrograde orbits. It's just now arriving at relative velocities of forty to sixty kilometers per second."

"Kersplat," Dagger said.

Emma smiled. "Also, we only use about ten percent of the mass we mine; the rest goes into orbiting slag piles, and they get hit, too, creating even more debris."

"Yeah," Dagger said. "We're doing something about that now. We've got all the mass from the next load in one slag pile, so the amount of exposed surface is way down. And we're gonna dump that right into Epsilon Eridani so we don't have to keep defending it from impacts."

Davra nodded. "I've got enough robots on the job that some can be spared to seek out and consolidate potential impactors too, even if we're not mining them.

Emma sighed. "We're already doing that—so much that I can see the increase in metallicity in the star's atmosphere."

Something in the back of my mind started wondering if that were entirely a good thing. I put it out of my mind. A star is not conscious, I thought, and so could not resent garbage being dumped on it, could it? Well, I was still uneasy, so, without telling a soul, I resolved to do a little checking of the history of the system since we started interfering with it.

••∞••

The *Admiral* and I fashioned a plaid and pleated skirt with a bit of mantle for my costume. I chose a traditional plaid from the Isle of Skye. In this I had the assistance of Kiri-Jean Stewart, a recently defrosted science anthropologist whose business was to study scientists as they studied the Universe. A big, cheerful, redheaded lass, she was actually from Christchurch, New Zealand, but she took her heritage seriously.

The bagpipe took a bit more work to assemble. Kiri-Jean said I fussed over the reeds for the pipe and drones a bit too much. Now I may have thought, Och, but does the lassie know! But I was very polite about everything as there was a bit of chemistry between us for our common interest.

Finally the day arrived.

The pseudo lamb dinner had been served. Davra and Weaver passed around a selection of synthesized single malt whisky and everyone settled back for my performance. I had Dagger sit just behind me for the last bit.

As luck would have it, Asgard had developed some of its own weather and greeted the evening with a dark cloud between us and the axis, from which a sprinkle of cold rain fell. Well, the plants had to drink too, so we crowded into our small theater.

I played a rendition of "Scotland the Brave," the one everyone thinks of when you hear a bagpipe band in a parade. Everyone clapped. Aye, I thought, and they'll clap for "Highland Laddie" as well.

Still, after three of the lesser airs, the audience applauded and asked for more. So I played two more energetic tunes then threw off my pipes in the general direction of Dagger to symbolize the music was of my soul and not from the pipes themselves.

I bowed to a wonderful round of applause and invited them all to "drink up!" I was feeling entirely too good and pleased with myself and had completely forgotten that the second shoe had not dropped, so to speak, from the escapade in the unfinished habitat. Ironically, I was probably not ten meters from where that ill-fated conversation had been held, now somewhere under the artificial landscape.

As I sat down, Weaver stopped by.

"A good rendition, Bruce. Thank you."

"My pleasure, sir!"

I could tell, though, that he had something more on his mind than the bagpipes.

No more had I reached down to pick up my drink when I discovered it was gone. Looking up, I saw serving robots disappearing with all the glasses, many like mine, still with a wee bit of whisky in them. I was about to register a protest when more bagpipe music wafted into the theater. It was a slow lament, "The Lament of Children," and it was played in the style of the old MacCrimmon family from Skye. I gripped the table to hold myself steady, remembering the legend, suddenly being transported back to Skye, to the pubs, to the college that was a dozen light years from here, I reminded myself. Tears balled up, I kept them back. Get a grip man, I told myself.

Emma stepped through the companionway with a tray of small port glasses filled with a dark fluid. Something strange was going on here. The tunic she wore was the genuine mustard-colored linen with the bellowing sleeves, and had no belt.

Of course. They'd wanted a Scot in a kilt and I'd not thought any further about it nor had Kiri-Jean. So I'd ordered up what they had been used to seeing.

But I had a sinking feeling this was much more authentic. Over the tunic, she had draped what was labeled a 'leine,' a mantle such as might have been worn by a 12th century warrior, held over her shoulder with a brooch that was no doubt as accurate a relic of the time. Her beautiful legs were covered in the traditional garter socks; that much I recognized.

I felt chagrined. The Isle of Skye's honor had been duly served, but not by me. Emma set the tray down, picked up a glass and gave it to me while taking one for herself.

"To Skye," she said, and the toast echoed through the hall.

The liquid poured down my throat and a smile spread across my lips. It was no whisky, but Bonny Prince Charlie's Drambuie and it melted its way down my gullet and into my stomach.

I turned to Kiri-Jean. "Well, it appears I've been upped."

Her eyes twinkled and she couldn't keep her face straight.

"Oh, no, lass, you're in on it?"

She laughed.

Well, it appeared that I indeed had been had and I'd best be a good sport about it.

I thrashed the glass to the table, stood and swept up Emma in my arms, carried her to the stage, and set her down beside me. She took this all with characteristic aplomb, I should add.

"Well, now," I told the audience. "I stand here upstaged in my own culture by this charming young English woman. What you are drinking is a recipe of Drambuie given to my fellow Isle of Skye islanders by the Bonnie Prince Charlie as we rescued him from the Redcoats. And, ladies and gentlemen, before you, on Emma, is a kilt from the 12th century, Scotland, far older than the one which I wear."

She laughed and spun around so they could see the whole thing.

"What Dr. Macready is wearing," she said, "was a version created in the 17th century so Scots workmen would safely work in a forge. It was, in fact, designed by an Englishman."

I looked down, mouth open. "Ye dinna say," I said weakly.

The *Admiral* confirmed it, as laughter cascaded through the audience.

Someone, who sounded a lot like Dagger, yelled from the back, "Time to kiss and make up." So I took Emma's hand and did so.

"Even?" I asked.

"Perhaps," she said with a smile, and turned and headed off the stage.

Well, the rest of the party went on very well. Kiri-Jean, I, and another couple who were actually from Glasgow helped get everyone dancing some simple jigs, inhibitions and muscles well lubricated with the ersatz whisky and Drambuie. Weaver, of all people, actually managed it quite well.

After cleanup, we 'Early Birds' plus Kiri-Jean went off to Weaver's ranch. He had half a dozen colts and fillies on some clear land about four kilometers from the central lake.

"I know how it was done," I said, "but I'm still amazed at how big a horse can get only six months from an artificial womb and bottle feeding."

Weaver smiled with the pride of a parent. "I started saddle training a couple weeks ago. No riding yet, but just to get them used to something on their backs."

"They are beautiful," Kiri-Jean said. "My family has horses back in New Zealand."

Everyone went to the corral fence to be near the horses except Emma, who stayed back, apparently lost in thought. Kiri-Jean was petting a colt with a white star on its forehead, both appearing to enjoy it immensely. I'd never seen anything more beautiful. With my normal inhibitions pretty much gone, I simply walked up and put an arm around her waist. She said nothing, but kind of melted against me to show the contact was entirely welcome.

Somewhat to my surprise, Davra moved over to my other side, and let her leg brush against mine. In a hundred and forty waking years, I'd never been in such a position. I just kind of kept my aplomb and smiled at each in turn as we played with the colt, who seemed to want all the attention for himself, snorting at any of his siblings that dared come close to us three humans.

It was too good a moment to end, but it did. I heard rapid footsteps come up behind us. It was Emma.

"Everyone, please, we have a problem. A planetesimal heading for the upper half of the array."

I looked at Weaver, who was already checking with the neural net, his frown growing deeper and deeper.

Dagger ran over to us.

"We'll meet in the Project Dome in an hour," Weaver said with a sigh, then went over to pat Star, having seemingly put the matter out of his mind.

••∞••

"The Project Dome" was a large video dome. A round table sat in the middle, causing local wags to call the building "Camelot." Depending on whom you asked, the table either had no head, or the head was wherever Weaver decided to sit. He waited until everyone else he called had sat down and then he entered. There were ten of us now, with two additional experts sharing in planetary astrophysics, robotics, and project engineering, working with Emma, Davra, and Dagger.

Emma had the *Admiral* circle one of a thousand comets displayed. Its statistics appeared beside it. "That one," she said, "is the threat."

The room fell silent. Emma, I knew was working orbital calculations, Davra was working out robot-replacement time factors. I dinna know what Dagger was thinking, but it looked grim.

C. Sanford Lowe ∞ G. David Nordley

Weaver broke the silence, his worry lines furrowed the more so. "How are we going to divert that? It's as big as Pluto."

"We have a Norse naming convention in this system," Emma said. "I've called it Skrymir. He was an ice giant."

"What I want to know is where did it come from?" Dagger asked. "Why is it a surprise?" He frowned and ran his hand through his hair.

Emma looked uncomfortable. "It was not on that orbit a week ago. It got hit by another smaller comet, one of thousands whose orbit changed due to increased out-gassing and due to the current anomalously high stellar activity. It will pass near the giant planet Loki in three weeks and Loki's gravity will greatly magnify the small change produced by the comet impact. The odds against this happening precisely this way were, well, astronomically high."

"If it's too big to move, maybe we can move the array," Davra said. "*Admiral?*"

"This would put us behind schedule again, but not impossibly so."

"Hey," Dagger said. "If a comet strike put it in this orbit, maybe another can take it out. Any options for that?"

"Yes," the *Admiral* answered, "assuming Skrymir stays on its present course." The *Admiral* circled a tiny dot on the dome. "This new comet will pass within about a billion kilometers of Skrymir, in three months. A velocity change of about 1.2 meters per second on this newer comet would cause it to strike Skrymir essentially head on. The comet should hit with enough energy to cause Skrymir to miss the trailing end of the array. Probably enough to make it hit the star itself so it won't be a problem on the other side of its orbit. Like this." Dotted lines on the diagram changed to show Skrymir being hit and falling into Epsilon Eridani.

"That appears to take care of the problem for now," Weaver said, nodding. "Make it so."

It so happened that Skrymir would strike Epsilon Eridani near the upper left of the star's disk as seen from Asgard; a potentially spectacular sight. But a problem with living on the inside of a rotating habitat is the lights in the sky at night are not stars, but the lights in the other houses above you. To see what's going on with one's own eyes, one must go outside.

Thus, the entire population of our tiny colony gathered in space suits on the sunward edge of the north pole despin platform. Our robots had temporarily repositioned the colony's main light-collecting mirror between us and Epsilon Eridani, creating the effect of a total solar eclipse.

The corona of the star was awesome, streamers going out several times the diameter of the disk. The array, a line of collectors nearly 40 million kilometers long at this point, was foreshortened to a brilliant dot from our point of view. It looked somewhat like an elongated version of the planet Venus as seen from Earth. One could still see the gas from Skrymir streaming away from the star and toward the array.

"They've collided," Emma announced. "We should see the effects as the light reaches us—in about six minutes. Watch the tail of Skrymir."

It seemed like a long wait. Then, an incredible brilliant white wave began to race up the comet's tail away from the star. A collective "Oh!" came from our helmet speakers.

"It isn't often one gets the chance to actually see the speed of light," Emma commented, her voice filled with awe.

Meanwhile, a brilliant dome began to peek above the edge of our artificial moon, casting sharp shadows surrounded initially by light that was nearly blue white. Its growth was like watching the Sun rise over a distant hill on a clear day back on Skye.

"Did that do anything to the star?" someone asked.

"Not that we know of," Emma replied. "What you see is an extremely thin plasma of star and planetesimal material that fluoresces and glows in the starlight. The amount of mass and energy involved are insignificant by stellar standards."

I was watching the band around my shadow change colors when I saw a second, fainter shadow appear. I looked back to the sky.

The array, bathed in the light of the impact, had become noticeably more brilliant, maybe two or three magnitudes brighter than Venus from Earth, I estimated.

Gradually, things began to fade and people, with other things to do, began getting back to the locks and vanished into the habitat. I lingered a while, with Davra, as the impact dome dissipated and its light faded to deep orange.

"We'll be moving the mirror back in a few minutes. Wouldn't do to get the habitat cold."

"Aye. Davra, I have a sense of déjà-vu about this." I would remember it in detail, of course, as soon as I recognized what it was that I was trying to remember.

CHAPTER 5

Asgard
Epsilon Eridani System
5 April 2274

The next problem resolution meeting was only eighty hours later.

"No warning for something this size, none at all," Davra was saying. She was talking about a major storm developing in Epsilon Eridani's magnetosphere.

"Well, how bad is it going to be?" Dagger asked.

"Bad," Emma said. "Very bad."

"How bad could a bunch of protons be?" I asked. "Surely the magnetic shielding will deal with it, aye?"

"What magnetic fields can hold back depends on the velocity and number of particles. We're getting much more of both than anticipated."

"Pull up Simulation D1238," Emma said.

I gave the *Admiral* the subvocal command and shut my eyes so I could concentrate on the images forming in my head. Simulation D1238 started with a schematic of the Epsilon Eridani system, showing things out to the habitat's orbit. The array was a long thin line enclosed in a blue fog that had a sharp boundary on the side toward the star and trailed off like a comet's tail behind it. As I watched, the sharp boundary pressed closer and closer to the array, almost as if something was blowing on it. Then it touched. Where it came into contact, the blue fog vanished. This process happened at multiple places along the array and continued until the blue fog vanished entirely.

Emma explained. "Where the magnetosphere—that's the blue—is blown into the array, the field generators themselves will be damaged. With enough generators out, the rest can't increase their fields enough to protect the array. The process will cascade, and the protective magnetosphere will be lost. The electronic systems and photovoltaic panels will be exposed to the full storm."

"The whole array?" I asked, not believing.

"The whole array. The panels will be degraded, not destroyed. We should be able to get them back to about half of what they were. The solid state electronics, however, will go. Also, about half the mobile robots in the system are on the array itself and will be damaged."

"Are we going to make it?" I asked. For the first time it sunk into me that what I would be reporting might not be a history of a major step toward one of humanity's greatest accomplishments, but a footnote to failure.

There was no answer to my question.

••∞••

We called it "the Inconstant Moon flare" after the Larry Niven story about the moon suddenly getting bright enough to make people think the Sun had become a nova somehow. We didn't have a moon, but the flare lit up the system's giant planet, Loki, so much that one could see by the reflected flare light. Indeed, we actually turned Asgard's mirror away from Epsilon Eridani and used Loki's light for a couple of days. It wasn't enough to provide heat or normal levels of photosynthesis, but it was easily enough to read by and our star was putting out a wee bit too much.

Wonders aside, the array was in ruins and we were all down a bit. The damage was so extensive, and so many robots had been damaged to so many varying degrees that it would be a week or two before we had a good handle on just how bad it was.

When we did, Weaver called the meeting.

"We all know what has happened," Weaver said. "Is it even possible to recover?"

There was a long silence.

Finally, Dagger spoke up. "We have twenty months or so before we have to launch the impactor. There's no shortage of raw material anywhere in this system. If we didn't have to deal with debris attrition—how fast could we build it, *Admiral?*"

"Assuming enough material, without degradation, 728 days," the AI said.

"We are supposed to launch the impactor in 640 days," one of the new experts said.

There was a great silence then; the cacophony of a room of furious thinking. Could it be that it was all over? I knew the political situation on Earth; it could be a long time indeed before another attempt was made. Perhaps with four different stars? Or would it be made at all? Would humanity turn inside, like China had a thousand years earlier, content with limits that did not risk upsetting the basis of rule?

"Now just hold on here," Dagger said. "We don't have to have the whole thing done to launch the impactor on time. What's the time to have the minimum needed to launch?"

"638 days," the *Admiral* replied.

"Well, then it's a lock," Dagger replied. "With two full days of margin."

Weaver coughed. "Given recent history, that is no margin at all. If we can't come up with anything better, our responsibility is to send out word that our impactor won't be coming."

"If I may," I asked, "what could they do with that information?"

Weaver shook his head. "As the impactors all approach the experiment vertex, they will run into a stream of particles sent out from the vertex facility, much like the streams sent out to decelerate starships. These streams will, of course, be much too thin to decelerate the impactors altogether, but the impactors will be able to use their lasers and magnetic fields to interact with these particle streams to adjust their position. If warned early enough, they could avoid impact altogether—it takes only a few centimeters. But an asymmetric impact would destroy the vertex facility and likely have other unintended consequences. The more warning we can give, the better."

There was a silence around the circle.

"Nuts!" Davra said. "We have to try. As long as there's any chance at all, we have to try!"

Weaver sighed. There didn't seem to be much fight left in him. "Okay," he said, finally. "Let's try again tomorrow."

••∞••

Nothing looked workable and we were facing a collective failure of unbearable magnitude. So small wonder that various people went a little farther afield than usual. In my case, I asked Davra over. I'd been dreaming about her often enough and was finally getting enough dating experience to question my assumptions that women like her were inaccessible to men like me.

Now that I had gone that far, I was nervous as I straightened out my couch for the fifth time and fluffed up two throws for the backrest.

She was due in twenty minutes. I pulled out my third and last bottle of real Talisker and poured three fingers in my "guest" glass and two fingers for myself.

"Lights at thirty per cent, please," I told the *Admiral*.

I pulled up some narrative files and went over them to kill the time. But the minutes passed until something told me she wasn't going to make it. There were only five minutes left until the appointed time, and surely she'd not cut it so close, would she?

Well, it had been a casual meeting we'd arranged, I explained to myself. Davra would be the first to renege on an appointment if something was even slightly amiss in her robotics area. And, there was plenty to be amiss, what with all the flare damage. Dagger joked a lot about the two of them, Davra and Emma, being sirens of disaster. But they were two of the brightest people I had ever met. Things had happened on their watch that shouldn't have. The team had to know that.

I should, I thought, pour my Talisker back into its bottle and pretend it was not a big matter. Davra's sexuality terrified me and her brain thrilled me. It was a dangerous mixture for me, and I wasn't as sure as Dagger was that I could make the grade.

I poured hers back and drank my two fingers.

I could have called her, but instead I left my house and hiked along North Central Lake path until I got to hers. There she was, just sitting in a lawn chair, staring at the sky with her eyes closed. She wore shorts and a loose tank top, and my heart ached to watch her chest rise and fall against its thin fabric.

"Asgard to Davra?" I said at length, not wanting to be discovered voyeuring, should she suddenly return to the here and now.

"Bruce!" She opened her eyes with a start. Then she sighed. "Sorry. Poring over modeling results... forgot the time. Can I take a rain check?"

The more things change, I thought, the more they stay the same.

"Ye sit here in a recliner, shut your eyes, and rearrange the heavens. It's quite an image, ye know."

She laughed, "I'm working on Weaver's idea of concentrating everything on making array-building robots, then rebuilding the array in a hurry."

"Does it work?"

"Four months short, but it's amazing it works that well. I'm looking for ways to close the gap. Weaver's kind of down, have you noticed? Spending a lot of time with Jill and Dagger down at the 19th hole."

"Aye." Like the good researcher I was, I filed away my personal desires and rearranged my priorities. How the management team functioned in crisis was grist for my mill.

"Maybe I'll head that way myself." I laughed. "It would be interesting to catch Dagger when he's given himself a wee bit of a handicap." I turned to go.

"Bruce," she said and turned so quickly that her long hair flung out around her head like a pleated skirt. "Not so fast."

I stopped.

"You shouldn't put me on that damn pedestal of yours."

"What pedestal?"

If I looked confused, I was. She needed to do her work, and I needed to leave her be. Isn't that what she'd just intimated to me?"

"Oh, forget it. Maybe I'll get down to the 19th hole later."

"Aye. See you later."

●●∞●●

At our next meeting, Weaver looked at the group, his face hard to read. "Has anyone come up with anything?"

Engineers in busy silence? Furious silence? Or, just silent silence, I wondered.

Weaver then looked at each person around the project dome as if trying to pull out something.

Finally, he turned to me, of all people. "Bruce, you're good at teasing ideas out of people. Think you can pull a miracle out of your brainstorming hat?"

I frowned; an observer such as myself shouldn't be taking a main role in events—it raises issues of objectivity in the end. Nonetheless, my help was being asked. It was just another departmental meeting, I told myself, though with higher stakes.

"I canna guarantee any results, but I'd be happy to give it a try. But first I think we might review some of the roads not taken in the last session. Dagger suggested building the array further out, using reflectors. Could we not do that, then angle the reflectors away if a big flare comes?"

Emma shook her head. "There's not enough time to move the array to an orbit far enough out. The modules would need to coast for a year. Then we'd need to figure out a way to push them in to circularize..."

"Why?" Dagger asked. "Why bother to circularize?"

Weaver looked at him sharply, then his features relaxed. "Doesn't make much difference, I suppose. No good to anyone after we're gone."

Emma frowned. "Even if we just let them go... But maybe, if we really don't care..."

We all looked at her.

"There is another planetesimal," she said, thinking out loud, "or maybe an escaped moon, inbound at high inclination. Loki sheds one sometimes, near periastron." Suddenly her voice took on an authority of knowledge and experience. "Call it Skrymir II. It will eventually get within a couple hundredths of an astronomical unit of Epsilon Eridani and likely be vaporized. But not until about four years from now."

Emma's eyes met Davra's.

"We have lots of robots now," Davra said. "We can get them out there quickly with the surviving array modules. Without any interference, our doubling period could get down to maybe twenty days." She held up a hand while she consulted the net. "Still not enough."

She looked at Dagger, eager to weigh in.

"Yeah, well, it would be enough to *start* the impactor," Dagger said. "Maybe we'll think of something else in the meantime."

"Yes, and maybe pigs will fly," Weaver said.

We went around this way for another three hours without really coming up with anything better. But with the *Admiral's* help and another brainstorming session, we somehow managed to convince ourselves that if we could get started, maybe something would come up.

••○○••

Soon everything was again in the hands of the automated systems. Heavy on our minds was that it would be the better part of a quarter-century before an attempt was made again. And at some point, we would have to admit failure and warn the central Project leaders that our impactor would be late. But, everyone was still trying to come up with a scheme to save the situation.

Three weeks after the "Inconstant Moon" flare, Weaver left a message. "New colt's a beaut. Come over Tuesday evening after my horseback ride and we'll trade horse stories."

Trading horse stories was Weaver-speak for getting us updated on the colts and getting him updated on what we were all doing. Tuesday, I took myself off the net to enjoy a walk and arrived shortly before our "sun" set behind the north end hills.

Weaver was still out riding when I got to his place. The colt had grown big enough to ride, Weaver had probably gone out among the sculpted crags and streams of the south end of Asgard, where the artificial land curved up toward its spin axis.

"Hi, Bruce." It was Dagger, leaning up against the rail and petting the jet-black new arrival.

"Weaver still out, eh?"

He nodded. I had a flask of ersatz Talisker with me, which I passed to him.

"Asked Davra out yet?" he asked, after a swig.

I laughed and shook my head. "I don't know. I don't think she's my type..."

Laughter as clear as a bell rang out. "Don't you guys ever learn anything?"

Davra sauntered into view wearing a cowboy hat, jeans and a bright blue halter with two big red stars on the only place big enough for big red stars.

"I'll decide who's my type..." Davra held up a hand as if listening on her neural net. Her smile vanished and her face turned into one of shock.

I put myself back on the net and instantly got an urgent incoming. I could see Dagger had one too.

It was Jill. *Not good news, everyone. I'm at the clinic. G. P. is dead.*

Dead! I sent. *How can anyone be dead anymore?*

They think it was a horse riding accident. He was off the net. When he didn't show up for our date, I sent an emergency message. He didn't respond. I called public safety and they found him with the survey cameras up in the rocks up by the north pole with his head bashed in and the colt nuzzling him. They had him in the clinic in ten minutes, but it was too late.

"I've got a car coming," Dagger said. "Five minutes."

How are you doing? I asked Jill.

There was a pause. *I feel awful. The horses aren't used to the low gravity up there. The trails aren't maintained as much. It's the sort of thing G. P. does to clear his mind when the burdens become overwhelming and he isn't careful. I should have said something to him. If I'd only called earlier...*

Jill, don't blame yourself, I sent.

"Damn!" Davra said. "He was awfully down. You don't think he arranged..."

Dagger shook his head. "Not Weaver! He'd think that was a coward's way out."

"Aye," I said. "But people with problems who would never think of killing themselves still might give death more of an opportunity to solve their problems than it would normally have. In the First World War, Churchill, fired from the Admiralty because of the Gallipoli disaster, went into the army and exposed himself to fire on the western front. He survived. Tchaikovsky, failing in personal relationships with women and men, drank tainted water. He died. An American President, Nixon I think, about to be forced from office, went on a strenuous foreign mission with blood clots in his leg. No such luck, mind you; he lived to be disgraced."

They stared at me.

"On the other hand, maybe it was just an accident," I said, but I wondered.

The fan car arrived and set down in a swirl of leaves. Everyone piled in.

••∞••

Whether by intention or premonition, Weaver had left final instructions only a few days old. He wished his remains to fertilize the soil of the uplands he loved, so we buried him on a rise of ground with a fine view of Asgard spread out below. Jill planted flowers from the same pot I'd seen in his quarters over the years. I played "Amazing Grace" on the pipes.

••∞••

"We need a leader," Dagger announced as we stared at each other across the circular table.

One chair had been left empty, not by any design; it had just happened that way and no one had come to fill it. Dagger had become acting director on Weaver's death, but made it clear that was temporary.

"There seems to be a consensus among the project people that it be one of us early birds," he continued. "In fairness, whoever it's going to be will probably have to tell the universe we failed."

"Isn't that a wee bit premature?" I asked. "We haven't tackled this one yet. Every time we do, we come up with something."

"Someone has to preside," Davra said.

"It just isn't my thing," Dagger answered. "I do better kibitzing. Anyone here have any management experience? Emma? You led the astronomy team."

She shook her head. "And my reputation hasn't suffered enough, has it?"

I thought to object, but held my tongue. She had a point.

"Davra?" Dagger asked.

She looked around the table at a number of frowns, then shook her head, too. "I have enough to worry about with the robotics. And besides," she lowered her voice, "it might interfere with my social life."

Though the remark was clearly meant for the laughs it got, she had a point also.

Jill stood up. She and Weaver had been close companions the entire mission. We all had great respect for her. "What we need is a generalist, someone who has an overall view of everything. The department heads already have their hands full." She paused and looked at me. "Bruce Macready is such a person."

My jaw dropped. I looked at Dagger, who raised an eyebrow; at Emma, who seemed to be looking somewhere else; then at Davra, who smiled as if she'd just swallowed the canary.

Jill continued. "He has personally chronicled every event from the time we left Earth. He has interviewed everyone here and he has a good working knowledge of our overall mission. At Broadford College, he chaired his department twenty-three times and served as chancellor for a decade. He's also been three times president of the International Science Historians Guild."

"Now wait a minute," I objected. "Yes, I've had a wee bit of what you might call management experience, but none of it at this level of responsibility."

They looked at me again. How had this happened? I asked myself. I'd come along to report on this thing, not to run it. Bruce, I told myself, they do not want a leader as much as a scapegoat. But I met Davra's eyes, and those eyes seemed to say yes, in several ways. Are you going to go for it, Macready? For once in your life, are you going to go for it?

Of course, maybe if I had fully appreciated the impossibility of completing the mission with success at that time, I would have shied away too. So I don't know. But either for Davra's eyes or out of ignorance and hope for something of significance to show for my time out at Epsilon Eridani, I decided to pick up this caber and try to stick it upright.

"Very well, I'll ride point for you—but not to be throwing in the towel just yet. We have almost a year, do we not, before we run out of power to push the impactor on its designated profile?"

The *Admiral* confirmed this.

"Then we shall meet again tomorrow with our thinking caps on, aye?"

They all nodded.

"Weel, I'm feeling a bit dry just now. Those who want, come over to my house and we'll lift a glass to the late Dr. Weaver."

••∞••

The wake was all that it should have been. Everyone brought a bottle of his or her favorite replicated liquor or drink and shared it around. One of Davra's people wailed away on an Irish fiddle while his wife dragged all the men to the center and taught them how to do an Irish jig. Bye and bye, we were all dancing and singing and having what Dagger called a whale of a wake.

Very late into the evening, Davra jigged into my arms. We danced until I needed a wee breath and so took her hand and led her out to the edge of my garden. She looked me straight in the eye.

"Something on your mind, lass?"

She laughed softly. "I've got to come up with some entirely new strategy for getting the project back on target tomorrow and you ask if I've got something on my mind? Well, besides that what I've got on my mind right now is I'm horny as hell."

Call it a death wish, but there is something about me that will not even walk through an open door to my dreams. "I dinna know if I have a cure for that, lass."

She laughed again, took my hand and led me away from the house and the commotion of the party.

About halfway on the path, surrounded by trees and singing birds, she stopped. "Bruce, Bruce. Look at me. The real me."

I stared into her eyes. "You're a beautiful lass, a lot more than I could..."

"Oh, stop making me unreachable. I'm a real woman who loves to love and I've always wanted to love you as much as anyone. Put me on the ground where I belong."

"The ground is it?" Thinking to make a joke of taking her literally, I looked around; there was a small grassy clearing just a few feet from the path.

I swear her eyes glowed, and her face split with a great grin. "Yes, on the ground, right now, oh yes!"

Summoning up nerve from I dinna know where, I took her hand. Her eyes glowed as she followed me through the brush, laughing. In the clearing, she kicked her sandals off and with one smooth motion, she pulled her long black dress over her head and stood before me naked.

She was beautiful, no doubt about it. This was a Davra I'd never seen before. Quiet, but excited, watching me, as I was her. Was she as nervous on the inside as I was, I wondered. I stepped to her and she grabbed my tunic and pulled it over my head, pressing her firm breasts against me as she did. The tunic fell to the ground, as in a moment did we. There, in the cool grass and soft leaves, we made love.

••∞••

The next day was all business. I have a degree of stubbornness in me, and an analyst's bent. Up until now I'd put all my work into historical studies of what people did and why. Now it was a star I was trying to figure out, a star that seemed to consciously fight our every effort.

Well, what was this star's pattern, this opponent of mine? I looked up the history of the entire project from the first robotic presence to the present day, and made graphs of its activity and ours. A correlation was no great surprise, but indeed... A chill went down my spine.

I called Emma. "If ye look at this, it seems that when we throw something big at the star, it throws something back a few days later."

Her image on my wall screen shrugged. "It's always throwing stuff out. So it's always throwing stuff out when we throw stuff at it."

"But it happens when other stuff hits it, too. Natural stuff. If ye look at the correlation."

She frowned. "You're saying it's not random?"

"So does the *Admiral*, Emma."

There was a long silence. Finally, she said, "Bruce, you might get a paper out of this when we get back. Astronomy is probably friendlier to contributions by amateurs than most sciences."

She was trying to let me down gently, but I was not to be deterred. "But don't you see it, Emma? It's us that have been making the star flare. Us! By dumping our waste on it."

She paused for a bit, then shook her head. "Possibly. But how? The material doesn't penetrate, really; it just sort of splatters on the photosphere."

"But it's all kinds of metal, heavy ions, current paths..."

She gave me a wan smile. "Well, maybe. I'll suggest to *Davra* that she direct the waste elsewhere. I don't suppose it could hurt. Not that anything's going to help now."

Were there tears in her eyes?

"I dinna want to make you feel bad, Emma."

The look she gave me was unreadable. "No, I don't suppose you did."

••◦◦••

There were long faces at Camelot. We all had a bit of a toast as our impactor, that billion-ton iron caber, started its journey to the implosion vertex. But we had to acknowledge a larger sobering thought. We would ultimately call it quits if we didn't find more power in another hundred and thirty days.

"Almost twenty percent more," Dagger said. "We could actually use one of those big flares now."

"Huh?" we all said simultaneously.

"Sure," he said. "Photovoltaics like light. It's particle radiation that hurts them, but that's all down in the magnetosphere. They'll take as much as double the illumination."

"So why don't we just build bigger concentrating reflectors?" I asked.

"That's how we're keeping up," Davra said. "Can't build 'em any faster. We've got the surface of Skrymir II covered with robots, and it's getting noticeably smaller as we take stuff away. That's a bottleneck. To get more light, you'll need to make Epsilon Eridani brighter."

My eyes met Emma's. Come on, Lassie, I thought. You say it. Make it your idea and get back some of yer self-respect.

"There may... may be a way of doing that," Emma said. "If we could dump a lot of mass in at the right time, it seems that flares should follow in a few days. Metallic ions affect currents beneath the photosphere, destabilizing it..."

"We've got a plenty of slag to push," Davra said.

Emma nodded, then shut her eyes. She'd be in a silent, furious conversation with the *Admiral*, I thought.

Finally, she said, "It will take about a hundred and thirty-two billion tons, if my model is right. Spread over several days with impacts maybe three hours apart."

"Well," Dagger added. "There's that much and more floating around this place. Let's get going." Then he looked at me with a curious expression on his face, as if he just remembered who was in charge.

I smiled and nodded. "Aye, let's do it."

As we left Camelot, Davra grabbed my hand. And Dagger took Emma's.

••∞••

Weeks later, with the pellets all safely on their way to the accelerating impactor, I walked out with Davra to the rise where we buried G. P. Weaver. He and I had been confidants of sorts over the years, and it seemed right to give his headstone an update, if nothing else but to clarify some of those details every once in a while.

I also needed to prepare a message to the Vertex facility concerning what we'd done. They'd get it a few weeks before the impactors all arrived. I sat on a rock and brought up my notes. Davra sat beside me, looking out over this vast inside-out green, white and blue Easter egg we lived in. In spite of everything, people were going to found an Epsilon Eridani colony. Davra and I had other plans, though. We were going with Captain Lee to Vertex to see how this all turned out, and then back to the Solar System and Skye—my whisky cache was about gone.

"You've sent the report?" Davra asked. "Emma's calculations were a bit conservative; a thousand massive bodies impacting the photosphere will..."

"Aye, I know. We need to let the Vertex facility know that, in spite of what they see, our impactor will arrive on time and with the right velocity. As for the rest of the galaxy, well, we can have a few days of fun with them." Galaxy was a wee exaggeration—only about a hundred settled star systems were involved.

Davra took my hand. "Oh, yes. I wonder how they'll take it on Earth when, all of a sudden, Epsilon Eridani becomes one of the brightest stars in the sky."

BOOK V

VERTEX

CHAPTER 1

The Barrel
a space colony orbiting Luyten 789-6
18 September 2274 SST

Hi Mom. I got fired. Went walking on a virgin kuiperoid without asking and it turned out someone else was supposed to get the honor. What bullshit! But guess what? Hilda talked me into taking charge of the Impactor launch at Lacaille 9352!

Katherine Avonford, sunning on the beach, grinned as she listened to the bioradio net message from Elizabeth. Her youngest daughter was far too much like her mother for the bureaucratic confines of the Solar System. Memories of her second baby's gurglings flashed into her head. Elizabeth. She remembered the day she first presented the baby to Wotan, his huge smile as the little girl took his finger, and her joy in that timeless ephemeral scene. The fact that Liz used Kate's last name instead of "Kremer" told her how *that* relationship had all gone after she'd left him again.

Little Hilda still bothered Kate's conscience. Wotan had been insufferable! She'd left at the first opportunity. Then Wotan, damn him, bless him, had sent Hilda away to Earth shortly thereafter. Hilda kept his name; she'd loved her father. Kate couldn't live with him, but couldn't stop thinking about him. She wondered what the old curmudgeon would do when he finished terraforming New Antarctica.

She felt the full spectrum artificial sun of *The Barrel*. It wasn't quite the same thing as lying out beneath a real sky with nothing but air between her skin and a real star—but for a tan, it did much better than the light of the red dwarf that fell on the outside of the space colony. She caught some teenagers ogling her from up the strand in front of her cottage and flashed them a smile. They'd probably guess she was born long before they were; but she wondered how many would guess two centuries.

"Big Red," they called the star. She'd gone into space when it was "Luyten 789-6," but the old Earth-based catalog names were used less and less. Some of the new names were her doing. As the captain of various starships, she'd planted three colonies, including this one. Out here you could build a space colony and be *free!*

She glanced sideways up the beach; from her sand level viewpoint, it was hard to tell she was on the inside of a rotating barrel rather than on a planet. The far shore of the equatorial sea was at least a kilometer away—barely a light line in the mist. Hazy clouds, backlit by the artificial sun, covered the opposite side of the colony. She might be on a Greek island.

This is pretty, she mused. The habitat was done; the colony was planted and ready to be lived in. She came here thinking it was time to give motherhood another try and maybe get it right, this time. Why then were the vast empty reaches of space calling her? She wrestled with her thoughts.

The Black Hole Project was part of it. Someday, with tame black holes to power them, starships might range through space independent of the beams needed to push them in the present era. Both of her older daughters were now part of the project, and she was bit jealous.

...as you read this, I'll be on the C. E. Singer *on my way to launch a piece of history and maybe pick up a squeeze.*

Oops! Kate thought. The *Singer* was Pete DeRoot's ship—as long as he stayed away from the Solar System. A brilliant star captain and leader of the first crewed expeditions to Barnard's Star and Ross 154, he had a dark side that was only whispered about when women who had starfared under him got together. A starship captain was a minor deity when light years from any threat of correction. Power corrupts, Kate thought ruefully, and she'd had her own temptations. DeRoot liked power. On top of that, Liz was headed for a colony governed by the equally power-hungry Aussie, Roger Gunheim, and his mistress, Cyan Mutori—and Liz would be displacing Cyan on the Black Hole Project.

Kate sat up. The grass no longer felt like an enjoyable luxury. What was Liz getting into?

••∞••

Uneasy weeks followed, made no less uneasy by the knowledge that because of light speed delay, what had happened, had already happened.

Hi Mom. DeRoot thinks he's a Casanova or something. I had to play up to him for a while, but my friend David helped me turn the tables, so that DeRoot shouldn't be any further problem. But what a disagreeable experience! Also, I understand that he and the System Council Chair at the Lacaille 9352 System—they're calling it Campbell now—are very thick and DeRoot's anger could be a problem for me there. I expect to be able to handle that. Meanwhile, David is a lot of fun, when he isn't being too principled.

Kate ran her fingers through her long flowing hair methodically as she scanned the other messages. One of the problems with living a very, very long time is the stories live a very long time too. Cyan Mutori and Gunheim went way back and had as prickly a relationship as the one she'd had with Liz' father, Wotan Kremer. Cyan was every bit as ambitious as Gunheim, if a little more subtle, and loved to play with fire.

But Liz would have to handle them without any help from her. The impactor would be launched and on its way, or not, before anything she said would reach Campbell. Would her daughter stay there? No, she'd probably head to Vertex to see what happened.

Maybe she should go, too.

••∞••

Over the next two months, Kate's worries subsided. Liz wasn't any better than most children in keeping a parent informed, but usually, no news was good news. On the morning of the fourth celebration of *The Barrel's* "Suits-Off Day," Kate had an early speech to give and woke early to get ready. As she stepped onto the shower platform and selected the standard program, she scanned on through the messages and smiled when she got to a message from Ivan Marenkov. Ivan had been her engineer on the *R. L. Forward* a hundred and twenty years ago.

Yo, love. Hope you are enjoying yourself at Big Red. We've got word that your daughter Liz is due here in a few weeks to supervise the BHP launch. Roger Gunheim's been paying a lot of attention to the BHP lately, wandering around asking questions like he was getting set to buy one. Or knowing his character, maybe steal it, if he could get away with it. Ha-Ha. Anyway, the good news is that people are a little sick of his act and just waiting for the next election. By the way, I'm single again if you're thinking of coming this way. The times with you were the best. Love, Ivan.

Kate smiled and shook water out of her hair. The drying cycle took over, and warm air gushed up from the grill. Gunheim? Stealing a black hole? Knowing Peter DeRoot's ego, Kate found the idea nowhere near as humorous as Ivan. Zhau Tse Wen was a dear, sweet man and extraordinarily competent in everything. But he had too rosy a view of human nature.

Stealing a black hole was an outrageous, absurd idea, but with DeRoot and Gunheim reinforcing each other's megalomania, it wasn't completely impossible. The very outrageousness of the idea might keep anyone from guarding against it. Zhau was not a sufficient worrier; he would philosophize. He would trust distance to keep his project safe.

Well, at least if De Root and Gunheim wanted the black hole, they wouldn't interfere with making it, so maybe Liz would be okay.

But what then? DeRoot had been out in the deep too long and become a law onto himself.

She laughed. The same, of course, could easily be said of her. She touched the net for the timeline. The Campbell projectile would be launching soon. Big Red was about the same distance away from Vertex as Campbell. Her lips curved into a what-if smile.

Decision made, she called down the hair robot and unconsciously selected braids, a style suitable for space. The bot floated down around her head like an oversize crown of thorns, and hundreds of tiny hands began braiding.

It would probably not be a good idea for DeRoot to know she was coming, but she would need a stream of pellets to decelerate her starship. Someone on site there would have to arrange it quietly. Pat Barrett had said his daughter Kelly was on her way to be a space operations shift leader at Shiva. Kelly had been her navigator's mate on the Tau Ceti expedition—a thoroughly competent officer. Kate sent the necessary messages on faith—she would have to be well on her way before any confirmation would be possible. Having former lovers on every other star in near-Earth space had some advantages. She could count on about half of them.

She would also need some extra mass, as much as she could get. She touched the net and made the arrangements. Big Red's arrays of photovoltaic generators and beam drivers would deliver more than momentum. What she would do with it, would depend on what developed. But, she'd have options.

The crew would have to be small, and all volunteers. She knew who to ask.

After the robot was done with her hair, she took a plain pin and wove it thoughtfully through her braided bun as she composed a few more lines.

Her Suits-Off Day speech would also be her farewell.

CHAPTER 2

Chandrasekhar Station
in orbit about Shiva
22 December 2284

Torsten Ried touched the net one last time for the facts on his *Popular Issues* interview subject, Kelly Barrett. An operations control shift leader, she'd been among the first to reach the Shiva system, betting fifteen years of her life that operations on four other stars would take place on time.

She'd very nearly lost the bet, he reflected, when the consolidationist coalition, headed by Torsten's half-brother, Lars, finally won the presidency of the Solar System's Interplanetary Association Senate. The coalition didn't have the votes to make the IPA kill the project, however, and Torsten and Ried operative, Anna Messenger, had left for Shiva on the *Giovanni Vulpetti* on the heels of the impactor from Sol, passing it and arriving a week ago.

The door announced Barrett's arrival. Torsten told it to open with a gesture.

It revealed a medium height brunette with long wavy hair that flowed dramatically over one shoulder. She wore a bright white jumpsuit with the tetrahedral BHP logo on the right shoulder, dramatically open in front. Amazing stuff, geckro, Torsten thought.

He beamed. "Nice of you to come, Kelly. I'm Torsten Ried, and this is my assistant, Anna." Except for hairstyle and clothes, he thought, they might be sisters. Anna had chosen a long, flowing Hawaiian dress.

"Hi, Mr. Ried," Kelly gushed, standing fixated like a deer caught in a spotlight. "Hi, Anna."

"You can call me Torsten." Torsten laughed. "You've never done an interview before, right?"

Kelly nodded nervously.

He smiled disarmingly. "Don't worry, I'll let you know when we're on the record. Just come on in and make yourself comfortable."

After she'd done so, he gave her a well-practiced, disarming smile. "Okay, let's start!"

He held still for a second, then introduced her for the audience and asked. "How has it been, Kelly, waiting here ten years for an event that may or may not happen?"

She nodded seriously. "We formed a very close knit community here at Chandrasekhar Station. In the early days, the complex was just a big empty ring."

"Kelly, our viewers will see us floating in front of a holographic cutaway view of the station with the giant planet Shiva behind us. But I'm mainly interested in all the uncertainty about the project. How did you folks handle it?"

She shrugged. "The physics isn't that uncertain. When the four impactors hit, the pressure exceeds what makes a neutron star collapse by an order of magnitude in an attosecond or so. So boom, you get an event horizon. The continuing pressure is enough to force the rest of the matter in past the Hawking radiation."

"Thank you, Kelly. I take it that you are confident the black hole will form."

"Huh? Oh, sure. The only thing to worry about was whether all the impactors got off, and we just got word they have. They even finished pushing Sol's impactor out here despite the political stuff."

Torsten winced. *Johnson, crop everything after "out here."*

He continued the interview. "It's been lonely for you, hasn't it?"

She giggled. "There are, uh, about forty-eight men and thirty-two women here. That is, there were until all the tourists from Campbell arrived. That was quite a surprise! Then the *Oberth's* inbound from New Antarctica. And that's not all..." She cut herself off abruptly. "I, uh, didn't say that last, okay?"

Torsten nodded. "I'll cut it." He'd been surprised himself to find a shipload of Campbell residents here. They were there, they said, as a tribute to Elizabeth Avonford, who'd lost her life in an effort to save a researcher from an asteroid impact, rather than divert BHP resources to prevent it. The whole thing smelled of a scandal to him. As for "...and that's not all...," he'd wait until Barrett's guard was down and probe in that direction again.

Anna came in, set Torsten's lemonade down and offered Kelly a glass, which Kelly drank eagerly.

"Kelly, what exactly do you do?" Torsten asked.

"I'm in charge of the operations room for six hours a day. A lot of times, decisions have to be made that can't be made by the AI because they involve competing human interests. So I make those calls, or now that Dr. Zhau is here, bump them up to him." She sighed.

Apparently, Torsten thought, she'd had a normal human reaction to project management showing up and starting to run the show. He smiled.

"So if, for example, some disastrous thing happened with the new black hole, you would jump into action? You must have protocols for every contingency, is that right?" Torsten asked.

"Oh, yes, we're trained to handle everything. Flight clearances, accidents, resource conflicts, that kind of thing." Kelly pulled at her neckline.

Oops, no geckro, Torsten noted. *Mark that, Johnson.*

"It's a bit warm in here, isn't it?"

Anna smiled. "I've lowered the room settings; you should be fine in a minute."

Kelly seemed much more relaxed now, even stifling a yawn. "Yeah. Look, what we'll get is a big explosion. If the black hole forms, we get a tiny bright speck where Vertex used to be, if not, nothing. There's not much in between that can happen..." She shook her head and took a deep breath as if trying to fight sleepiness. "Sorry. I'm awfully tired all of a sudden."

Torsten shot Anna a look. Had she drugged Kelly, hoping to get more information out of her? Utterly unethical, and it looked like she'd given the woman too much.

"Anna," he said sharply, "would you get some coffee?"

Kelly smiled. Then she yawned again. "Don' unnerstand this." She shook herself. "Could we continue this another time..." She fell back onto the couch with her eyes rolled upward.

"Kelly," Torsten said hurriedly, realizing that he was losing her. "Just one more thing for now. You mentioned the Campbell ship wasn't all. Is there something else coming? Another ship? We know about the ship from New Antarctica, is that it?"

Kelly's eyelids flickered and then she was sound asleep.

"Don't call the medics," Anna said. "I doped her."

"I should have figured that. Anna, first you got the dose wrong, and second, we don't do that. Ever. If anyone finds out... God! What are you doing?!"

Anna took off her wig and pulled the muumuu over her head, revealing an outfit identical to Kelly Barrett's. Then she sprayed herself with something.

"You can't..." he started.

"I can. I'm covered with her DNA markers," she flashed her fingers, "I've got her fingerprints, and I'm going to take her place."

"Anna, they'll lock me up!"

She shrugged. "Sometimes sacrifices are needed. But you can finish off her lemonade and call the medics when you wake up. Say we all had the lemonade, fell asleep, and you woke up alone. Maybe they'll buy it." Anna took a white ring with a tiny tetrahedral logo from Kelly's finger. "This opens doors and keyboards—a fail-operational hedge against the system going down."

"Anna, those people know her. You can't pull this off."

"I can. Kelly Barrett basically does what the position description says. I've studied her job." She beamed a Kelly Barrett grin at him. "And I'm a really good actress!"

"But security..."

"They don't have any real security systems here; they counted on the Solar System's outbound checks. I'll use the keyboard, which isn't so unusual in Ops because people don't multitask well when their heads are in the net. I've got my own access to any net info I need. Piece of cake." She raised an eyebrow, daring him to say something. He knew better.

She laughed and pointed to Barrett's unconscious body. "Dump her."

"Me?"

"You're in this up to your neck now. Your brother expected you might grouse a bit, but he trusts you to follow orders first and recriminate later." Anna stared him in the eye.

Torsten took hold of his cousin's arm and held it tight. "Anna, I want her alive. No funny business like last time."

"That was Vitali's idea." Anna tantalized him with a finger under his chin and patted his cheek. "Anyway, your precious Hilda survived, blew our plans up in Vitali's face, and he got the blame. Then she went to New Antarctica and made a mess of the backup plan as well. So, no, dear, she didn't get killed and here we are with one last chance."

Hilda Kremer. A diffident, modest, intriguing scientist with a brilliant mind, utterly dedicated to the project. Twenty years ago, Anna's sabotage team had misjudged what "brilliant" meant. He sighed.

"She's coming here, too, you know," he told her.

"Huh? Who?"

"Hilda Kremer. Her father kicked her out of New Antarctica for overstepping her authority—probably something to do with Vitali's fake schedule change message. Her ship won't get here before the impact, though."

Anna laughed and shook her head. "Thank God for small favors. I keep telling Lars that you're too sensitive. Anyway, you don't have to kill Kelly Barrett." She gave him a wicked grin. "I just wanted to see if you would. We can put her in my Cold Sleep Unit; it's self-contained, I've got it off net, and its controller isn't sentient—no Asimovian laws of robotics apply."

Anna, he remembered, had arranged to arrive in the coffin-shaped CSU from the *Vulpetti* and wake up in her room. No one on the starship had seen her and the CSU was still conveniently in her quarters. How was he going to get out of *this* when she got caught?

He sighed. "I see why Lars sent you out here, Anna. You're three steps ahead of everyone else. But look, the election is over and the BHP is just a science story now. Why not leave it alone?"

She smiled. "Torsten, Dr. Zhau has become increasingly political. If he succeeds in this, he'll return a hero. It would be better if something went a little wrong."

Torsten shook his head. "Sabotage? Lars would never..."

Anna shook her head. "You poor, dear wimp. Lars has to play the statesman. That doesn't mean he's given up. Anyway, this is personal with me, now. When I undertake something, I don't give up, either. Anyway, we're all opportunists—you, me, Lars. There's an opportunity to sabotage the impact and make political hay with this, and I'm grabbing it."

Torsten nodded dumbly.

"Now let's get her in the CSU, okay?"

••∞••

Anna bounced into the operations area. It was the biggest room on Chandrasekhar station, large enough that the curve of the floor was visible. The entire north wall of the room was a video screen with three banks of virtual consoles that rose from floor level half way up the south wall of the room. The saddle-shaped ceiling glowed white.

The duty controller's position was in the middle of the top rank of consoles. Only a couple of the other consoles were active; all spacecraft were docked until after the impact, and most of the other controllers were getting some sleep now. The impact was in twelve hours and nobody, but nobody, would want to sleep through that.

Security was almost nonexistent, as advertised. Nonetheless, Anna was nervous and excited. It was performance time—now or never. By luck, the shift officer was a George Muller; one of the few men in the station whose name wasn't in any of the very busy Ms. Barrett's private files. She took a breath, walked up him and tapped him on the shoulder. He turned, his eyes passing only briefly at her face on their way down to more interesting scenery.

"Hi, Kelly." He grinned. "Early for a change?"

So far so good. Anna grinned back at him and nodded to the 1.5-meter-long, half-meter-wide console display of graphics and touch zones, putting on as serious an expression as she could.

Muller paused as if he wanted to say something else, but thought better of it. He started his briefing. "The impactor from Campbell is a bit hot; it's on full braking mode and we added all the pellet mass we could to its approach lane. It's tight, but if nothing else goes wrong, we'll have a hole. It might have some residual momentum, though. The other three impactors are on phase within a couple microradians. The hole retrieval vessels are ready. Nothing much else to do. The *C. E. Singer*, with some of the Campbell tourists, will be headed toward a position beyond the impact site opposite Campbell in a couple of hours. They want pictures of the impact with their star in the background." He shook his head. "If that Campbell impactor stays hot, they may get more than they bargained for. Are you okay for taking the board through impact? The rest of us will be over in the science section."

Anna nodded and whispered huskily, "Sounds like a party. I drank some really hot coffee. Scalded my tongue, so I need to keep quiet a while, anyway."

"Sorry to hear that. Well, all's quiet here now, but we'll probably have more people soon. We have a ship coming in from New Antarctica at 2100 and another from Epsilon Eridani still a day out. Reggie Terry over at services has it covered. I suspect some of them might want clearance to visit the hole, if we get one. If you need anything, check the on-call list." He got up, glanced down at her chest one last time, and headed for the door with a grin. "Good night."

Anna smiled and waved him goodbye. Then she surveyed the console display. It was close to what she'd studied—only two different keys and a new gauge—she looked those up quickly enough. She found the beacon controls. The impactor from Campbell was already on the knife-edge of being too early and was dragging at maximum thrust. If she were to move the guidance null just a couple of picoradians, it should deflect just enough to cause the implosion to fail. But she had to do it quickly, and without attracting notice. For practice, she sent an attoradian change—pushing the center point a few micrometers west of dead on. The AI asked if she was sure, but accepted her affirmative response. She started typing in the modifications to the beacon calibration.

"G'd evening, Miss," said a male voice from somewhere in the remains of the British Empire.

Anna whirled around in her chair to see an amiable-looking heavyset man in trousers, turtleneck, and jacket, his hand in the jacket pocket.

"I'm Roger Gunheim from Campbell. Came by Ops to make sure everything is okay."

Anna flashed her come-hither smile. "Is that so? Are folks from Campbell supervising us now?"

He eased himself into the seat beside her and laughed. "The BHP project sent someone in to take over our operation, so we thought we'd return the favor."

Anna measured the man up and down. So this was Roger Gunheim, the former Campbell chief executive she'd heard about. It would be fun to discuss Nietzsche and the will to power with him some day, but that would be out of character for Kelly Barrett.

She arched an eyebrow. "Everything appears normal." She smiled seductively, "Is there anything you need?"

He smiled back. "Only to find out what your intentions are..."

Alarm bells started to ring in Anna's head. Hoping that was just a pick up line, she gently raised her chest to distract him. "I see a man of action. When and where?"

Gunheim laughed, pulled out a trank gun, and waved it in her face. "Not so fast there, sheila. Hands off the keyboard. You're not Kelly Barrett, you're Lars Ried's cousin, Anna Messenger."

Anna froze, then relaxed a little. He knew, but he hadn't shot her or called the authorities.She had easily penetrated what passed for the security of these absent-minded scientists. But she hadn't counted on running into another player. What was his game?

She lifted her chin. "How did you know?"

Gunheim gave a short laugh. "I've compromised the net. Item one, Anna Messenger is listed on the news staff and present in the Operations Center but seems invisible. Item two. Kelly Barrett is supposed to be on duty but is not on the net. Item three, Lars Ried never gives up—commendable. I always liked his style, never liked his politics, but he did a few favors for me once. Item four, Peter thought he recognized you despite your disguise. He did you at Earthport, about thirty years ago? It must have been memorable."

Anna groaned. There was a downside to looking too much like your impersonation target. Well, it had seemed like a good idea at the time. Gunheim might have compromised the system, but maybe not the press encryption within it. She filed a dispatch. *Torsten, I've been caught.*

Gunheim seemed to like the sound of his own voice; maybe she could string this out for a while. "*I* did *him*," she responded at last, with a bit of vamp.

Gunheim laughed. "I just might believe that."

She smiled ruefully.

"Okay, you haven't shot me or called security. Why? What do you want?"

Gunheim folded his arms. "My suggestion is that what we have planned might be as useful to Lars Ried as your sabotage. More useful, even."

Anna turned to look at him. The trank gun was a palm-sized Cavalli twin-barrel of the kind that had been standard issue for security forces for the last half-century. It fired two-millimeter flechettes that dissolved in blood.

"More useful?" she asked, coolly.

He nodded, looking her over. "If the experiment fails through sabotage, and that becomes known, there would be a political backlash of the sort he might not survive. Whereas, if some of the darker predictions come true, he'll look like a bloody prophet."

"Darker predictions?"

Gunheim just smiled.

Anna raised an eyebrow. "I have to take that on faith?"

"For now." His smile vanished. "You just keep your Kelly Barrett persona and do nothing she wouldn't do until the impact. And after the impact, you do *nothing* she would do and everything I tell you to do. Is it a deal?"

"Hi, Kelly!" Torsten said, finally arriving.

Gunheim smoothly pocketed the Cavalli.

Just play it cool, Anna sent to Torsten. *Distract him. I only need second or two.*

Anna, You're nuts!

Do it!

Her cousin's expression resolved itself into a media man's public mask. "Good evening, Mr. Gunheim," Torsten said, affecting his best Ried smile. "What brings you to operations?"

"I'm busy, Ried." Gunheim glanced toward him.

While he did, Anna silently finished her inputs.

A woman's voice boomed from across the room. "Messenger, move away from the console."

Anna froze. The computer was flashing at her, asking if she really wanted to do the guidance change. She had only to acknowledge the command with a touch. She moved her arm.

The dart felt like a wasp had stung her. With her hand inches from the console, she went numb. As she fell, she heard Roger Gunheim's answer to Torsten.

"What's going on, Mr. Ried, is perhaps the most significant event in human history. With a few changes. As you have probably gathered, we are taking over the station. This is Magda Lobacz, who will be in charge while my party heads out to collect the black hole."

So that was their game! Even lying paralyzed on the floor, Anna was thrilled by the audacity of it. Yes, indeed, it would be one of Lars' worst propaganda nightmares confirmed. And if everything people said they could do with tame black holes was true, Roger Gunheim would become the most powerful man in the universe. Maybe, just maybe...

Lobacz was a grim-faced butch-cut blonde at least two meters tall and not in the least bit willowy. Her jumpsuit was solid black and she had a full security belt. She picked Anna up off the floor as if Anna were a feather, placed her in the chair, and slapped pieces of yellow tape around her to pin her arms and keep her there.

"Next time I say something to you, you do it and ask questions later, understand?"

Anna found she couldn't move her mouth. The question, of course, was purely rhetorical. But if she read Lobacz' tone of voice correctly, a long line of power-seeking females lay between her and Roger Gunheim.

Torsten, answer 'yes' to the system prompt. Now. Do it even if they shoot you!

"Mr. Gunheim, Ms. Lobacz," Torsten said. "Uh, I see the board's calling for an automated guidance adjustment to be okayed. I hate to bother you, but if you want a black hole, you probably shouldn't hold it up."

Lobacz turned and looked at the board, then at Gunheim.

Gunheim stared at the panel for a minute, looked at Anna, then looked back at the board.

"It's routine," he said, finally. "I studied this setup on the way in; the adjustments are automatic, but the system gets a human okay to let them think they're doing something. Best give it the okay."

Trust Torsten to know people, Anna thought. Gunheim apparently liked to impress people and pretend he knew what was going on. Lobacz nodded obediently and hit the okay herself.

●●∞●●

Dr. Bradford Adams watched data from the impactors pour into the science gallery and felt the tension mount. Ten hours and counting. Over a century of work behind them. His mouth was dry. They'd replicated a Melbourne pub in the recreation area of Chandrasekhar Station, and he intended to spend some time with a Victoria Bitter there when this was done.

He tore his eyes from the displays. Gunheim's people were everywhere. Why weren't they all on the *Singer*? The starship turned excursion boat had just left for the impact point. Maybe these were just the cautious ones.

"Dr. Adams?"

"Yes?" He turned and saw an Asian woman of medium height.

"Kim-Soh Young," she introduced herself with a big smile, "representing InterplaNet News. How do you feel about making the black hole tonight? You are working on this a very long time."

Brad smiled. "You might say we all have our fingers crossed."

Kim smiled. "Everything is coming out okay, then?"

"She'll be right. Some problems with the Campbell Impactor, but..." He looked at the board just to be sure. "Now what's that? Pardon me, Miss."

Brad couldn't believe his eyes. *Sarah, Tse Wen. Check Hilda's impactor.*

Brad, this is Sarah. It's right down the pipe.

Brad, Sarah, Tse Wen here. Brad's concern, I believe, is that it should not be right down the pipe. It was under full deceleration only two hours ago. It may be wise to question the instruments.

"What's going on?" a new voice said.

Brad turned and saw another Campbell person, a tall grim-faced man with short hair. Brad frowned. "Could you wait a moment, mate. I've got an interview in progress."

He looked at the data again—normal. Something was bloody rooted. *System, who's on Ops Control.*

It is Kelly Barrett's shift; however, Anna Messenger, of Popular Issues magazine, is currently occupying the control seat.

What did that mean? A news interview? *Who else is there?* he asked.

Magda Lobacz, a Campbell visitor.

Brad shot a look at the Campbell person near him. *Where is Barrett?*

She is not responding.

We have an emergency! Get someone on the staff there!

Magda Lobacz is authorized staff, the system replied.

Since when?

"Problem happening now?" Kim asked.

"Do you have a problem, Dr. Adams?" the Campbell man asked.

Brad was on the point of wheeling around and yelling that yes, he bloody well had a problem—but caught himself in time. If he did something like that, he'd likely end up wherever Kelly Barrett was.

"No," he said evenly. "Just some adjustments need to be made." He changed the view field from the Campbell impactor to the one from Earth, which had a dramatic effect on the screen and did nothing whatsoever to the impactors. "There, Ms. Kim. It'll be right."

He turned to see the Campbell man looking over his shoulder and gave him a big phony smile. Kim had vanished.

"Nothing special here, *mite*," he said, laying his Australian accent on a bit heavy, hoping they would underestimate him. "Lots to look at, but she's all nominal, right down the pipe. Here, why don't you sit down yourself for a bit? Something to tell your *wallies* about, right?"

The man smiled, nodded, and sat down eagerly. "Is that one of the impactors?" he asked, pointing to a long line in an upper left-hand screen.

"Sure is, mate. That's the one from Earth. Up the mag and look on the front end."

He did so. "It's dark out there. How can I see it?"

"We're illuminating it with lasers and we've got a synthetic aperture a million kilometers across staring at it. The big can on the front end is the brains. We send out a string of pulses, kind of like road signs on a rally. The impactor has to pass each road sign at just the right time."

"What if it doesn't?"

"The big mag sail off the back—you can't see it at this magnification—is set to drag at thirty kilonewtons, but it can increase or decrease that to make up a difference. That's not much thrust for a billion tons, but we'd only need to move it a few wavelengths back or forward. Let's go max on the magnification,"

Brad's mouth dropped open as the video magnified. The bloody idiots back home had done just what he'd done on the sim and painted his initials, B.A., right on the nose of the thing, like it was a bomb in some old war. He shook his head, laughing.

"What's so funny?"

"Just what the guys painted on the thing's nose." Brad laughed. Then the laugh died in his throat as he saw an "S2" below the initials. That stood for "simulation 2." That wasn't the real impactor. It couldn't be.

"Something wrong?"

"No, no, mate. Just gotta run for the bloody loo, I've been sitting here five hours, worrying and drinking coffee."

The man laughed. "I know how that goes."

"See if anyone else has painted stuff on the noses of the other ones. I'll be right back."

Whoever hacked that image could probably listen in on anything he sent to Sarah or Tse Wen. He didn't dare let anyone know he'd caught on. Even so, he might have only a few minutes. He gave a quick look at Sarah, whose head was buried in her displays, and then Tse Wen, who looked up at the right time. Their eyes met. From the frown on his face, Brad thought Tse Wen clearly knew things were amiss as well. Brad tossed his head ever so lightly at the exit and Tse Wen gave a barely perceptible nod. The exchange might have taken two seconds.

Brad then turned away and headed out of the operations room. He passed the rest room, headed for the elevator, opened the service panel and pulled it off the net. He then told the lift to take him to the maintenance floor; elevators were designed to work autonomously in emergencies.

At maintenance, he picked up a spare central processor for the *Martinez*, an in-system shuttle equipped for monitoring the black hole.

That would be duly reported, but as he was scheduled to be on the post-event inspection crew, it probably wouldn't ring any AI alarms. He could only hope the Campbell crowd hadn't anticipated everything. Worried that any exceptionally hurried activity might trigger concern, he pulled himself along with the handholds at normal speed through the access tube to the lock. Once aboard the *Martinez*, he headed right for the engineering bay and threw the manual comm disconnect. He had the processors swapped in seconds and touched the local net secure. Would this work? He bit his lip and touched the ship's net.

Martinez, Bradford Adams commanding, secure. We have a hijacking emergency involving the Chandrasekhar Station AI. It must not know I am aboard and am giving instructions.

Understood. Bioradios were self-authenticating; no two were alike any more than fingerprints. But Brad sighed with relief anyway. Halfway there. *I'm declaring an emergency. The station AI has been compromised.*

You have authority for such an emergency bypass.

Right. Can you get us pumped down and out of here without the station knowing in time to stop us?

I can perform the tasks in 200 seconds. The rest is uncertain.

Bloody damn right it was uncertain. Adams managed a chuckle at himself.

Okay. I'm going to restore comm. Give them a couple minutes to think that everything is okay and I'm heading back to shuttle ops. Then get us out of here.

He scrambled back to the comm access panel, through the switch, then headed for the nearest seat in Engineering.

Prepare for acceleration in two minutes. Where are we headed?

Good question. He quickly abandoned any notion of trying to attack the *Singer*. Its AI was probably fully compliant to DeRoot and Gunheim at this point. Even without a beam to ride on, a starship still had three hundred megawatts of nuclear-powered lasers and fusion torch drives to play with. There was no point in trying to challenge that in a runabout. The *Oberth* from New Antarctica was less than a light minute out and decelerating. He didn't know her captain, but Hilda was on board. It would be good to have her head on this.

Rendezvous with the Oberth, minimum time trajectory. I'll take the acceleration. Get a direct link to the Vertex site. Transfer control here without notification to central. Did he have sufficient authority? Had the site been hacked, too? Seconds of light speed lag passed.

Emergency transfer authenticated.

Various audible clanks and whirs confirmed the *Martinez'* departure. He strapped in, shut his eyes and scanned the data flowing into his head—the real data. The Campbell impactor was still hot, though decelerating on schedule. But it was also off track, almost a hundred nanometers—barely a quarter of the wavelength the guidance beacons used, but a huge error given the requirements. The Campbell takeover, a consolidationist in the ops chair—what the hell was going on? He had to put that out of his mind and concentrate on the impactor. What was making it go off course? Something to do with the phase of the guidance beams? What was the command history? He read. He checked. He thought. He checked again.

"Prepare for deceleration," the *Martinez* said over audio speakers.

"Deceleration? When did we bloody accelerate?"

"Almost two hours ago, at point four gravities."

Bradford Adams laughed. "Well, that's concentration for you."

An unmagnified view of the *Oberth* filled his screen. It was a standard three spheres on a solenoid ring design, with long grazing incidence cones ahead of each sphere. A smaller coaxial "choke ring" that improved the plasma reflection performance lay about fifty meters forward of the main ring. A docking trolley ran on its inside, catching the runabout. Inside the ring, shielding water would be redistributed to maintain the ship's balance as the trolley brought the mass of the runabout into sync with the ring. Brad monitored the process with interest.

When he turned back to the problem, he thought he knew what was going on and why.

CHAPTER 3

Near Vertex in orbit around Shiva
23 December 2284

Brad and the *Oberth's* captain, Ada Chenhansa, scanned a virtual screen showing current locations of each of the four impactors, Gunheim and DeRoot's ship, theirs, and Chandrasekhar Station. A petite woman with shiny black hair, Chenhansa moved and spoke with grace, economy and deliberation. The aura of command, he thought.

She pointed to one of the impactors. "From Campbell, on time?"

Brad nodded. "It's a bit off center and has a little too much energy. I did what I could about that. But it will be on time. With three groups of human beings playing tug of war for it."

The *Oberth's* AI called for attention with the soft and deep tone of a large gong.

"Yes?" Chenhansa said.

"Dr. Adams wished to be notified when Hilda was about to awaken."

Chenhansa caught his eye and nodded.

Brad hurriedly left the captain for Hilda's stateroom, threading his way down from the dome to the deck below and into the tube connecting the *Oberth's* spheres. How many years had it been? About twenty-five since the Ten-Ten experiment validated her model. Most of that in relativistic spaceships for her. It would only be like a year or two for her, fifteen for him.

A robotic attendant met him at the door. "She's awake and expecting you. It may be a few minutes before she's fully oriented."

"Understood. If I might? It is urgent." The machine smiled and stepped aside, somewhat more slowly than Brad thought was necessary, which was silly because it was just part of the *Oberth* which bloody well knew what was going on. Probably just impatience on his part. Hilda, looking a little dazed, was rubbing her limbs. Her eyes focused on him.

"Brad!"

"How's it going, Hilda?"

"Bones and muscles ache. Brain's intact. I'll be on the net in a moment." She looked at him carefully, then zeroed in on his eyes. "You're not supposed to be here. Something's happened."

He told her what, ending with, "If I'm right, they intend to take possession of the black hole."

"My sister, Liz, is at Campbell..."

She wouldn't know yet. Of course not, he realized. He'd have to tell her. Oh, what the hell had he been thinking? This should be Tse Wen's job, but Tse Wen wasn't available just now. A knot formed in his stomach. Things couldn't wait; he would just have to tell her and pick up the pieces later.

Hilda looked at him dumbly after he finished. "Dead?"

"It's too big a thing," he said softly. "Too big to think we weren't going to pay a price. Bloody rotten thing for you to wake up to. I'm really sorry."

She tottered to her feet and fell into his arms. "Brad, people just don't die anymore." Tears were beginning to form in her eyes.

He nodded and held her, rocking her gently back and forth. That was what biological immortality was supposed to be all about, to live for bloody ever. "I pray to whatever runs this crazy universe that I'm wrong, but I'm not entirely sure it was all an accident."

She sobbed softly, then seemed to come out of it. "How did eliminating Liz help them? There should be a small armada of robotic craft around the impact site to take data. You've taken control of that."

Brad shook his head. "When Mutori took back the project, she arranged for the Campbell impactor to be just a little hot. The extra momentum will pop the black hole out beyond our containment arrangements and off toward where Gunheim's positioning his starship." He explained the fake data from the Science Section video feed. "Nobody would have painted 'S2' on them, for 'simulation two.' They bummed that video right from the sim, and I almost dropped the load when I recognized it."

He watched anger flow over Hilda's face as if it were morphing in some video. When she looked up, her eyes burned and her jaw was set. Brad had only the sketchiest details of what Hilda had been through on New Antarctica, but the coldness and resolution in her voice told him that, if anything, she had changed more in her last three waking years than he had in fifteen.

He shook his head. "I do have a surprise for them. I couldn't fully correct the perturbation from Anna Messenger's sabotage attempt, so this hole is going to squirt out a little sideways of what they thought. We can be there first."

"How long do you think before they catch on?" Hilda asked.

Brad shrugged. "The system AI's got a split personality now, half of it helping us under the security emergency codes, the rest of it pretending nothing's going on. I suspect something will give it away, eventually."

The robot came in with clothes.

"Give me a few minutes."

He nodded, and with a quick hug, left. As he did, a cold cramp grew in his stomach. There had never, in any history that had reached him, been a fight between starships before. One of them may have been modified in anticipation of it—and that wasn't the one he and Hilda were on.

••∞••

Peter DeRoot stood in the center of *C. E. Singer's* dome looking at the impact site. The tiny moon seemed curiously soft in the shadowless glow of amplified starlight.

Roger Gunheim walked over to him and put a hand on his shoulder. "Do you feel like bloody Caesar looking across the Rubicon, Peter?" he asked.

DeRoot smiled and nodded. Roger might play the *boerenkinkel*, but from time to time let on that he knew more of the world. "A good analogy," he whispered. Caesar, not Moses. A lout would have said Moses.

Gunheim waved a hand toward the left of the impact site. "The *Oberth's* coming on."

A tiny speck of light lay at the head of a trail of glowing gas. He touched the net and got the flight plan. Captain Chenhansa was stationing herself safely away from the line of any impactor. DeRoot shook his head. "Magda has Operations under control?"

Gunheim paused a moment to get a report. His fellow Aussie, Dr. Bradford Adams, was apparently missing and being looked for, but otherwise Magda had no problems. "Yeah, she's right there. That bloke, Adams, is missing, but we've got him locked out of the system; there's nothing he can do there. So no worries."

"Then I would say that Hilda Kremer has come to see the show. She will see more than she's bargained for."

Gunheim laughed, perhaps a little too loudly. "Bloody right about that! Still, we're ready to deal with it if she tries something."

DeRoot gave a quick smile. They had been busier than normal during the passage from Campbell. The *Singer* now boasted a laser array a hundred times more powerful than what was needed to ionize debris in her path. They'd also manufactured some forty homing missiles. The one-meter layer of shielding water surrounding three of the *Singer's* spheres had been jelled with fullerene tubes and frozen steel-hard at three degrees above absolute zero.

It had all been unnecessary. Their surprise had been complete, there were no station security forces to speak of, and they had complete control. In a few minutes, they could even be magnanimous.

●●∞●●

Hilda arrived at *Oberth's* Sphere One and took the lift up to the park dome. The screens showed the exterior view, starlit objects amplified to dim ghosts, and symbology labeling everything. Brad and Captain Chenhansa were sitting in lawn chairs, staring at the display. Dotted lines raced across the dome to a convergent point. Hilda touched Brad's hand as she took a seat next to him, and he squeezed back.

"If Captain DeRoot were to capture the black hole first," Captain Chenhansa asked, "what can he do with it? He cannot go anywhere tied to a four-billion-ton astronomical anomaly!"

Hilda shook her head. "It's big enough that its gravity can overcome resistance to compression and the pressure of its Hawking radiation. You can dump mass into it, and then it should act like other spinning black holes; it will spit most of the mass back out in plasma jets from its poles at relativistic velocity and most of that from the pole opposite the incoming mass. From the starship's point of view, it should act like a pulse fusion drive with a higher exhaust velocity. All DeRoot needs is a mass roughly equivalent to that of the hole, and he can reach a significant fraction of the speed of light."

"A ring rock?" Brad asked.

Hilda shrugged. "Or something." She thought a couple of moments. "Acceleration may have to be low, however, depending on how much radiation he's ready for."

"What is he going to do?" Captain Chenhansa asked. "Build a fleet of black hole-powered starships and conquer the Solar System? What is he thinking?"

Thankfully, Torsten had never thought to ask *that* question. "We don't know with any certainty that one black hole can make others. But if it can, they don't need to conquer the Solar System; they just need to make it irrelevant."

"A bunch of dingoes trying to put their own piss on the cosmos, if you ask me," Brad added.

Hilda touched his arm. "Chaos, Brad, the consolidationists will let them. They'll say 'we told you so' and use it to stay in power in the Solar System, which is all they care about."

Captain Chenhansa sighed. "There is so much at stake... but I have a ship full of passengers in cold sleep who cannot be risked."

They were all silent.

"We can put them on the *Martinez*," Brad said. "You'll need to give them enough fuel to get home."

Chenhansa frowned and nodded. "We will wait until we are at lower relative velocity."

Hilda went over Brad's contingency plan and the trajectories of the impactors again, adding every factor she could think of. Unfortunately, it all came up with DeRoot closer than them. There was something she could try. In theory, it would work; in practice, it would be taking an awful risk.

"Brad, I'm thinking of a drag reduction on the Groombridge 34 and Epsilon Eridani impactors. They're coming in with the nominal drag allowed by the mission rules, but it isn't zero. Less, and they would come in slightly faster and produce a component of post-impact momentum in the Earth direction. Watch."

Lines converged on the dome again, coming together at a spot somewhat further away from them but at less of an angle to their present course.

"We should get another kilometer per second or so of reserve," Captain Chenhansa remarked. "I like that."

Brad touched the net and pulled up the project sim. In principle there was some margin for off center impact, but it was literally measured in nanometers. "We can try. If anything goes wrong..."

Brad looked at Hilda. Almost a century of work was at stake and the political environment was such that it might be centuries from now before it was attempted again. If ever. Twenty years earlier, Hilda would not have taken the chance.

"It already has gone wrong," Hilda said. "We have to try to make it right. Tse Wen?"

Brad shook his head. "We don't dare try to talk to him."

"I shall wake the rest of the passengers and get the evacuation under way," Chenhansa informed them. She closed her eyes for a moment, then said, "It's done. I've ordered a lighter to meet the *Martinez* at a rendezvous point."

"Did they ask why?" Brad asked her, worried about alerting Gunheim.

Chenhansa smiled faintly. "I did not bother the duty controller, and the computer did not ask why. They seldom do."

Brad nodded and smiled. He was beginning to like this captain.

"Are Tse Wen and Sarah okay?" Hilda asked.

Brad thought of all the Campbell people around. Not tourists at all, but, essentially, Campbell government forces. No, he amended that. Pirates. They were bloody pirates. He smiled at Hilda darkly. "As okay as any people staring down the barrels of loaded guns are okay."

Her eyes went wide. "Hostages?"

Brad winced. He hadn't thought of that one. Not at all.

••∞••

Anna watched the main display, biting her lip. Torsten stood behind one of the consoles in the amphitheater of the Science Section, quietly speaking into his news feed, too softly for Anna to hear. He had actually asked Magda's permission to continue with the news operation. The Campbell security people laughed and said go ahead, even letting him have her to assist him.

And why not? Any reaction from Earth would take nearly twenty years to get back here, thirty or so to get to Campbell. By then, one way or another, the situation would be entirely different. The broadcasters were still, of course, being watched very carefully.

The Campbell people, all in red coveralls now, were everywhere in the Operations Section, and everywhere else. A glance behind her showed that her own personal minder—a dark, narrow-faced man with no hint of a smile—had his full attention on her. The guidance change had been sent, but she'd had no console access since.

One minute now. It would either work or it would not. If it did not, and if the Campbell people got the hole, Lars would be furious. He would self-righteously scream, "I told you so," to everyone who would listen.

It would be a short-term political bonanza for him. But in the long term? Would the Solar System itself be safe from DeRoot and Gunheim? Conventional wisdom was that interstellar war was impossible. She looked around her as if seeing what had happened for the first time. Impossible? She was sitting in the middle of what was arguably the first attempt at interstellar warfare, and one that looked to be completely successful.

Whatever the political benefits of "I told you so," the Rieds would become irrelevant. The future now looked to be Gunheim's. Ultimately, Gunheim and DeRoot would want someone who knew the Solar System, knew where the keys to power were hidden, someone whose will to power might match their own. Gunheim had women waiting in line, but DeRoot was rumored to be insatiable. She smiled to herself. She knew how to use her body. Perhaps...

Torsten's voice became loud with excitement. "If ever there was a time when everyone in the known universe was focused on one single moment, this would be it. We are in the last six seconds."

"...four, three, two, one..."

••∞••

Someone on the *Singer* started counting backwards from twenty. "...nineteen, eighteen."

Conversations hushed. "...twelve, eleven..."

"...two, one..."

Peter DeRoot may have seen the slightest flash. For the tiniest fraction of a second, the tiny moon did nothing. Then it turned into a perfect, shining sphere of plasma, only slightly marbled, which first lit up the spacecraft arrayed around the impact site then expanded through them at incredible speed.

He caught his breath as the huge translucent plasma bubble struck the *Singer*, and rocked it firmly. Behind the bubble, a miniature nebula formed and also expanded, though much more slowly.

The prize for all their efforts should be in there somewhere. It should be a brilliant spark coming right toward them. He strained to see it.

••∞••

It had already happened, Anna thought. The light had just not gotten here yet.

There was a brief flicker as the impactors zipped across the screen and vanished into the targeted moonlet, which, after a fraction of a second was replaced by a rapidly expanding glowing bubble. It was translucent. Anna could see stars through it. Where was the hole?

"...we have impact."

"Look at Shiva!"

Heads turned in unison to the right as the ringed planet and its moon system flashed into view from the light of the implosion. A giant blue Saturn, slightly gibbous, with huge broad white rings hung over them, or was it below them? It faded quickly back to black.

Anna glanced back at the impact site; the plasma shell generated by the impact moved more slowly than light, but now filled a quarter of the large screen and rushed toward them. Such a perfect, pearl-like sphere, she thought. A cosmic soap bubble. A new universe? Death?

Before she could complete the thought, the front passed them without any discernible physical effect. So much for five decades worth of propaganda!

She looked toward the *C. E. Singer* and saw an invisible speck of light, unrecognizable on the screen except for the symbology that floated along with it. The hole should be brilliant, glowing with megawatts of Hawking radiation. It wasn't there.

Had she succeeded? She gripped the arms of her chair in excitement.

"The instant of impact itself was an anticlimax," Torsten announced to posterity. "The impactor rods flashed through the field of view, end to end, and vanished into the moonlet in thirty-three millionths of a second. At the vertex, what happened was done in three millionths of a second. That seems a very short time to us, but as these physicists tell us, that is an eternity of three trillion attoseconds at the nuclear scale.

"In the first few million attoseconds, the center of the impact fills up with collision-produced matter to make a nut so dense not even neutrinos can penetrate it. Nor can the force of any one impactor move it against the force of the other impactors. A stream of matter flows into the implosion at five billion tons a second, but is brought to a halt in a little less than a centimeter.

"There are no common words to describe the central pressure. Dr. Kremer's calculation was that at 4.3 with thirty zeros after it times standard atmospheric pressure, the last resistance to compression is exceeded and the entire mass collapses into one irreducibly small loop, or set of loops, separated by fractional dimensions of Planck scale. Something like that, anyway. Maybe. We can't tell what happens actually, because at that density, gravity has produced a black hole.

"Which won't be black because of something called Hawking radiation which I will not attempt to explain, but which will make this object not black but a tiny quantum scale star that radiates its mass away with a power of millions of watts!

"So it is supposed to have happened. Most of the outer layers of the moon were vaporized and blown away in the spectacular bubble of plasma you saw. This was expected. We are not, however, seeing the brilliant speck that should be there in the center of where the moon was."

Murmuring and muttering filled the room.

Anna could hardly contain herself. Had she won? Had she? Oh yes, it had worked! She'd prevailed! *Her* will had trumped all the others! A manic grin began to spread across her face. This was better than sex. Better than sex with drugs. Oh, she would savor this moment!

••∞••

Zhau Tse Wen looked from his guard, a burly mustachioed man introduced to him as "Micky," to the stateroom wall screen, then back. After Brad had escaped to warn Hilda, the Campbell people had removed all the project management from the net. There was nothing for him to do but watch. He must be content with that. For now.

There was irony, Tse Wen reflected, that this stateroom had originally been assigned to Anna Messenger, the cousin of Lars Ried who had probably been the mysterious woman who had impersonated Hilda Kremer in a previous sabotage effort. Messenger's modus operandi, apparently. She had reappeared after the conservative coalition had gained power and was now on station, ostensibly to assist reporter Torsten Ried. Whatever plans she'd had must have been preempted by the Campbell takeover. The usurpation seemed to be fairly complete and did not, apparently, include sabotaging the project.

"Micky, could I have a view of Shiva?" he asked.

The minder pulled on his moustache. "Instead of the impact? After all these years?"

"It may succeed, or it may not. Either way, there will not be that much to see. But when the flash of light from the implosion hits Shiva's rings, that will be a sight unlike any other."

"Yeah? Okay if I keep a corner of the screen on the vertex?"

Tse Wen nodded. "As you wish."

He almost missed the impactors' flash across the screen by blinking, but a couple of seconds later, the light echo of the implosion racing across the rings and body of Shiva was, indeed, a wonder to behold. The rings and the few high clouds on the planet changed color as the flash faded from violet to deep red. The bulk of the planet itself was momentarily a brilliant blue which darkened and darkened until it seemed that a few ruddy-gold clouds floated in the darkness of the void itself.

He looked at the Campbell man again. He was big enough, but there was a softness about him. He nodded to the man and smiled. "Imagine that for several weeks."

The man frowned, "A supernova?"

"A hypernova. That is the way nature makes black holes."

"You just want to study it, right?"

Tse Wen shrugged his shoulders innocently.

"Maybe the boss man will let you do that, if you behave yourself."

Tse Wen allowed himself the slightest frown. He had conceived the project and managed it to fruition across four star systems and this lone planet. Now, "maybe" he would be allowed to study its results. But the game was not over yet. There were hidden strategies in this game, moves placed in advance to stand guard against an unknown. A step here and a gesture there, and everything could change. But he would have to wait his turn.

"I shall have to ask him," Tse Wen said mildly.

"Do you know where the black hole is?" the man said. "I don't see anything."

Tse Wen frowned. "The light echo was beautiful. We can return to a full screen view of the implosion area now."

••∞••

Hilda Kremer braced herself. Even ten thousand kilometers away, the wave of plasma from the vaporized moonlet grabbed their magnetic fields like a gust from a hurricane as it swept by them. The floor felt like it had been shoved sideways and everything trembled.

In a few seconds, they each gained almost a kilometer a second of velocity away from the implosion center. Both the *Oberth* and the *C. E. Singer* were fully prepared for this, of course, and the velocity increment was factored into their plans.

The plasma cleared in seconds.

Where is it? she thought as the star field faded in through the last aurora-like shreds of implosion debris. Oh, please, please, where is it?

Their eyes, and every instrument in the ship, scanned the area in front of them.

"Since when," Captain Chenhansa said, very softly, "does Orion's belt have four stars?"

"Tallyho!" Brad cried as the clearing plasma revealed an impossibly brilliant spark heading right for them. "It's coming right at us!"

Hilda's estimate hadn't been perfect, but they hadn't gotten to the predicted point in time, either. The errors had canceled almost exactly. "The *Oberth* has acquired it. We're maneuvering to match velocities."

The maneuver went smoothly; the only thing Hilda noticed was a slight increase in weight as the rockets came on before spin reduction was complete.

Hilda glanced at the *C. E. Singer*, less than five thousand kilometers away. It continued to scud away on its too-high velocity vector, but was braking at its maximum thrust.

"We will be on it about fifteen minutes before they get here, assuming they decelerate," the captain said. "Two hundred megawatts of Hawking radiation. Magnetic moment... chaos!"

Hilda nodded, unable to take her eyes off the tiny star in the viewscreen. "The Campbell impactor was at max deceleration, its field fully inflated, for the better part of a month in its frame. It went in magnetized and a lot of that was compressed to nuclear dimensions. Its angular momentum is astronomical, but that will decay fairly rapidly. The higher Hawking radiation means we got less mass in the hole than expected. But enough. It's enough to be with us a long, long time." Forever, perhaps, as they would feed it more mass. A permanent monument. Decades of effort, determination, and sacrifice made real. But its existence felt surreal to her, too big to grasp fully in the instant.

"It doesn't matter how long we live, a day like this, she'll never come again." Brad said, quietly.

A gong sounded both in Hilda's ears and in her head.

We are beginning the capture sequence, the *Oberth's* voice said. *Please lie down, sit, or otherwise secure yourselves. There may be transient accelerations peaking at approximately fifteen gravities.*

"It has the mass of a bloody asteroid," Brad said with a laugh. "And with that field, we go where it goes, quickly."

They lay down on the grass and looked up at their version of the night sky. It was disconcerting to Hilda that when the acceleration came, it was in the opposite direction of the relative movement of the hole. The cameras, of course, were pointed backward. The bump was more like falling out of bed than a sustained acceleration, though. After it was done, she saw the brilliant point floating between the *Oberth's* field generators.

Hilda touched the net for instrument reading. "We're picking up frame drag on the accelerometers."

"It's a ring singularity?" Captain Chenhansa asked.

"Kerr geometry," Brad stated.

"Near the limit, I'd think," Hilda said. "It's too small for any charge to speak of."

"We have secured it. Or, rather, we have secured the ship around it," the captain said. Then she looked from Hilda to Brad and back to Hilda. "Now what do we do?"

CHAPTER 4

Chandrasekhar Station
in orbit about Shiva
24 December 2284

Torsten watched events unfold with the sort of awe one has for a superlative player of any sport, even if on the opposing team. In spite of everything, and it had been quite a lot in his estimation, Hilda Kremer appeared to be in possession of a mini black hole.

"Damn, damn, damn, damn," Anna said in front of him.

She had almost literally wilted when the black hole had finally turned up. He put a hand on her shoulder. She shrugged it off.

He looked around. The Campbell people were grim-faced. Magda Lobacz went from urgent conversation to urgent conversation, then left the room.

On the screen, it looked as if two starships were about to contest for ownership of a black hole. Neither answered to Lars' interest. "Anna..."

"Go to hell."

"Anna, you need to let go."

She spun and looked at him. "Well, they might still knock each other off out there."

Torsten shook his head. Gunheim had anticipated even that. "Then the Campbell people here pick up the pieces."

Anna motioned him closer and whispered, "*If* they are still in charge. This is still a Solar System government project. I am, kind of, a Solar System government agent. Maybe I should be in charge."

Torsten's jaw dropped at the audacity of it. Was she now considering a rebellion here to save the project she came here to sabotage? He glanced at their minder. The man's eyes were riveted to the unfolding drama on the big display screen.

"What are you thinking?" he asked.

She grinned madly at him. "Watch. Just watch," she whispered.

Then she turned to the minder. "I need to use the head."

He motioned for one of the Campbell women to escort her, a gangling dark-haired woman with an earnest expression on her face.

His power-mad cousin could easily kill her. Or vice versa—the other woman was armed. He should say something. Stop this before it made even more of a mess. What would Lars want him to do? He opened his mouth.

The minder looked at him expectantly.

He shook his head and turned back to the screen. What would happen, would happen. It was none of his doing, he told himself.

Roger Gunheim's image appeared on the screen. He was dressed casually, seated at a clean desk with a starscape behind him.

"I am addressing all of you in the Shiva system. The Campbell government that I represent is claiming possession of the black hole on behalf of the Campbell system as compensation for the Black Hole Project's interference in Campbell's internal affairs. But beyond that immediate objective is the need, indeed the destiny manifest, for the control and direction of the expansion of the human race to come under the control of those of us who are already out here.

"Imperial Earth is a thing of the past. This marks the end of the Interplanetary Association Senate's attempts to dictate events light years beyond its natural setting and the beginning of an era in which the colonial worlds stand up to the home planetary system as equals, and claim the right to make their own destinies.

"We know that in the hands of the government of the Solar System, the near limitless power that black hole technology will bring would be used to further the ends of that government in places far beyond its natural reach.

"We ask for your support in this effort. Under the Campbell government, genuine scientific study of the black hole will not be inhibited. Indeed, it may proceed with more freedom than the present consolidationist Solar System government would allow.

"Most of you have expansionist sympathies. We ask you to join us, or at least not impede what we must do to secure the future for all independent men and women.

"Specifically, we plead with Captain Chenhansa to withdraw from the hole. Our ship has been prepared, as hers has not, to move it to a more suitable location. It is also prepared, as misunderstandings were anticipated, to disable spacecraft operated in such a way as to interfere with such progress. We will do this only with great reluctance, given the risk to life involved.

"I repeat. Please withdraw peacefully.

"Those at Chandrasekhar Station who wish to declare allegiance to our cause need only explain this to one of the uniformed officials of our administration. Their declaration will be noted and, with reasonable precautions, of course, they will be integrated into the new operations; in most cases with positions and authorities similar to those exercised prior to the advent of the new administration.

"This is all I have to say for now. G'day all."

Torsten looked around him as Gunheim's larger-than-life image faded from the screen. Already, here and there, researchers and technicians were talking to their red-shirted minders.

A chill went down his spine. The world of science and technology was still a little distant and difficult to comprehend for him, but this he understood only too well. Napoleon, Hitler, Marsdale and Ramachandra must have sounded like that at some point in their careers.

So Lars now had a rival whose skill, ambition and ruthlessness seemed limitless in time and space, and who was, or shortly would be, in possession of a power that not even the Solar System's hundred-billion person economy could match. The seven light years between here and home seemed not to matter so much—a speed bump. Whatever Anna had in mind, he suddenly wished her luck.

●●○○●●

Brad glared back at Gunheim's image on the wall of Chenhansa's wardroom. Buried in the center of Sphere One and equipped with padded chairs and elastic restraints for use in zero gravity, it seemed a better place to ride out whatever. "That's a bunch of bloody nonsense! Catch a beam out of here!"

Gunheim's image was replaced by DeRoot's.

"This is Captain Peter DeRoot. I have been commissioned by the System Government of Campbell to take possession of the black hole. Disengage from the black hole."

"I don't believe this," Brad said. "DeRoot, just what is it you intend?"

"I have weapons and will use them. I also note that Dr. Zhau, Dr. Levine and all the others, including those passengers you dropped off, are guests of our security people at the station."

"It's been over a hundred and eighty years since one spaceship took a shot at another; and neither of those had crew aboard! You'll be put away for the rest of eternity."

DeRoot raised an eyebrow and laughed. "I'm betting not. You have, what shall we say, thirty minutes? DeRoot out."

Hilda called up a magnified image of the *Singer*. "Brad, Captain, look at the *Singer's* deflector cones."

As they watched, sections slid away to reveal ranks of tubes. Missiles. The starships were still about four thousand kilometers from each other—too far to use lasers effectively.

Brad looked at Hilda.

"It could be an empty threat," she said. "Or not. It may matter, politically, if we do not give in until he actually commits an act of violence, rather than merely threatens. Personally... Liz died for this. I can take the risk."

Brad nodded. "If it were me, I'd call his bluff, too. But it's not really our call. The people on this ship didn't sign up to fight a bloody war."

Captain Chenhansa shook her head. "Dr. Adams, I am commissioned by the IPA. With Dr. Zhau unavailable, you are the legitimate representative of the Project and carry, I think, the authority of the Solar System government in this place. My ship and I are at your service. Those who stayed aboard were volunteers. We are all of one mind. *Oberth*, notify everyone to find vacuum suits and helmets. Secure the ship for despin and zero gee."

Chenhansa looked at him and Hilda. "He is, unfortunately, positioned in our roll plane. Neither our dust deflection lasers nor the particle detonator lasers can bear on him or his missiles in this geometry."

That was a challenge to Brad. How could they bend the laser light sideways? With mirrors! "Look. We can rig up a mirror to redirect one of the anti-debris lasers and send a robot up the deflector cone with it. Not much compared to what he's got, but he won't be expecting it."

Chenhansa barely paused for a moment. "I have directed it be done."

Chenhansa's *sang-froid* surprised Brad. "We can't fire first," he said. She was silent.

A robot brought them their helmets and vacuum suits. They put them on in silence.

Precisely thirty minutes later, DeRoot's image was on the screen.

"Brad Adams here. Mate, what is all this nonsense? This is a research station. Everyone gets to share whatever we find out here. There's not a bloody imperial thing about it."

"Where is Captain Chenhansa?"

"I am here. We have decided that Dr. Adams' authority is highest in this matter. He speaks for the Black Hole Project and the Solar System government."

DeRoot laughed. "Which is seven light years away and has no say in the matter. Very well. It is your ship, Captain, and on your shoulders rest the consequences. Ada, we were friends once, very good friends. You know I wish harm to no one."

Chenhansa's face was unreadable. "I was eighteen, Captain. However much I idolized you then, what happened was not friendship. I have a different role to play now."

Brad looked back and forth between them, realizing they had a history. The fraternity of starship captains was a small one, filled with large egos.

"Look, no one's been hurt yet," Brad said. "You can still back off. Take the long view, if you will. History would never see this as anything but piracy."

"That depends on who writes the history. It would be interesting to ask Francis Drake. Begin to disengage from the hole. Now."

"No," Brad said, before he could double and triple-guess himself. This is what we planned, so this is what we do, he thought.

The *Oberth's* gong sounded. *Missile launch, fifteen gravities acceleration. Helmets on, now. Prepare for loss of air pressure!*

"You bloody bastard!" Brad screamed.

I am depressurizing to ten millibars, Captain Chenhansa sent. *This will prevent a blowout and still leave enough pressure to let us check for leaks.* She looked at Brad, then Hilda, her lips tight and her eyes narrowed. *Our mirrors are deployed and we will fire on the missile when it is close enough.*

As they watched, the approaching missile fragmented into a large number of submunitions. One vanished in a vapor that let them see laser beams striking the others, reducing the swarm, but not rapidly enough.

There was a shudder throughout the ship and a great groaning noise as if the ship itself were crying out in pain. The deck rolled in a sickening fashion. The screen blinked momentarily, then showed a cloud of vapor expanding around part of the smaller, forward magnetic field generation ring. Suddenly, as terajoules of magnetic energy became heat, the whole ring sprouted a crown of mist that was blown away by the black hole's Hawking radiation.

"The forward ring has quenched destructively," Chenhansa said, stating the obvious. "They've also taken out primary power in hulls one and two. I suggest we have no choice but to back off now."

Brad nodded. DeRoot had damned himself; there was no point now in losing lives.

"I'm quenching the main loop," Captain Chenhansa informed them. "We can use its stored energy to stay at full power for another half an hour. We can back away from the hole as soon as its magnetic field is down to zero."

Brad ran through the spacecraft systems status. The main drive solenoid ring ran through all the spheres; an uncontrolled quench of that much energy would be like setting off a line charge through the middle of each of them.

Without the forward ring intact, the ship's structural integrity would be badly compromised. The structure screamed like a wounded animal as auxiliary thrusters attempted to counter the angular momentum imparted by the attack.

"DeRoot, this is the *Oberth*," screamed Captain Chenhansa. "We are leaving. Cease firing! We have to clear the black hole."

Another explosion shook the ship, and they lurched downward, then back up as the black hole's magnetic field tried to snap them back into alignment.

The floor below lurched sideways and buckled up. He felt queasy. Lights blurred and dimmed. Brad's chair broke free and he slammed into the ceiling. Everything went black except the red lights on his helmet heads-up display.

●●∞●●

This, decided Zhau Tse Wen, was the appropriate and auspicious time to act. His guard, Micky, was fully occupied watching the drama playing out on the screen of the stateroom.

It was a small matter to step up behind the man unnoticed and close his hand around Micky's trank gun.

Regretfully, Micky chose to resist. Unable to point the gun, he tried to pull away. Tse Wen placed a leg behind Micky's ankle and Micky lost his balance. He also lost his grip on the gun as the edge of Tse Wen's hand broke the bones in his wrist.

Tse Wen did not hesitate, once he had the gun. He calmly shot tranks into the three other armed men before they finished turning from the screen to see what the commotion was, moving as he did so to complicate any possible return fire. There was none. He saw Micky writhing in pain on the floor and shot him, too. The tranquilizer charge would ease the poor man's discomfort until medical help could reach him.

Then he went into the bedroom and shot the two Campbell women who were minding Sarah Levine and the three other project personnel. Sarah rushed up to him, and after a brief but embarrassingly intimate hug, said, "So, you think we have a chance."

Tse Wen nodded and motioned to the CSU parked along the bedroom partition. "Kelly Barrett, one of the duty controllers, is in there. She would be most helpful. I need to go to cybernetics before they react. The Campbell AI program is looking for a way out of the box that the contingency program Brad activated has built around it. As things stand, orders from both sides are being ignored. We need to gain full control, from here."

Sarah nodded. "Tse Wen, you might grab a red shirt on your way out."

He smiled. "It is not my color. But one of you should do so and replace the person I will shoot outside the door."

Tse Wen did so and moved quickly. No Campbell person stood outside cybernetics when he reached it, a somewhat surprising circumstance, but he heard footsteps in the corridor and moved quickly to the door, hoping. It slid open. In one motion, he stepped through, moved to the side, shot the person in a red Campbell uniform shirt in front of one of the consoles and dropped into a crouch. The person, a woman, turned in surprise. As she did, two other Campbell people entered the door, aimed at Tse Wen, missed and shot the woman.

There was no time to do anything but react. Tse Wen shot the Campbell people before they could react. As the door slid shut, he scanned the room; a fourth Campbell man lay on the floor not too far from him. He locked the door manually and rushed to the fallen woman who had, by this point, received a potentially lethal dose of tranquilizer.

It was Anna Messenger. If Tse Wen called for medical assistance now, she might be saved, but he would be unlikely to have time to regain control of the system. With great regret, he turned to the more important task.

His part of the system had informed him that while the Campbell AI was distributed throughout the system, an essential part of it was physically located in maintenance memory module eighteen. He located the maintenance memory rack, a box barely the size of his hand installed over the maintenance console. Its access panel had already been removed.

He reached in and pulled out number eighteen. He should be in full control now.

Medical emergency, trank overdose, this location. Do not notify Magda Lobacz.

He waited beside the door in a crouch. It hissed open and a robot gurney entered.

There were no Campbell people with it.

●●∞●●

For Kelly Barrett, doing her job from a plush chair in front of an ordinary stateroom screen seemed surreal. But the main operations and science amphitheaters were now, essentially, prisons from which people were being released only with due screening. And she had a lot to do.

Two starships were inbound, one on a vector from south of Campbell, and the other from Epsilon Eridani. Neither radiated anything, not even a beacon, on her instructions. Her heart pounded; they were flying into a hornet's nest and she had to keep the hornet ignorant long enough for these ships to finish deceleration.

The Epsilon Eridani ship was scheduled, but vulnerable. On closed beam, she advised them of the situation and recommended a slow approach.

The other ship was coming from the right part of the sky, but way early and well off her deceleration beam. Was it Captain Avonford? With only starlight and the black hole's Hawking radiation to work from, it took almost a second to build up the image. Tendrils of worry began to pick at her. It did not look like any human starship she had seen before. Four rings—three of them arranged small-to-large in *front* of the ship. The structure connecting the rings was skeletal and the rings seemed thicker than normal. The aft ring looked almost familiar, with a sphere at the base of each connecting truss, but the cones were truncated, with various pieces of equipment exposed. *Identify?* she asked.

Unrecognized, the system said.

She smiled. The ship transformed as she watched it. The strange structures began to vanish as if being eaten away. But the empty space that replaced it seemed distorted somehow.

What is that star field? she asked.

It is the one that lies behind us, as if reflected from a spherical mirror.

Or a shield, Kelly thought. A shield. It had to be her. "Dr. Levine, come look at this. Peter DeRoot isn't the only starship Captain who can rebuild his ship in flight!"

Sarah Levine looked at the strange ship, eyes wide. "Who...?"

"That is, or was," Kelly said, "the *Farseeker* out of Big Red, Kate Avonford commanding."

"How do you know?" Levine asked.

"I was one of her mates on the Tau Ceti mission. She wanted to come in unannounced, so she asked me to get the deceleration trail laid and tell no one."

"So here comes the cavalry," Sarah whispered, her voice full of wonder.

••∞••

In the *Singer's* wardroom, Gunheim looked grimly at DeRoot. "What are you bloody waiting for, Peter?"

"Patience. I want a little more clearance between the wreck and the black hole."

Gunheim frowned at him. "Magda's lost control of the station. It's only a matter of time before they come up with something effective."

"We are the only armed spacecraft in the area, and in a few hours, we will be the most powerful armed spacecraft in history. We will deal with that situation then. This has to be done right. While the hole is minute, it has enough gravity to exceed all countervailing forces. It can, and will, suck in any matter that comes within a meter or so."

"Huh? The electron shells of atoms withstand..."

"The electron shells of atoms will be eaten first, then electrostatic forces will add to gravity. I must proceed carefully. If I do not..."

An attention tone from the *Singer* interrupted him. *A mass of about four thousand tons is approaching at twenty kilometers per second. On its present trajectory, it will pass... has passed, by within three kilometers.*

"What the bloody hell? On screen, magnify."

The screen showed nothing but a distorted star field.

It is almost perfectly reflecting, the *Singer* told them. *Doppler measurements indicate the reflections are decelerating at eight gravities.*

"Bloody aliens, Peter. They must have been watching."

"That doesn't seem reasonable to me, but if so, there will be very little we can do. If they want something, they will let us know. More likely, Hilda Kremer is playing some kind of trick."

The *Singer's* approach to the hole was agonizing. Two minutes went by, then four.

Finally, they were hailed. A stern woman in a full vacuum suit stared from the screen at them. Incredibly, there was music in the background.

"Captain DeRoot, Roger Gunheim, crew of the *C. E. Singer* and occupation forces aboard the Chandrasekhar Station. This is Captain Katherine Avonford of the Solar System Starship *Farseeker.* I am declaring this area to be under martial law under IPA code, Chapter Four. Any Lacaille 9352 residents holding weapons are ordered to put them down now. *C. E. Singer*, close your weapons bays."

Gunheim turned to DeRoot. "What the bloody hell is *she* doing here? What kind of starship is that? And why the background music?"

DeRoot looked at Gunheim in surprise, then straightened his face. "I would venture that what we see reflects modifications she made while traveling here. That was Wagner's *Ride of the Valkyrie*; she's probably trying to psyche me. But I think she means to fight."

Gunheim raised an eyebrow. "Then we should shoot first, Peter." Gunheim flipped his hand as he would against a fly.

"There's a problem, Roger. That mirror is over ten kilometers across. The *Farseeker* is only two hundred meters across. I don't know where she is behind there."

"Well, shoot the bloody missiles through it. They'll find 'er."

"Not in time to prevent her from shooting back, Roger."

Gunheim laughed. "Well that's why we built this fort, isn't it, mate. You're giving her too much time to think. Get rid of 'er."

Peter nodded. He had much less confidence in the result than Roger, but it was either fight, or lose the whole effort. And if to fight, best to strike first.

••∞••

Kate Avonford sat tense in front of her screens. Hailing was a calculated risk, designed to save lives. DeRoot knew his classics; *Valkyrie* should unsettle him a little, reinforce the notion that she was crazy enough to fight. So he should know he was in deep trouble—but there was always a chance that wouldn't matter to him.

"*Oberth*, this is *Farseeker.* Katherine Avonford in command. How are you doing, Ada?"

Kate heard Chenhansa's distinctive voice, "Kate, Ada. Please stand by... We're a mess. Didn't get the main quenched in time to detach from the hole, and the last blast from DeRoot got us resonating with it. The spheres are intact, but everything inside shifted up and down again. Sphere Two is leaking, Three has minor damage, and our floor got bent up and back again, with lots of open metal and torn composite. Muck from the park pond is all over everything."

Kate's jaw clenched; DeRoot would pay for this. Oh. Would. He. Pay! She set aside anger for a moment and absorbed the intelligence; that kind of damage was something she had anticipated; The *Farseeker's* parks were frozen solid. "Sorry to hear, and damn them to hell. I'll try to give you some time. Hilda?"

"Mother, I'm here. I know about Liz."

She'd gotten the message. *To Captain Katherine Avonford on whatever starship she may be flying to wherever. Mom... You've probably heard what happened...* Oh, to want to hold your child, or have her hold you! And there was no time, no time.

"A heroine's death, Hilda. We honor it now. Are you injured?"

"I got a bump on the head, but it seems okay now."

About the same time as Hilda said bump, Kate felt a hard pull to the left.

Incoming missiles. Six, ten, fourteen we are initiating evasive maneuvers and engaging them with lasers, Farseeker's AI announced.

Kate's blood ran cold. "Later, Hilda, I'm under attack."

She would have to launch her counterstrike while she still could.

She'd left a hundred relativistic kinetic energy weapons trailing behind her. Those were now entering the Shiva system at fifteen-minute intervals in groups of five at a gamma of 2.1, about 90% of light speed. The tennis-ball-sized objects were calculated to punch crippling holes through targets, not destroy—but that was only a calculation. People would die. She sighed.

Activate the trailers, two groups. Take out the forward ring, and the missile magazines in the cones, she sent. The weapons would use almost most of their mass making the targeting corrections, but what remained might as well be pure antimatter.

Kate was shoved down and forward as she sent that. Behind its reflective screen, pushed by the thrust of its fusion engines in two directions, the *Farseeker* began to accelerate on a complex compound curve with continuous random changes designed to confuse the guidance of incoming missiles.

But there were limits. The homing missiles were literally a million times more agile than the massive *Farseeker*. Despite evasion, lasers, and last-second warhead-disabling magnetic pulses, three of DeRoot's' missiles got lucky. One cone-based laser battery, then another, went off line. The third smashed the fusion rocket module off the bottom of Sphere Two, with shrapnel damage to the other two. The *Farseeker* was down to lateral thrusters only until repairs could be made.

The flood of missiles stopped. The screen was essentially intact—the pinprick points where the missiles went through healed themselves in seconds, and the magnetic fields kept the screen in shape and in its well-off-center position. With luck DeRoot wouldn't even know the results of his strike.

The trailer command system is off line, the *Farseeker* reported. *Mode A went with the Cone Two laser battery, and Mode B was damaged by shrapnel from the Cone Three hit. Estimate time of repair, three hours.*

Kate bit her lip. Until then she had one laser battery and a flimsy mirror. Reality sank in. Bravado had not worked, her brilliant bubble had not worked, and she was down to her last chance and only one shot at that. Meanwhile, another strike from DeRoot could arrive at any moment. She told the crew to abandon ship while the robots did the repairs.

●●∞●●

"Did we get her?"

Peter DeRoot frowned at Gunheim, hesitated, then nodded. "The mirror screen's still there, but there's been no response. I think so."

"Okay, now let's stop yabbering and take the black hole before anything else happens!"

A warning clang and red lights erupted through the ship. *Interstellar debris deflection system activated,* the *Singer's* AI announced.

"What the bloody hell? We aren't moving," Gunheim said.

But Peter, trained to react instead of question in such circumstances, already had his helmet on.

One, two, three, four loud explosions echoed through the ship in rapid succession before a brilliant flash filled the room followed by a deafening blast from the bulkhead behind Roger. It threw Roger's body into DeRoot with a force that knocked the wind out of him. Chairs tore off their mountings. Debris flew past him and bounced off walls, ceilings and floors. As his hearing returned, a tremendous, low-toned howl drowned out all other sounds.

Incredibly, in the direction of the blast, Peter glimpsed a patch of empty space, maybe six centimeters across, through the metal and ice. Objects streamed out through it. He turned around and saw another one in the opposite direction. A relativistic kinetic energy weapon, he thought, an RKEW. A grim smile spread over his face. Too fast, actually. The real explosion must have taken place a kilometer or so beyond where the mass flew through the ship.

What was left of the wardroom filled with damage control robots. Moving with incredible rapidity, they plugged the holes and began taking out the debris.

One look at Roger confirmed the worst. The RKEW had punched a hole right through where the man's heart might have been.

"Thanks for the ride, Roger," he said to himself quietly, and left the cleanup to the robots.

Damage, casualties, status? he asked the ship.

The forward ring quenched, estimate six days to return to operational. Major damage to all missile batteries. After repair, we may have ten missiles left.

There would, he thought, probably be a second wave of RKEW.

Shed the cones and fly the rest of us away from them on fusion rockets. Casualties?

Five dead by decompression. All in this sphere.

I'll move command to Sphere Two, if the passage is clear. What's the status elsewhere?

There's another starship inbound, unannounced until now. The Admiral Byrd, *from Epsilon Eridani.*

Captain Lee. As cold-headed as Kate was hot-blooded. There was only one way to success now. The black hole itself could be used as a power source and a weapon, with the proper preparations. They had made such preparations—once they had the hole, they would be invincible. But they had to get it now.

After getting out of the wreckage of the Sphere Two wardroom, DeRoot was a little more heartened. The structure had pretty much held two meters away from the strike line.

There, he watched the second wave of RKEWs punch holes through what was left of the *Singer's* cones and his remaining missiles. He addressed the remaining crew.

"I have every reason to believe that was the *Farseeker's* best shot, and it may well have been posthumous, because we have heard nothing from that direction since our missile volley. Our maneuvering engines are intact. We have three batteries of lasers, two intact spheres with one repairable. Once we possess the hole, nobody will be able to interfere with us. We are going to proceed with the mission. Just in case Avonford is not done, we will approach the black hole so the wreck of the *Oberth* lies between us and the direction of her RKEWs. Once in position, we'll use the sphere base laser batteries to quench the *Oberth's* main ring, blow holes in her spheres and vaporize her shielding water. The reaction of escaping steam should be sufficient to push it away from the hole. DeRoot out."

CHAPTER 5

**On the *Oberth*
in orbit about Shiva
25 December 2284**

What was left of the ship was a complete wreck, Brad thought. Utilities were off line; there was still energy in the main ring, but no way to distribute it. Cybernetics had fallen off line for lack of power. Some robots were still active, uselessly trying to bail an ocean of debris. Captain Chenhansa, to do something, was trying to help them.

Kate Avonford, in the immobile *Farseeker*, was trying to keep them informed over their suit radios. "What's left of him is coming for you," she said. "Can you get out of the way? I should be maneuvering again in ten minutes. I may outgun him now."

Captain Chenhansa answered. "Almost everything here is down from the shaking. Our maneuvering engines are probably intact, but we can't get power or data to them. This ship was not designed to fight battles."

"The two that were, kind of, are wrecks as well," Kate said. "In hindsight, this was all a very bad idea. Fortunately, so far, everyone was shooting to disable. So you're still stuck to the black hole?"

"With our systems down, we have no way to quench the ring fields," Chenhansa replied, "so we're still coupled to the black hole's field. That is just as well—we do not want to drift into it."

"Also," Hilda added, "the particle component of the Hawking radiation would be bad if it were not for the field's protection."

Brad unstrapped himself and pushed himself away from the chair. The ceiling above was almost touching the wardroom's small central table. "There's more elbow room here near the walls, mates. I've got an idea. It's a bit dicey, but if we dump some water on that thing, it should behave like a small version of a galactic nucleus, with a bipolar pair of plasma balls."

"I can't do any simulations," Hilda said as she joined him, "but I don't think you get symmetric outflow unless the input is equatorial."

"Exactly. If I dump stuff in the north end, it gets spit out the south end faster. We get a big plasma ball behind us and that should push us away from the hole with more force than the magnetic field holds onto it."

"It could work... if the ship can take the stress," Hilda said.

"It should if the stress is small, steady, and on-axis," Captain Chenhansa said. "Large oscillations are the problem." There was a creak and a groan as the captain pushed a piece of intruding partition out of the way, and joined Brad and Hilda.

"Hi everyone, Sarah Levine here. Sorry for the delay, we had some fun figuring out the *Oberth's* suit radio protocol. The Project is fully back in control of the base. We're trying to come up with a way to aid you with the propulsion beam drivers, but they aren't pointed anywhere near the right direction. It takes hours to rotate them a milliradian. Brad, Hilda, we *can* do simulations and your mass dump into the hole will work, though exactly how well is very dependent on initial conditions. Brad, more help is on the way. *Admiral Byrd* is inbound. Captain Lee Hyun Sil and Dr. Bruce Macready."

"Brad Adams here. Hi, Sarah. Our ship won't endure another blast from DeRoot, either. He's taken casualties and my guess is he won't be aiming to wound this time. Regards to Dr. Macready, and tell them to bloody *hurry*."

"Zhau Tse Wen on. The *Admiral Byrd's* arrival may have already forced this move on DeRoot's part. He may believe that gaining the black hole is his only option now. Unfortunately, he would not be incorrect."

"Captain Chenhansa on. At this point, we would give it to him, but it is magnetically stuck to us. Dr. Adams... Dr. Adams has left the area."

There was very little time, Brad realized. He pulled himself out of the wardroom into the central section of the sphere. The park floor had split, dumping tons of wet soil and dirty water into the area. It was pitch black and turning on his helmet light didn't improve things.

"Adams on. I'm going to try to find some way to throw water into the black hole. The resulting plasma blast should push us free." It also might do a number of other things, Brad thought, but there was no time for analysis. "I'm on my way to the rotary joint between the sphere and the ring. That's the strongest place on these ships and should be intact. There's a galley and a head there, so maybe water and something to put it in."

"Chenhansa on. I'll try to get some people there to help. We have several with extra vehicular activity experience, but as you can tell, it's difficult to move around."

"Adams on. Roger that. No problems there, but I'll likely have as much EVA time as anyone."

He didn't add that he was inventing what to do as he went along, and that it would go more efficiently if he did the task himself. He worked his way through debris and around a collapsed floor section to the galley. The part near the sphere's hull was reasonably intact, but everything was badly bent and twisted inboard.

He felt a hand on his shoulder and turned his body to see a long spacesuited figure.

"Dr. Adams, Jomo Oboto," the male voice was very faint in the rarefied atmosphere. "I'm a botanist, but cooking's my hobby. I was hoping to salvage something, but..."

"It's a bloody mess," Brad said, in sympathy. "Look, we're looking to feed some mass into the black hole. There's plenty of water, but we need some kind of container. Something that will hold up to a lot of radiation for a few seconds, at any rate."

"Understood. One of our standard trash bags might do. They're designed to withstand a drive flare long enough to avoid splattering the hull. Maybe 5% of the visible gets through, not much at all in infrared or UV—just transparent enough so you can see what is in them.

Properly sealed, they might hold up to a dozen atmospheres in vacuum."

"That sounds good," Brad said. It would have to do.

Oboto rotated his body and reached for a cabinet door under the counter. The whole structure was warped and it wouldn't open. He motioned for Brad to help. "Grab the sink with one hand and hold my belt with the other."

Brad maneuvered into position, and grabbed Oboto's belt firmly.

Oboto gave a mighty kick at the reluctant door. It broke open with a loud snap.

"Kremer on. Careful of Ada's spaceship, Brad."

That produced a round of ironic laughter.

They were able to pull the pieces off separately. In the cabinet were three rolls of bags in different sizes. The shiny material glinted in the available light.

"Looks good," Brad said. "Where do I get water?"

Oboto tried the kitchen tap. Nothing. "Safety valve probably cut off the line. There's a feed/drain line outside the main connecting ring that will open mechanically from inside the ring opposite the emergency access hatch. You'll need a hose." He reached under the sink, disconnected one of the water lines and handed it to Brad. "Standard push/pull fitting."

Brad recognized it and smiled to himself about the contrast between this ordinary object and the extraordinary circumstance in which it would be used. "Right. Bag sealers?"

Oboto shook his head. "Just twist it around and stretch it a bit. The stuff will bind itself. Permanently."

"Right. I best get at it."

Hilda Kremer appeared. "Nothing to do where I was."

It took all three to push open the door from the sphere into the connecting tube just outside the rotary joint. In contrast to the devastation in the sphere, the passageway in the tube showed no sign of damage. They closed the door after them to limit air loss to the connecting passage.

Brad found the emergency exit in the "forward" side of the tube that would be overhead under thrust. He removed the access panel, revealing a tiny view port and a levered sliding seal designed to be opened manually against pressure.

"We'll need a tether," he said.

Oboto nodded. "There should be an emergency kit in a red box near the hatch. In it will be a tether spool, space tape, a spare recycle catalyst canister, an EVA maneuver pack, and a net."

"Roger that," Brad said. He found the red box and opened it.

"Let's see. Hilda, you can belay the line while Oboto operates the valve."

"That sounds like a plan," Hilda said.

Brad nodded and Oboto opened the hatch, creating a small gale as what was left of the atmosphere in the connecting tube rushed into space.

They put the net out first, and shoved the roll of water bags into it. Hilda attached the EVA maneuver pack over the life support unit on Brad's back. Its telltales blinked green in Brad's helmet display as it came on line. She gave him a hug and touched her helmet to his.

"Brad, if we get out of this..."

He gave her a brief, one-armed squeeze back. "She'll be right. Just you watch."

Then he exited the hatch feet first, letting himself be blown into the net on top of the water bags. His radiation alarms went off—the Hawking radiation was still over limits with the black hole a hundred meters away.

That, he thought grimly, was nothing compared to what he was about to get.

The rush of air from the hatch helped push him out and gave him the feeling of hanging down. They handed him the tether reel, and he clipped its free end to a stanchion near the hatch and the reel to his belt. Then they shut the hatch.

He had no time to feel isolated. He found recessed handholds in the connecting tube hull and used them to pull himself over to the outboard side of the ring. With the ring between him and the hole, it was suddenly very dark. As his eyes adapted, the stars blazed forth. As it happened, he was looking toward Leo, only slightly distorted; its rear triangle pointed toward Sol, now the first star of a brilliant arc through Virgo; Sol, Spica, and Alpha Centauri. The sight steadied him.

"Helmet light," he whispered. It came on, illuminating an almost featureless hull. Where was the spigot? He spotted a maintenance panel about ten meters from where he'd come round the hull.

"Adams on," he sent. "Got the spigot."

The cover popped open at his touch, revealing a handhold as well as the spigot. He attached the hose Oboto had given him and felt the connector click hold.

"Adams on. Give me just a bit of water, mate," he said, holding the thumb of his suit glove over the end of the line.

"Oboto on. Wilco."

When Brad felt the tube stiffen with pressure, he released his thumb and a cloud of steaming water jetted out. The temperature of the water was barely over freezing, but that was enough to make it boil in vacuum.

"Close," he said.

"Oboto. Wilco."

Brad hooked his toes under the handhold to steady himself, pulled a bag off the roll and worked the end of the tube into the open end. Then he gathered the material around it and wrapped space tape around that.

"Adams on. Okay, give me a little again." The bag inflated instantly with water vapor, rigid and spherical. It looked like it might hold almost a cubic meter of water, if it would fill.

It was too dark to see anything in the bag. He would just have to trust. "Okay, more."

The line vibrated and the bag began to feel heavier if he moved it. The volume of vapor would get less, condensing back to liquid as the pressure in the bag increased. With luck, he would end up with a bag full of cold water.

He did. As his eyes adapted to the night, he could see the brighter stars through it, distorted as if through a great lens. The internal pressure kept it stiff, more like a huge basketball than a blob of jelly.

He filled four bags altogether and put them into the net. Then he worked his way back over the hull into the brilliance of the black hole's Hawking radiation.

The gravity of the black hole was very slight at the distance of the ring, but enough to give direction and pull the tether taut as Brad lowered himself and the water bags toward it.

"Hilda on. Brad, we've got AI restored. I can give you guidance."

Her face filled the tiny view port in the emergency hatch. She sounded much more confident, Brad thought. She'll be right, they both will be.

He used his maneuvering unit to gently push himself a little bit forward of the spin plane. He stared through one of the bags. It formed an ersatz lens, providing a distorted, magnified view of DeRoot's *C. E. Singer*, approaching.

"Adams on. I can see the *Singer*. It's missing its cones. No radiator area—they'll be limited in how much power they can use."

"Avonford on. We're maneuvering, but not fast. Maybe thirty minutes to laser range. Give us some time if you can."

"Chenhansa on. Roger that. We're going to try to push ourselves free of the hole."

Brad watched the *Singer* approach. If it kept on that course, he thought, it would be within a degree or two of the black hole's spin axis in a minute. Of course. Since they meant to get the hole, they would approach on its spin and magnetic axis. There was no saying for sure, but the results could be bad. Should he warn the *Singer*? It was a volunteer crew, he told himself.

"Kremer on. Come forward four degrees if you can, tether taut."

"Adams. Roger."

Damn, he told himself. Keeping silent would be murder. Simple bloody murder. "Adams on. Check the geometry. If we get polar jets, we might toast the whole mob."

"Kremer on, roger that. Brad, push the bag directly toward the hole from your present position. I'll start the countdown."

"Starship *C. E. Singer*. This is Captain Chenhansa, *Oberth*, issuing a maneuver exhaust warning. Clear aft. Now. Repeat, maneuver warning. Clear our aft now."

"Kremer on. Four, three, two, one..."

Brad released the bubble forward with a gentle push as Hilda hit zero, and held his breath. The bubble moved toward the hole with ever-increasing speed. He immediately began reeling in tether, damping the swing with his maneuvering unit. He wanted to be in the equatorial plane of the hole when the bag hit. "Hilda, the bag is rotating. Will it..."

"It's on course. Hang tight, Brad. Watch through the other water bags."

"Wilco." At twenty meters, the bubble began to accelerate. It took on the shape of a teardrop, pointed end at the hole. The back end of the bag burst as it accelerated into the hole, but it was too late for any of the mass to escape. Suddenly it was gone.

••∞••

Captain Peter DeRoot played the message again with a sardonic grin on his face. "Starship *C. E. Singer*. This is Captain Chenhansa, *Oberth*, issuing a maneuver exhaust warning. Clear aft. Now. Repeat, maneuver warning. Clear our aft now."

"Don't believe it," Peter DeRoot told his crew. "They just want us to give the next waves of RKEWs a clear shot at us. This we are not going to allow. We will fire presently."

DeRoot's view of his target was not clear. The black hole's brilliant Hawking radiation cast everything in harsh contrast, and the area was cluttered with all sorts of debris. The main spheres and ring of the helpless *Oberth* showed up well enough, however. He would fire his three laser weapons in two rounds. The first would quench the *Oberth's* main ring, releasing the hole. The next would turn the habitat spheres into steam rockets, pushing the remainder of the doomed ship away.

He'd known Ada Chenhansa for over a century. If circumstances were different... But this was no time for sentimentality—the project people were back in control of the operations base, all his bridges were burned, and Roger's legacy was at stake—the vision of a humanity spurred on by great thoughts and great deeds, rather than the mundane compromises of timorous bureaucrats. No, this was no time for weakness. Still, he did not want Ada on his conscience for eternity. The great man controls events to his will, he told himself, rather than lets events control him.

"Ada, Peter. Sorry, but this is a bigger thing that I am about than either of us. Abandon your ship now if you can. Someone will pick you up in... what?"

The black hole appeared to have exploded, with brilliant plasma covering everything before the screen went dark. Alarms and red lights burst out everywhere.

"Oh, shit." He felt like he had a terrible fever and saw objects all around bursting into flames. In one last moment he saw that he, himself, was burning and lifted one flaming hand in wonder. Then a thunderous boom ended it all.

••∞••

Brad found himself suddenly in a shadow. It was as if the black hole had vanished for a moment. Then two violet searchlights lanced out from where it had been—along the ship's and the hole's lateral axis. The rearward one might have been the brighter, but he couldn't be sure. The tether jerked him firmly. In a moment of recovered focus, he dumped the net and jetted forward and out toward the ring hatch. He had only time for a glance in the *Singer's* direction, and saw only what looked like a cloud at the end of the violet beam.

The emergency hatch opened as he arrived, and a robot's arm reached out and pulled him in with ruthless, painful efficiency. He realized he was hot and feverish. The robot pulled him along into the galley. He felt queasy, sick. He couldn't see.

Someone jammed a hypo against his arm, right through the pressure suit.

"Hey, ouch..."

He was suddenly, tired, very tired. He managed to retch once into his helmet.

"Sorry for the mess..."

••∞••

Zhau Tse Wen watched the expanding cloud of vapor that had been the *C. E. Singer* fill the main screen in the Operations Section amphitheater. Somebody cheered. It was, he reflected, his fault in a way. Had he anticipated an effort to steal the black hole, rather than simple sabotage, the people on that ship might still be alive. He raised a hand for silence and sent his voice through the address system.

"Friends. Whatever the flaws of his last adventure, Captain Peter DeRoot was legend among the stars. He was an extraordinary astronaut who opened five new planetary systems, rescued three disabled starships, and had a vast love for the history and continuity of the urge for humanity to explore and seek beyond what we know. What has just happened is tragic on many levels. I ask all to observe a moment in silence for those who are no more, and to contemplate our own misadventures."

Quiet spread among the project staff, newspeople, and Campbell people who had surrendered weapons and pretense of authority—some literally ripping the red shirts from their bodies.

After what he thought was a decent time, Tse Wen set people about the work of adjusting the carefully prepared post-implosion plan to actual events.

Kelly Barrett was still on station.

"You seem to need no rest," he observed.

She turned to look at him with a smile that took any sense of irritation out of her words. "Dr. Zhau, I slept through the most important event in human history, damn it. I may never sleep again!"

He had to smile at that.

"*Farseeker* is in her final approach to Dock Seven. The hatches should be open in ten minutes. The *Admiral Byrd* is due in fifteen minutes, at Dock Three."

"Thank you," Tse Wen said. "I will go to the Science Section and get Dr. Levine. We shall go up to meet it together."

The door to the Science Section slid open as he walked in. The mood here was one of quiet business. They had lost a heartbreaking amount of data, but what they had still filled banks of qubit memory files. There was not a little element of tension in here; if any radically new science was to be found, the chances were that it would show up in these first hours, and everyone wanted to be the first to spot it.

Sarah walked by Torsten Ried, who was talking to his pickup. He turned toward her, but she passed by, barely acknowledging his presence. Tse Wen frowned.

"He gives me the creeps," Sarah said when she reached him, as if she had read his mind.

"He is still a chronicler of the event and an important person in the long run."

"When the whole story gets back home, they'll lock him up."

"Forever?" Tse Wen asked. "He can write."

Sarah gave him a wicked grin. "So can I!"

Forever? he thought again, but didn't say it. He simply nodded and followed her to the central docking complex to await the arrival of *Farseeker* and its load of radiation and trauma casualties from the *Oberth*.

When the lock opened, the crews of two damaged starships emerged, some heavily bandaged, others obviously not feeling well, many seeming dazed, but almost all with smiles of a victory that at least for now anesthetized their discomfort. Tse Wen greeted each of them with a handshake, thanking them for their efforts and sacrifice. Sarah Levine gave a hug to everyone who seemed willing to receive one. Finally, Hilda Kremer and Ada Chenhansa came out. Sarah got to Hilda first, so Tse Wen took Captain Chenhansa's hand.

"We haven't met before. I am honored," he said.

Her eyes glistened. "And I as well," she said.

Sarah brought Hilda over to them. Hilda looked like she should be on a stretcher. And had she not been in zero gravity, Tse Wen thought, she might well be.

Then a ghostly parade of coffin-like CSUs emerged. Many inside were clinically dead before freezing, though for a short enough time that revival in some form at least seemed possible. Moving on magnetics and turning with flywheels, they floated out of the *Farseeker*, across the anteroom, into the cargo lift door, rotated ninety degrees, and vanished down the tube headed for the station infirmary.

Bradford Adams would be in one of those. *Which one?* Tse Wen asked the AI.

F29. It is exiting the lock now.

Tse Wen pointed to it and Hilda rushed forward to put her hand on it, then walked it across the anteroom with tears in her eyes. Tse Wen touched the CSU briefly as it went by. He collected Hilda at the exit and gently pulled her back to the group.

As the last CSU left, an average-sized man in a trim dark tunic and trousers entered.

"Glad I'm nae in one of those!"

His accent identified him instantly. Dr. Bruce Macready, the Scottish science historian who had inherited leadership of the Epsilon Eridani impactor project and managed his way to a successful launch under extraordinary difficulty.

"Bruce!" Tse Wen exclaimed. "You help lift a heavy heart. Welcome!"

"Aye, but if we could have only been a bit earlier."

Tse Wen stepped forward to embrace the Scot—a gesture so out of place for both of them that it signified the most profound of circumstances. They released each other and shook hands.

"Do you have any left?" Tse Wen asked.

"One bottle," Macready said, shaking his head. "Which I fear will be gone tonight!"

Sarah smiled and held her hand. "Okay guys, I have some physics news. You heard it here first. They've just finished the before-and-after mass and energy totals for the water Brad dumped into the black hole. And, by the way, we need to thank Peter DeRoot for putting his starship where it could provide a calibration point in the bipolar flow."

"Sarah," Tse Wen said, reprovingly.

She laughed and a brief smile flashed across Chenhansa's face.

"Anyway," Sarah continued, "we're short about three kilograms."

"Three?!" Tse Wen was intrigued. While it might sound small, it was, in fact, enormous. If the result held up, two hundred seventy thousand terajoules of mass-energy had simply vanished.

"Where did the rest of the mass go?" Captain Chenhansa asked.

Tse Wen shook his head. "For almost three hundred years, people have speculated that there is no way to know what happens to mass that enters a spinning, charged black hole along its polar axis. The singularity is ring-shaped. There is an event horizon, but it is essentially flat within the ring—what goes that way is not crushed into a three-dimensional singularity."

"For all we know, it may have left this universe without a trace," Sarah said.

"Left this universe?" someone asked.

Tse Wen smiled. "That is very speculative. We will have to review the bookkeeping of mass-energy very carefully."

"Tse Wen, Sarah," Hilda said. "If that can happen here, it would happen elsewhere. Much of cosmology assumes the mass-energy density of the universe is constant. If it can change like this, cosmological issues that have been thought settled for centuries will be open again."

Tse Wen still felt very skeptical about this, but it was good to see some life in Hilda's eyes.

"Well, maybe," he said. "There is no good model for what happens on the other side of a Kerr-Newman geometry."

Captain Chenhansa smiled benignly, hands folded. "I have always wanted a wormhole drive."

"We would not know how to build one," Tse Wen said.

"Yet," Hilda added, pensively. "But we've paid a high enough price for one, I think."

"Hello from Big Red!" Kate Avonford's voice rang out as she walked from the access tube. She wore a tight-fitting, coal-black jumpsuit with a flashing diamond Captain's badge over her left breast. Platinum hair cascaded dramatically over her shoulders. She looked around and shook her head. "Come on now, people. You would have thought you'd lost the battle instead of saving the culminating achievement of human history!"

"Mom!" Hilda said, and rushed forward to embrace her.

"Hilda, dear, cheer up," Kate said, tears in her own eyes. "The dragon is dead, the would-be gods are vanquished, our fallen will be immortalized, our wounded are being cared for, and we Rhine maidens have our ring back! You have a pub here?"

"The Melbourne," Sarah said, grinning.

Kate raised an imaginary tankard to her.

"So let's head for the pub and raise a pint to Brad, who is going to be just fine. Five sieverts of radiation hasn't killed anyone in a hundred years. I'm thirsty!"

Even Tse Wen had to smile for a moment. Kate had her own way of seeing the world, and making it stick. That, he thought, might be a useful quality over the next few years.

But his mind went back to questions of missing mass, missing people, and the enormity of what lay spinning in the vacuum nearby. The culminating achievement of human history? He considered Big Red, a star that would still be shining a trillion years from now. They stood, he thought, not at the culmination of human history, but at its very beginning.

The End

GLOSSARY

Abbreviations
(G) — General Background
(KL)— Kremer's Limit
(IG) — Imperfect Gods
(SP)— Small Pond
(LR) — Loki's Realm
(Vx) — Vertex

- A -

anisotropic

Not the same in all directions. Opposite of isotropic, isotropism. (G)

artificial intelligence (AI)

A computer program advanced enough that people can have general conversations with it. AI's are not quite human; they are motivated by programmed priorities, constrained by Asimov's laws of robotics, and are limited in creativity, self-concern, and ability to act on their own volition. (G)

Asimov's laws of robotics

Three rules programmed by law into all artificial intelligences. The AI must not actively harm a human being or allow one to be harmed through inaction, it must follow the orders of human beings, and it must protect its own existence consistent with the first two laws. Named for the 20th century scientist, educator and writer, Isaac Asimov, who wrote down their first formulation in a work of fiction. [See "Runaround" in *Astounding*, March 1942.] (G)

- B -

BHP interstellar communications facility

A communications facility in the solar system asteroid belt dedicated to the Black Hole Project. (KL Chap 4)

bioradio

A part of the human brain genetically engineered to transmit and receive radio signals. Also, the system of information networks and transceivers that communicates with people by bioradio. Bioradios are individual and self-authenticating; like fingerprints, no two signals are alike. This is one of a number of changes made to the human genome in the early 22nd century. (G)

black hole

A mass large enough or dense enough that its space-time geometry causes the trajectory of any photon or particle originating or crossing an "event horizon" to stay within that horizon. Non-rotating black holes are characterized by their "Schwarzschild radius," $Rs = 2MG/c^2$, where M is the mass of the black hole, G is the universal gravitational constant (=6.672e-11 m^3 /kg/s^2) and c is the speed of light (=3.00e8 m/s^2). Actually, the distortion of space-time near a black hole is such that "radius" presents definitional problems, so some physicists prefer to talk of a Schwarzschild surface or circumference.

Mass	object of similar mass	Schwarzschild radius	object of similar size
4,000 tons	ship	5.94e-21 m	?
4 million tons	skyscraper	5.94e-18 m	?
4 billion tons	hill	5.94e-15 m	atomic nucleus
4e+15 kg	small asteroid	5.94e-12 m	proton-antiproton orbit
4e+18 kg	large asteroid	5.94 nm	molecule
4e+21 kg	moon	5.94 µm	bacterium
4e+24 kg	Earth	5.94 mm	insect
4e+27 kg	Jupiter	5.94 m	dinosaur
4e+30 kg	bright star	5.94 km	asteroid
4e+33 kg	galactic cluster	5,938 km	planet
4e+36 kg	globular cluster	5.94 Gm	giant star
4e+39 kg	small galaxy	5.94e+12 m	solar system
4e+42 kg	Milky Way	5.94e+15 m	light year

Black holes evaporate by a process known as Hawking radiation. The smaller the hole, the brighter the radiation. Massive holes last a very long time.

Mass	Luminosity	Lifetime
4,000 tons	21 billion GW	1.6 hours
4 million tons	21,000 GW	180,000 years
4 billion tons	21 megawatts	180 trillion years
4e+15 kg	21 watts	1.8e+23 years

4e+18 kg	21 microwatts	1.8e+32 years

Black Hole Project (BHP)

The project started by physicist Zhau Tse-Wen to create a black hole with a mass on the order of a billion tons. Four billion-ton iron rods from four different stars would be accelerated to relativistic velocities and crashed together in a symmetric implosion. That would momentarily generate a pressure at their meeting point that far exceeds what even quantum mechanics can resist. The four star systems and the implosion site are:

Planetary system	Local name	Local habitat	Title of system story
Sol	the Sun	Earth	Kremer's Limit**
Groombridge 34A	Erebus	New Antarctica	Imperfect Gods
Lacaille 9352*	Campbell	Minot	Small Pond
ε Eridani	Epsilon Eridani	Asgard	Loki's Realm
Shiva	Shiva	Chandrasekhar Station	Vertex

*Lacaille 9352 is also known as Gliese 887 and HIP 114046.

**The Ten-Ten experiment is located in Sol's asteroid belt beyond Mars.

Black Hole Accretion

Black holes above a certain mass, if fed compressible matter, accrete rapidly and form high temperature accretion rings and polar jets. The radius at which the hole's gravity overcomes thermal and atomic forces to produce a nuclear density accretion disk depend in a complex way on its mass, its rotation, its electric charge, its Hawking luminosity, and the relative velocity, density, and pressure of the medium in which it is immersed. In one of the first applications of the Opticor 1000 parallel qubit machine, Black, Popov and Chen (2074) demonstrated that, contrary to prior estimates, spinning holes as small as 2.3 gigatons could produce such behavior. (G)

Black Hole Project History

The entire history of the Black Hole Project (BHP) spans nearly 250 years, five star systems, and light years of distance or time/space.

- ⊏ -

Can, The

See Ten-Ten experiment station habitat. (KL Chap 4)

Cold Sleep Unit (CSU)

The coffin-like module which contains people in suspended animation for various reasons, including interstellar travel or to stabilize injuries pending treatment. (G)

Conservative Union Party

Lars Ried's consolidationist-leaning party. It generally opposes cultural changes, experiments like the BHP and greater interstellar expansion that leads to them. (KL Chap 2)

consolidationists

A broad name for conservative political groups at the time of the BHP. Their basic ideology holds that the effect of too-rapid technological progress has been damaging to traditional human values, and that human culture should have a period without the introduction of any new potentially disruptive ideas or technologies, such as the BHP would generate, to allow the consolidation and incorporation of the last century's changes into traditional institutions.(G)

CSU

See Cold Sleep Unit. (G)

- D -

Duluth Station

An abandoned asteroid research station near the Ten-Ten experiment site. Named after Sally Duluth, a famous 21st century astronaut, it was the original BHP research station before the Ten-Ten habitat was built. (KL Chap 4)

- E -

Epsilon Eridani

A young, rapidly spinning, chromospherically active main sequence star of spectral class K2 with large flares and a planetary system in a stage of evolution comparable to the late bombardment era of the solar system. Its mass and radius are about 80% of Sol's and its bolometric luminosity is about a third of Sol's. A minimum beam-projection starport was established in 2210, but due to its radiation environment, Epsilon Eridani was not considered prime colonization material. However, it occupies one of the corners of the best tetrahedron of stars for the black hole project, so a robotic mission was sent in 2247 to establish a BHP infrastructure. Only one of these planets was known before the Sagan Interferometer Array began operation in 2037. The planet "Loki" was discovered in the late 20th century, but not named until 2042. (G)

The Epsilon Eridani planetary system circa 2270 CE

The ε Eridani planetary system circa 2270 CE

Name	semi-major axis, AU	orbital period years	inso-lation* Earth=1	mass Earth=1	mean radius Earth=1	surface conditions			
						pressure Earth=1	temp.* K	atm. comp.	surface type
Glut	0.1270	0.0518	24.1879	0.0049	0.1639	~ 0	507.4	He, S2	rock
Fenris	0.2940	0.1823	4.5135	0.0535	0.3785	~ 0	327.0	H2, He	rock
array	0.4800	0.3803	1.6933	n/a	n/a	n/a	n/a	n/a	artificial
Asgard	0.6120	0.5475	1.0416	4.7e-14	7.8e-5	n/a	288.5	N2, O2	artificial
Loki	3.3100	6.8867	.13-.02	253.677	10.0348	(1)	322.1	H2, He	gas, ice
Freya	8.3582	27.633	0.0056	60.2705	7.2483	(1)	263.9	H2, He	gas
Idun	12.4490	50.231	0.0025	11.7385	3.52	(1)	251.4	H2, He	gas
Sigyn	17.6400	84.726	0.0013	0.5157	1.129	14.5	293.7	H2, N2	rock

*global mean. (1) "surface" at 1 atmosphere pressure level for giant planets.

- F -

flare (stellar)

A significant brightening of part of the surface of a star, lasting a day or so. Flares are associated with huge loop-shaped filaments of glowing gas that extend into the star's corona, tracing magnetic field lines generated by currents inside the star. The brightening comes from sudden changes in currents thus in the fields they generate. The rapidly changing fields accelerate charged particles to high velocities. These particles hit atoms in the stellar atmosphere, making them glow. The energy released is roughly similar in all stars, so that when flares occur in M stars (red dwarfs), the amount of light produced can be comparable to the total quiescent luminosity of the star.

Flare activity declines as the stars age and their rotation slows. Stars with frequent major flares are typically less than a billion years old, though occasional flares may occur through the life of the star, as they do with the Sun.

Flares are also associated with "coronal mass ejections" which are plasma clouds of high energy protons and other nuclei. These are blasted away from the star with velocities on the order of a percent of the speed of light, and present a significant radiation hazard to unprotected astronauts.

What triggers flares is not well understood, but by the late 23rd century, most astrophysicists had come to think that the current reconfigurations that cause flares were a chaotic, stochastic phenomena of internal stellar weather. Like earthquakes, rogue waves, and tornados, they were not predictable more than a few weeks in advance, and then not with much accuracy or specificity. (G, LR)

- G -

gamma

A measure of relative velocity, from the Greek letter gamma (γ) generally used to represent the Lorentz factor. (See Lorentz factor). (G)

gamma radiation

Electromagnetic radiation (i.e., light) with wavelengths less than 0.1 nanometer. These wavelengths are much more energetic and damaging than x-radiation. Historically, when nuclear reactions were first investigated, three kinds of radiation were discerned and labeled by the first three letters of the Greek alphabet: alpha, beta, gamma. Alpha rays proved to be the nuclei of helium atoms (two protons and two neutrons), beta rays proved to be electrons and positrons, and gamma rays proved to be very high energy light. (G)

grazing incidence

Impact and reflection from an otherwise penetrable surface at a very low angle, like a stone skipping across water. Use of grazing-incidence surfaces includes mirrors to focus x-rays, high energy exhaust nozzles, and deflectors for neutral interstellar particles. (G)

Groombridge 34 (Erebus & Bee)

A pair of red dwarf stars about 11.6 light years from Sol toward the constellation of Andromeda. The stars are about half the age of the sun. The main star (A), called Erebus by its colonists, is about 2.7% as luminous as Sol. The companion, "Bee," is about a tenth as bright and circles the primary in a long, loose orbit about 163 AU in average radius. A Neptune-sized giant planet around A was discovered in 2031.

Groombridge 34 occupies a corner of the best tetrahedron of stars for the black hole project, and the third planet of the larger star, New Antarctica, was found to be the most Earthlike planet known beyond the solar system. For these reasons, the system was colonized in 2200 and the New Antarctica terraforming project, led by Wotan Kremer, was started. None of its planets were known in the 20th century. (G)

The Groombridge 34A planetary system circa 2270 CE

Name	semi-major axis, AU	orbital period years	inso-lation* Earth=1	mass Earth=1	mean radius Earth=1	surface conditions			
						pressure Earth=1	temp.* K	atm. comp.	surface type
Palmer	0.0818	0.0402	4.3975	0.0005	0.0722	~ 0	392.0	H, He	rock
array	0.1298	0.08	1.7600	n/a	n/a	n/a	n/a	n/a	artificial
New Antarctica	0.2636	0.22	0.4233	0.9200	0.9641	0.97	257.2	N2,CH4	ice, rock
McMurdo	0.2636	0.22	0.4233	3.26e-6	0.0176	~ 0	210.4	N2,CH4	rock
Vostok	0.2636	0.22	0.4233	0.0006	0.0972	~ 0	216.7	N2, Ar	rock, ice
Wilkes	0.3872	0.38	0.1962	1.1300	0.9884	1.65	221.6	H2,He	rock, LNH3
Ellsworth	0.3872	0.38	0.1962	0.0012	0.1304	0.21	203.1	N2,CO2	ice
Enderby	0.3872	0.38	0.1962	1.26e-4	0.0696	0.00	182.1	N2, CO2	rock
Ross	0.7695	1.0812	0.0497	0.1304	0.5637	11.10	611.3	N2,CH4	H2O
Amundsen	2.8100	7.50	0.0037	12.4950	3.5083	(1)	96.7	H2,He	H2 gas
Scott	4.4642	15.03	0.0015	8.2950	2.8423	(1)	98.3	H2,He	H2 gas
Byrd	7.3020	31.4323	0.0006	0.0634	0.6002	26.59	308.5	N2, CH4	ice, LCHx
Kreitzer	9.3800	45.7610	0.0003	0.0018	0.1676	2.3e-5	60.3	N2,He	ice

*global mean. (1) "surface" at 1 atmosphere pressure level for giant planets.

- H -

halo orbit

A quasi-stable, repetitive, out-of-plane path of an object around the first or second Lagrange points (L1&L2). Viewed from the Earth, for instance, an object in a halo orbit around the Earth-Sun L1 point appears to circle the point as if it were drawn toward it. Spacecraft in halo orbits can stay in the vicinity of the otherwise unstable L1 or L2 points for extended periods of time with minimal fuel consumption. (G)

Hawking radiation

Black holes evaporate by a process known as Hawking radiation. The smaller the hole, the brighter the radiation. Massive holes last a very long time. See black hole. (G)

- I -

Interplanetary Association (IPA)

The main governing body for the Solar System and, in principle, of its extrasolar colonies. Beyond the solar system, by practical necessity, the authority of the IPA is invested in starship captains and local governments, except in extraordinary circumstances. The legislative authority of the IPA is vested in the IPA Senate and its executive authority in the president of that body. (G)

isotropic

The same in all directions. The gravity field of a stationary point mass with zero spin is isotropic. The luminosity of a star is approximately isotropic. (G)

- K -

kelvin

A unit of temperature equal to one Celsius (centigrade) degree on a scale starting at absolute zero and abbreviated by "K". Zero kelvin is absolute zero. Ice melts at 273.15 K and water boils at 373.15 K. The smallest true stars have effective temperatures of about 2300 K; the surface of the Sun is about 5870 K. The scale is named for William Thomson, Lord Kelvin, a 19th century UK physicist. It is the temperature scale of the "System International" (SI) set of units used in physical formulae. (G)

Temperature unit	Conversion equations	Examples
Kelvin to Celsius:	C = K - 273.15	257 K = -16.1 C = 2.93 F
Celsius to kelvin:	K = C + 273.15	40 C = 313 K = 104 F
Fahrenheit to kelvin:	K = (F + 459.67)/1.8	-100 F = 199.8 K = -73.3 C

Kuiperoid

Portmanteau of "Kuiper belt" and "asteroid." Also: "Kuiper belt object" (KBO) or "Edgeworth-Kuiper belt object," (EKO). A small (say less than 1000 km in radius), icy (density generally around 1 to 1.5 tons/cubic meter) object found in the outer reaches of a planetary system. The existence of a belt of such objects in the solar system was predicted independently by 20th century astronomers Kenneth Edgeworth and Gerard Kuiper. Kuiper's predictions, though later, gained more notice leading to the more common "Kuiper Belt" appellation. (G)

- L -

Lacaille 9352 (Campbell)

The second nearest BHP star to the Sun at 10.73 light years. Also known as Gliese 887, HIP 114046, and Campbell by its colonists. The star name is its number in a catalog compiled by French astronomer Nicolas Louis de LaCaille (1713-1762). It is an early red dwarf of spectral class M0.5 with a luminosity of 0.024 Suns and a mass of 0.304 Suns. The colony was established in 2170 in anticipation of the BHP. None of its planets were known in the 20th century. (G)

The Lacaille 9352 (Campbell) planetary system circa 2270 CE

Name	semi-major axis, AU	orbital period years	inso-lation* Earth= 1	mass Earth= 1	mean radius Earth= 1	surface conditions			
						pressure Earth=1	temp.* K	atm. comp.	surface type
Sunbeam	0.0713	0.0389	2.422	0.0052	0.173	5.0e-16	291.5	He, S2	rock
array	0.0713	0.0389	2.422	n/a	n/a	n/a	n/a	n/a	artificial
Canning	0.1133	0.0779	0.961	0.0676	0.415	6.60e-4	226.7	CO2,He	rock, ice
Carlisle	0.1798	0.1558	0.381	0.9877	1.035	3.71e+1	371.4	CO2, N2	rock, ice
Minot	0.1798	0.1558	0.381	9.2e-12	7.8e-4	(1)	288.5	N2, O2	artificial
Martin	0.2854	0.3115	0.151	0.086	0.483	4.50e-1	151.9	N2, CO2	rock
Munro	1.4270	3.482	6.1e-3	11.9764	3.520	(1)	132.0	H2, He	H2 gas
Spencer	4.6400	20.420	5.7e-4	10.8458	3.428	(1)	121.2	H2, He	H2 gas
Ray	9.2430	57.412	1.4e-4	0.0019	0.174	2.06e+1	21.0	N2, CH4	ice
Lenore	13.7480	104.15	6.5e-5	1.01e-7	0.006	1.25e-7	20.2	N2	ice

*global mean. (1) "surface" at 1 atmosphere pressure level for giant planets

Lagrange points

In the rotating frame of reference of the orbit of one mass around a much larger one, five locations where the combined centrifugal and gravitational forces balance. Labels vary, but the usual convention in astronautics is to label the points as follows: L1: between the two bodies, L2: beyond the smaller body, L3: on the far side of the large body from the small body and at a greater distance than the small body, L4: in the orbit of the small body, leading by 60 degrees (so that the L4 point and the two bodies form an equilateral triangle), L5: like L4, but trailing the small body by 60 degrees. Orbits in the L4 and L5 points are "stable" with respect to small perturbations, which result in cyclic motion about those points. The other three points are unstable with respect to radial perturbations, which will cause a body there to slowly accelerate away from the point. (G)

Lorentz factor

The multiplier for mass increase and time dilation due to relative velocity, generally symbolized by the lower case Greek letter gamma (γ) γ = 1/(1-(v/c)^2) where v is relative velocity and c is the speed of light. Named for Dutch physicist Henrik Antoon Lorentz, who realized that contraction in length and gain of mass of moving particles was needed to explain their behavior and provided the formula (later explained by Einstein).

"The peculiar thing about this apparent mass is, moreover, that it is not constant, but depends on the velocity; consequently the study of the motion of the electron differs in many ways from ordinary dynamics." (H. A. Lorentz, Nobel Lecture, 11 Dec. 1902) (G)

Lu superposition theory

A model for allowing limited superposition of subnuclear particles in multidimensional space. Named for 22nd Century Chinese physicist Lu, J. Z.,

"A useful model is to consider our three dimensional space-time continuum as a surface embedded in a four dimensional space. Superimposed particles are, somehow, forced up into that embedding dimension. Now imagine a four dimensional spirit of some kind whose job it is to stack Planck-scale rings or loops up into the embedding dimension over one small patch of three-space. It is easy at first, but as the stack grows higher, the spirit's job becomes increasingly difficult." (Lu, J. Z., Hawking Award Lecture, 11 Dec. 2108) (KL Chap 1)

- M -

Macrocollider Experiment Station (MES)

The ten-meter-radius sphere at the vertex of the Ten-Ten experiment that houses the instruments recording the experimental results. (KL Chap 3)

Minot

A large space colony constructed to house the population of the Lacaille 9352 (aka "Campbell") planetary system. It is named for a character in the John W. Campbell novel, *The Mightiest Machine*. (SP Chap 2)

- N -

neutron

A neutral subatomic particle with approximately the mass of a hydrogen atom and no electrical charge. Neutrons are found in the nuclei of atoms where they help hold protons together with the "strong force." A neutron is composed of three quarks and is approximately 3.4e-16 m in radius under normal nuclear conditions. (G)

neutron star

A star composed almost entirely of neutrons and held together by extreme gravity. A typical neutron star has a density of about 1e18 1e18 kilograms per cubic meter. (G)

Neutronium

Coined by Andreas von Antropoff in 1926 before the discovery of neutrons, neutronium stood for the element of atomic number zero and was placed at the head of the periodic table. Today it refers to a substance of extremely dense matter composed primarily of neutrons, as in a neutron star or a conjectured ultradense material sometimes encountered in science fiction. (G)

- P -

panspermia

The 20th century concept of microbes being transported between planets, reproducing and evolving where conditions are suitable. Also called "paleopanspermia." The observed process of the ejection of intact rocks from planets in large impact events and the survival of certain microbe spores for thousands of years in rocks lends credence to this idea, but it remained unverified at the time of the BHP. (G)

pascal (Pa)

A unit of pressure named for 17th Century French mathematician and natural philosopher Blaise Pascal (1623-1662). It is equal to one newton (N) per square meter. As the newton is a fairly small amount of force (only about 2/9 of a pound), pressures in pascals tend to be high numbers; average terrestrial atmospheric pressure at low elevations is about 100,000 Pa.

"In order to show that a hypothesis is evident, it does not suffice that all the phenomena follow from it; instead, if it leads to something contrary to a single one of the phenomena, that suffices to establish its falsity." Blaise Pascal (letter to Estienne Noel circa 1648) (G)

pellet accelerator

A device, generally a coaxial linear accelerator, designed to accelerate tiny pellets of matter to very high relative velocities. Pellet accelerators, also called "beam drivers," are used to push starships up to relativistic velocities in a system first described by 20th century Physicist C. E. Singer. (KL Chap 3)

periapsis

The nearest point to the gravitational center in the orbit of any satellite. The suffix "apsis" may be modified to indicate a specific central body, thus perigee (Gaea=Earth), perihelion (Helios=Sun), periastron (astra=a star), etc. (G)

photon

A finite and strongly localized distribution of electromagnetic wave energy (basically, light), also called a "wave packet," which has a discrete energy, wavelength and frequency. Light can only be emitted and absorbed in these discrete quantities. (G)

"In the year nineteen hundred, in the course of purely theoretical (mathematical) investigation, Max Planck made a very remarkable discovery: the law of radiation of bodies as a function of temperature could not be derived solely from the laws of Maxwellian electrodynamics. To arrive at results consistent with the relevant experiments, radiation of a given frequency f had to be treated as though it consisted of energy atoms (photons) of the individual energy hf, where h is Planck's universal constant (6.626e-35 joule-seconds). During the years following, it was shown that light was everywhere produced and absorbed in such energy quanta. In particular, Niels Bohr was able to largely understand the structure of the atom on the assumption that the atoms can only have discrete energy values, and that the discontinuous transitions between them are connected with the emission or absorption of energy quantum. This threw some light on the fact that in their gaseous state, elements and their compounds radiate and absorb only light of certain sharply defined frequencies." Albert Einstein, "On Quantum Theory" (1940) (G)

pion

A transient particle composed of a quark and an antiquark. Charged pions decay first into muons which then decay into electrons or positrons. A neutral pion is composed of a quark and its own antiquark; these quickly self-annihilate into gamma rays. (G)

Planck, Max

20th century German quantum physicist. (G)

Planck scale

Also called the Planck length, this is the distance scale at which random quantum fluctuations are thought to dominate the geometry of space-time ($Lp = 1.616e-35$ m.). Even a neutron is huge on the Planck scale, being about 5e20 Lp. (G)

Planet

Historically, an object that moved across Earth's sky, as opposed to remaining in a fixed stellar position. In common usage, the term refers to any large substellar object that doesn't orbit another large substellar object. Administratively, however, inhabited satellites, asteroids, and space colonies that are independently governed are considered *de jure* "planets" (Luna, for instance).

The history of a more technical definition is a case study in the politics of science and the futility of categorizing a continuum, with significant efforts being made in 2006, 2014, 2034, 2102, 2178, and 2230. The intuitive divisions within our own solar system were blurred by discoveries in others, and definitions based on assumptions of how or where an object was formed were eventually abandoned because this could not be determined with any certainty in many systems. The latest (2230) IPA commission on terminology relied only on what can be currently observed. It recommended that the term "planet" be used for substellar objects not gravitationally bound to a more massive substellar object and which have masses between 3E20 kg and 3E28 kg. The lower mass limit corresponds, approximately, to the mass needed for an isostatically compensated ellipsoidal surface and the upper limit to the mass needed to initiate significant deuterium fusion, i.e., to make a brown dwarf. In cases of "double planets," the larger object is the planet, the lesser, the satellite. Marginal situations are to be addressed individually and may include other factors. (G)

posigrade

Moving, revolving or rotating in the same direction. For example, motion in the direction of the orbit of the planet is called posigrade. If a planet is rotating counterclockwise as seen by an observer, a satellite revolving counterclockwise about it is called posigrade while one revolving clockwise is called "retrograde." (G)

Prometheus

(1) A satellite of Saturn (2) In Hellenic mythology, a Titan who steals fire from heaven for the benefit of mankind.(G)

quagma

A portmanteau word from QUArk - Gluon - plasMA. "It's what you get when neutrons under extreme heat and or pressure dissolve into an undifferentiated sea of quarks." -Dr. Brunhilda Kremer (G)

quark

A subatomic building block of neutrons, protons and other nuclear particles. There are "up," "down," "strange," "charmed," "bottom" and "top" quarks, but normal stable atoms contain only up and down quarks. The up quark has a charge of 2/3 and the down quark, -1/3. Two up quarks and a down quark compose a proton, and one up quark with two down quarks make a neutron. Lu superposition theory (2135) allows quark compression and "stacking" at extreme energies. (G)

quark star

Predicted by 20th century physicists, and first unambiguously observed in 2058, it occurs when a neutron star reaches just the right density and pressure that neutrons lose their individuality and their quarks interact to create exotic matter not massive enough and they stay neutron stars; a little bit more massive and they collapse into black holes. According to Dr. Brunhilda Kremer's Limit, a central pressure of a non-rotating quark star of 3.18 solar masses is enough to cause that collapse. (KL Chap 1)

- R -

Ragi probes

Radiation and Gravity Integrated probe: High energy particle detectors. The 23rd century version measures nanogal accelerations as well primary and secondary electromagnetic radiation at wavelengths longer than 97 nm. (G)

- S -

Schwarzschild radius

Projected radius of a black hole event horizon. See "black hole" (G)

space colony

A large self-sustaining artificial environment for human habitation in space. Many architectures are used, but the most common in the 23rd century is an ellipsoid of revolution (roughly the shape of a rugby ball). Large toroidal structures are also used. These structures are spun for centrifugal gravity and use large mirrors or nuclear power sources or light and energy. They range in size from on to a hundred kilometers in length and house a few dozen to several million people.(G, SP, LR)

SST (Solar System Time)

Date and time coordinates in a frame of reference at rest with respect to the center of Sol, with the length of the second adjusted to correspond with and account for Earth's rotation, mean orbital velocity, and sea level surface gravity.(G)

starship

A spacecraft designed to travel between stars. At the time of the BHP, starships are pushed up to relativistic velocities by Pellet Beams from orbital projectors powered by vast solar arrays. The typical starship design has three or more spheres spaced evenly along a hundred-meter-diameter super-conducting solenoid ring, with long grazing incidence cones ahead of each sphere. A smaller, coaxial "choke ring" that improves plasma reflection performance lies about fifty meters forward of the main ring. (G)

strange matter

Exotic matter composed of strange quarks that may be found within a quark star. See also quark. (KL Chap 1)

- T -

telomerase

An enzyme in living cells that protects telomeres at the ends of DNA strands and can aid tissue and organ regeneration. Telomerase treatments became standard by the late 21st century. By the time of the BHP project stories, genetic engineers have improved maintenance of telomeres as part of an overall genetic modification to end cell aging. (G)

Ten-Ten Experiment

A preliminary experiment to test the models being used to design the BHP. In the final run of the experiment, two ten-gram pellets will be collided at a Lorentz factor of ten, hence the name Ten-Ten. The location of this experiment is in the Solar System's main asteroid belt, beyond Mars. Two pellet accelerators mounted end to end are used to create the high-energy collision in the Ten-Ten experiment. (KL)

Ten-Ten Experiment Habitat

Also known as "The Can," this cylindrical habitat and control center is at the site of the Ten-Ten experiment. It is tethered to a tiny, rapidly rotating (1 rpm) asteroid about ten kilometers from the planned collision vertex to produce centrifugal gravity. The Can is about thirty meters in diameter with staterooms arranged in rings around the outside of each of the first nine levels. The center sections are given over to equipment, labs and common functions. There are three elevators spaced equilaterally. The tenth level is a domed combination of park and vegetable garden, with a swimming pool. (KL Chap 3)

Tsiolkovsky, Konstantin

Russian space pioneer. Generally credited to be the first person to publish serious non-fiction about traveling and living in space. His late 19th and early 20th century writings include accounts of liquid fuel rockets and rotating space habitats. "The Earth is the cradle of the mind, but we cannot live forever in a cradle." - Konstantin E. Tsiolkovsky (Kaluga, Russia, letter, 1911) (G)

Vaterführer

Literally it means father-leader. One who has the vision for how the family will function as a whole. The term became common in 22nd century Germany following governmental problems and social crises. (G)

vertex

In high energy physics, the point at which a collision occurs, as indicated by a spray of particle tracks that originate at that point. The name "Vertex" is the satellite of Shiva where the BHP implosion is planned. (G)

- W -

Whipple, Fred

20th century astronomer and comet expert. (G)

Note that as glossary items extend well into the 23rd century, parts of it are necessarily fiction. However, the intent is for those parts of it dealing with things known before 2006 to be as accurate as time and space permit.

DRAMATIS PERSONAE

Abila, Naomi
Deputy Director of BHP on New Antarctica, Erebus (Groombridge 34A) System (Imperfect Gods)

Abila, Sasha
Macroarchitecture graduate student on New Antarctica, Erebus (Groombridge 34A) System (Imperfect Gods)

Abila, Ted
Engineer working on the BHP at Groombridge 34A. (Imperfect Gods)

Adams, Bradford "Brad"
BHP Engineer, from Earth (Kremer's Limit, Vertex)

Avonford, Elizabeth "Liz"
BHP Manager, Lacaille 9352 (Small Pond)

Avonford, Katherine "Kate"
Captain of the Starship *Farseeker* (Vertex)

Chenhansa, Ada
Captain of the Starship *Oberth* (Vertex)

Davenport, Jill
Head of Biology on the Epsilon Eridani expedition (Loki's Realm)

Davra, Dr. (no surname)
Head of Robotics on the Epsilon Eridani expedition (Loki's Realm),

DeRoot, Peter
Captain of the *C.E. Singer*, brother of Director Vitus DeRoot. (Small Pond, Vertex)

DeRoot, Vitus
Director of Explorations Division of the ISA, brother of Captain Peter DeRoot. (Small Pond)

Dickson, Daggert "Dagger"
Project staff engineer on the *Admiral Byrd*, expert in propulsion systems. (Loki's Realm)

Hassan, Shira

Moslem resident of New Antarctica and elementary school friend of Hilda Kremer's

Gunheim, Roger

Head of the executive council at Minot Colony, Lacaille 9352 (Campbell) System (Small Pond, Vertex)

Kremer, Brunhilda "Hilda"

Chief theorist on the Black Hold Project (Kremer's Limit, Vertex); Sister of Liz Avonford (Small Pond)Chief scientist for the BHP on New Antarctica (Imperfect Gods); Daughter of Kate Avonford and Wotan

Kremer, Wotan

Chief Terraforming Engineer at New Antarctica, Chairman of the Erebus System Commonwealth Council. (Imperfect Gods); Father of Hilda Kremer and Liz Avonford.

Lalande, Judi

An astrophysicist (Small Pond)

Levi, David

Bio-Nanotechnologist first in the Explorations Division of the ISA, then at Minot, Lacaille 9352 (Campbell) System. (Small Pond)

Levine, Sarah

BHP project scientist, specializing in experiment design and data analysis. Close friend of Hilda Kremer (Kremer's Limit, Imperfect Gods, Vertex)

Lewis, Emma

Epsilon Eridani mission's astrophysicist. (Loki's Realm)

Lobov, Brian

Professor and head of the Physics Department at the University of New Antarctica. (Imperfect Gods)

Macready, Bruce

Longtime professor of the history of science and technology at Broadford College on the Isle of Skye in Scotland, on leave of absence as historian of the Epsilon Eridani mission. (Loki's Realm, Vertex)

Messenger, Anna

Actress and impersonation specialist; cousin of Torsten and Lars Ried and sometime covert Conservative Union Party operative. (Kremer's Limit, Vertex)

Mutori, Cyan

Liz Avonford's BHP deputy at the Campbell system. Apparently one of many women used by Minot executive Roger Gunheim (Small Pond, Vertex).

Peal, Terry

An unbalanced roboticist and robot war gamer at the Lacaille 9352 mining site supporting impactor fabrication. (Small Pond)

Ried, Lars

Torsten Ried's half-brother, noted consolidationist and Conservative Union Party member of the Solar System's Interplanetary Association Senate. (Kremer's Limit)
Later, President of the Interplanetary Association Senate. (Vertex)

Ried, Torsten

Reporter for *Popular Issues*, brother of Lars Ried. (KL, Vertex)

Rossov, Vitaly

The MES' new site engineer, Ph.D. in Physics (Kremer's Limit)

Weaver, Dr. George. P.

BHP Project leader on Epsilon Eridani. (Loki's Realm)

Zhau, Tse Wen, Ph.D.

Overall head of the Black Hole Project, based on Earth. (Kremer's Limit, Vertex)

Visit variationspublishing.com
for information about the authors, plus
non-fiction articles and documentation
on the science of
The Black Hole Project.

ABOUT THE AUTHORS. . .

G. David Nordley is an astronautical engineer whose second career is writing. His main interest is the future of human exploration and settlement of space, with stories typically focusing on the dramatic aspects of individual lives within the broad sweep of a plausible human future. His research fuels also nonfiction articles. He is a four-time winner of the AnLab, the *Analog* reader's award for best story or article of the year, and a past Hugo and Nebula award nominee.

C. Sanford Lowe (pen name of Candace S. Lowe) is a science fiction writer, and, formerly, a newspaper reporter in Boston, a deputy sheriff in Arizona, and an airline pilot in New Mexico. Lowe currently works in IT at Stanford University. She is a winner of the best short story for the New England Science Fiction Association. When not writing, she collaborates on experimental music with her husband, and tutors students studying English as a second language.